NORTHUMBERLAND COUNTY LIBRARY

You should return this book on or before the last date stamped below unless an extension of the loan period is granted.

Application for renewal may be made by letter or telephone.

Fines at the approved rate will be charged when a book is overdue.

Copper Beach

Jayne Ann Krentz is the critically-acclaimed creator of the Arcane Society world. She also writes as Amanda Quick and Jayne Castle. Jayne has written more than fifty *New York Times* bestsellers under various pseudonyms and more than thirty-five million copies of her books are currently in print. She lives in the Pacific Northwest.

Copper Beach

A Dark Legacy Novel

Jayne Ann Krentz

piatkus

PIATKUS

First published in the United States in 2012 by G. P. Putnam's Sons,
A member of Penguin Group (USA) Inc., New York
First published in Great Britain as a paperback original in 2012 by Piatkus

Copyright © 2012 by Jayne Ann Krentz

The moral right of the author has been asserted.

A CIP catalogue record for this book
is available from the British Library.

ISBN 978-0-7499-5622-6 [HB]
ISBN 978-0-7499-5617-2 [TPB]

Printed and bound in Great Britain by CPI Group (UK) Ltd, Croydon, CR0 4YY

Papers used by Piatkus are from well-managed forests
and other responsible sources.

MIX
Paper from
responsible sources
FSC® C104740

Piatkus
An imprint of
Little, Brown Book Group
100 Victoria Embankment
London EC4Y 0DY

An Hachette UK Company
www.hachette.co.uk

www.piatkus.co.uk

For Steve Castle, with love and thanks

for the background on rare earths.

Great brothers like you are even more rare.

Sure glad we made it into the same family.

Copper Beach

1

THERE WAS NOTHING LIKE THE DRAMA OF A DEATHBED SCENE to expose the skeletons in a family's closet. You never knew what would fall out when you opened the door, the nurse thought. Lifelong conflicts, absolution, regret, long-held grudges, enduring love or unrelenting hatred, whatever had been hidden for decades or generations was suddenly made visible at the end.

The night-shift staff was gathered at the nurses' station, drinking coffee, snacking on vending-machine munchies and speculating on the sexual orientation of the new orthopedic surgeon, when the dying man's son arrived. Emotions in the small group ranged from cynical to relieved.

They had all watched patients die without family at the bedside. It happened more often than most people realized. Everyone who did this kind of work understood that family dynamics were often convoluted and messy and sometimes downright evil. There were often very good reasons why relatives turned their backs on a family member who was dying. And there was no getting around the fact that the patient in 322 was seriously wasted not just from the cancer but from years of hard living and major addiction issues.

"Knox probably wasn't anyone's idea of a great father," the orderly said. "Still, it's about time someone from the family showed up."

The middle-aged nurse watched the visitor disappear through the darkened doorway of 322. Then she checked the computer file.

"He signed in as Knox's son," she reported. "But there are no relatives listed on the chart."

One of the orderlies popped a handful of potato chips into his mouth. "Guess it's safe to say it's not a close family."

Lander Knox knew what the crowd at the nurses' station was thinking. *The prodigal son shows up at last.* It amused him, but he had been careful not to let his reaction show. He understood that humor was not appropriate to the occasion.

He had learned long ago to fake the correct emotional responses for a wide variety of situations. His acting talent was worthy of an Oscar. He had gotten very good at pretending to be one of the sheep. He moved among the weak, emotional, easily duped creatures that surrounded him like the wolf he was.

He had considered taking a moment to charm the staff at the nurses' station. It would have been simple to give them a clever story about how he had been on the other side of the world in a war zone when he got word that his father was dying. He could have told them that he had spent three days without sleep trying to get back before the end. But it wasn't worth the effort. He was planning to stay only a few minutes, just long enough to take his revenge.

Shadows pooled inside room 322. The machines hummed and hissed and beeped like some high-tech Greek chorus heralding the inevitable. Quinn Knox's eyes were closed. He was hooked up to an IV line. His breathing was harsh, as if it took everything he had just to grab the next breath. He looked exhausted beyond bearing. The outline etched by the sheet revealed a painfully thin body. The cancer had been gnawing on him for a while now.

Lander went to the bed and gripped the rail. There was very little that could arouse strong emotion in him, but looking down at the father who had betrayed him, he felt something familiar and powerful stir deep inside. Rage.

"Surprise, I'm alive," he whispered. "But, then, I'll bet you've known all along that I didn't die in that boating accident. Hey, you're psychic, after all. But you sure hoped I was dead, didn't you? Well, I'm here. I won't stay long. Just stopped in to let you know that you lost and I won. Are you listening, you son of a bitch?"

Quinn's eyelids twitched. One withered hand moved slightly. Lander smiled. A euphoric satisfaction twisted and melded with the old fury.

"So you can hear me," he said. "That's good. Because I want you to go to your grave knowing that I know everything, how you lied to me, how you tried to cheat me out of my inheritance, *everything*. I'm on the trail of that lab notebook. I've traced it to the Pacific Northwest. Once I have that book, I'll be able to find that lost mine."

Quinn's eyelids fluttered and opened partway. Faded gray eyes, glazed with morphine and the oncoming chill of death, looked up at Lander.

"No," Quinn rasped.

"A couple of years ago I found the one crystal that you kept as a souvenir. What's more, I've learned how to use it to commit the perfect murder. I've run a number of successful experiments so far. Very useful, that crystal. But now I'm going after the whole damn mine full of those stones, and there's nothing you can do to stop me."

"No, listen . . ."

"You're a dead man, or you will be very soon. They probably got a pool going out there at the nurses' station, betting on whether or not you'll make it through the night."

"Lab book is psi-coded." The breath rattled in Quinn's chest. "Try to break it and you'll destroy your senses. Maybe kill yourself."

"I heard the rumors about the code," Lander said. "But I haven't told you the best part yet. I've already located a code breaker in Seattle. She's a freelancer in the underground hot-books market. I'm going to use her to acquire the book for me and break the encryption. Sort of a two-for-one deal."

Quinn stared at him with an expression of gathering horror. Lander smiled, pleased.

"You don't fear death, but you're terrified that I'll get my hands on that lab notebook, aren't you?" he said. "And I will, old man, I will. I am so very close."

"No," Quinn wheezed. "You don't understand. The crystals are dangerous. You can't reopen the mine."

"The Phoenix Mine was my inheritance. You had no right to keep it from me. But I'm going to find it now. I've been working on my plan for months. Now everything is in place in Seattle. I almost wish you were going to live long enough to see me reopen that mine. Almost."

Quinn moved his head restlessly on the pillow. "You don't know what you're doing."

"You're wrong." Lander stepped back from the bed. "I know exactly what I'm doing. I'm going to claim what belongs to me."

"Please, listen . . ."

"Good-bye, you pathetic bastard." Lander started to turn away but paused, eyeing the IV lines. "You know, it's tempting to put a pillow over your face and finish you off right now. But I want you to have a little more time to think about how you failed to cheat me out of what's mine. I want you to suffer a little longer, *Dad*."

Lander turned on his heel and walked swiftly out of the room. If he stayed for even another minute, he would give in to the rage and the urge to pull the plug on the old man.

Once out in the hall, he went quickly toward the elevators. He could feel the eyes of the medical staff boring into his back. *Screw them.* He was never going to see any of them again.

In room 322, Quinn's head cleared a little as he raised what was left of his old talent. The effort dumped a small jolt of adrenaline into his bloodstream, countering the effects of the drugs. After three fumbling attempts, he managed to press the call button.

The nurse appeared. Quinn dredged up the name out of his failing memory banks.

"Nathan," he rasped.

"Are you in pain, Mr. Knox?" Nathan came to stand beside the bed. "I can give you another injection."

"Forget the damn drugs. Help me make a phone call."

"All right. I can dial it for you, if you like."

"Number's in my wallet. It was with me when I got here."

"You aren't supposed to bring valuables with you to the hospital," Nathan said.

"Nothing valuable in my wallet except that phone number. Get it."

Nathan went to the closet, pawed through the meager assortment of personal belongings and produced the aged, well-worn wallet. He brought it back to the bed and opened it.

"Dial the number on that old card," Quinn said. "Elias Coppersmith. Hurry, man, I don't have a lot of time."

Nathan punched in the number. A man picked up. The voice had a faint, Western edge to it, the kind of voice you associated with cowboys and pilots. The classic Chuck Yeager twang, Nathan thought. The voice also had the ring of authority.

"Coppersmith."

"I'm calling from Oakmont Hospital," Nathan said. "A patient named Quinn Knox wants to speak with you, Mr. Coppersmith. He says it's urgent."

"Quinn? Put him on."

Nathan helped Quinn grip the phone and maneuver it to his ear. Quinn pulled on the last of his fading strength and his talent. He got one last rush of energy.

"Elias?" he croaked. "That you?"

"Damn, it's good to hear from you, Quinn. It's been at least twenty, twenty-five years. Didn't know you had my number."

"I kept track of you," Quinn said.

"Glad to hear it, but you should have stayed in touch. You sound awful. What the hell are you doing in the hospital?"

"Dying," Quinn rasped. "What the fuck do you think I'm doing? Shut up and listen, because I don't have a lot of time. I'm down to hours here, maybe minutes. I think someone may have found Ray Willis's notebook."

"Are you serious?"

"I just told you, I'm dying. Turns out people get real serious when shit like that happens."

"Quinn, where is that hospital?"

"Florida."

"I'll be on a company plane within the hour. Be there by morning."

"Forget it," Quinn rasped. "Not gonna last that long. Here's what I know. There's some rumors floating around in the hot-book market that the notebook has surfaced somewhere in your neck of the woods."

"Sedona?"

"Last I heard you bought yourself a whole damn island up there in the San Juans."

"Still got the island, but Willow and I just use it as a spring and summer getaway place. Moved the main headquarters of the company down here to Arizona years ago. There's one division left in Seattle, the R-and-D lab. My oldest son, Sam, is the only one who lives year-round on the island."

"You had another son and a little girl, too."

"Judson and Emma. All grown up now. Judson and Sam run their own private consulting firm. And Emma is . . . Emma. Lives in Portland, Oregon. Willow says she's still finding herself. I say it's time she got serious about life, but that's a whole other issue."

"So you're in Sedona." Quinn tried to smile. The smile turned into a painful, breathless, hacking cough. "You always had a thing for the desert."

"Tell me about the notebook, Quinn."

"Not much more to tell. But here's the thing you need to know. My son is going after it."

"I heard your son died a few years ago. Some kind of boating accident."

"Hate to say it, but it probably would have been better if that were true. But he's alive, Elias. He came to see me tonight. Says I deprived him of his inheritance. He's got my talent, Elias, but he's got a hell of a lot more of it than I ever had. And he's sick in the head. Evil sick. Be careful. That's all I can tell you. Gotta go now."

"Quinn, wait. For God's sake, man, don't hang up."

"You were the best friend I ever had, Elias. Always thought of you as a brother. All these years I tried to keep our secret, but I made the mistake of holding on to one of the crystals. Now Lander has it. I failed you."

"No, Quinn," Elias said. "Listen to me, you didn't fail me. You had my back forty years ago when Willis tried to kill both of us. And now you've given me the warning I need to handle this situation. I'll take it from here."

"Just like last time, huh?"

"Just like last time," Elias said.

"Good-bye, brother."

"Good-bye, my brother."

The phone fell from Quinn's hand. A strange calm settled on him. He had done what he could to protect the secret that he and Elias had vowed to keep forty years ago. It was up to Elias now.

In spite of the oncoming darkness, Quinn realized that he felt at peace for the first time in maybe his entire life. He could go now. He closed his eyes.

2

A CRAZY MAN AND A GUN WAS NEVER A GOOD COMBINATION. A crazy man with paranormal talent and a gun made for a very bad start to the day.

Abby Radwell watched the terrifying scene taking place in the library from the shadows of the doorway. The intruder holding the pistol on Hannah Vaughn and her housekeeper could not have been older than twenty-one or twenty-two. His eyes were fever-bright. His long hair was matted and disheveled. His jeans and ragged T-shirt looked as if they had not been washed in a very long time. He was becoming more agitated by the second.

The intruder's voice rose. "I'm not playing games, lady." He waved the pistol in an erratic pattern. "I know *The Key* is here in this room. You have to give it to me, and then she has to unlock it."

"You are welcome to take *The Key*," Hannah said, somehow managing to maintain a calm, soothing tone. "But I can't unlock it for you. I don't know how to do that."

"She's supposed to unlock it," the intruder said.

"Who are you talking about?" Hannah asked. "Surely you don't mean my housekeeper. Mrs. Jensen doesn't know anything about unlocking encrypted books."

"Not the housekeeper," the intruder said. He used the back of his arm to wipe the sweat off his forehead. "The woman who is working for you here in this library. She knows how to unlock hot books."

"I don't understand," Hannah said. "Mrs. Jensen and I are the only people in this house. Please, take my copy of *The Key* and leave before this situation gets out of control."

Hannah was doing a magnificent job of lying, Abby thought. But the situation was already out of control.

Hannah Vaughn was eighty-two years old and confined to a wheel-chair. She was helpless against the armed intruder. She was doing her best to defuse the mad tension in the room, but her tactics were not going to work. Mrs. Jensen was pale and shaken. She looked as if she was about to faint.

Abby's senses were wide open. Her intuition was screaming at her to rush back downstairs and out onto the street. The intruder was not yet aware of her presence. She could call nine-one-one once she was safely outside. But by the time the police arrived, it might be too late for Hannah and Mrs. Jensen.

Abby spoke quietly from the doorway. "I'll get *The Key* for you."

"*What?*" The intruder whirled around to face her, eyes widening in shock. "Who are you?"

"My name is Abby. I'm the one you're looking for, the woman who can unlock *The Key*."

"Huh." The intruder blinked several times and shook his head as if to clear it. He was shivering, but he managed to steady himself some-what. He gripped the gun with both hands, aiming it at her. "Are you sure you're the right woman?"

"Yes. What's your name?"

"Grady." The response was automatic.

"All right, Mr. Grady . . ."

"No, my name is Grady Hastings." Grady looked confused for a few seconds. He wiped his forehead again. "That's all you need to know. Get the book. Hurry. I don't feel too good."

"The book you want is encrypted?"

"Yes, yes." Excitement heightened the fever in Grady's eyes. "*The Key to the Latent Power of Stones.* They told me you could unlock it."

"It's in the crystals section, up on the balcony," Abby said.

"Get it. Hurry."

"All right." She walked into the room and headed toward the small spiral staircase that gave access to the balcony which wrapped around the library. "How did you know that it was in Mrs. Vaughn's collection?"

"The voices told me. Just like they told me that I needed you to break the code. I have to have that book, you see. It's vital to my research."

"You're doing research on crystals?" Abby asked.

"Yes, *yes.* And I'm so close to the answers, so *close.* I gotta have the book."

"Okay," Abby said.

Mrs. Jensen whimpered softly. Hannah had gone very quiet. She watched Abby with a sharp, knowing look. Her anxiety was a palpable force in the room.

"All right," Grady said. "That's good. Okay, then." He seemed to regain a measure of control. "But I'm coming with you. No tricks. You have to break the code. *The Key* is no good to me unless you unlock it. That's what the voices in the crystal told me, you see."

"I understand," Abby said soothingly. She started up the spiral staircase.

Grady gave Hannah and Mrs. Jensen a quick, uncertain look and seemed satisfied that neither of them would cause him any trouble. He followed Abby up the staircase. Abby was aware of his heavy, labored breathing. It was as if he was exerting enormous energy just to hold the gun on her.

"You're ill," Abby said. "Maybe you should leave now and go to the emergency room."

"No. Can't leave without the book."

"What sort of crystal research are you doing?" she asked.

"Know anything about latent energy in rocks?"

"Not a lot, but it sounds interesting."

"So much power," Grady said. "Just waiting for us to figure out how to tap it. I'm almost there. Got to have that book."

Abby reached the top of the spiral steps and walked along the balcony to the section of shelving that contained Hannah's fine collection of volumes devoted to the paranormal properties of crystals. Many of the books were filled with the usual woo-woo and occult nonsense. Hannah said she collected those volumes for historical purposes. But a few of the titles contained the writings of researchers, ancient and modern, who had done serious work on the power of crystals, gemstones and amber.

The most valuable book in the Vaughn collection was Morgan's *The Key to the Latent Power of Stones*. Written in the eighteenth century, it was locked in a psi-code that added enormously to its value. In the world of antiquarian and collectible books that had a paranormal provenance, encrypted volumes were the rarest of the rare.

Abby stopped and ran her fingertips along the spines of the books on the shelf.

"Quit stalling," Grady said. The gun shook in his hand.

"Here it is." She pulled out the old leather-bound volume. The energy locked in the book whispered to her senses. "Morgan's *Key*."

Grady eyed the worn leather cover warily. "Are you sure that's the right one?"

"Do you want to see the title page?"

"Yes. Show me."

Cradling the heavy book carefully in one hand, she opened the cover. Grady took a step closer and looked at the title page. He frowned.

"I can read it."

"Yes, you're lucky it was written in English. A lot of the old alchemists used Latin."

"No, I mean I can *read* it. *The Key to the Latent Power of Stones.*" Grady reached out and gingerly turned a page. "I can read this page, too. This isn't the right book. The voices in the crystal told me that the book I need is encrypted."

"Oh, right," Abby said. "You think that because you can read the text the book is not locked in a code. But that's exactly how psi-encryption works. It camouflages the real text in subtle ways, just enough to distort and conceal the true meaning. You could sit down and read this book cover to cover and think you were reading the original text. But in the end, it would be just so much gibberish."

"Break the code," Grady demanded. "Let me see if the text really does look different."

Abby braced herself for the inevitable shock and focused on the layers of energy that shivered around the old book. Few sensitives possessed the ability to lock a book or other written material in a psi-code; fewer still knew the oldest and most powerful techniques. Talents like her who could crack such codes were even more scarce. The whole business was a dying art. Encrypting a book or a document required physical contact with the item that was to be encoded. In the modern world, people tended to store their secrets in digital form in cyberspace, a realm where old-fashioned psychic encryption did not work.

It figured that she had chosen a career path that was fated to go the way of buggy-whip manufacturing, Abby thought. But she hadn't been able to help herself. The old books filled with ancient paranormal secrets called to her senses. And those wrapped in psi-encryption were irresistible.

She found the pattern of the code. It was not the first time she had unsealed the old volume. She was the one who had acquired it for Hannah's collection in the first place. She had unlocked the book twice already, once to verify its authenticity and again to allow Hannah to make some notes. Hannah had requested that the book be relocked after she had read it, in order to maintain its value.

"Done," Abby said. "I broke the code."

"Are you finished already?" Grady eyed the book with a dubious expression. "I thought psi-encryption was tricky stuff."

"It is, but I'm good."

"I can still feel a lot of hot energy coming off that book."

"Strong encryption energy leaves a residue, just like any other kind of energy," Abby said.

"So I can read the real text now?"

"Yes. Take a look."

She held the book out. Grady's hand closed around it. The physical contact was all she needed. She channeled the darkly oscillating currents of the encryption energy into Grady's aura.

The atmosphere was suddenly charged. Grady reacted as if he had touched a live electrical wire. His mouth opened on a silent, agonized scream. The gun dropped from his hand. His eyes rolled back in his head. He stiffened for a timeless moment. Then he shuddered violently. He tried to stagger back toward the spiral staircase, but he collapsed to the floor of the balcony. He twitched several times and went still.

There was a moment of stunned silence.

"Are you all right, Abby?" Hannah asked.

"No. Yes." Abby took a deep breath and silently repeated her old mantra, *Show no weakness.* She gripped the balcony railing and looked down at Hannah. "I'm fine. Just a little shaken up, that's all."

"You're sure, dear?" Hannah's face was etched with concern.

"Yes. Really. Breaking a code is one thing. Using the energy in it to do what I just did is . . . something else altogether."

"I knew you were strong," Hannah said. "But I hadn't realized that you were that powerful. What you just did was extremely dangerous. If that sort of energy got out of control . . ."

"I know, I know," Abby said. "I couldn't think of anything else to do." She glanced at the housekeeper, who was crumpled on the floor. "What happened to Mrs. Jensen?"

"She fainted. There was an awful lot of energy flying around in here a moment ago. Even a nonsensitive could feel it. What about that dreadful man? Is he alive?"

Dear heaven, had she actually killed someone? Horrified at the possibility, Abby went to her knees beside Grady. Gingerly, she probed for a pulse. Relief swept through her when she found one.

"Yes," she said. "He's unconscious, but he's definitely alive."

"I'll call nine-one-one now."

"Good idea." Abby drew a deep breath. She was already starting to feel the edgy adrenaline-overload buzz that accompanied the use of so much psychic energy. In a couple of hours she would be exhausted. She focused on the immediate problem. It was major. "How on earth am I going to explain what happened here?"

"There's nothing for you to explain, dear." Hannah rolled her chair to the desk and picked up her phone. "A mentally disturbed intruder broke into my home and demanded one of the rare books in my collection. He appeared to be on drugs, and whatever he took evidently caused him to collapse."

Abby thought about it. "All true, in a way."

"Well, it's not as if you can explain that you used psychic energy to take down an armed intruder, dear. Who would believe such a thing? The authorities would think that you were as crazy as that man who broke in here today."

"Yes," Abby said. A shuddery chill swept through her, bringing with it images from her old nightmares, the ones filled with an endless maze of pale-walled corridors, sterile rooms and locked doors and windows. She wasn't going to risk being called crazy, not ever again. "That is exactly what they would think."

"I have always found that when dealing with the authorities it's best to stick with the bare facts and not offer too much in the way of explanations."

Abby gripped the railing and saw the understanding in Hannah's eyes. "I came to the same conclusion myself a few years ago, Mrs. Vaughn. Those are definitely words to live by."

Hannah made the call and put down the phone. She glanced up at Abby.

"What is it, dear?" she said gently. "If you're concerned that word of what you did with that encryption energy might get out into the underground market, you needn't worry. I won't ever tell anyone what really happened here, and Mrs. Jensen passed out before she witnessed a thing. Your secret is safe with me."

"I know, Hannah. I trust you. Thank you. But there's something about this Grady Hastings guy that is bothering me."

"He is obviously mentally unbalanced, dear."

"I know. But that isn't what I meant. He was sweating so hard. He seemed on the edge of exhaustion. It was as if he was struggling against some unseen force."

"Perhaps he was, dear. We all have our inner demons. I suspect that Grady Hastings has more than most people."

. . .

The new nightmare started that same night.

She walked through the strange glowing fog. She did not know whom or what she was searching for, only that she desperately needed to find someone before it was too late. Time was running out. The sense of urgency was growing stronger, making it hard to breathe.

Grady Hastings materialized in the mist. He stared at her with haunted, pleading eyes and held out a hand.

"Help me," he said. "You have to help me. The voices in the crystal told me that you are the only one who can save me."

She awoke, pulse racing. Newton whined anxiously and pressed his furry weight against her leg. It took her a few seconds to orient herself. When she did, she was horrified to realize that she was no longer in bed. She was in the living room of her small condo, looking out the sliding glass doors that opened onto the balcony. The lights of the Seattle cityscape glittered in the night.

"Dear heaven, I've started sleepwalking, Newton." She sank to her knees beside the dog and hugged him close.

The first blackmail note was waiting for her when she checked her email the next morning.

I know what you did in the library. Silence will be maintained for a price. You will be contacted soon.

3

"YOU'VE PROBABLY HEARD THE RUMORS ABOUT SAM COPPERSMITH."
The water-taxi pilot eased off the throttle, allowing the boat to cruise
slowly into the small marina. "Don't pay any attention to 'em."

Abby pushed her sunglasses higher on her nose and took a closer
look at the man at the helm. Half an hour ago, when he had picked her
up at the dock in Anacortes, he had introduced himself as Dixon. He
looked to be in his mid-sixties, but it was hard to be certain of his age
because he had the rugged, weathered features of a man who had spent
a lifetime on the water.

Dixon Charters was painted on the white hull of the boat. The name
of the business was accompanied by a logo depicting an orca leap-
ing out of the waves. Images of the magnificent black-and-white killer
whales that prowled the cold waters of the Pacific Northwest in pods
were ubiquitous throughout the San Juans. Orcas graced signs above

bookstores, souvenir shops, real estate offices and restaurants. They decorated menus, greeting cards and calendars. Parents bought cute, cuddly stuffed orcas for their children.

Abby had grown up in the region. She understood the significance of orcas both culturally and historically. And they were certainly magnificent. There was nothing like the thrill of watching the sleek, powerful creatures launch their multi-ton bodies out of the depths and into the air and then plunge back beneath the surface. But in her opinion, most people tended to forget that orcas were anything but cute and cuddly. They were intelligent, powerful, top-of-the-food-chain predators. *Just ask a salmon,* she thought.

"I'm here on business," she said coolly. "I can assure you that the very last thing I care about is Mr. Coppersmith's personal life."

"That's good," Dixon said. He nodded once, satisfied. "Because the gossip about him being the one who murdered his fiancée six months ago is pure bullshit. Pardon my language."

Okay, didn't see that coming. Abby's pulse kicked up for a few beats. She had already figured out that Sam Coppersmith was probably somewhat eccentric, but that hadn't bothered her. Eccentric collectors made up a good portion of her clientele. She had not, however, heard about the murdered fiancée. She'd taken time to run a quick background check on the Coppersmiths, but she had been in a hurry this morning. Maybe she should have done a little more research before coming to Legacy Island.

"Is that so?" she said politely, going for noncommittal.

"You know how it is when a woman dies under mysterious circumstances," Dixon said. "The cops always look at the guy she was sleeping with and the one who finds the body. In this case, that man just happened to be one and the same."

"Sam Coppersmith?"

"Yeah. But the sheriff cleared him. It was those damn bloggers with their conspiracy theories who tried to stir things up. It was the Coppersmith name that got their attention. When your family operates a big business like Coppersmith Inc., there's always folks who'll suspect the worst. No one here on the island believed a single damn word of what they wrote about Sam, though."

"I gather the Coppersmith family is respected here," Abby said. She kept her tone politely neutral.

"Well, sure," Dixon said. "But it's more than that. The Coppersmiths have been a part of the local community for damn near forty years. That's when Sam's parents' bought the old mansion out on the bluffs. Named it Copper Beach. There was hardly anyone else living on the island when they arrived. They pretty much founded the town. The first mayor and town council voted to name the town Copper Beach."

"If no one lived on Legacy Island before the Coppersmiths arrived, who built the mansion you just mentioned?"

"Man named Xavier McClain. He made a fortune in shipping and lumber back in the early nineteen-hundreds. Bought the island and built the big house. According to the legend, he was downright strange."

"Everyone has a different definition of strange," Abby said politely. *Trust me, I know whereof I speak,* she thought.

"The old stories say that McClain was really into the woo-woo stuff, you know?" Dixon aimed a forefinger at his temple and made a few circles. "He claimed he saw things other folks couldn't see. There are a lot of tall tales around here about how he got up to some real weird shit, I mean stuff, in the basement of the old house."

"What happened to Xavier McClain?" Abby asked.

"No one knows for sure. His body was found when it washed ashore in the cove below the big house. Most folks assume he fell from the bluff. Others say he jumped. A few think he was murdered. The kids like to tell you that his ghost still walks the bluff on foggy nights, but I don't hold with that nonsense. Anyhow, after McClain died, his descendants didn't want the house, let alone the island. Way too expensive. They sold out to Elias Coppersmith."

"Wait a minute. Are you telling me that the Coppersmith family *owns* Legacy Island, not just a house?"

"Well, they don't exactly own the town. They gave that property to the local residents. And folks around here own their own homes, of course, on account of Elias Coppersmith subdivided some of the land and sold it. But yeah, the family still owns most of the island. The only one who lives here year-round now is Sam, but the rest of the Coppersmiths are always coming or going. They've all got their own houses out there on the bluff now. Sam took the old house on account of no one else in the family wanted it. His mom never did like the place. Willow and Elias live down in Sedona; that's where the main headquarters of the company is located."

"Willow and Elias are Sam's parents?"

"Right. They'll be coming up here soon," Dixon said. "They always show up for the R-and-D lab's annual technical summit and staff family weekend. On the last night there's a real fine barbecue. The locals are invited. It's a big deal around here."

Abby examined the boats in the marina slips. The majority appeared to be hardworking craft of one kind or another. Several were rigged for serious fishing. The green plants and the curtains in the windows of others spelled live-aboards, people who lived full-time on their boats. Unlike the marinas on some of the other islands that catered to summer tourists, there were no luxury yachts.

One sleek, clean-lined boat caught her attention. The name on the hull was *Phoenix*. Dixon followed the direction of her gaze.

"That's Sam's boat." He said. "I'm surprised he didn't pick you up himself today. But he only leaves the island when he has to these days."

"Is Sam involved in the family business?"

"Sort of. He and his brother run their own consulting firm, real high-tech stuff, you know? But they do a lot of their consulting for the family business so I guess you could say they are involved."

She had learned a little about the family business in the course of her cursory online research this morning. The Coppersmith fortune had been built on the mining and research-and-development of so-called "rare earths," the elements and metals that provided the sophisticated materials and crystals so vital to modern technology. Rare earths with unfamiliar names, such as lanthanum and cerium, were used in everything from computers and cell phones to X-ray machines and self-cleaning ovens.

"Sam was always a bit of a loner, even when he was a kid," Dixon said. "But after he found his fiancée's body he really started keeping to himself in the old Copper Beach house. Lot of folks, including my wife, swear that losing the love of his life about broke his heart. They say his family is worried about him. They think he might be depressed or something, you know?"

Great, Abby thought. Thaddeus Webber had sent her all this way to hire a reclusive mad scientist with paranormal talents who was suffering from some form of depression due to the death of a fiancée he might or might not have killed. The long trip from Seattle today was looking more and more like a waste of time. She glanced at her watch, wondering if she should tell Dixon to turn the water taxi around and take her back to Anacortes, where she had left her car.

Dixon eased the boat against the dock. A gangly-looking boy in his teens trotted up to help with the lines. He gave Abby a curious once-over. She gave him a vague smile in return and turned to study the small cluster of weathered buildings that surrounded the marina. There were a few more structures along the short waterfront, but all in all there wasn't a lot to the town of Copper Beach. It barely qualified as a village. But that was typical of most of the remote communities scattered across the San Juans.

People moved to the islands for any number of reasons. Some sought privacy and a simpler, slower way of life. Others came looking for a serene environment that encouraged contemplation and meditation. The islands had been home to various cloistered orders, religious sects and assorted communes and marijuana entrepreneurs for years.

A lot of folks who chose to live in the San Juans arrived with one paramount objective in mind—to get off the grid altogether. Their goal was to get lost and stay lost. It was not all that hard to do, because in the islands people minded their own business. Outsiders were stonewalled if they got too curious. Which only made Dixon's gossipy comments about Sam Coppersmith all the more intriguing, Abby thought. It was as if he felt some responsibility to defend Sam against the lurid rumors that had evidently circulated at the time of the woman's death.

Dixon and the teen finished tying up the boat. Abby stepped cautiously off the gently bobbing craft onto the planked dock and looked around, wondering if she was supposed to walk to her destination.

"Can I pay someone to drive me to Coppersmith's house?" she said to Dixon.

"You won't need a lift," Dixon said, angling his head. "Sam's here to get you."

A chill of awareness stirred the hairs on the back of her neck. Automatically, she raised her senses and turned to watch the man who was coming toward her along the dock. His dark hair was a little too long. A pair of black-framed sunglasses shielded his eyes, but the hard-edged planes and angles of his face told her a great deal about him.

It was the currents of raw power that burned in the atmosphere around Coppersmith that compelled her senses. She could literally feel the heat, both normal and paranormal, even from this distance. When he drew closer, she glimpsed a small spark of fire on his right hand.

She took another look and concluded that the flash of light had been caused by sunlight glinting off the stone of his ring.

Her initial shiver morphed into a charged thrill. She could not decide if she was more excited than she had ever been in her life or merely scared out of her wits. It was a classic fight-or-flight response. There was obviously more than one kind of top-of-the-line predator living here in the San Juans.

She looked at Dixon. "I have one question for you, Mr. Dixon."

"Sure."

"Why are you and everyone else on the island so absolutely convinced that Sam Coppersmith did not murder that woman?"

"Simple," Dixon said. He winked. "Coppersmiths are all real smart, and Sam is probably the smartest of the bunch. If he had killed that woman, there would have been nothing at all to link her death to him. He sure as freaking hell wouldn't have left her body in his own lab. She would have flat-out disappeared. No problem making that happen here in the islands. Lot of deep water around these parts."

4

"THADDEUS WEBBER INDICATED THAT YOU HAD SOME experience with this sort of thing," Abby said.

"Obsessed collectors who send online blackmail threats to innocent antiquarian book dealers?" Sam Coppersmith leaned back against his desk and folded his arms. "Can't say that I have. But an extortionist is an extortionist. Shouldn't be all that hard to find the one who is bothering you."

"I'm glad you're so optimistic," Abby said. She drummed her fingers on the arm of her chair and glanced uneasily at her watch for the third or fourth time. "Personally, I'm getting a bad feeling about this meeting. I think there may have been some mistake. Thaddeus Webber must not have understood my problem."

"Webber wouldn't have sent you to me if he hadn't thought you needed me."

Sam had said very little during the short drive from town. But she had known that his senses were slightly jacked for the whole trip because her own had been fizzing. They still were, for that matter. It was an unfamiliar sensation. She wondered if her intuition was trying to send her a warning. Or maybe she was simply sleep-deprived. Regardless, she was quite certain that Sam was assessing her, measuring her reactions, testing her in some way.

Her first view of the gray stone mansion that was the Copper Beach house had not been reassuring. The place was a true gothic monstrosity. It loomed, bleak and shadowed, in a small clearing on a bluff overlooking a cove and the dark waters of the San Juans. From the outside, the windows of the old house were obsidian mirrors.

She had concluded immediately that Sam and the house deserved each other. Both looked as if they belonged in another century, one in which it was considered normal for mysterious men to live in dark mansions that came equipped with attics and basements that held scary secrets.

Her sense of unease had deepened when she had gotten out of the SUV and walked to the front door with Sam. She had watched while he did something with his ring that unlocked the door.

"I've never seen a security system like that," she said. "Some kind of variation on a card-key security system?"

"Something like that." Sam opened the door. "My own invention."

She had anticipated another tingle of alarm, or at the very least uncertainty, when he ushered her into the shadowy front hall. But to her astonishment, the ambient energy whispering in the atmosphere had given her a small, exciting little rush. She knew that Sam noticed.

"I've got a lot of hot rocks down in the lab," he explained. "After a while, the energy infuses the atmosphere and gets embedded in the walls."

"That happens with hot books, too," she said.

"Not everyone is okay with the sensation. Gives some people the creeps, I'm told."

"Don't worry about my reaction, Mr. Coppersmith. I'm accustomed to being in the vicinity of paranormal energy."

"Yeah, I can see that." Something that might have been satisfaction had edged his mouth. "Call me Sam."

She had not offered her own first name. This was a business arrangement. The safest thing to do was to maintain at least minimal formality, at least until she figured out how to handle Sam Coppersmith.

He had removed his dark glasses at that point, revealing eyes that were a startling shade of gemstone green.

When he closed the door behind her, she had taken another look at his ring. It was made of some darkly gleaming metal and set with a small crystal. The stone was a deep, fiery red in color.

Sam had led her along a hallway and opened a door to reveal a flight of stone steps.

"Lab's in the basement," he had explained. "We can talk there."

She still could not believe that she had followed him downstairs into a windowless basement lab like some naive gothic heroine. Maybe she had been dealing with eccentric collectors for a little too long.

The cavernous, dimly lit chamber below the house was unlike any lab she had ever seen. It was crammed with display cases and drawers filled with crystals and stones and chunks of raw ore. If it were not for the low simmer of energy in the room, she could have been in the hall of gems and minerals of a world-class natural history museum.

But unlike the specimens in a museum, most of the stones around her were hot. The vibes in the atmosphere were unmistakable. She was no expert in the field of para-rocks, but like most strong talents, she could sense energy that was infused in objects, especially when there was a lot of it in the vicinity.

In addition to the crystals and stones on display, there were a number of state-of-the art instruments on the workbench. There were also some devices made of iron, brass and glass that she was certain qualified as antiques. Several appeared to be from the seventeenth or eighteenth century, but a couple of the objects looked as if they had come from the laboratory of a Renaissance-era alchemist.

The low lighting in the room added to the weirdness factor. Unlike most modern labs, there were no overhead fluorescent fixtures. The stone chamber was lit only by the desk lamp and the faint paranormal glow of some of the charged rocks. Abby got the impression that Sam preferred the shadows.

She cleared her throat discreetly. "No offense, Mr. Coppersmith, but are you a real investigator?"

"Depends on how you define *real*."

"Do you have a private investigator's license?"

"No. But I do a lot of consulting work, if that makes you feel any better."

"What kind of consulting?"

"Technical consulting."

That did it, she thought. Thaddeus had sent her on a wild-goose chase. She did not have time to waste on mad scientists and gothic mansions. She gave Sam a cool smile and got to her feet.

"I'm afraid there's been some mistake," she said. "I need a real private investigator."

"You need someone like me. Webber wouldn't have sent you here otherwise."

"You're a technical consultant, for Pete's sake."

"Trust me when I tell you that technical consulting covers a lot of territory. You're here now; you may as well sit down and tell me about the blackmail threats."

She did not sit down. But she did not grab her shoulder bag and jacket and head for the door, either. As a compromise, she walked to stand in front of a glass display case and looked down at a chunk of what looked like blue quartz inside. With her senses still slightly heightened, she could perceive some of the energy locked deep inside the crystal. She wondered what the lab looked like to Sam. With his strong psychic sensitivity to para-rocks, the place probably glowed as brightly as if it was lit by sunshine.

She made her decision. Sam was right. She did not know where else to turn. She had to trust Thaddeus Webber's judgment. He had been her friend and mentor for years.

"Here's the situation," she said. "I'm a freelancer in the underground hot-books market. Collectors in that market tend to be somewhat eccentric, especially those who possess some real talent."

Sam looked amused. "Are you saying those who collect paranormal books are crazy?"

She gave him what she hoped was a quelling look. "What I'm saying, Mr. Coppersmith, is that there are some collectors who are obsessed to the point of being quite dangerous. Others are just plain weird. And then there are those who actually believe in the occult. Witches, demons, sorcery, that sort of nonsense."

"Your clientele must be very interesting."

"For obvious reasons, I have to be careful. At the start of my career, Thaddeus Webber advised me to work only by referral. I have stuck to that advice. I do not accept commissions from collectors I don't know unless they are referred to me by someone I trust. And even then, I always check them out with Thaddeus. I go out of my way to keep a low profile. But word gets around in collectors' circles. The result is that once in a while a determined person manages to get my email address."

"That's how clients contact you?"

"Yes. I use a false name with that email address, of course."

"What name?"

"My clients know me as Newton. And that's all they know about me. When I do get a message from someone seeking my services who has not been properly referred, I never respond. That's usually the end of the matter. People who don't hear back from me tend to conclude either that I'm something of a myth or that I'm a complete fraud. But yesterday morning I received the first blackmail note. The second one came in last night. Both were sent to my Newton address."

"How hard would it be for someone to dig up that address?"

"Probably not hard at all if they hang out in the right chat rooms and hot-books sites. That's not what worries me. What freaked me out is that the blackmailer knows way too much about me. When I contacted Thaddeus to ask for advice, I got a one-line email back from him. He told me to contact you, and he gave me your email address."

"Let me see the notes."

"I printed them out for you." She turned away from the blue quartz and went back to her chair. Leaning down, she reached into the large shoulder bag, took out the manila envelope and handed it to Sam.

He opened the envelope and removed the two printouts inside. He studied the first one without comment. He read the second one aloud. *"In addition to knowing what you did in V's library, I also know about your past and why you attended the Summerlight Academy."*

Sam looked up from the page. "I assume V is Hannah Vaughn and that the incident referred to is the home invasion at her house that took place a couple of days ago?"

Startled, she watched his face very carefully. "You know about that?"

"Thaddeus Webber sent me an email, too."

In spite of everything, Abby found herself smiling. "To vouch for me? I gather you work by referral also."

Sam's mouth edged upward at one corner. "Whenever I can."

"In that case, you must have done some research on what happened in Mrs. Vaughn's library."

"According to what I found online, a mentally unstable man with a gun invaded Vaughn's home. He claimed to hear voices and may have been tanked up on drugs, which, in turn, caused him to collapse at the scene. He was taken into custody and is now sitting in a locked ward at a psychiatric hospital, undergoing observation to see if he is sane enough to stand trial. Statements were taken from the owner of the home, Mrs. Vaughn; her housekeeper, who fainted at some point; and an unnamed woman who was there at the time. That would be you?"

Abby took a deep breath and let it out slowly. "You seem to have all the facts, Mr. Coppersmith."

"Like you, I don't take every job that comes my way. And I do not have all of the facts, but I intend to get them." He slipped the printouts back into the envelope. "Any idea what the blackmailer wants from you?"

"Not yet."

"In that case, tell me what he has on you."

Abby began to pace the chamber, weaving through the maze of display cases while she composed her thoughts. She had known this was coming, she reminded herself. It had been highly unlikely that she would be able to hire Sam without giving him all the information he might need to find the extortionist.

"Everything in the police report concerning the Vaughn home invasion is true," she began.

"That makes me very interested to know what is not in the report."

"Right." She took a deep breath. "What's not in those reports is that I'm the one who caused the intruder to collapse that day."

Sam inclined his head once, as if she had confirmed a conclusion he had already reached.

"Thought so," he said.

"*What?*" She stopped and stared at him, slightly stunned.

"The convenient collapse of an armed intruder in the middle of a home invasion was a bit of a red flag," he said mildly. "You somehow used your talent to take down the intruder, didn't you?"

"Yes," she said quietly.

"You knew going in that you could do that."

"I knew that if I could manipulate him into touching one of the heavily encrypted books at the same time I was holding it, there was a good chance that I could channel some of the energy into his aura and temporarily destabilize his pattern, yes."

Sam looked intrigued. "So do you do that kind of thing on a regular basis?"

She glared at him, outraged and maybe even scared now, although she was loath to acknowledge it. *Show no weakness.*

"Of course not," she said. She clasped her hands tightly behind her back and resumed pacing. "But for obvious reasons I do not want rumors of my ability to channel energy like that to start circulating in the collectors' market."

"You think it would hurt business?"

She whirled around to face him again. "Gossip like that could destroy me."

"How?"

"Look, Mr. Coppersmith, I work both sides of the book market, the normal side and the true paranormal side. My normal clients are mostly legitimate private collectors who are interested in the history of the study of the paranormal."

"Those would be your non-talent clients?"

"Yes. But to be honest, a small-time freelancer like me would starve if she catered only to that clientele. Talk about a niche market. The money is in the genuine hot-books world, which is, for the most part, an underground market. Deals conducted in that market have to be kept very low-profile. A lot of the most serious collectors prefer to remain anonymous. If they do invite me into their homes to appraise their collections, as Mrs. Vaughn did, they expect me to be extremely discreet. Generally speaking, the underground market pays well, but the clients tend to be a difficult bunch."

"Define *difficult*," Sam said.

"The spectrum of difficult clients starts at eccentric and moves on through secretive, reclusive and paranoid, all the way to dangerous. But I try to leave that last category of client to my competitors. The true hot-books market is a pool that is very deep at one end. I stick to the shallows."

"Sounds like a smart business plan."

"There's less money at my end of the market, but it's definitely safer swimming. The point I'm trying to make, though, is that in my business, reputation is everything. Aside from the fact that I'm very good at what I do, my most important credentials are that I am considered one hundred percent trustworthy and that I am not perceived as a potential book thief. I regret to say that there are some freelancers in my business who are not above accepting a commission to acquire a particular hot book by any means possible."

"But if it got out that you can walk into someone's private library, zap the collector unconscious and walk out with any item you care to take, some would-be clients would be reluctant to hire you, is that it?"

"What do you think?"

"I think you're right," Sam said. "Power of any kind is always interesting, but people tend to react to it in one of two ways. Some folks are compelled and attracted or even obsessed by power. Others get very, very nervous."

"Exactly. I'm glad you understand what I'm facing here. When it comes to my underground clients, I walk a fine line. Like them, I try to keep a very low profile, and not only because I value my reputation. I do not want to become the subject of someone's research experiment or, worse yet, attract the sort of freaks who want to fire up a cult."

For the first time, surprise narrowed Sam's brilliant green eyes. "You've had trouble with one or both of those types?"

"When I was in my teens, and again in college, I attracted the attention of some people who wanted to study me. It was not a pleasant experience. And even though I try to vet every client carefully, once in a while one becomes obsessed with me because of my talent. Fortunately, no one has tried to get me to channel some ancient spirit, thank heavens, but my friend Gwen had some trouble in that department a while back. It was scary."

"Sounds like your talent-obsessed clients and the would-be cult founders have the potential to turn into stalkers."

"Yes." Abby paused. "I don't suppose you Coppersmiths have ever been bothered with problems like that."

"No, can't say that we have."

She gave a small sigh. "Must be nice to be part of a family that can insulate you from that sort of thing."

"Moving right along, whoever sent you the threatening notes mentioned something about keeping your old secrets as well as the new ones. What did he mean?"

"To tell you the truth, that was what made me contact Thaddeus." She cleared her throat. "When I was in my early teens and just coming into my talent, my family concluded that I had some major mental-health issues."

"I can see where that might happen if you grow up in a family that doesn't acknowledge the existence of the paranormal."

"In my case, there were some unfortunate incidents that confirmed their worst fears."

"Incidents?"

"Yes. As a result of those incidents, I was sent to a school for troubled teens. It was either that or a juvenile-detention facility. My father made sure my legal file was sealed, but obviously the bastard who sent those blackmail notes is aware of at least some of my history."

"What kind of incidents?"

"Nothing serious, really." She unfolded her arms and waved one hand in a vague way. "I accidentally set a couple of fires, one of which partially destroyed a bookstore."

"No kidding?"

"But the owner was only mildly injured, I swear it," she said quickly. "And there was the time I did some damage to my family's house. Very minor damage, really. It was the water damage that occurred when the fire department put out what was a very tiny fire that was the biggest problem afterward. Well, that and the smoke damage."

Sam watched her with a fascinated expression. "You can do that? Set fires with your talent?"

She raised her chin. "I told you, the fires were accidents."

"Right. Any other incidents I should know about?"

"Nothing of significance. Look, this conversation is not going in a good direction. Let's get back on track. The problem here is that I've got a complicated past, and whoever is trying to blackmail me knows about it. He's threatening to spread gossip about me. That would be bad enough if the gossip was confined to the collectors' market, but I'm afraid that he'll go to the media."

"Why would the media care about your troubled childhood?"

She spread her hands apart. "My father is Dr. Brandon C. Radwell."

"A psychologist who specializes in family counseling. Wrote a book on marriage. Does some talk shows. I know. That much came up when I checked you out online."

"Clearly you haven't been paying attention to those talk shows."

"Guilty as charged," Sam said.

"My father has become one of those TV guest experts on families, child-rearing and marriage. His new book, *Families by Choice,* is being released this week. He is in serious talks with a television producer about a reality TV series. It would be similar to those shows that feature the dog experts who go into people's homes and deal with bad dogs, I think, except that he would go into people's homes and tell them how to fix their family problems."

"Okay, I see the picture here," Sam said. "If it gets out that the hot celebrity expert in family psychology has a daughter with a troubled past who thinks she has paranormal powers, it could kill book sales and the TV deal."

"And it would be all my fault. On top of that, the whole family would be horribly embarrassed. I'm the crazy daughter they would have preferred to keep stashed in the attic. That sort of thing isn't done much these days, though, so everyone, including me, goes out of their way to pretend that I'm normal. As far as the media is concerned, the Radwells are just one big happy family. Specifically, we are the perfect example of the modern blended family."

"You sound like you're quoting someone."

She wrinkled her nose. "Yeah. Dad."

"Your father and the rest of the family don't realize that you actually do have some true talent?"

"No, of course not. How do you prove a paranormal talent like mine to someone who isn't sensitive to that kind of energy?"

Amusement gleamed in Sam's eyes. "Setting fires wasn't proof?"

"That is not funny. My family concluded that I was not only delusional but seriously deranged. Hence my time in the Summerlight Academy, where I learned how to pass for normal. They like to think the intensive counseling and therapy were effective. I prefer to let them believe that. It works better for all of us."

"What do they think you do for a living?"

"As far as they're concerned, I'm a small-time online bookseller. I'm the official underachiever in the family, but that's better than having everyone think I'm still delusional." Abby glanced at her watch again. "I don't have any more time to waste, Mr. Coppersmith. Will you take the job?"

"Let's see what we've got here," Sam said. "You had a difficult childhood, you set a few fires, spent some time in a special school for troubled teens, and you currently live a double life that has a secret side involving the underground hot-books market. You have zapped at least one individual with your talent, and I'm betting there have been others."

Alarm flashed through her. "What makes you say that?"

Sam gave her a wicked smile. "Because you admitted you knew you could take down the intruder before you confronted him. That implies some prior experience, or at least a little practice."

She swallowed hard. "Okay, there may have been a couple of other similar incidents, but I can explain all of them, really. One involved the owner of the bookstore that I accidentally burned down, and there was this creepy assistant professor in college who wanted to run experiments on me and tried to rape me when I refused. And a couple of years ago, a client became obsessed with me, but . . ."

Sam held up one hand, palm out. "No need to explain, Abby Radwell. You are my kind of client. I'll take the job."

5

NOT JUST MY KIND OF CLIENT, SAM THOUGHT. *MY KIND OF woman.*

He watched from the dock until Dixon piloted the water taxi with Abby on board out of the harbor and out of sight beyond a cluster of small islets.

He was still feeling the rush when he climbed back into the SUV and started along the narrow winding road to the Copper Beach house. He flexed his hands and took a tighter grip on the steering wheel. Stirred by the energy that was still splashing through him, the Phoenix stone in his ring burned with a low, deep fire. He could not remember the last time he had responded to a woman this way. *Never,* he concluded.

Abby Radwell had hit his senses like sizzling, sparking, flashing heat lightning produced by some exotic, unknown crystal, one with incredible properties that he could not wait to investigate, that he was *compelled* to investigate. It was not curiosity or even just physical desire that energized him now, although desire was definitely a big factor in the mix. There was something else going on. Whatever it was, he had a hunch the prowling, hungry awareness was going to keep him awake tonight. Fine by him. It beat the hell out of the recurring dream that had plagued him for the past six months.

When he walked back into the big house, he discovered that a strange silence, a sense of emptiness, had settled on the old place. It was not the kind of silence that was associated with the lack of sound. The stone walls echoed, as they always did, with his footsteps. The thick oak floors creaked in places. The refrigerator hummed faintly in the kitchen.

But there was something different about the atmosphere now. It was as if an invisible hand had hit the paranormal mute button after Abby departed.

He went downstairs into the lab, cranked back in the chair and stacked his heels on the corner of the desk. He steepled his fingers and thought about his new client.

He summoned a mental image first, concentrating on what it was about her that had fascinated him. It was not any single aspect of her appearance, he decided. Warm copper and gold glowed in the depths of her auburn hair, which formed a vibrant cloud of curls around an animated, fascinating, intelligent but not classically beautiful face. Eyes the color of dark amber tilted slightly upward at the outer corners. There was a firmly etched nose and a soft, sensitive mouth to go with the eyes.

She was not tall, no more than five-foot-four at most, but what there was of her was curvy and feminine and healthy-looking in all the right places. She carried herself with the self-confidence of a woman who was accustomed to dealing with her own problems, a woman who was capable of handling a lot of talent. An aura of energy and power brightened the atmosphere around her.

After a while he took out his phone and hit a familiar code. His father picked up halfway through the first ring.

"Did she show up?" Elias demanded.

"She was here," Sam said. "Just left. She's on her way back to Seattle."

"Well? Were you right? Is she involved in this thing?"

"I think so, but I'm not sure how, yet."

"Webber sent her to you. He wouldn't have done that if there wasn't some connection to the lab notebook."

"I agree, but all I've got for certain at the moment is that an anonymous person has sent Abby two notes that qualify as blackmail threats. The sender is trying to coerce her cooperation. He wants her to do something for him, but he hasn't made any specific demands, just issued a few threats."

"What kind of threats?" Elias asked.

"Nothing physical, at least not yet. Abby has some stuff in her private life that she would prefer to keep secret for the sake of the family image. Also, she definitely does not want the news of what happened in Vaughn's library to become widespread gossip in the underground book market."

"So you were right? That intruder did not go down because of a drug overdose?"

"Abby broke the psi-code on one of the books in Vaughn's collection, and then she channeled the energy into the intruder's aura. The currents knocked the guy unconscious."

Elias whistled softly. "Takes a lot of power to channel energy that hot."

"It does."

"And the blackmailer *knows* she did that?"

"It's not clear if he knows that she took down the intruder. The blackmail notes are a little vague. But I think we can assume he is aware that Abby can unlock psi-codes. My gut tells me that is what is important to him."

"Lander Knox," Elias said urgently. "Got to be him. He needs someone like Abby to acquire the lab book and break the code."

"I'd say there's a definite possibility that the guy who sent the notes is Lander Knox, but we're still in the theory-and-speculation stage. The rumors that the lab book has surfaced have been circulating for months now, according to Webber. There are a few other folks who would like to get their hands on that book."

"Helicon Stone." Elias's voice hardened. "Yeah, we have to assume that if that SOB Hank Barrett has gotten wind of the lab book, he'll be looking for it. Probably send his son out to do his dirty work."

Sam almost smiled. The feud between Elias and Hank Barrett, the owner of Coppersmith's biggest competitor, was legendary. No one knew the origins of the quarrel, but over time the hostility between the two men had helped fuel two empires.

There was a great fallacy taught in business schools. It held that successful multimillion-dollar companies were run by smart executives who based their decisions on hard data and logical marketing strategies.

The truth, Sam thought, was that, as with all the other endeavors that human beings engaged in, business was conducted by people who let emotions, egos and personal agendas rule the decision-making process. Sometimes it worked.

"I know how you feel about Hank Barrett, Dad," he said. "But blackmail isn't his style, and it's not Gideon's, either."

"Huh." Elias was silent for a beat. "Wonder why the blackmailer didn't just try to hire Abby Radwell outright?"

"She only works by referral, and she vets all potential clients through Thaddeus Webber."

"Must make for a small client list," Elias said.

"But a relatively safe list. You know as well as I do that there are some dangerous people in the underground market. Abby described it as a very deep pool. She told me that she prefers to swim in the shallows."

"Looks like somebody just tossed her into the deep end. Too bad Judson isn't available. You're on your own with this."

A week ago, Judson had taken what had looked like a routine consulting assignment for a regular client. He had sent one brief message indicating that the situation had become complicated and that he would not be in touch for a while. There had been no further word from him. That was not unusual with consulting jobs for this particular client, a no-name government agency that paid well for talent and discretion.

"Keep an eye on Radwell," Elias ordered. "We need to locate that lab book. For now, she's our best lead."

"Keeping an eye on Abby won't be a problem," Sam said. "She hired me to find the blackmailer."

"*Hired* you?" Elias was flabbergasted. "What the hell do you mean by that?"

"I thought you'd be pleased that I have a new consulting job. I know you and Mom have been worrying about me lately."

"Now, just one damn minute. Your job is to find that old lab book before Lander Knox does."

"Got to go, Dad. I'm on my way to Seattle. I'll update you later."

Sam ended the connection and went upstairs to pack an overnight bag. Anticipation crackled through him. He would be seeing Abby again soon.

6

ELIAS TOSSED THE PHONE ONTO HIS DESK AND WENT DOWN the glass-walled corridor that overlooked the patio, the pool and the great red rocks beyond.

He paused at the door of his wife's study. Willow was at her computer. He knew she was working on foundation business. It had been her idea to set up the Coppersmith Foundation twenty years ago. Although she staunchly denied having any psychic talent, her intuition combined with her financial expertise ensured that the foundation was managed brilliantly. No one in the Coppersmith Inc. accounting department could follow the money the way Willow could. As a result, no one got far trying to scam the foundation.

When he went through the doorway he felt the familiar sense of rightness that always thrilled him when he was in Willow's presence. He'd experienced that same thrill the first time they met. Nothing had changed over the decades.

He had fallen hard for Willow all those years ago, but he was pretty sure that he loved her more now than he had at the start, assuming such a thing was even possible. He had not had a dime to his name back in those days, just the land and mineral rights to a chunk of desert that everyone else thought was fit only for rattlesnakes and growing cactus. But Willow had believed in him. She had made a home for him in a secondhand trailer out there in the desert, never complaining about the lack of money, the blistering heat or the fact that the nearest mall was several hundred miles away. And Willow had kept his secrets. He counted himself the luckiest of men.

Life was very different now. It had taken several years and a lot of sweat before the mining venture proved successful. But in the end, the rare earths that his small company had pulled out of the ground had formed the foundation of the family empire.

He and Willow could afford anything they wanted these days. They enjoyed the money and lived well. But every time he looked at Willow, he knew an unshakable truth that warmed his soul. If he lost the company tomorrow and had to start over again, she would be by his side the whole way, even if it meant going back to that damned trailer.

"He called her Abby," Elias said.

Willow looked up from the computer. She took off her reading glasses with a slow, thoughtful motion and contemplated him with her knowing eyes.

"You're talking about the young woman in Seattle who freelances in the book market? The one Thaddeus Webber sent to Sam?"

"Abigail Radwell. Sam met with her today. Looks like someone is trying to blackmail her. I'm betting it's Lander Knox. Somehow he found out she can break psi-codes. He thinks he can force her to help him find the lab book."

"There are other people who are after that book," Willow said.

"Yeah, Sam reminded me of that, too. But Quinn warned me that his son was sick in the head. Evil sick. Blackmail is the kind of shit an evil man would try."

"Maybe. How does the situation stand now? Did this Abby Radwell agree to help Sam find that notebook?"

"Not exactly. As far as I can tell she hired him to find out who is blackmailing her."

Willow blinked. "She *hired* Sam?"

"That's what he told me."

"Hmm." Willow pushed back her chair and got to her feet. She went to stand at the window. "Well, I suppose that might work. Sam will persuade her that locating the book and getting it off the underground market is the best way to neutralize the blackmailer."

Elias joined her at the window. "That must be the plan. He said he was on his way to Seattle right now."

"He'll get the lab book, Elias." Willow reached out and took his hand. "It will be all right."

"For the past couple of decades, I've been telling myself that the lab book must have been buried in the explosion along with Willis. But deep down I always knew that it was out there somewhere. And now it's surfaced at last. If it falls into the wrong hands—"

"Stop blaming yourself for what happened at that old mine all those years ago. It was not your fault. You and Quinn Knox were nearly killed that day."

"I'm the one who found that vein of crystals. I'm the one who insisted we run those first tests to see what we had."

Willow tightened her grip on his hand. "What's done is done. You had no way of knowing how dangerous those rocks were."

Elias exhaled slowly. "I still don't. That's one of the things that makes that lab book so damn dangerous."

"Sam knows that. He'll find the book. He's smart, and his talent will be an asset in this thing. You'll see."

Elias pulled her closer and wrapped his arm around her shoulders. Together they watched the fading sunlight splash across the red rocks. He knew they were both thinking about the past and the deadly explosion at the mine.

The repercussions of the paranormal energy that had been released that day had echoed down into the future, creating the greatest of all the Coppersmith family secrets, the one secret that he and Willow had never told Sam, Judson or Emma.

After a while, Willow turned her head to look at him with a speculative expression.

"He called her Abby?" she said.

"Yeah. After meeting her for all of maybe one hour. And now he's on his way to Seattle." Elias paused, trying to find a way to explain what he had heard in Sam's voice. "He sounded *energized,* Willow. As if he was looking forward to something."

Willow smiled. "In that case, regardless of how this turns out, I'm already grateful to Abby Radwell."

7

"ARE YOU OUT OF YOUR MIND, ABBY?" GWEN FRAZIER LEANED
forward across the restaurant table and lowered her voice. "According to what I found online, Sam Coppersmith was implicated in the murder of his fiancée six months ago. You have no business hiring a man like that. He might be very, very dangerous."

"Relax, I'm employing him, I'm not sleeping with him. Big difference."

"That's supposed to reassure me?"

"Well, it certainly makes me feel better about the whole thing," Abby said.

They were in a booth in the bar section of the restaurant. It was seven-thirty. The after-work crowd that had drifted in earlier had come and gone. The place was now filling up with the locals from the nearby condos and apartment buildings. Several stylists from the hair salon on the corner, which closed at seven, were celebrating a birthday. The low rumble of conversation and the music playing over the sound system provided a layer of privacy.

Gwen Frazier was the same age as Abby. Tall, dark-haired and hazel-eyed, she was an aura-reading talent who made her living as a psychic counselor. Her abilities allowed her to work with talents and non-talents alike. As she had explained to Abby, there was no real difference between the two groups of clients. Those with real psychical abilities of their own believed her when she explained that she worked by reading their auras. Those without talent wanted to believe that she could see their energy fields. It was a win-win situation for a woman in her line.

"This isn't a joke," Gwen said.

"I know. Sorry. It's been a very long day. The drive back from Anacortes took longer than usual. Accident on the interstate." Abby swallowed some of her wine and lowered the glass. "If it helps, I have been informed that there is no way Sam Coppersmith could have murdered his fiancée."

"Who told you that?"

"The water-taxi guy."

"He's an authority?"

"He certainly seemed to think so. Evidently, no one on that island thinks Sam did it."

"And what proof do they offer?" Gwen demanded.

"They seem to feel that if Sam had murdered someone, he would have done a better job of it."

"I beg your pardon. What's that supposed to mean?"

"He would have made the victim disappear." Abby waved one hand in a now-you-see-it-now-you-don't motion. "And he would have taken care to make sure that there was nothing left behind that pointed back to him."

"And you believed this water-taxi guy's theory?"

Abby looked at Gwen over the top of her glass. "Having met Sam Coppersmith, yes, I believe that theory."

"You do realize that there's a lot of money in the Coppersmith family," Gwen said ominously. "With money comes the kind of power it takes to make sure someone in the family does not go down for murder."

"Your cynical side is showing, Gwen."

"It's my best side. Is this Sam Coppersmith a real private investigator?"

"He described himself as a technical consultant."

"Oh, that's just wonderful," Gwen said.

"But I do think he's the best man for the job."

"Why, for heaven's sake?"

"Because this situation involves a very hot book, and I need an investigator who at least takes the paranormal seriously. Not a lot of those floating around, in case you haven't noticed. Besides, you know as well as I do that Thaddeus Webber would never have sent me to Coppersmith if he had believed there was a better option."

"Point taken." Gwen sat back. "Have you received any more email from the blackmailer?"

"No, thank goodness. But there's something else I want to talk to you about."

"What?"

"I've had a really weird dream two nights in a row. They both featured Grady Hastings."

Gwen frowned. "The crazy guy who staged that home invasion in your client's house?"

"Yes."

"Well, it's not surprising that you would have some bad dreams for a while. That was a very frightening situation."

"True, but what is freaking me out about the dreams is that I've started sleepwalking. I've never done that in my life."

"There is nothing unstable about your talent," Gwen said, "if that's what's worrying you."

"You're the one who told me that a disturbance in the dreamstate can be an early indication of serious problems with the para-senses."

"It's true, but that kind of disturbance is visible in the aura. You're fine."

Abby framed the base of her glass in a triangle formed by her thumbs and forefingers. "Take a look. Please."

"Okay, okay."

Gwen heightened her talent. Abby felt energy shiver gently in the atmosphere. A few feet away, a middle-aged businessman who was slouched on a bar stool suddenly turned his head and looked around, as though searching for someone or something. Abby knew that he had felt the tingle of psi in the vicinity but probably did not know what it was that had lifted the hairs on the nape of his neck. Over in the corner, a redheaded stylist drinking a cosmopolitan glanced uneasily around the room before turning back to her colleagues.

Abby waited while Gwen did her thing. After a couple of minutes, the energy level in the atmosphere receded.

"I'm not picking up any bad vibes," Gwen said. "Just the indications of stress that I've mentioned before. There is some deepening in the intensity of ultralight coming from the hot end of the spectrum, but nothing alarming. I didn't see anything that I associate with instability of the para-senses. Also, for the record, I didn't see the kind of dream-light that is associated with regular sleepwalking."

"Then what in the world is going on?"

"I've tried to explain to you that what happened to you in the Vaughn library was the equivalent of a category-five hurricane, as far as your para-senses are concerned. You channeled an enormous amount of volatile energy. For heaven's sake, you managed to render a man unconscious. There was bound to be some blowback, to say nothing of the fact that you could have been killed that day. You need to give yourself time to recover from the shock."

"I can't continue sleepwalking," Abby said. "What if I open the sliding glass doors and decide to take a walk off the balcony?"

"Calm down. You're not going to do that. Your para-senses would kick in fast if you tried to do anything that might put your life in danger."

"You have more faith in my senses than I do."

Gwen grew thoughtful. "In this dream, do you have any sense of where you're going or what you want to accomplish?"

"I see Grady Hastings. He's reaching out to me, begging me to help him. He tells me I'm the only one who can."

"Is that all?"

"Pretty much."

"Okay, I'm sticking to my theory that the fugue states you're experiencing are being triggered by stress you experienced the other day. But there is another possibility that you should not overlook."

"What?"

"Your intuition may be trying to tell you something important."

"Such as?"

"I don't know," Gwen said. "But you're too smart to ignore the implications. Try turning the dream into a lucid dream, and then take control of it."

"Easier said than done."

"Well, it's certainly easier for a strong talent than it would be for someone who doesn't have much psychic sensitivity," Gwen said. "Before you go to sleep tonight, set your psychic alarm clock to alert you when you start dreaming. Then take control of the dream."

"That will work?"

"Yes, if you do a good job of setting the alarm. The trick works on the same principle that makes it possible for you to tell yourself that you have to wake up at a certain time in order to catch an early plane. Lots of people, even people with very little talent, do that all the time."

Abby took a slow breath and reminded herself that this was Gwen's area of expertise. "Okay, I'll give it a shot."

Gwen aimed a finger at her. "You know what you really need?"

"Please don't say a new boyfriend."

"You need a vacation. You should come with me to Hawaii tomorrow. It's not too late. I'll bet we can find you a seat on my flight. There are always last-minute cancellations."

"Sure, at full fare. You know I can't afford that. Besides, leaving town now is out of the question. How can I enjoy a vacation if I know there's a blackmailer waiting for me when I get back?"

"I guess that would put a damper on things," Gwen conceded. "But you've hired Coppersmith to take care of the extortionist for you. Let him do his job while you relax on a beach."

"I don't think you can just hire an investigator and then go merrily off on vacation while he cleans things up for you."

"Why not? You're finished with the Vaughn job, and speaking as your friend and psychic counselor, I'm telling you that you need some time off to let your senses recover. Put the ticket to Hawaii on your charge card and tell your investigator to file reports of his progress by email."

"I don't like the idea of turning Sam Coppersmith loose, unsupervised, on what is essentially my very personal and private business."

Gwen smiled knowingly. "You like to be in control."

"Who doesn't? But trust me, if you ever meet Sam Coppersmith, you'll know why staying in charge is a very sensible idea."

"What's he like?"

"Think mad scientist with a basement lab."

"Doesn't sound like the typical profile of a private investigator."

Abby picked up her glass again. "There's nothing typical about Sam Coppersmith."

When they emerged from the restaurant, a light misty rain veiled the Belltown neighborhood. The wet pavement glowed with the reflected light of the streetlamps. Neon signs illuminated the windows of the innumerable restaurants, pubs and clubs that lined both sides of First Avenue.

Gwen shoved her hands deep into the pockets of her trench coat. "I'm thinking that maybe I should cancel Hawaii tomorrow. I don't like leaving you here alone to deal with Coppersmith and a blackmailer."

"You are not going to cancel. Your new client is paying you a huge fee and all expenses just to have you go there to do a reading. You can't turn your back on that kind of money."

"Screw the money. I'm worried about you, Abby."

"I'll be fine."

"Promise me that if you start to feel like you're in more trouble than you can handle you'll call Nick, first, because he'll be the closest. And right after you call him, you'll call me. I'll be on the next plane back to Seattle."

"I promise," Abby said.

Neither of them mentioned the possibility of her going to her family for help. It was not an option, and they both knew it. Gwen and Nick Sawyer constituted her real family, Abby thought. The bond among the three of them had been forged in the fires of their years together in the Summerlight Academy. Nothing could sever it.

She was about to add more reassurance, but a flash of intense awareness stopped her cold in the middle of the sidewalk.

"Abby?" Gwen stopped, too, concerned. "Are you okay?"

"He's here," Abby said quietly.

"Who?" Gwen asked.

Abby watched a shadowy figure detach itself from a darkened doorway and walk forward into the light. The man wore a black leather jacket open over a dark crewneck pullover and dark trousers. The collar of the jacket was pulled up against the chill and the rain, shadowing his features.

He carried a black leather gym bag in one hand. With her senses on alert, she had no difficulty at all perceiving the faint heat in his eyes. A thrill of excitement fizzed through her veins.

Sam looked at her, eyes heating a little. "I've been waiting for you. You know the old saying."

"What old saying?" Abby asked.

"You can run, but you can't hide."

Abby looked at Gwen. "Meet Sam Coppersmith."

8

SAM HEARD THE CLICKS OF DOG CLAWS ON A WOODEN FLOOR before Abby got her door unlocked.

"That's Newton," Abby explained. "He isn't keen on strangers, especially strange men."

"I'll try to make a good impression," Sam said.

She turned the key and pushed the door open. A scruffy gray dog of uncertain ancestry lunged forward to greet Abby as if she had been gone for a year.

"Sorry I'm late, Newton." Abby leaned down to scratch the dog affectionately behind the ears. "We've got company."

Newton regarded Sam with an expression of grave misgivings.

"I'm with her," Sam said.

"Generally speaking, he doesn't bite," Abby said.

"You don't have to make that sound like a character flaw," Sam said.

Newton was on the small side, but that was about all he had in common with the typical condo dog, which, in Sam's experience, tended to come in two versions: tiny, white and fluffy or chunky pug. Newton was a condo-sized version of a junkyard dog.

"Where did you get him?" Sam asked.

"The animal shelter." Abby gave Newton an affectionate smile. "It was love at first sight, wasn't it, Newton?"

Newton spared her a brief glance, acknowledging his name. Then he turned his attention back to Sam.

Sam set the leather duffel bag on the floor, crouched and extended his hand toward Newton. The dog tilted his head slightly to the side and pricked up his ears. He sniffed Sam's hand and then condescended to allow himself to be patted a few times.

"Congratulations," Abby said. She slipped out of her coat and turned to hang it on the red enamel coat tree. "Newton approves of you. He doesn't take to everyone."

Sam got to his feet. "I think it's more a case of tolerating me."

"Well, yes, but at least he doesn't look like he's going to go for your throat."

"He's a condo dog," Sam said. "The most he could go for is my ankle."

Abby glared. "Do not, under any circumstances, underestimate Newton. He picks up on vibes in the atmosphere. He knows when he's being insulted."

Sam looked at Newton. "Is that so?"

Newton gave a disdainful little snort and trotted off down the hall.

Sam looked at Abby. "Since your guard dog has decided to allow me over the threshold, is it okay if I take off my coat?"

Abby flushed. "Yes, of course. Sorry. I didn't mean to be rude, it's just that I wasn't expecting to see you again so soon."

"I got that impression."

He shrugged out of his jacket and handed it to her. When she took it from him, her fingers brushed against his, sending an intimate little thrill of awareness across his senses. He knew she felt the small flash because her brilliant eyes widened slightly in surprise. She gave him a startled look and then just as swiftly looked away.

She hung his jacket on the coat tree and led the way down the short hall to the living and dining area.

A few minutes ago, Gwen Frazier had discreetly vanished in a cab to her own apartment a couple of blocks away. Sam had felt the energy shiver in the atmosphere when Abby had introduced him to her friend. He was fairly certain that Gwen had used some talent to make a judgment call. She had evidently decided that Abby was safe with him, at least for now, because she had not tried to hang around.

Things were looking up, he decided. He had managed to get through two lines of defense tonight, the protective friend and the protective dog. He was on a roll.

"Your friend is also a talent, isn't she?" he asked.

"Yes. Gwen is a psychic counselor. She does aura readings in a shop in the market."

"Aura readings. Right."

Abby gave him a severe look. "I know what you're thinking."

"Do you?"

"You think Gwen is using her talent to con people. For the record, she doesn't do fortune-telling or palm-reading. And she certainly doesn't pretend to talk to the dead. She really can read auras. Her clients come to her for advice and guidance. She analyzes their energy fields and tells them what she sees and makes recommendations. She's a kind of therapist."

"Got it."

Abby sighed. "I'm probably overreacting here. It's just that so many people think Gwen is a fraud. Storefront psychics aren't exactly held in high esteem by psychologists and traditional counselors. Would you like some herbal tea? I'd offer coffee, but I don't drink it at night, at least not lately."

And that was all the information he was going to get on Gwen Frazier, he thought. "Tea will be fine. Thanks."

"I'll get the water started." She hesitated, as if she wasn't quite sure what to do with him. "Please, sit down."

He studied his options. The condo was small, but it was a corner unit with an open, flowing floor plan. The walls were a sunny Mediterranean gold with dark brown accents. The floors were hardwood. There were two area rugs decorated with modernistic designs in deep red, teal, green and yellow. Newton was lounging on the one near the window. He watched Sam with deep suspicion, but he showed no signs of going for the jugular or the ankle.

There was a comfortable-looking L-shaped sofa, a reading chair, some bookshelves, a lot of healthy-looking plants and a glass-topped coffee table. There was a book on the table. He took a closer look. *Families by Choice: A Guide to Creating the Modern Blended Family* by Dr. Brandon C. Radwell.

"That's my father's new book," Abby said.

He picked up *Families by Choice* and turned it over. The back-cover photo showed a smiling Brandon C. Radwell holding hands with an elegant-looking woman who had to be his wife. Behind the beaming couple stood Abby, a man about her age, and two very attractive women who appeared to be nineteen or twenty.

"This is your family?" Sam asked, holding up the book to show the photo.

"That's the Radwells, the perfect modern blended family," Abby said. She turned away and became very busy with the teakettle. "That's my stepbrother, Dawson, and my half sisters standing with me behind Dad and Diana."

"Your half sisters look like twins."

"They are. They're in college." Abby set the kettle on a burner. "I was twelve when they were born. Dawson was thirteen."

He put the book down on the coffee table and finished his examination of the room. One corner had been turned into a home office outfitted with a desk, a computer and some storage cabinets.

The tiny balcony and wraparound floor-to-ceiling windows took full advantage of the cityscape view. The lights of the Space Needle glittered in the night.

The whole place glowed with a cozy, inviting warmth that suggested a very personal touch. A lot of time and attention had been lavished on the little condo to transform it from a living space into a home.

"Nice," he said.

Abby smiled, the first genuine smile he had gotten from her. She was suddenly radiant. Deep satisfaction and delight lit her eyes. "It's my first home. I've been renting forever. But I finally managed to save enough for a down payment. Moved in three months ago. Did the decorating myself. My friends helped me with the painting and built-ins."

There was more than just pride of ownership in her voice. "It's my first home" said a lot. The little condo was very important to Abby. Something else she had said struck him, too. Her friends had helped her paint and decorate. There was no mention of any assistance from her stepbrother and half sisters.

He walked to the granite counter that divided the living area from the kitchen and angled himself onto one of the bar stools.

Abby took a canister down out of the cupboard. "I assume you came to see me tonight because you've made some progress on the investigation?"

"Nope. I've got zip."

For a heartbeat or two she did not move or even blink. Her stillness was absolute. She recovered quickly and frowned.

"Then what in the world are you doing here?" she asked.

He folded his arms on the counter. "My job. I told you I don't have any startling revelations, but I do have a few questions."

"You could have called."

"I prefer to get my answers face-to-face." He smiled. "Less chance of a misunderstanding that way."

"Fine, whatever." She removed the lid of the canister and started spooning loose tea into a pot. "Ask your questions."

"You said you don't know what the blackmailer wants."

"I told you, he hasn't made any specific demands."

"Do you have any theories?"

"I assume he's after some very hot, probably encrypted, book. He wants me to get it for him."

"But you don't know which book?"

"Not yet." She put the lid back on the canister. "At any given time, there are always a few extremely rare volumes with a paranormal provenance floating around in the underground."

"Did Thaddeus Webber give you any clue?"

"No." She opened another cupboard and took down two mugs. "Our communication on the subject thus far has been via email. Thaddeus lives alone in the foothills of the Cascades. He's very reclusive. Quite paranoid. He doesn't have a phone. Says they're too easy to tap. When he insisted that I contact you immediately, I emailed him a couple of questions, but the only response I got was 'Talk to Sam Coppersmith. He'll know what to do.'"

"I think he's right. I have a better idea of what may be going down than you do."

She gave him a wry smile. "I've come to the same conclusion. Talk to me, Sam."

"I'm pretty sure that Thaddeus Webber sent you to me because he thinks your blackmailer is after an old lab notebook that my father spent years trying to find."

"For the record, whoever he is, he's not *my* blackmailer, but go on."

"Eventually, Dad concluded that both the notebook and the man who had recorded the results of his experiments in it had been buried in an explosion in an old mine called the Phoenix. But now there is reason to believe that the notebook has surfaced in the collectors' market. We know of at least one very dangerous man who is after it."

Abby raised her brows. "I assume that you are not referring to yourself?"

For a second, he didn't comprehend. Then it hit him that she had just let him know that she considered him dangerous.

"No need to insult me," he said, going for offended. "I'm on your side in this thing, remember?"

"Actually, it's starting to sound like you've got your own agenda, but I'm good with that. Everyone has an agenda, right?"

He did not dignify that with a response. "What I'm trying to explain here is that it's reasonable to assume that Webber sent you to me because he thinks that you're in danger from someone who is after that notebook. He understands that I'm the best-qualified person around to look after you until we find that damned book and get it off the market."

"Okay, I get that, but remember that you're supposed to be working for me."

"Trust me, I am not going to let you out of my sight until we find the notebook and the person who is trying to blackmail you."

"I'm not sure that translates into working for me."

"You will have my full attention until this is over," he assured her gravely.

For a long moment, she studied him with deeply shadowed, unreadable eyes. The shriek of the teakettle's whistle broke the tense silence. She turned away to pour the hot water into the pot.

"All right," she said. "I guess that's the best deal I'm going to get. You find my blackmailer and make him go away. In exchange, I will find the lab notebook for you."

Irritation sparked through him. "This isn't a business arrangement."

"Yes." She set the kettle down."That is exactly what it is. Never mind. I take it you think this lab book is locked in a psi-code?"

"According to the rumors, yes. We don't know when it was locked or who did the encryption."

"This man you mentioned, the one who kept the records of his experiments in the notebook, you say he died in a mine explosion?"

"Yes."

"When?"

"About forty years ago. His name was Ray Willis. He and my father and another man named Quinn Knox were mining engineers who all had some intuitive sensitivity for the latent energy in rocks and crystals and ores. In addition, they had the vision to see that the future of technology was going to be dependent on the so-called rare earths. They formed a partnership and went into the exploration business. They hit pay dirt, literally, when they picked up the mineral rights to an old abandoned mine out in the Nevada desert. Whoever sank the shaft originally was probably looking for gold. There wasn't any there. But Dad and his partners were after twenty-first-century gold."

"The rare earths."

"Right. They were all convinced that the Phoenix was the modern equivalent of a gold mine."

"Did they find the minerals and elements they were looking for in the Phoenix Mine?"

"Yes, but they found something a lot more interesting and, according to Dad, a lot more dangerous. They discovered geodes filled with quartzlike crystals unlike anything they had seen before. There was no data on them in the research literature. But they eventually turned up a few old references to similar crystals in some ancient books on alchemy."

Abby made a face and poured the tea into the mugs. "Alchemy. That figures. The old alchemists were always coming up with secret formulas and running experiments with para-crystals and amber and other stones in an effort to enhance their powers."

"Dad, Willis and Knox could sense the energy locked in the rocks, but they had no idea how to access it, let alone figure out how to use it. They set up a small on-site lab and started conducting experiments."

Abby set one of the mugs on the counter in front of him. At least she was no longer looking skeptical. Instead, she appeared to be reluctantly fascinated.

"They found out that the crystals had paranormal properties?" she asked.

"Yes. But they soon realized that they were playing with fire." He was suddenly very conscious of his ring. "Maybe literally. All they could tell in the field lab was that the energy in the stones was volatile and unpredictable, and that it was paranormal in nature. Dad and Knox wanted to stop the experiments until they could get some of the specimens to a properly equipped facility. But Ray Willis was obsessed with the stones. He was convinced they had enormous value, and he decided that he didn't want to share the potential profits."

Abby picked up her own mug. "There was a falling-out among the partners?"

"You could say that. Ray Willis tried to murder Knox and my father. Dad never told us exactly what happened in the mine shaft that day, but in the end there was an explosion. Knox and my father escaped through an air shaft. Willis didn't make it out."

"What happened?"

"Afterward, Dad and Knox made a pact. They decided that for the foreseeable future, the crystals should stay in the ground. Those rocks were just too dangerous. There was no telling what would happen if they fell into the wrong hands. They agreed to keep the location of the mine a secret, and they tried to destroy all traces of its existence."

"The foreseeable future has turned into forty years?"

"Yes, but Dad still hasn't changed his mind about the Phoenix. He does not want it found, not yet at any rate. He says if the time comes to reopen that mine, Coppersmith Inc. will handle the job."

"Meanwhile, your father is committed to keeping the secret."

"His old partner, Quinn Knox, kept the secret, too. But he died a couple of weeks ago. Before he passed on, however, he warned us that his son, Lander Knox, who is evidently a full-blown bad guy with a lot of talent, is on the trail of the lab book."

"You say your father and Knox searched for the book after the explosion?"

"Not just the notebook. Several of the crystals that Ray Willis was using in his experiments went missing, too. Dad and Knox couldn't find the book or the stones. Eventually, they gave up and told themselves everything had been buried with Willis in the explosion. But over the years there have been occasional whispers that indicated that the book and at least some of the crystals survived. In the beginning, Dad chased down every lead. Now my brother, Judson, and I do it. But until now, nothing has ever come of any of the rumors."

"What happened to your father's partnership with Knox?"

"They worked together for a while. Found a new mine, one that produced copper. They sold out to a big mining company and split the profits. That was the end of their partnership. My father spent his share of the money on exploration and development of another rare-earths mine that became the foundation of Coppersmith Inc."

"What happened to Quinn Knox?"

"He and Dad lost contact over the years. Knox evidently had a problem with gambling and a few other addictions. But Dad heard from him for the first time in decades when Knox called from his hospital bed to warn him about Lander Knox. Apparently, Lander found one of the crystals that Quinn had kept and learned about the existence of the

Phoenix Mine. He has concluded that he was deprived of his rightful inheritance, and he's determined to find it. To do that, he needs the lab book."

"You really think this Lander Knox is the person who is trying to blackmail me?"

"I think there's a very high probability that he's the blackmailer, yes. But we have to assume that there may be others who will do whatever it takes to get that book."

"Wow, a lost mine and a missing lab book." Abby looked genuinely amused. "You know, if it weren't for the blackmail part, this would actually be one of my cooler gigs."

"I'm glad you can see the positive side of this situation."

He studied the tea she had placed in front of him. Normally, he never drank tea, herbal or otherwise. But this tea was a mysterious golden green. He picked up the cup and swallowed cautiously. The brew tasted oddly soothing. He could feel the warmth flooding through him, and it felt good. It occurred to him that he had been cold for a while now. Strange that he had not been aware of it until tonight.

They drank the tea together in silence. Eventually, he put down the cup.

"By now you've probably heard the rumors about me," he said.

9

SHE DIDN'T PRETEND THAT SHE DIDN'T KNOW WHAT HE WAS talking about.

"Well, sure," she said. "Even my friend Gwen has heard them."

"I didn't kill Cassidy Lawrence."

"I know."

That was not the response he had expected.

"How do you know that?" he asked.

Abby shrugged. "Gwen would never have left us alone together if she thought you were capable of that kind of thing."

He frowned. "She's that good?"

"She's that good."

"Huh."

So much for the fantasy of Abby throwing herself into his arms and swearing a vow of unqualified trust. *Take what you can get, Coppersmith.*

"There's one other thing I'd like to clarify," he said.

"Yes?"

"For some reason, a lot of folks seem to believe that Cassidy and I were engaged."

"Not true?"

"No," he said. "We saw a lot of each other for a while, and people made some assumptions. We had an affair, but she was not my fiancée."

"I see."

Abby's phone chimed into the sudden, acute silence. She flinched, clearly startled, and picked up the device. She glanced at the screen, smiled and took the call.

"Talk about a psychic intercept," she said. She walked out from behind the kitchen counter, heading toward the small desk. "We were just chatting about you, Gwen. . . . Yes, that's what I told him. You can take off for Hawaii without having to worry about me."

Abby stopped in front of her desk and began to flip through a small stack of mail.

"Yes," she said. "I promise I'll call Nick if I think I need backup. But I'll be fine. . . . Yes. . . . Good night. Safe trip. I know it's a job, but try to have some fun in Hawaii, okay? . . . Yes, I promise I'll call with updates."

She closed the phone and set it down. "Good news. Gwen just gave you a clean bill of aura health."

"I appreciate that," Sam said.

Abby tossed the last of the mail aside and reached for the small package that sat on the desk. "I don't remember doing any online shopping recently."

A visible shiver went through her when her fingers closed around the parcel. She gave a sharp, audible gasp. Energy sparked in the atmosphere.

"Oh, my," she breathed.

Newton jumped to his feet, ears sharpened. He whined softly.

Sam was already moving, crossing the room to where Abby stood, gazing raptly at the package that she held in both hands.

"What's wrong?" he asked.

"Nothing is wrong." She had recovered from the initial shock. Anticipation sparkled in her eyes. "I think someone sent me a very special gift, a book, judging by the energy. An old one."

He could sense the subtle shiver of energy around the package now. "Whatever is in there is hot."

"Yes, indeed," she said. She began to unwrap the package with great care. "Very hot."

The hairs lifted on the nape of his neck.

"Who sent it?" he asked.

"I don't know yet. There's no return address. Maybe there will be a note inside. I have a hunch that it's a thank-you gift from one of my clients."

"Your clients have your home address?"

"No, of course not. Too many crazies in my line. All of my business correspondence goes to an anonymous private post office box and is then forwarded here."

She got the outer wrapping off, revealing an ornately carved wooden box.

"Those are alchemical designs," Sam said.

"They certainly are."

Abby opened the hinged lid of the box. There was a small leather-bound book inside. She used both hands to take it out. She smiled.

"What?" Sam asked warily.

"It's encrypted with a delicate little psi-code." Abby opened the cover with great care and studied the title page. Pleasure and a little heat illuminated her eyes.

Sam looked over her shoulder and studied the Latin. "What does it say?"

"The title translates to *A Treatise on the Herbs and Flowers Most Useful in the Art of Mixing Perfumes*. It's a guide to perfume making, written by someone who obviously had a psychic talent for the craft. According to the title page, it contains some of Cleopatra's own personal recipes. Isn't it lovely?"

"Abby," Sam said, "it wasn't mailed to you."

"Yes, I know. I told you, my mail goes through a private post office."

"That's not what I meant," he said evenly. "It wasn't mailed anywhere. There's no postage on it. That package must have been hand-delivered."

Abby looked up at last. Her eyes narrowed faintly. He realized he finally had her attention.

"Well, I do have a few friends," she said tentatively. "I suppose one of them could have dropped it off."

"Is there a note?"

"I didn't notice one." She looked at the wooden box. There was a small white envelope inside. "Wait, there it is."

She put the book down and opened the envelope. She pulled out the small card inside and read the handwritten message: *"Please accept this small gift as an expression of my admiration for your unique talents. I wish to commission your services with a view to acquiring a rare item that is rumored to be coming onto the market. Price is no object. There will be a generous bonus if you are successful. Regardless of your decision, the herbal is yours to keep."*

"Someone is trying to bribe you to take him on as a client," Sam said. "And he knows where you live."

"Oh, crap," Abby said.

10

ICY ENERGY ELECTRIFIED THE ATMOSPHERE. ABBY KNEW THAT Sam was jacked. So was she, but in a different way. It made her uneasy to realize that a potential client had found her home address, but she could not bring herself to believe that the little herbal represented a truly dangerous threat.

"I take precautions," Abby said, "but everyone knows that these days you can find anyone if you look hard enough. I would point out, for instance, that you found my address tonight. I don't recall giving it to you this afternoon."

"I had your license plate," Sam said.

"I beg your pardon? I left my car in Anacortes when I went to see you." Then it struck her. "Oh, for heaven's sake, it was Dixon, wasn't it? He made a note of my license plate when he fetched me at the marina. You used it to trace me."

"My family takes precautions, too," Sam said. "How many of your clients have gone to the trouble to track you down like this?"

"It's never been much of a problem, to be honest. Everyone knows my reputation. There's no point approaching me unless you have been referred by someone I trust. Even if someone got as far as the front door of this building, none of the doormen would let him in unless I gave my approval."

"Mail and packages are delivered to the lobby. How did these get up here today?"

"I was supposed to be out of town for the next few days. I had a job down in Portland that I rescheduled after the blackmail threats arrived. The day doorman, Ralph, always brings up my mail and waters my plants when I'm gone. I forgot to tell him that my plans had changed."

Sam picked up the note and read it silently. "This isn't the same guy who is sending you the threatening notes."

"No, I'm sure it isn't. Whoever sent me this herbal is trying to impress me. This is a very generous gift. I could probably sell it for several thousand dollars, enough to cover my mortgage payments for a while and pay off my new furniture."

"*Are* you impressed?" Sam asked softly.

She drew one finger across the elegantly hand-tooled leather cover. Hushed power locked in stasis stirred her senses.

"Oh, my, yes," she whispered. "No one has ever given me anything like this in my whole life. The book is valuable in and of itself as an antiquarian text, but the psi-encryption makes it worth much, much more to the collectors in my market. Who knows what secrets may be hidden inside."

Sam's jaw hardened. "In other words, the person who sent it to you is wooing you."

She smiled. "You could say that. Giving me this book is the equivalent of giving another woman a very nice set of diamond earrings."

She could see that Sam did not like hearing that. She wondered why it bothered him so much. She had merely been trying to illustrate a point.

"It's not personal," she said quickly. "I mean, it's not like he wants to have an affair with me or anything. He just wants me to know that he can afford my services and that he'll pay well for them." She touched the herbal again. "This gift also tells me that he respects my talent."

"Don't get any ideas about dumping me and taking him on as a client," Sam warned. "You and I have a deal."

She sighed. "Yep, I'm committed."

"You don't have to act like it's a tragedy. That blackmailer is still out there, remember."

"Believe me, I haven't forgotten."

"Can I have a look at that herbal?" Sam asked.

"Sure." She handed it to him with some reluctance. The energy of the book was mildly intoxicating. Like an exotic perfume, she thought.

Sam opened the book with due care. "I can feel a little heat, but nothing that would warn me that it's encrypted."

"Whoever locked that book was very skilled with the old techniques. You probably wouldn't notice anything at all unless you actually tried to concoct some of the recipes. Then you would find out, probably the hard way, that the perfumes you created were all off in some fashion."

Sam looked up. "The hard way?"

"The results might vary, from foul-smelling concoctions to some that are downright poisonous. It would depend on just how serious the person who set the code was about protecting her secrets."

"You think a woman locked this book?"

"Yes," Abby said. She smiled. "Every psi-code is unique. It's like a fingerprint in that it reveals a lot about the individual who set the encryption. You'll have to take my word for it when I tell you that you do not want to re-create any of those recipes unless the code is broken first."

"I believe you." Sam put the book down on the desk. "What are you going to do with the herbal? Keep it?"

"No, I really can't do that. The person who sent it was very gracious and very generous about insisting it was a gift, but I could never accept such a valuable item for services that haven't been rendered."

"How will you return it?" Sam asked. "You don't know the sender."

"I'm sure that won't be a problem. I'll give the book to Thaddeus Webber. He'll find a way to return it to whoever sent it. Thaddeus has connections throughout the hot-book market. Unlike me, he works the deep end."

"Do you think that the person who sent you the herbal is a deep-end collector?"

"Yes." She placed the herbal carefully back into the box. "I do."

"Think he knows you'll arrange to return the book if you don't accept him as a client?"

"Certainly." She smiled. "I told you, I have a reputation in this business."

"In other words, he didn't take much of a risk when he gave you the herbal."

"No. But it was a very elegant gesture, regardless."

Sam watched her close the lid of the box. "You know, I had no idea until now how delicate business negotiations are in your world."

"I thought I made it clear. In my line, reputation is everything. All my transactions involve an element of trust."

"Well, that attitude explains why you aren't yet ready to hold hands and jump off the edge of a cliff with me," he said, without inflection.

She blanked for a couple of beats. Then she chuckled. The chuckles turned into laughter, and she was suddenly laughing harder than she had in some time.

"That's hilarious." She wiped the corners of her eyes. "You are a very unusual man, Sam Coppersmith."

"You want to know the sad part? I wasn't trying to make a joke. I need your trust to do my job, Abby."

She sobered and blinked a few times to clear her eyes. "Oh. Sorry. I didn't realize. Never mind. As you just pointed out, we have a deal, and I do trust you to honor your part of the bargain. I give you my word I'll honor my end. I'll do my best to find that lab book. Speaking of my little problem, just how do you plan to go about finding the blackmailer?"

Sam looked as if he wanted to pursue the topic of trust, but he must have concluded that the conversation was not going to be useful. He turned away and went to stand at the window, looking out into the night. Newton joined him.

"A chat with Thaddeus Webber would be a good place to start," Sam said. "But I'd like to do it in person, not via email. Unlike you, he isn't so easy to find. Think you can get him to agree to talk to me?"

"Yes, I'm sure I can. I want to see him, myself, in order to give him the herbal. I'll email him tonight and set up a meeting. He's quite security-conscious, though, so he'll want to choose the time and place."

"Fine by me, so long as he makes it soon, preferably tomorrow."

"I doubt that will be a problem. Thaddeus is the one who sent me to you in the first place, after all. He'll be as helpful as he can."

"Good."

She waited a beat. Sam did not say anything else. He and Newton continued to contemplate the night.

She cleared her throat. "So do you plan on returning to Copper Beach tonight? It's a long trip."

"What?" Sam sounded distracted, as if she had interrupted his train of thought. He turned around. "No, I'm not going back tonight. I thought I made it clear I'll be sticking close to you until this is finished. Got a spare blanket for your sofa?"

Blindsided. She stared at him, speechless. A tiny tingle of panic iced her spine. *Should have seen this coming.*

"I really don't think it's necessary for you to spend the night here," she said quickly. "It's not like there is an immediate threat to my safety."

"Sure there is."

"I don't see it."

"Let's review," Sam said. "You are suddenly very hot, in more ways than one. Every time I turn around, someone else is either trying to bribe you or trying to blackmail you into working for him."

"Just two people," she said. "Three, counting you."

"That's two too many. Sooner or later, someone may decide to take more direct action. This place is not exactly a fortress."

"I've got Newton," she said. But she was grasping at straws, and she knew it.

"I'm sure Newton is a fine animal, but he's not exactly a pit bull or a rottweiler. Tonight, I sleep here."

She thought about the black leather duffel he had left in the entry hall. "I'm guessing that whatever is inside that bag you brought, it's not your gym stuff."

"Overnight kit, a change of clothes and some of the equipment I use in my consulting work. I never leave home without it."

"You came prepared."

"We're in this together, Abby."

"Right." She took a deep breath. "Actually, there are three of us involved in this thing. You, me and Newton. And right now Newton has priority. It's time for his late-night walk."

"Please don't tell me that you make a habit of going out onto the street alone at this hour every night?"

"No need for that," Abby said. "The main reason I chose this partic- ular condo building is because it has a lovely dog garden on the roof."

Newton bounded toward the front door, claws skidding on the floor.

"He knows the word *walk*," Abby explained.

"Maybe you're right," Sam said. "Maybe he is a little bit psychic."

"All dogs have a psychic vibe," Abby said. "But Newton has more talent than most. I knew that the instant I saw him in the animal shelter."

Some time later, she closed her bedroom door, turned off the lights and pulled back the covers. The curtains were open, allowing the nighttime glow of the city to spill into the room.

Newton jumped up onto the foot of the bed and settled down.

"Feels weird knowing he's out there in the other room, doesn't it?" Abby whispered.

Newton regarded her alertly, his proud, intelligent head silhouetted against the city lights.

She pulled the down quilt up to her chin and contemplated the shadows on the ceiling. She should have been more uneasy about the situation, she thought. She was not accustomed to having a man spend the night. Her dates were never invited to stay until morning. Even with Kane, she had not taken that step. Maybe that had been a sign that the relationship was doomed, she thought. A woman should long for that kind of domestic intimacy with the man she was thinking of marrying. But she had never felt the need to have Kane stay. And in the post-Kane era, she had been living something of a cloistered life. There had been no other relationship that had even come close to being serious.

Her new home was her refuge, her fortress, her private, personal space. It was the first place that had ever truly belonged to her. She had filled it with things that had meaning to her. She had decorated it with the colors and fabrics and furnishings that she loved. And tonight a man she had known for less than a day was sleeping on her new sofa. She was still making payments on that sofa.

"I probably won't sleep well tonight," she said to Newton. "But what if I have that damn dream and go sleepwalking out into the front room? It would be so embarrassing."

Newton put his head down on his paws.

Abby looked out into the night and thought about the lucid-dreaming advice that Gwen had given her. *Set your psychic alarm clock to alert you when you start dreaming. Then take control of the dream.*

11

"Help me." Grady Hastings was barely visible in the swirling mist. He reached out a pleading hand. "Please help me."

Abby looked at him through the eerie light that illuminated the dreamscape and knew that she was dreaming. The strange fog that ebbed and flowed around Grady was different tonight. It burned with an inner radiance that she had not noticed in the previous dreams. She could move through it, get closer to Grady.

She was dreaming, but she was aware that she was dreaming. Her psychic alarm clock had gone off right on time. She could take control.

"Tell me what you want from me," she said, speaking in the silent language of dreams.

The mist thickened around Grady. It was getting harder and harder to see him, but she sensed his desperation and despair.

"Help me," he said. "You're the only one who can."

She tried to grasp his hand. . . .

ABBY CAME FULLY AWAKE IN A RUSH OF ENERGY, HER SENSES sparking and flashing like dark fireworks in the night. The primordial instincts of childhood kicked in. She tried to hold herself utterly still, not daring to move, but she could not stop the shivering that racked her body.

Heart pounding, she opened her eyes, searching the shadows. No one leaped out of the closet. No monster crouched at the foot of her bed. Newton was not there, either. That was not right, because she could feel his warm weight pressed against her leg.

In the next heartbeat she realized that she was on her feet beside the bed. At least her psychic alarm had awakened her before she had actually started to walk out of the bedroom.

There was something very wrong with the shadows in the room. They seethed and shifted. It took her a few seconds to figure out that the pulsing, roiling ultralight was coming from the small, hot storm brewing on her dresser.

"Oh, crap," she whispered to Newton. "It's the herbal. I accidentally ignited it in my sleep."

Newton growled softly.

She rushed to the dresser. Hot currents from the herbal were seeping out of the wooden box. She realized that she had inadvertently tapped some of the encryption energy in the old book when she tried to take control of the dream.

She looked at the box with a sense of dread. Currents of hot psi from the darkest end of the spectrum twisted and wreathed around it. Any minute now she would start to smell charring wood. And then the smoke alarms would go off. If the condo building's fire-detection systems were activated, the fire department would be called automatically. Even if no real damage was done, her neighbors and the condo board of directors would want to know what happened.

Disaster loomed.

She opened the box very carefully. Energy flared higher. Gingerly, she put her hand on the leather cover of the herbal. Shocks of paranormal electricity crackled through her. She ignored them and channeled her talent, dampening the currents. She could only hope that Sam was a really sound sleeper.

The last of the hot energy had almost winked out when the bedroom door opened abruptly. She looked over her shoulder and saw Sam's shadowy frame silhouetted against the city lights that illuminated the living room. Icy energy chilled the atmosphere. The room was suddenly very cold.

"What's going on?" Sam asked. His eyes burned. The strange crystal in his ring glowed with an inner fire.

Newton spared him a brief glance, ears sharpened, and then returned his full attention to Abby and the hot book.

Abby winced and stifled a groan. So much for the faint hope that Sam would sleep through the disturbance.

"Nothing is wrong," she said. Her voice sounded half an octave too high, even to her own ears. The book was almost dark now. She got the lid back on the box and turned to face Sam. "I had a bad dream and got up to walk off the energy. You know how it is with nightmares."

"Yes," he said. His tone was as cold as the energy that enveloped him. "I know how it is with nightmares. I also know that you're lying through your teeth. Why are you trying to hide the herbal?"

"Excuse me," she said. Her voice was firmer now. It would have been easier to pull off stern and deeply offended if she had not been standing there in a plain, unadorned cotton sleep shirt that fell to her knees. "In case it has escaped your notice, you are in my bedroom and I did not invite you in here."

He ignored her and glided toward the dresser. When he moved into the light slanting through the windows, she saw that he was barefoot but still partially dressed in his trousers and a black T-shirt that molded to his sleek, strong shoulders. She felt very vulnerable, not to mention seriously underdressed. She was aware of another sensation as well, an excitement that was decidedly sensual in origin. *Just the fallout from all the energy that you were using a minute ago,* she assured herself.

A heavy dose of adrenaline and psi often had a stirring effect on all the senses, although she could not recall feeling sexually aroused when she had gone into the zone on previous occasions. Usually, she just felt jittery and agitated afterward.

It was Sam's fault, she decided. All that powerful masculine energy emanating from him was messing with the natural wavelengths of her own aura. It was annoying. It was also unaccountably exciting.

Sam came to a halt and looked at the open box. She was intensely aware of him and the heat coming off him. He was so close now. It took an enormous amount of willpower not to touch him.

"You did something to the book, didn't you?" Sam said. "I can sense some of the residue of the energy. You're still jacked, too. What the hell were you doing?"

She abandoned the attempt to kick him out of the bedroom. The man was very focused.

"The book was a little hot, yes," she admitted. She cleared her throat. "But it has gone cold now, as you can tell."

Sam glanced at her, his eyes still burning a little with psi. His ring continued to heat with a fiery light.

"What triggered the energy in the book?" he asked.

"You know how it is with old objects that are infused with a lot of encryption energy," she said smoothly. "It doesn't take much to kick up a little heat."

"This thing didn't switch on all by itself. You got it hot, didn't you?"

"That's not exactly what happened."

"What the hell were you doing? Running an experiment? Trying to break the code? You should know better than that. You're the expert on para-books. Tests on objects known to be infused with unknown energy should be done under carefully controlled conditions, and never at night."

He was right, she thought ruefully. As a rule, paranormal energy was usually more powerful after dark. It could also be a lot more unpredictable at night, something to do with the absence of normal daylight energy waves. But the fact that Sam was quoting one of the laws of para-physics to her while she was engaged in putting out a fire was infuriating. She was so not in the mood for this.

"You are correct, I'm the expert here," she said, in her coldest voice. "You have absolutely no right to lecture me on the care and handling of old books."

"So you figured you were qualified to conduct a night experiment on a highly encrypted book?"

"I was not running an experiment." She angled her chin. "For your information, I did not deliberately trigger the energy in that thing. I was sound asleep. I woke up and saw that it was giving off some psi-light, so I got up and shut it down."

"If you expect me to believe that book ignited all on its own, you can forget it. Tell me what the hell is going on here."

"It's complicated . . ."

Sam clamped his hand across her mouth. Furious, she glared at him. But he was not looking at her. He was watching the bedroom doorway.

The room was suddenly much, much colder. *Sam's energy,* Abby thought. He was running very hot, but the bedroom was deathly cold. Something sparked at the corner of her eye. Sam's ring.

She realized Newton had gone very still, very alert. He, too, was gazing fixedly at the doorway, looking down the short hall and into the living room.

Sam put his mouth very close to her ear. "Keep Newton quiet."

She nodded once to show that she understood.

He took his hand off her mouth and gripped her shoulder. He squeezed gently, silently warning her to stay put. She nodded again to show she had got the message. When he took his hand off her shoulder, she was once again aware of the icy chill in the atmosphere.

She crouched beside Newton, wrapped one arm around him and put her hand over his muzzle. Newton shivered, not with fear, she thought. The energy crackling through him was the tension of the hunter.

Sam crossed the room and disappeared through the shadowed doorway.

12

IT WAS THE FAINT CLINK OF METAL OUT ON THE CONCRETE
balcony that had alerted him. Even a very small amount of impact
noise traveled in steel-and-concrete buildings.

Sam waited in the kitchen, watching the balcony from the shadows
of the refrigerator. He gripped his most recent invention in his hand.
It resembled a cell phone, but the crystal-powered device had a very
different purpose. He was pretty sure that the theory behind the design
was solid, but he had not yet had a chance to conduct any real-world
experiments. Tonight promised to provide the opportunity for a field
trial.

His intuition had been riding him hard all day. It had spiked into
the hot zone after dark. He had the sense that things were moving fast,
and that Abby was in danger. He had not even tried to sleep tonight.
He had spent the night mentally and psychically standing guard.

Out on the balcony, a dark shadow appeared. It dropped easily down
from the floor above. For a second or two, the newcomer dangled on

the rope he had used for the descent. Then he stepped nimbly onto the railing and down to the floor of the balcony. It was clear he had done this kind of thing before. An expert.

He left the rope dangling and moved swiftly to the sliding glass doors. A small tool of some kind appeared in his gloved hand. A moment later, the sliding glass door slid silently open.

Chilled night air and faint currents of psi whispered into the room when the intruder entered. A talent of some kind, Sam concluded, and definitely a professional. It was a good bet that he had gained access to the building via the parking garage, always the weak point in the security system of any condo tower. Once inside, he would have had access to every floor and the roof.

The intruder moved across the room, going directly to Abby's desk with the certainty of a man who knew his way around the condo. That raised some intriguing questions, Sam thought.

The guy had a second-story man's sense of style. He had definitely nailed the cat-burglar look. He was dressed from head to toe in tight black clothing. A black stocking cap concealed his hair and all of his features except his eyes.

At the desk, he stopped, flicked on a small penlight and began to sort through the mail.

Sam walked out of the kitchen and around the end of the dining counter.

"No need for that," he said. "Abby went through her mail earlier this evening."

"What the . . . ?" The intruder swung around, spearing the shadows with the penlight. "Who are you?"

"A friend of Abby's."

"No, you're not. Abby doesn't have any boyfriends. Who are you, and what are you doing in her place?"

"I was just going to ask you the same question."

"Like hell."

The intruder sprinted for the open slider. Sam was already moving. He managed to seize the man's shoulder and succeeded in touching the crystal device to his arm. He sent energy into the fake cell phone. There was a small flash of paranormal lightning. The intruder grunted and started to crumple. He struggled to straighten and resume his flight to the balcony, but he fell slowly to his knees, arms wrapped around his midsection.

Sam yanked off the stocking cap, revealing platinum-blond hair cut in a short, crisp, vaguely military style.

"What the h-hell d-did you do to me?" the intruder got out, teeth chattering.

There was a sharp, excited yip. Newton charged into the room. He went straight to the intruder and started licking his face.

"Hell of a guard dog, all right," Sam said.

Abby appeared. She had taken the time to pull on a robe. She had a large object clutched in her hands.

"Sam." Her voice was tight and anxious. "Are you all right?"

"Yes," he said. "Get the lights."

She flipped a wall switch, illuminating the heavy lamp she carried. Her eyes widened, first in shock and then in outrage, when she saw the man shivering in the middle of her living room.

"Nick?" She put the lamp down on the coffee table. "What in the world are you doing here?"

Nick gave her a disgusted look and continued to shudder. "Your taste in boyfriends is going downhill, Abby. This one just tried to kill me."

Abby glanced at Sam, frowning. "Whatever you're doing to him, you can stop, at least until I decide whether or not to call the cops."

"He'll be all right in a few minutes," Sam said. "Probably." He pocketed the crystal device. "I just temporarily shocked his senses. You know this guy?"

"Nick Sawyer," she said. She regarded Nick with seething irritation. "And yes, I know him. You could say we're colleagues of a sort. We both work the book market, but Nick isn't quite as selective as I am when it comes to clients. I was, however, under the impression, until tonight, that he was my friend."

Nick muttered something unintelligible. Newton bounced around him, waiting for the new game to begin.

"Give him a minute," Sam said.

Nick managed to get to his feet. He was still shaky. He was about the same age as Abby, a lean, athletically built man with the sort of clean, chiseled features that could have ensured him a successful career in modeling. His silver-white hair and artificially tanned face served to enhance the vivid blue of his eyes.

He shot a hooded look at Sam, did a quick assessment of the situation and evidently concluded that his best option lay in an appeal to Abby.

"Sorry about this, sweetie," he said. "I thought you were out of town."

"That's supposed to excuse what you just did?" Abby waved a hand toward the open slider. "You just broke into my home. You'd better start talking, and fast, or I'm going to call the police, I swear it."

Nick exhaled heavily and leaned over to scratch Newton behind the ears. "Take it easy, sweetie. I can explain everything. You know you're not going to call the cops."

"Before you say another word," Abby warned, "if you call me sweetie one more time, I will use that lamp on your head."

"It's a little complicated, sweet—uh, Abby."

"I think we can uncomplicate this thing real fast," Sam said. "Tell us why you broke in here tonight."

Nick scowled. "Who is this guy, Abby? I can't believe he's a new boyfriend. Definitely not your type."

"Talk," Sam said. "Fast."

Nick shot him an irritated look. "I didn't break in, I let myself in."

"That wasn't a key you used to open the slider," Sam said.

"Abby and I are old friends." Nick turned back to Abby and flashed a smile that was as brilliant as his hair. "Isn't that right?"

"We both know that I never gave you a key to my home," Abby said. "Gwen has a spare, but you don't. Why are you here?"

"Believe it or not, just looking out for you. There's a real hot book floating around. Some kind of lab notebook dealing with crystal experiments. It's supposed to be about forty years old, and rumor has it that it's encrypted. If that's the case, there's a good chance that some of the people who are after it will be trying to hire you."

"Don't give me that blather about looking out for me," Abby snapped. "You're trying to locate that book yourself, aren't you? You came here hoping that you would find a lead."

"So you are working that job." Nick jerked a thumb at Sam. "He's a new client, isn't he? What's going on here? You never let clients into your home."

"You know, I really don't have to answer your questions," Abby said. "You are supposed to be explaining why you are here in my living room."

Nick shrugged. "Like I said, just looking out for your best interests."

"I got that much," Abby said, bristling with impatience. "Tell me the rest of it."

"Okay, okay, calm down. I don't know a whole lot more than what I just told you. I don't have a client yet, but the word on the street is that the book is worth a fortune to more than one person. Figured if I got to it first I could hold an auction. This could be the big one for me."

"Where did you hear the rumors of the book?" Sam asked.

"Like I'm going to tell you that," Nick muttered.

Sam took the aura-suppression device out of his pocket.

Nick looked bored. "The rumors cropped up in the usual places online. Tell him, Abby."

Abby folded her arms. "There are chat rooms where collectors and dealers exchange gossip and leads. I haven't had a chance to check out the usual suspects lately, because I've been preoccupied with my own problems. Guess I'd better visit some of the online sites."

"What have you heard about the collectors who are after the encrypted book?" Sam asked.

"Damn it, who is this guy, Abby?" Nick demanded.

"The name is Sam Coppersmith," Sam said.

He was still trying to get past the comment about not looking like Abby's type. It occurred to him that no one would think it odd if a cat burglar fell from a tenth-floor balcony while engaged in an act of breaking and entering. Stuff happened. Abby, however, would probably not approve of that disposal plan. She clearly had a history with Nick Sawyer. So did Newton.

"Coppersmith." Nick frowned. "Name rings a faint bell. How did you find Abby?"

"She found me," Sam said.

"You're a talent of some kind." Nick gave him an accusing look and then turned back to Abby. "You never trust strangers."

"Sam was referred to me by Thaddeus," Abby said. "Or maybe it would be more correct to say that I was referred to Sam. Either way, Thaddeus vouched for him."

"Okay, so Webber approved him. That still doesn't explain what he's doing here in your apartment at two o'clock in the morning. You never let your dates stay over."

Abby flushed. "I thought I made it clear, Sam is not a date. My arrangement with him is strictly business."

"You never let clients do sleepovers, either. What the hell is going on here, Abby? Why did Webber send you to him?"

"If you must know, Thaddeus thinks I may be in some danger because of that book you're looking for," Abby said.

"Damn it, I *knew* this had something to do with that lab book. You should have come to me."

"I've been a little busy," Abby said. "Someone is blackmailing me."

"Shit," Nick growled. "Who?"

"That's where I come in," Sam said. "I'm going to find the bastard."

Nick frowned. "But you're after that old lab book, aren't you?"

"That, too," Sam said. "But the two projects go together."

Nick looked at Abby. "Sounds like you've fallen into the deep end."

"Yes," Abby says. "It appears that is the case."

"There are some real sharks out there. Are you sure you trust this guy to take care of you?"

"Yes," Abby said.

Sam told himself that he should take heart from that simple response.

"What is the bastard using as the extortion threat?" Nick said. "You've always been squeaky-clean. You don't even get parking tickets."

"He knows about my time at the Summerlight Academy and why I was sent there, and he knows who my father is. You know what would happen if my past suddenly became an issue in the media. It could ruin Dad's chance at the reality series."

"Screw it," Nick said. "Let your father take care of himself. You don't owe him or anyone else in that family a damn thing. They don't deserve your loyalty. Hell, even if they knew that you were trying to protect them, they wouldn't appreciate your efforts."

"It's not just about protecting them," Abby said. "We're not entirely certain yet, but it looks like the blackmailer may know exactly how I took down Grady Hastings in Mrs. Vaughn's library. If he knows what I can do with encryption energy and decides to fire up rumors about me in the chat rooms, he could destroy my business."

"Okay, that would not be good," Nick said. "But according to the rumors, this lab book is attracting some dangerous collectors. I don't want to see you get hurt."

"She won't," Sam said. "That's why I'm here."

"I'll be okay, Nick," Abby said. "I think you'd better leave. It's late."

"All right, I'm going." Nick gave Sam one last glare and then turned back to Abby. "But promise me you'll call me if you need backup."

"I will," she said. "By the way, please use the stairs on your way out. I don't want any of my neighbors to wake up and see you climbing past their balconies from this floor. I've got my reputation to consider."

"Yeah, right." Nick coughed. "I, uh, left some of my stuff out on the balcony."

"Get it," Sam said. "And then go."

Nick pretended not to hear the order, but he went out onto the balcony and collected the rock-climbing equipment. When he came back inside, Sam followed him down the short hall and into the small foyer. Newton accompanied them.

Nick opened the door. The outer hall was empty. He gave Newton one last pat and then straightened to give Sam a hard, cold look. He lowered his voice.

"If anything happens to Abby, I'll be holding you responsible," he said.

"Understood," Sam said. "Believe me, if I thought she would be safer far away from this situation, I would have arranged that. But running wouldn't do her any good. Problems like this tend to follow a person. And even if you escape for a while, they're lying in wait when you return."

Nick thought about that for a few seconds. Then he nodded. "You're right. Guess that makes you her bodyguard."

"That's pretty much what it comes down to," Sam said.

"That gadget you used on me is sort of impressive. Can I assume that you've had some practical experience in the bodyguard business?"

"I've done some occasional consulting work for a private firm that gets most of its business from a government agency."

Nick widened his eyes. "You've got experience as a *consultant*? Gosh, darn, that sure makes me feel a whole lot better. Which government agency are we talking about? The post office?"

"Close enough. Time to leave, Sawyer."

Nick looked down at Newton. "At least you've got Newton to help you."

"Right."

Nick narrowed his eyes. "Don't underestimate the dog. Or Abby."

"I won't."

Nick went out into the elevator lobby and vanished into the emergency stairwell.

Sam closed the door, threw the dead bolt and looked down at Newton. "Just you and me, pal."

Newton looked hopefully at the leash hanging on the coat tree.

"Forget it," Sam said. "It's two o'clock in the morning."

He went back into the living room. Abby was in the process of closing the sliding glass door. The chilly breeze stirred the wild curls of her hair and caused the hem of her robe to flutter around her ankles. She had very nice ankles, Sam thought. Dainty, feminine, sexy.

Abby got the door locked and turned around to face him.

"So do you date a lot of cat burglars?" he asked, before he could stop himself.

Abby made a face. "That is not amusing. But just to be clear, Nick and I never dated."

"Why not? Seems like you two have a lot in common, what with being in the same business and all."

Why was he pushing her like this? he wondered. They had more important things to talk about, such as the lab book. But he knew the answer. He had been feeling increasingly territorial all afternoon and evening. Watching Sawyer come through the balcony door and then act as if he had every right to do so because of his personal relationship with Abby had triggered some very primal responses.

"Nick is a friend," Abby said quietly. "He and Gwen and I go back a long way together. The three of us are like family. For the record, Nick is gay."

"Huh." Okay, now he felt like a certified ass. That's what the old primal-response thing did to a man, he thought. It made him stupid.

Abby watched him with her mysterious eyes. Energy continued to swirl gently in the atmosphere around her. He realized that he was still running a little hot. An edgy hunger stirred things deep inside him.

"That gadget that you used to stun Nick," she said after a while. "Is that your own invention?"

"Works on crystal energy. But it can only be triggered by psychic currents."

"In other words, only someone with talent can use it?"

"Yes. I think of it as a bug zapper." He rubbed the back of his neck, trying to suppress the restlessness. "This isn't a good time to talk about technology. We both need sleep."

Newton appeared from the hallway. He looked plaintively at Abby.

"He wants to go out," Abby said.

"He went out earlier. I can't believe you're in the habit of taking him out at two in the morning every night."

"Of course not," Abby said. "But we don't usually have so much excitement going on in the living room at this hour. Now he's wide awake, and so am I. We could both use a stroll to work off some of the adrenaline. I'll take him up to the garden."

"In your nightgown and robe?" It dawned on Sam that he sounded like a scandalized husband.

Abby was amused. "Calm down. I'll put on a coat and a pair of shoes. No one will know that I'm in my nightgown."

Sam thought about saying something along the lines of "It's the principle of the thing" but decided that it would only make him look like a Neanderthal.

Abby went down the hall and opened a closet door. Newton trotted enthusiastically in her wake.

"Hang on," Sam said, resigned. "You're not going up there alone."

They took the elevator to the rooftop terrace, went through a set of glass doors and out into the crisp summer night. Low-level lamps marked the winding path through the elaborately planted rooftop garden. Abby and Newton went ahead, to the gate of the section that had been set aside for dogs.

Sam pulled up the collar of his jacket. At least it wasn't raining, he thought. Abby was bundled up in a long trench coat. She had on a pair of shoes that his sister, Emma, would have called slides, but they looked a lot like slippers to him.

He watched her stoop down to unclip Newton's leash. As soon as he was free, Newton hurried through the gate and began to investigate a row of bushes, selecting just the right spot. *Choices, choices,* Sam thought. It seemed like there were always choices to be made in life. And once a man had made his decision, he was committed.

He moved to stand beside Abby, savoring her scent and her unique vibes. She did not try to put any distance between them.

"Sorry I zapped your friend tonight," he said.

"Nick had it coming. He had no business sneaking into my home tonight to go through my mail. As long as there was no permanent harm done."

"He'll be fine. At least I think he will."

"I beg your pardon?"

"Relax. According to my design calculations, there won't be any permanent damage."

She looked up at him, her eyes pools of mystery in the darkness. "Have you ever used that gadget on anyone else?"

"No. Haven't had the opportunity. But I've had some experience with a prototype."

"Great. Wonderful. I'm so relieved to hear that."

He exhaled slowly. "Nick asked me if I was qualified to act as a bodyguard."

"You're not my bodyguard," she said quickly. "You're my hired investigator."

"Comes down to the same thing. And you have a right to know my qualifications."

"As a bodyguard or as an investigator?"

"Both. I told Nick that I've done some consulting for a private contractor that does some work for a government agency."

She smiled. "The post office?"

"You know, you and your friend have a warped sense of humor."

"Nick already made that joke?"

"Yeah."

"Sorry. Couldn't resist. Go on."

"I'm trying to explain that I do have some experience in this kind of work. Thought it would make you feel better."

"You don't need to tell me your credentials," she said. "Although I admit I'm curious. But the bottom line is that I know you can handle my situation. I wouldn't have let you spend the night under my roof if I thought otherwise."

"What makes you so sure I'm qualified for the job?"

"My intuition, of course. Hey, I'm psychic, remember? You give off all the right vibes."

He turned to face her. "What kind of vibes would those be?"

"I knew the moment I met you that you're the kind of man who does what he says he's going to do. No excuses. In some ways, you're as hard as any of those rocks in your collection, but you can be counted on to complete the job or go down trying, and it would take a lot to bring you down. You've committed yourself to protecting me while we hunt for the blackmailer and the lab book. You would not have made that commitment unless you thought you could carry it out. I realize you have your own agenda, but that doesn't mean you won't honor your commitments."

"You've known me for less than twenty-four hours. How can you be so damn sure of me?"

"I don't know," she admitted. "Just something about your energy. But I'm not basing my conclusions entirely on my own intuition. Thaddeus Webber thinks you're the right man for the job. But more to the point, Gwen and Newton approve of you. And Nick, for all his faults, is a pretty good judge of character, too. He has to be, because he deals with some very shady clients. He wouldn't have left without a struggle tonight if he thought you couldn't be trusted to do your job."

"In other words, you trust me because your friends and your dog signed off on me."

"They're my family, Sam. I've got another, picture-perfect family, but it's not the same thing. Gwen, Nick and Newton are my real family. Do you understand?"

"Yes." He reached out and framed her face between his hands. "But there's something you need to understand. The lab book is important, but you are my number-one priority in this thing. I give you my word on that."

Her eyes burned with a little heat. "That's good to know."

"Is there any other man who might climb through your window tonight?" he asked. "Some other guy who might feel he has a claim on you?"

"No," she said. She rose slowly on her toes, as if she was making her decision on the way up. The energy around her got a little hotter. "No one else. Not tonight. Anyone I should know about who might feel she has a claim on you?"

"No," he said.

"That's all right, then."

She put her arms around his neck and kissed him lightly, carefully, as if she was conducting a delicate experiment, the outcome of which was designed to satisfy her curiosity but not to oblige her to make a commitment.

Fire roared through him. He lifted his head.

"Don't know about you," he rasped, "but as far as I'm concerned, we are not running a field test or a lab experiment here."

Her eyes widened. "What do you mean?"

"I'll show you."

He crushed her close and kissed her hard and deep, making it clear that he wasn't running a test. This was the real deal, and he wanted to make sure she knew it.

She was clearly startled, and for a terrible moment he thought she would retreat. But she gave an urgent little gasp and tightened her arms around his neck. Her mouth softened invitingly under his.

Heat lightning snapped and flashed in the atmosphere. He was suddenly more aroused than he had ever been in his life. It was as if the energy of his aura was resonating with hers in a way that made every sensation more intense, more volatile, more vital.

He was trying to decide how to get her out of the coat and down onto one of the loungers when she planted both hands against his chest and pushed herself a little distance away. She was breathless.

"Newton," she managed.

He looked down. Newton was sitting at their feet, his head tipped to one side with an expectant air. He had the leash between his teeth.

"Your dog has lousy timing," Sam said. "But he's got a point. It's too cold out here for this kind of thing."

Abby giggled. Her laughter sparkled in the night. Sam grabbed her hand and made for the glass doors. Newton, leash still in his teeth, dashed after them, excited and enthusiastic.

"He thinks we're playing a game," Abby said. She punched the elevator button.

The elevator door opened. Sam pulled her inside. Newton trotted in with them.

Sam hit the button for the tenth floor and pinned Abby to the wall.

"No games," he vowed.

She struggled a bit. He held her still and kissed her fiercely.

When the elevator doors opened, he was forced to release her. She clamped a hand over her mouth and looked at him with laughter-filled eyes.

"What's so funny?" he asked.

In response, she pointed up at the ceiling of the elevator. He saw the security camera and realized why she had resisted a moment ago. He laughed and yanked her back into his arms, making sure that he was kissing her as the elevator doors closed, making sure that the last image recorded on the security camera was that of Abby in his arms.

Staking his claim.

13

SHE WAS HOT AND COLD AND SHIVERING SO HARD SHE COULD not even get the key into the lock. What was wrong with her? It was as if she was in the grip of a raging fever, but she did not feel ill. Just the opposite. She was wildly exhilarated. She was flying.

The key fell to the floor.

"This is embarrassing," she said.

Sam scooped up the key, opened the door and propelled her inside. She was vaguely aware of Newton's nails clicking on the floor behind them. He disappeared down the hall to the living room. Sam got the door closed, peeled off his leather jacket and immediately went to work unfastening Abby's coat.

Part of her was shocked by the force of her response. It was as if the physical contact had awakened something deep inside her that had been dormant all these years, as if she had been *waiting* for this encounter.

Sam wrenched off her coat, hurled it in the general direction of the coatrack and closed his hands deliberately, powerfully, around her shoulders. Yet for all the strength that she sensed in him, both physical and paranormal, there was an exquisite tenderness in his touch that was incredibly seductive. *As if he was handling fine, delicate crystal,* she thought.

She slipped her hands up under his black T-shirt and flattened her palms on his chest. The feel of sleek, hard muscles beneath his warm skin excited her senses. She could see the heat in his eyes. He tangled his fingers in her hair and kissed her throat. For the first time in her life, she understood what it meant to be thrilled.

"Yes, yes, *yes,*" she whispered.

He pulled back just long enough to tug off his T-shirt. With her fingertips, she traced the outline of an elegant bird with wings of fire that covered his left shoulder.

"It's a phoenix, isn't it?" she said.

"Yes."

"You know, I would never have pegged you as the type to get a tattoo."

"I was nineteen," he said.

He cradled her jaw in one hand and used his thumb to tease open her mouth, tasting her, drawing her deeper into the embrace. The world spun around her. It took her a few heartbeats to realize that Sam had picked her up in his arms. He angled her carefully and carried her down the hall, through the dimly lit living room and into the darkened bedroom.

He tumbled her down onto the bed and sprawled heavily on top of her, anchoring her with his weight. His mouth moved over her as if he craved her.

She could feel the damp warmth gathering between her legs. He had done little more than kiss her, but her body was already preparing for him. The sheer urgency of her need should have made her hesitate, pull back. And somewhere a faint alarm was sounding, warning her that what she was doing held all manner of unknown risks.

But she was in no mood to pay attention to the weak protests that emanated from the part of her mind that was still trying to think rationally.

Sam dragged his mouth across hers one last time and then wrenched himself free. He rolled off her and sat up on the edge of the bed.

"Give me a second here," he said. His voice was low and husky, and his breathing was rough. He stripped off his pants and fumbled briefly in a pocket. "Damn. My hand is shaking so hard it will be a wonder if I can get this thing on."

She exulted in the knowledge that she was the reason he was having problems with the logistics of the situation. A sense of her own feminine power arced through her. Tonight she was a goddess.

Sam managed to sheath himself in the condom. He came back down on top of her, crushing her into the bed. In the darkness, his eyes were ablaze with a desire that crossed the spectrum from normal to paranormal. On his right hand, his ring glowed with a muted coppery radiance.

Her own senses were spiking wildly now. She was unbelievably sensitive to the slightest touch. She flinched when he pushed her nightgown up to her waist and pulled it off over her head. And then his mouth was on her breast, and she would have screamed with the intense pleasure of it all if she had been able to catch her breath.

"You are on fire," he said. The words were filled with wonder and awe.

"So are you." She stroked the contoured muscles of his back. His skin was streaked with sweat. "You're burning up."

"Never felt better in my life."

A sliver of uncertainty pricked the lush fog of sensation at last. She clutched his taut upper arms.

"I'm not sure this is normal," she said.

"So what? Neither of us is exactly normal."

He was right, she thought. She pushed the concern to the back of her mind and abandoned herself to the exhilarating resonance of the energy in the bedroom.

He cupped her hot core and stroked her. Fire and ice sleeted through her. She twisted beneath his touch, straining into the embrace, trying to pull him into her.

He kissed the curve of her shoulder. "I can't wait any longer. I need you now."

"Yes," she said. "Now."

He moved, making a place for himself between her thighs. She gasped when she felt him pushing slowly, heavily, into her. Once again she thought she heard a whisper of warning. *This isn't normal.* Something more was happening here, something she did not fully comprehend. Whatever it was, the meaning was still encrypted.

But he was inside her now, filling her completely, and it seemed to her that their auras were resonating together in some unimaginable way. Then she could not think about anything else except the overpowering need that was building inside her.

Sam began to move. She raised her knees to let him sink deeper. Until tonight, she would not have believed that she was capable of experiencing such intense sensations.

In the next heartbeat, her release cascaded through her in waves of energy that defied easy descriptions of both pleasure and pain. *Not normal,* she thought again. *But incredible.*

She cried out and sank her nails into Sam's back. He went rigid, and then his climax broke free, surging through him in heavy waves. His fierce growl of triumph and satisfaction echoed in the shadows.

In that senses-shattering moment, she could have sworn that the flaring ultralight currents of their overheated auras had established a harmonic link, a breathtakingly intimate resonance.

She had just time enough to think, *Such a thing isn't possible.*

And then they were collapsing together into the damp sheets, and she could not think coherently at all.

14

SHE AWOKE TO THE INTOXICATING FRAGRANCE OF FRESHLY brewed coffee.

Sam.

She opened her eyes to the early light of a Seattle summer morning and bolted upright on a tide of adrenaline. *Sam had spent the night in her bed.*

She knew he had not gone back to the sofa, because she had a distinct recollection of him returning from the bathroom after the heated lovemaking. Mentally, she corrected herself: *the heated sex.* No love involved on either side. They barely knew each other.

It came down to a one-night stand. She never did one-night stands. Too risky.

Newton was nowhere to be seen. A shiver of alarm shot through her. He was always there to greet her first thing in the morning.

As if on cue, she heard Newton in the hall. He trotted into the bedroom, put his front paws up on the bed and licked her hand.

"Well, good morning to you, too," she said.

She rubbed his ears. Newton gave her another perfunctory lick on the hand and bounced off, tail high. He disappeared back down the hall, as if he had more important things to do.

She forced herself to focus on the chain of events during the night. When Sam had returned to the bed, he had pulled her close and fallen into a profound sleep. She had expected to spend the short time left until dawn lying awake, worrying about the weird, unsettling sensations she had experienced and the possible ramifications of what had happened.

But the exhaustion that had come over her had been beyond any normal postcoital languor. *Probably because there had been as much paranormal as normal energy involved,* she thought. She had never before engaged in sex with all of her senses wide open. Until last night, she would not have believed such an encounter was even possible.

Her phone chimed, snapping her out of her reverie. She scooped it up off the nightstand and glanced at the screen. The familiar caller ID calmed her. Ralph, the day doorman.

"Good morning, Ralph," she said. She glanced at the clock again. "Early-morning package delivery?"

"There is a gentleman here to see you." Ralph spoke very quietly into the phone. "A Mr. Strickland."

"Dawson? Are you sure?"

"Says he's your brother, but you never mentioned a brother."

"Dawson is my stepbrother," she said. She spoke automatically while she tried to think. "What does he want?"

Sam came to stand in the doorway of the bedroom. Newton was at his heels. Sam had obviously showered and shaved. His dark hair was still damp. He wore a charcoal-gray pullover and a pair of black trousers. He had a cup of coffee in his hand and a little heat in his eyes. She was suddenly very conscious of her wild hair and the faded nightgown.

"Mr. Strickland says he wants to talk to you," Ralph said, his voice still barely above a whisper. "But if you'd rather not see him, I'll be happy to tell him that you're not at home. After all, you were scheduled to be out of town this week, anyway."

She smiled a little at Ralph's protective tones. He knew she had spent the night with a man and that said male was still under her roof. The door staff knew everything that went on in the building. He was trying to shield her from any possible awkwardness that might result if her stepbrother walked in on the situation. *As if Dawson has ever shown any interest in my social life,* she thought. So long as she kept a low profile and did not embarrass the clan, Dawson and the rest of the perfect blended family pretty much ignored her.

"I appreciate that, Ralph, but it's okay," she said. "Tell Dawson that I'm just heading into the shower. I need about thirty minutes to get dressed. If he wants to wait that long, you can send him up then."

"Let me see if he'll wait," Ralph said.

There was some mumbled conversation on the other end of the connection. Ralph came back on the phone.

"Mr. Strickland says he'll go down the block to Starbucks and get a latte," Ralph said. "He'll be back in half an hour."

"Thanks, Ralph." She ended the connection and tossed the phone down onto the nightstand. She looked at Sam. "Dawson will be coming up here in thirty minutes."

Sam walked to the bed and set the coffee on the nightstand. "Who is Dawson? Or should I ask?"

"Technically speaking, he's my stepbrother. He's the son of my father's current wife by her first marriage."

"The man standing next to you in the back-cover photo of your father's new book."

"Right."

"I get the feeling you're not close."

"No kidding," she said. She grabbed her robe off the foot of the bed. "Which is, as Gwen has pointed out, a real shame, because Dawson is the heir to a fortune on his mother's side. His Strickland ancestors made a ton of money in the lumber industry and later did some very shrewd investing in commercial real estate here in Seattle."

"Dawson is connected to those Stricklands?"

"Yep, those Stricklands. His grandmother, Orinda Strickland, controls the family money now. Dawson and his mother, Diana, are the only heirs." She pulled on the robe and picked up the mug. "Thanks for the caffeine."

He gave her a slow, sexy, intimate smile that raised the hairs on the back of her neck in an exciting way.

"Any time," he said.

She flushed and looked toward the dresser, searching for a distraction. The old herbal was gone. Suspicion slashed through her. She whirled around.

"Where's the book?" she asked.

"In my duffel bag. Figured it would be safer there."

"What, exactly, do you mean by 'safer'?"

"By 'safer,' I meant a little more secure than it was lying on top of your dresser." Sam's voice hardened. So did his eyes. "I'm not planning to steal the damn thing, if that's what you're thinking."

She reddened. "I didn't mean to imply that you would do that."

"Sure you did. It was the first thing that popped into your mind when you noticed that the book was missing."

"Sorry," she mumbled. "That was rude." She sipped some coffee.

"Do you always wake up this suspicious after a date?"

Shocked, she choked on the coffee and sputtered for a few embarrassing seconds. Eventually, she managed to compose herself.

"That wasn't a date," she managed weakly. "Not exactly." She fumbled to a halt.

"Let's see, there was tea and conversation, a kiss in a garden, and there was sex. Really great sex, I might add. I admit that the late-night prowler in your living room, the burning herbal and taking the dog out for a walk at two in the morning were a little unusual, but aside from that, I'd say we met most of the requirements for a date."

"Or a one-night stand," she said.

"Or that," he agreed, a little too readily.

She was feeling cornered, and she knew she sounded surly. She did not dare look in a mirror. Her face was probably scarlet. She drew herself up and squared her shoulders.

"Excuse me. I need to get into the shower and get dressed," she said.

She fled toward the bathroom.

"Coward," Sam said behind her. He sounded amused.

She closed the door very firmly.

15

SAM DID A QUICK SURVEY OF THE FREEZER, CUPBOARDS AND refrigerator. The refrigerator was mostly empty, but he located half a loaf of bread and some eggs. He unearthed a package of frozen soy sausages in the freezer and scored a jar of peanut butter in a cupboard.

Newton sat alertly in the middle of the kitchen, watching each step of the breakfast preparation process with rapt attention. Sam tossed him half a slice of toast slathered with peanut butter. Newton snagged it neatly out of the air and wolfed it down.

Abby finally emerged from the bedroom. Sam punched the button on the microwave to nuke the pale gray sausages. He glanced at the clock.

"We've still got a few minutes before your brother arrives," he said.

"My stepbrother," she corrected. She walked into the kitchen and picked up the coffeepot. "And I'm glad we've got some time, because I think I need another cup of coffee before I deal with him. I can't imagine why he wants to see me. Something bad must have happened. Maybe someone fell ill or is in the hospital. But I would have expected a phone call if that was the case."

He watched her carry the mug around to the other side of the counter and perch on one of the stools. She was wearing a pair of snug-fitting brown trousers and an amber sweater that was about the same color as her hair. Her eyes were shadowed with anxiety.

The microwave pinged. He opened the door and took out the fake sausages.

"You're sure you don't have any idea of why your stepbrother is here today?" he asked.

"Nope." She watched him place the sausages on the two plates that held the fried eggs and slices of toast smeared with peanut butter. "That looks good. I think I'm hungry."

He set the plates on the counter and walked around the corner to sit down beside Abby. He eyed the soy sausages and reminded himself to keep an open mind. "I take it you're a vegetarian?"

"Not entirely." She took a bite out of a slice of the toast. "I eat fish."

He picked up a fork. "When was the last time you saw Dawson?"

"A couple of months ago. He's got a house on Queen Anne. We ran into each other by chance in a restaurant here in Belltown. I was with Gwen and Nick. Dawson was having dinner with his fiancée. We said hello. Introductions were made, and that was about it."

"You meant it when you said that you aren't close, didn't you?"

She shrugged. "We have nothing in common, certainly not a bloodline. I was twelve and he was thirteen when I went to live with my father and his new family. That happened because my mother died. Dad didn't have much choice except to take me in. Dawson and I both developed immediate resentment issues. I didn't like his mother, Diana, trying to parent me. Dawson didn't like my father trying to parent him. Things got even more complicated when the twins were born later that year."

"Okay, I think I'm seeing the dynamics here."

"And then there was the inheritance issue. Dawson's grandmother did not approve of her daughter marrying my father. She insisted on a prenuptial agreement and made it clear that when it came to the Strickland money, I was not considered family. Not that I gave a damn about the financial aspects of the situation. I was just a kid, but by then I already understood that money follows blood. I didn't have a problem with that fact of life. The little lecture that Orinda Dawson gave me when I turned thirteen was entirely unnecessary, however."

Sam winced. "She gave you the talk about inheritance issues when you were just a kid?"

"The financial stuff wasn't a big deal. Like I said, I already understood how that worked. But Dawson's grandmother is one scary lady. She certainly scared the daylights out of me, at any rate. But in hindsight, I think it's only fair to say that she was horrified by me. Actually, everyone was."

"Because of your talent?"

"I was just coming into it when I moved in. But within the year, it was obvious that I was going to be a little different. Orinda did not want anyone to think that the family bloodline was tainted by weirdness."

"She didn't understand what was going on with you?"

"No, and neither did the others. I made them all very nervous. I saw a series of counselors and shrinks, and made the fatal mistake of trying to convince each of them that I really did sense paranormal energy in some books. And then there were the incidents I mentioned."

"The fire-setting stuff?"

"You wouldn't believe how that kind of thing upsets folks. Eventually, the decision was made to send me to the Summerlight Academy. That's where I learned to pass for normal. Mostly."

The doorbell chimed. Newton growled softly and glared down the length of the front hall.

Abby sighed and set down her cup. "That will be Dawson."

She slipped off the stool and went down the hall. Newton followed, hovering near her in a protective manner. Maybe Abby was right, Sam thought, maybe the dog was a little bit psychic.

A moment later, he heard the front door open. Polite greetings were exchanged, not the relaxed, familiar sort that friends and colleagues employed, and not the more intimate kind typical of family members. The relationship between Abby and Dawson fell into another category altogether, he decided, one that was not easy to identify.

Abby reappeared. Newton was still at her heels.

"Sam, this is Dawson Strickland. Dawson, Sam Coppersmith."

Dawson looked exactly as he did on the back cover of *Families by Choice*. Medium height, brown-haired and endowed with what, in another era, would have been labeled patrician features. He had the toned-and-tanned look that spelled expensive athletic clubs and a lot of time on ski slopes, golf courses and private yachts. His shirt and trousers bore all the hallmarks of hand-tailoring. His watch had cost as much as a European sports car. He carried an Italian leather briefcase in one well-groomed hand.

But it was the anxious, edgy energy that shivered invisibly in the atmosphere that interested Sam. Dawson was nervous. It was clear he was not looking forward to the conversation ahead.

Sam came up off the stool and offered his hand. "Strickland."

"Coppersmith." Dawson shook hands briskly, frowning a little in polite concentration. "Name sounds familiar. Any relation to Coppersmith Inc.?"

"Some."

"A pleasure to meet you." Dawson bestowed a dazzling smile on Abby. "I didn't know you were seeing anyone."

"Of course you didn't." She gave him a polite smile. "Why would you? It's been a couple of months since we last met. How's the engagement going? Have you set a date for the wedding?"

"Next month." Dawson affected an air of surprise. "Didn't you get an invitation?"

"No."

"Must have been an oversight. Carla is handling that end of things. I'll make sure you get one."

"Don't worry about it," Abby said. "I think I'm going to be out of town on that date, anyway."

Dawson frowned. "How would you know that if you don't know the date?"

"Just a wild guess. Would you like some coffee?"

"Sure, thanks. Had a latte down the street, but I could use some more caffeine." Dawson set down the briefcase and took the stool that Abby had just vacated. "So how long have you two been seeing each other?"

"Not long," Abby said, before Sam could answer. She put the coffee in front of Dawson. "What is so important that you had to track me down at this hour of the morning?"

Dawson stopped smiling.

"Sorry about the timing," he said. "I came in person because I don't like to have these kinds of business discussions over the phone."

"You're starting to scare me," Abby said.

But she looked irritated and maybe a little apprehensive, Sam thought, not frightened.

"Relax." Dawson flashed a closer's smile. "I want to hire you."

Abby stiffened. "What are you talking about? You don't collect books of any kind, let alone the type I handle."

"Let me explain," Dawson said. He grew serious again. "I'm in the middle of some very high-level negotiations with a potential investor.

This guy is hugely important to me and to my firm. Needless to say, I've got some competition. Evidently, the man has a thing for old books."

"Oh, crap," Abby said very softly.

She looked at Sam. He knew what she was thinking, because he was thinking the same thing. *There are no coincidences.*

Oblivious, Dawson pressed on, very intent now. "It has been made clear to me that I can improve the odds of bringing this very heavy hitter on board if I can produce a certain book that is rumored to be coming up for sale in the paranormal books market. That's your market, Abby."

Icy fingers brushed the back of Sam's neck. He was suddenly jacked, all senses on alert. He knew that Abby was running a little hot as well.

"What old book would that be?" she asked, without any inflection.

"Not what I'd call a real antiquarian book," Dawson said. "It's only about forty years old. Hang on, I'll get the details." He got off the stool and hoisted the briefcase onto the counter. Opening the case, he took out a sheet of paper. "Let's see. It's a laboratory-style notebook containing the handwritten record of experiments that were conducted on various specimens of ore and crystals taken out of a mine in the Southwest. Exact location of the mine is unknown. Whoever kept the notebook evidently believed that the crystals possessed paranormal powers." Dawson grimaced. "In other words, he was some kind of nut job."

Abby raised her eyes to the ceiling. "Why me?"

Dawson put the paper back into the briefcase. "Because you're the only expert on rare books dealing with the occult that I know."

Anger flashed across Abby's face. "I do not deal in the occult. I've explained that."

"Paranormal, the woo-woo thing, whatever," Dawson said quickly. "You're not just the only paranormal–rare-books expert I know, you're the only rare-books dealer I know. Naturally, I came to you."

"Sounds like the man you're negotiating with is aware that you have a connection in the paranormal-books market," Sam said.

"Sure," Dawson said. "Probably why I was invited to the negotiating table. In my world, you use whatever edge you've got."

"So you decided to use me?" Abby asked.

Dawson had the grace to redden. "Sorry. That didn't come out right. I'm not trying to take advantage of you, Abby. I'll pay you for your time. In fact, I'll give you a very hefty bonus if you can turn up that lab book before my competitors get hold of it."

"Any idea how many other people are looking for the book?" Sam asked.

"No," Dawson said. "But I have to assume that at least a couple of the other players who want the account have hired their own experts. What do you say, Abby? There's a lot of money at stake, and a big chunk of it can be yours if you find that book for me. I'm on a deadline, by the way. I need to get it as soon as possible."

Abby shook her head. "I'm sorry. I realize the account is important to you, but you don't know much about my world. Some books are dangerous. Some collectors are ruthless. Your investor may be one of the bad guys."

"The bad guys in my world are focused on the money. They operate Ponzi schemes. They don't set up elaborate scenarios just to acquire old lab books."

"The fact that your investor knows enough about you to figure out that you're connected to me is not a good sign," she said. "That means he knows he can't approach me directly, because he can't get a referral."

"He needs a referral to get you to broker a deal for an old book?" Dawson asked, incredulous.

"Yes," Abby said. "That's how I work."

"That's crazy."

Abby said nothing. She just looked at him. But there was suddenly energy in the atmosphere. Sam heard a low growl and looked over the counter. Newton was on his feet now, very still, very focused. His whole attention was fixed on Dawson.

Dawson flushed. "I didn't mean anything personal. Just an expression. Come on, Abby, it's just an old lab notebook. I know it's valuable to this particular collector, but we're not talking illicit drugs or the arms trade here. People don't kill each other over forty-year-old notebooks."

"Actually, they do from time to time," Abby said. "Which is why I try to stay out of that end of the market."

Dawson's face was a study in outraged disbelief. "You expect me to believe that this book is that valuable?"

"I don't know," she said. "But I do know that it is associated with the paranormal, and collectors in that market are often eccentric and unpredictable."

"Abby, this is supposed to be your specialty. You find weird books for weird people who believe in the paranormal, right?"

She smiled faintly. "Something like that. It's nice to know you have so much respect for my professional expertise."

Dawson grimaced. "Come on, I know you're holding a grudge because of the past. And let's face it, you did have some serious issues when you were in your teens. Remember the time you came home with that old book you picked up at a yard sale? That night you set fire to it in the bathtub."

Abby's shoulders were rigid. "That was sort of an accident. But no one believed me."

"Because you scared the hell out of everyone and set off the alarm," Dawson shot back. "We ended up with a house full of firefighters and a lot of water on the floor. Mom was furious. You embarrassed her in front of the neighbors. That was when Grandmother said you should be put into an institution."

"I'm well aware of your grandmother's opinion of me," Abby said.

"It's not like that was the only scary incident. You exhibited some very bizarre behavior when you were in your teens. Mom had every reason to worry about the twins."

"No, she didn't. I would never have hurt anyone."

"What about the time you disappeared for nearly two whole days? Mom and your father were frantic. The police wouldn't look for you, because they said you were probably just a runaway. Then we got that call from the cops saying you'd been found at the scene of a fire that had started in a bookstore. The dealer was injured and had to be taken to the hospital. The only reason you didn't end up in juvenile detention was because your father got you a good lawyer who got the charges dropped."

"Got news for you, Dawson," Abby said. "The Summerlight Academy was only about half a step up from jail. The doors and windows were locked. There were forced therapy sessions. There were counselors who wanted to test me and my friends, over and over again."

"What was the family supposed to do? They couldn't risk keeping you at home. The shrinks told us that you really believed you had paranormal powers."

Abby's smile was edgy and cold. "I do believe that. Which is why I'm in a position to warn you that the lab notebook is dangerous."

"It's just a damn book." Dawson's voice hardened. "I need to find it. I'm not fooling around here."

"I realize that the account is worth a lot to your firm, but there are other gazillionaires out there," Abby said. Her voice softened. "Let this one go. Find another."

"Damn it, this is business. I'm not asking for a favor. I told you, I'll make it worth your while."

"Thanks, but I can't take the job."

"This is about the past, isn't it?" Dawson's face reddened with anger and frustration. "About the fact that your father married my mother for her money and found out too late that my grandmother had it locked up in a trust."

"Believe it or not, this is not about the past."

"It is all about the past and the money. Don't you get that? Grandmother saw through your father right away, but Mom wouldn't listen."

Newton had stopped growling. More than ever, he resembled a scaled-down version of a junkyard dog. He looked remarkably dangerous. There was a little wolf in every dog, Sam thought. People who forgot that sometimes had nasty encounters with teeth.

"It's all right," Abby said to Newton. She stooped and touched him lightly with her hand. "It's okay."

Newton did not take his focus off Dawson.

"Whatever happened in the past isn't important here," Abby said. "Everyone has moved on, including me. We're the perfect blended family now, remember?"

"Bullshit."

Her mouth curved slightly. "True. But family is family."

"This isn't funny," Dawson said tightly. "You've had it in for me from the start because Grandmother made sure you and your father would never get a dime of her money."

"I don't suppose it will do any good to tell you that I never cared about the money," Abby said.

"If there's one thing I've learned, it's always about the money," Dawson said. Bitterness edged his mouth. "And right now you're letting the past get in the way of both of us making a hell of a lot of it. Want some brotherly advice? Grow up and get over it."

"I repeat, this isn't about the past." Abby locked her arms beneath her breasts. "It's about you getting involved in something you know nothing about."

"I realize I don't know anything about rare books," Dawson said, exasperated. "That's why I'm here. What I know is that I need this investor and you're the only one who can get him for me." He closed one hand into a fist. "Name your price, damn it."

"No," Abby said.

Dawson's jaw twitched. "You know, don't you?"

"Know what?" Abby said.

"You know that my firm is in trouble."

She frowned. "No, I wasn't aware of that."

"I took a real hit a couple of months ago when a major project, a sure thing, went south. It was a Ponzi scheme, and I fell for it. My clients don't know about the losses yet. I can juggle the numbers for a few months while I recover. But the only way I can dig myself out of this hole is with new capital. I have to close the deal with this investor. If I don't, I'll go under."

"Oh, damn," Abby whispered, shocked.

"Lawsuits will be the least of it. You think some of your clients are dangerous? I've got a couple who will go to the Feds. I could wind up in prison."

"I'm sorry," Abby said. Her tone was surprisingly gentle. "But you can recover. You're good at investing."

"Abby, I'm standing on the brink of bankruptcy and maybe looking at jail time. I need to land this account."

"I'm sorry," Abby repeated. "I'm sorry, but I can't help you."

"Why not?"

Sam picked up his coffee. "For one thing, she's already got another client for that lab book."

Dawson swung around, jaw working. "You?"

"Me," Sam said.

Dawson pulled himself together immediately. "I'll buy the book from you. Just name your price."

"I don't have the book yet," Sam said. "If and when I do get it, I won't be selling it."

Dawson turned back to Abby. "This is your idea of revenge, isn't it?"

"No," she said. "I swear it's not."

"I hope you enjoy it." Dawson slammed the briefcase shut, picked it up and went down the hall.

The door closed behind him.

"Excuse me," Abby said.

She rushed out of the kitchen and disappeared into the bedroom. Newton hurried after her.

Sam got up and followed the pair, not sure what he should say or do. It was clear that Abby was accustomed to handling her problems all by herself or with the help of her close-knit circle of friends. But he happened to be the one who was here today.

He walked into the bedroom. Abby was sitting on the edge of the bed, clutching a tissue. She was not crying. She had one hand on Newton, who had his front paws propped on the bed beside her.

"Please go away," she said, a little too politely. "I'll be fine."

Sam went to the bed. He pulled her to her feet and into his arms.

"We're a team now," he said. "That means you're stuck with me."

She pressed her face into his shoulder and sobbed.

16

AFTER A WHILE SHE REALIZED THAT THE HUMILIATING BOUT of visible weakness was finally over. She stopped crying. The temptation to stay where she was, wrapped warm and tight in Sam's arms, was almost overwhelming. It took everything she had to push herself away from him.

"This is so embarrassing," she said. She stepped back and managed a shaky, rueful smile. "Sorry about the drama. Sorry about your shirt, too."

He glanced down at the damp spot. "It'll dry."

"I'm okay now. Just lost it there for a while." She grabbed another tissue and blew her nose. "I haven't been sleeping well lately, and now there's the blackmail thing and that stupid lab notebook and Dawson facing bankruptcy and . . . and last night."

"I thought last night went well," he said neutrally. "It certainly did for me."

"I didn't mean that. Not exactly." Utterly mortified now, she tossed the tissue into the little wastebasket and rushed past him toward the bathroom. "Never mind. Give me a few minutes to wash my face."

"Sure," he said.

She fled into the bathroom, closed the door and turned on the cold water. She winced when she saw her tear-swollen face in the mirror. She was not one of those women who cried in an attractive way. But, then, it wasn't as if she'd had a lot of experience. She rarely cried these days, and when she did, she made certain that she was always alone.

It was the stress. She'd been under a lot of it lately. She had to get a grip.

She leaned over the sink and splashed the cold water on her face for a couple of minutes, then turned off the faucet and grabbed a towel. When her face was dry, she took another critical look at the wan features of the woman in the mirror. *Show no weakness.* She reached for a lipstick and a compact.

A short time later, feeling back in control, she went into the front room. Sam was standing at the window, looking out over the rain-dampened city. He turned around when he sensed her approach.

"You can't stay here," he said. "Not now."

She stopped in the middle of the room. "What?"

"There are too many people after that book, and a lot of them have decided you can get it for them. I'm going to take you to a different location, one that is more secure. You'll be safe there, while I look for the blackmailer."

"What on earth are you talking about? I can't just disappear."

He smiled. "Sure you can. You'll see."

"What are you proposing to do with me? Stash me in a hotel room under a different name?"

"No. I'm going to take you to the Copper Beach house. I've got good security there. In addition, strangers stand out like sore thumbs on the island. It's hard to get ashore without being noticed."

"Whoa, whoa, whoa." Horrified, she held up both hands, palms out, and waved him to silence. "Thanks but no thanks. I appreciate the thought, but that is not going to work."

"Why not?"

She lowered her hands. "You said it yourself a few minutes ago. We're a team. We're going to have to work this thing together. You don't stand much of a chance of finding that lab book, let alone breaking the code, without my help. And I need you to track down the blackmailer. Let's face it. Finding out that my stepbrother is under a lot of pressure to come up with that book really put the icing on the cake, didn't it? I'm in this thing up to my neck now, and there's nothing either of us can do about it except see it through."

He looked at her for a long time.

"Do you always get to the bottom line this fast?" he asked finally.

"Believe me, if there were viable options, I'd be running for the exit by now. You need me, Sam Coppersmith. And I need you."

He raised his brows. "Like I said, we're stuck together."

She smiled. "Well, we do have Newton."

Sam looked at Newton. "Good point."

Bored, Newton trotted into the kitchen and began to slurp water out of his bowl.

Abby walked across the room to stand directly in front of Sam. "But I can't think of anyone else I would rather be stuck with in this situation."

"You're sure about that?"

"Absolutely certain," she said.

"Okay," he said. He stroked her cheek with the back of the finger on which he wore the fire-red crystal. "I agree we're in this together. But I'm not changing my plans. We're going to Copper Beach."

"Why?"

"We need a secure base of operations. Copper Beach is built like a fortress. Most of your work is done online, right?"

"Well, yes."

"Looks like a lot of my work will be done that way, too."

"You're going to try to find Dawson's major investor, aren't you?"

"It's a solid lead. Worth pursuing."

"I can't just walk away from my life here in Seattle. Among other things, I need to put in an appearance at my father's book-launch event. That's on Friday night. He's giving a talk and signing *Families by Choice*. There will be media. Dad has made it clear that it's very important that the whole family show up."

"You're not going into exile. You're just going to Copper Beach. We can get back here for the book-signing event."

She looked around, searching for other excuses not to leave her new home.

"All of my stuff is here," she whispered. Okay, that sounded excessively juvenile. She squared her shoulders. "But you're right. No reason I can't leave for a while. Like going on vacation, right?"

He smiled. "That's one way to look at it."

"Newton will enjoy the country. He loves to visit Thaddeus because he can run around in the woods." She turned toward the bedroom. "I'll go pack."

She was in the process of folding her nightgown, the lacy new one that she had bought on impulse and had been saving for some special occasion that had never seemed to come, when she heard the chimes that told her she had new email.

She put the nightgown into the small suitcase and picked up her phone. She recognized the code instantly. For no good reason, a chill of apprehension iced her senses.

"Thaddeus," she said softly.

She opened the email and read the brief, cryptic note. She hurried out into the living room. "We need to see Thaddeus right away. He says he wants to talk to both of us in person. Something about an auction for the lab book."

Sam tossed his two soy sausages to Newton and dumped the dishes in the sink.

"Let's go," he said.

17

"DID HE GIVE YOU ANY DETAILS ABOUT THE AUCTION?" SAM asked.

He was at the wheel of his SUV, driving into the foothills of the Cascades along a narrow, winding road. The terrain was turning steeper and more heavily wooded. Abby was strapped into the passenger seat, her attention focused on the view through the windshield. Newton was in the backseat.

Abby had been unusually quiet since she had locked up her condo and stowed her suitcase and her dog in his vehicle. He had sensed how hard it was for her to accept that her home was no longer safe. He wanted to tell her that she could trust him to take care of her, but he knew that would not make up for the temporary loss of the one place that was hers, the small, cozy space where she was in complete control. He understood about control issues. Hell, he had them, too. Who didn't?

"No, but obviously rumors are circulating that the lab book will soon be up for auction," Abby said. "That's good news and bad news."

"What's the good news?"

"I know how to track that kind of chatter. I don't usually do business with the dealers who work the deep end, but thanks to Thaddeus and Nick, I know who they are and I know how to contact them. I'll try for a preemptive bid for the lab book. Failing that, I can guarantee that my client will top any other offer." She gave him a quick, searching look. "That's right, isn't it?"

"Yes. I want that lab book." He tightened his hands around the wheel. "Price is no object. What about the bad news?"

"Once the announcement of the auction is made, one or more of the high rollers who want the book will be able to drive the price sky-high."

"Not a problem."

"That's nice to know. What has me worried is that we are now officially in the deep end of the market. Like I told Dawson, some of the collectors are dangerous. If one of them decides he won't be able to buy the book, he may go after it some other way."

"He'll try to steal it?"

"To do that, he would have two likely options. The book is most vulnerable during a transaction. So he can try to identify the current owner or the dealer who is brokering the sale. That won't be easy. If that doesn't work, he'll get a second shot at acquiring the volume if he can ID the new owner."

"Me."

"Your problem is that you are not exactly a low-profile collector in my world. Dawson, for instance, now knows that you are trying to acquire the book. If he tells his investor . . ."

"I see where you're going with this. But once I have the book, I'll make sure it's secure. The word will go out that it is permanently off the market. Even if some people know that my family has it, there won't be many collectors who will take the risk of trying to steal it from Copper-smith Inc. We've got some serious security and an even more serious interest in making sure that notebook stays locked up. We'll take good care of it."

"Okay," she said. But she did not look satisfied.

"What's wrong?" he asked.

She hesitated. "I'm not sure. I've got a bad feeling about Thaddeus's last email."

"We'll be at his place soon."

"Take the next left."

"There's no road sign."

"Thaddeus likes it that way."

He slowed and turned left onto an even narrower strip of badly cracked pavement. The trees loomed close on either side. "Mind if I ask you a personal question?"

"Depends on the question."

"I'm pretty sure I know what happened when you accidentally started the fire in the bathtub. You tried to unlock a book, and the energy got out of control."

"I had no idea what I was doing, let alone that it might start a fire."

"Paranormal fire is unpredictable. Get it burning hot enough and it will affect the energy in neighboring bands on the spectrum, all the way to the normal." Sam whistled softly. "Must have been a lot of energy released when you broke that code."

"Uh-huh."

"What about the time you disappeared for a couple of days and nearly got arrested for trying to burn down a bookshop?"

"That was a little more complicated," Abby said slowly. "I thought the owner of the bookshop was just a nice old man who recognized my talent and wanted to help me learn how to handle it. I realized later that he wanted to use me to unlock an old volume that he had in his collection."

"Did you?"

"No. And to this day, I'm not sure why. When I picked up the book, I got the overwhelming sensation that whatever was inside was dangerous, or at least it would be in his hands. I just knew that I did not want him to be able to read that book."

"What was it about?"

"Hypnotic poisons. So I lied and told the bookshop owner that I couldn't break the code. He went a little crazy. He locked me inside his rare-book vault and told me that he wouldn't let me out until I agreed to break the encryption."

"The son of a bitch imprisoned you?"

"I was terrified. I held out for as long as I could. I had some fantasy that someone, my dad or the police, would realize what had happened and rescue me. But eventually it dawned on me that no one knew where I was and that I was on my own."

"You told the bastard that you would break the psi-code."

"Yes. When he opened the door I told him I had done what he wanted. I handed the book to him. When he touched it, I channeled some of the energy into his aura. I was acting entirely on intuition. I had no idea what would happen. He screamed and collapsed. The next thing I knew, the book was on fire."

"A shop full of old volumes and manuscripts. Talk about a firetrap."

"I had no idea how to put out the flames. I pulled the fire alarm and managed to drag the owner out of the vault. That's where the firefighters and the cops found me. When the dealer recovered, he claimed that I had attempted to burn down his shop."

"And you ended up in the Summerlight Academy for troubled youth. What happened to the dealer who forced you to decode the book?"

"He died of a heart attack a few months later." Abby held up one hand. "I had nothing to do with it. I was locked up at the Summerlight Academy."

He flexed one hand on the wheel, aware of the cold tension simmering in him. "Wish I could have taken care of him for you."

Abby looked disconcerted. "That's very . . . sweet of you."

He smiled. "Sweet?"

"I didn't mean to offend you. It's just that no one has ever offered to do anything like that for me before. I'm touched, truly I am. So, uh, have you done anything like that before?"

"Most of the time I prefer to use less permanent methods."

"In other words, you have done that sort of thing before."

"Maybe."

"When you work for that private contractor you mentioned? The one who does some business with the post office?"

"To be clear, the post office is not the client," he said. "It's a different agency."

"When was the last time you worked for the contractor?"

"About three months ago." He paused. "But I was on an assignment the night Cassidy was murdered."

"Ah," she said softly. "No wonder you had a hard time establishing an alibi."

He did not respond to that. It was enough that she believed him, he thought.

"Take that gravel road to the right," she said.

He slowed the SUV and turned into a rutted lane that wound through the trees and dead-ended in a small clearing. A high steel security fence protected a run-down house and a yard filled with large stone pots. As far as he could tell, the only things growing in the planters were weeds.

He brought the vehicle to a halt and studied the scene. "You're sure this is the right place?"

"I told you, Thaddeus is a bit eccentric." Abby unfastened her seat belt and opened the door.

"Doesn't look like he's much of a gardener."

"The pots and the weeds are all that remain of an experimental garden he planted years ago. He was trying to grow some exotic herbs that he found for sale online. Supposedly, the herbs had psychical properties. But they didn't do well in this climate."

Sam got out of the car. "How do we announce ourselves?"

"There's an intercom at the gate." Abby started forward. "I'll let Thaddeus know we're here. He'll disarm the security system and let us in." She opened the rear door of the SUV. "Come on, Newton. We're going to visit Thaddeus."

Newton bounded down, but he did not look like his usual enthusiastic self. Instead, he flattened his ears and moved close to Abby.

"Maybe he's not a country dog at heart, after all," Sam said.

"I don't understand it," Abby said. "Usually he loves to come up here."

Small shards of ice touched the back of Sam's neck. He jacked his senses a little and looked around, trying to decide what it was about the scene that was bothering him.

"Wait," he said, making it an order.

Abby stopped and looked back at him. "What is it?"

"Looks like the gate is unlocked."

"That's impossible. Thaddeus always keeps the gate locked." She took a closer look. "Good grief, you're right. It's not like Thaddeus to get sloppy with his security system. He's totally paranoid, and he's got reason to be. He deals with some very dangerous collectors."

Sam went back to the SUV, opened the cargo-bay door and unzipped his duffel bag. He took out the small pistol, shut the door and went back to the gate.

"That's a gun," Abby said. She sounded oddly shocked.

"Good observation."

"But I thought you used that crystal gadget for self-defense."

"Sometimes a gun works better. It gets people's attention faster."

He gave the gate a cautious shove. It swung open easily enough. He walked into the yard. Abby followed quickly. Newton trailed behind. He whined softly.

"Something is wrong," Abby said.

"Yes," Sam said. "But I think the trouble has already come and gone."

"You can tell things like that?"

"I've got pretty good intuition when it comes to this kind of stuff." He glanced at Newton. "So does your dog."

"Maybe Thaddeus fell ill or took a fall," Abby said anxiously. "If he managed to call an ambulance or a neighbor, that would explain why he unlocked the security system."

"Maybe." But he knew before he went up the three concrete steps that whatever he found inside the little house was going to be bad.

The front door was ajar. He pushed it wider.

Abby eyed the open door. "This isn't good."

"No," Sam said. "It isn't."

Sam took another look at Newton. The dog's ears were flat, and his tail was down. He stayed close to Abby, but he did not have the go-for-the-throat vibe he'd had earlier, when Abby had confronted Dawson.

Sam moved across the threshold. An all-too-familiar miasma iced his senses. He knew that Abby felt it, too. But, then, most people, psychic or otherwise, could sense death when it was close by.

"Dear heaven," she whispered. "Not Thaddeus, please."

Sam went along the small front hall. The house felt empty and filled with the silence of the dead. There was no other sensation like it. He heard Abby and Newton behind him.

The place looked like the home of a hoarder, but as far as he could tell, the only things Thaddeus Webber had ever hoarded were books.

There were thousands of them on the floor-to-ceiling shelves. Hundreds more were stacked on the floor.

"It's hot in here," he observed. "Psi-hot."

"Most of the books in this house have a paranormal provenance," Abby said. "Get enough hot books together, and you can feel it. If you think it's warm up here, you should see the vault."

"Where is it?"

"Downstairs in the basement. That's where Thaddeus keeps his most valuable books."

Sam turned the corner at the end of a row of shelving and stopped at the sight of the crumpled form sprawled on the floor.

"Thaddeus," Abby said.

She said the name with grim resignation. She had known this was coming, Sam thought.

She slipped past him and hurried to the end of the aisle to crouch beside the body. Newton hung back, whining a little.

Abby touched the dead man's throat. Sam knew there would be no pulse. He was sure that Abby knew that, too.

She drew her fingertips away and looked up at him. There was a forlorn sadness in her eyes that he knew he would not soon forget. He walked to the body and hunkered down beside it.

"I'm sorry," he said quietly.

"There's no blood," Abby said. "I don't see any wounds. Perhaps he died of a heart attack or a stroke. He was eighty-six, after all."

"The authorities will conclude that the death was due to natural causes, but you know as well as I do that is probably not what happened here."

"He was just an old man who loved his books," she said.

An old man who loved his books so much that he was willing to do business with some very dangerous people, Sam thought. But he did not say it.

He turned Webber faceup. The body was surprisingly heavy. *They always are,* he reflected. There was a reason the term *dead weight* had been coined a long time ago.

Scraggly gray hair and a wildly overgrown, unkempt beard framed sunken cheeks and a bulbous nose. Webber was dressed in a tattered robe and ancient pajamas.

"He heard an intruder during the night," Sam said. "Came out of the bedroom to see what was going on."

"Someone got past his security system." Abby rose and looked around. "It would have taken a lot of digging to find this place. He did all of his business anonymously over the Internet."

"As you pointed out, if you want to find someone badly enough, it's usually possible. Even the most sophisticated computer security systems are vulnerable."

"I know," Abby said. "Thaddeus shelled out for a high-end system, but it's not like he was a large corporation or the military."

"Which, as we all know, get hacked, too. The thing that narrows our list of suspects in this situation is the cause of death."

"What do you mean?"

"I've seen this kind of thing before, Abby. This was death by paranormal means. Not many people could kill this way. It almost always involves physical contact."

"Are you certain?"

He got to his feet. "This is the kind of crime I investigate for that private contractor I told you about. No, I can't be absolutely certain yet, but death by paranormal means is my working theory until proven otherwise. A heart attack would be way too much of a coincidence."

Abby took a deep, shuddering breath. "Maybe someone used one of his encrypted books to do this, someone with my kind of talent."

"It's a possibility, but I doubt it."

"Why?"

"For one thing, there just are not a lot of folks who can do what you do. For another, being able to short-circuit someone's aura long enough to knock him unconscious is one thing. The ability to actually stop a man's heart with psychic energy is something else. It would take a whole different level of talent."

"Maybe not." Abby rubbed her arms as if she was cold. "If the victim was old and frail and was having heart problems, a severe shock to the senses might be all it would take."

"There is that. Let's take a look at that vault you mentioned."

"All right."

She led the way to the small kitchen, Newton hanging at her heels, and opened what looked like a closet door. Sam saw a flight of stone steps that went down into darkness. Abby flipped a light switch, revealing a concrete chamber piled high with cartons, crates and shelves of books.

"I don't see a vault or a safe," Sam said.

"That's because Thaddeus took care to make it as invisible as possible. The door to the vault is in the floor."

She went down the steps ahead of him, wove a path through the crowded space and stopped at what looked like a nondescript section of the concrete floor. She shoved aside a heavy book cart and revealed a small computerized lock set into the floor. She crouched, entered a code and stepped back.

"Webber gave you the code?"

"I think I'm the only one he ever trusted," Abby said.

A large square section of the floor rose on invisible hinges. A heavy wave of psi poured out of the lower basement, jangling Sam's senses. At the top of the basement steps, Newton whined again.

"I see what you mean about the heat in the vault," Sam said. "It would take at least some degree of talent just to push through that high-energy atmosphere."

"Thaddeus kept all of his most valuable items down there." Abby descended a few steps and flipped another switch. She looked around. "I don't think the killer got this far. Nothing appears to be disturbed."

"Whoever killed Webber was not interested in anything except the lab book."

"Which Thaddeus did not have." Abby turned off the lights and climbed back up the steps. "The bastard killed him for no reason."

"Not necessarily. The killer may have been after information."

Abby entered another code into the vault lock. She watched the section of floor glide back into place with an expression of pain mingled with anger. "Such as?"

Sam took a few seconds to put himself into the mind of the killer. "If it were me, I would have come here to get the identities of the most likely auction dealers."

Abby gave him an odd look.

"What?" he said.

"Nothing. It's just that for a moment there you sounded like you actually knew what the killer was thinking."

He said nothing.

Abby blinked and collected herself quickly. "Right. That's certainly a reasonable assumption. Thaddeus knows all the players. If there is an auction about to go down, he would have known the dealers most likely to handle it."

"The question, then, is whether or not Webber gave up the information before he died."

"He would have had no reason to risk his neck to save his competitors. In the deep end, it's every man for himself. Yes, if he felt threatened, he would have given the killer a few names and contacts. I'm sure the monster got what he wanted, and then he went ahead and murdered poor Thaddeus anyway."

"Let's go."

She turned quickly and went up the steps to the main floor of the house. Sam followed her. Newton was waiting for them. He seemed relieved to have them aboveground again. Sam closed the basement door.

Abby surveyed the crowded shelves. "It won't be long before everyone in the rare-book community knows that a cache of extremely valuable books has been left unguarded. But only a very small number of people know the location of this house."

"The killer found Webber," Sam pointed out. "That means others can find this place, too."

"What are we going to do about Thaddeus? We can't just leave him there."

"Yes," Sam said. "We can, and we will. As soon as we get to an anonymous phone, we'll call nine-one-one and tell the authorities that we're concerned neighbors who are worried about Webber because no one has seen him outside his house for a time."

She frowned. "Why does the call have to be anonymous?"

"At this stage, I don't want anyone to know that we found the body. We need to leave. Now." He started toward the front door and stopped.

"What is it?" Abby asked.

He looked back toward the body. "What was Webber doing in that aisle when he died?"

"He was probably trying to flee the killer. He staggered that far and collapsed."

"Yes, but that row of shelving dead-ends at the wall," Sam said. "This was his home. He knew every inch of it. He must have realized that if he fled in this direction, he would be trapped."

"He was dying. He would have been terrified. At the very least, terribly disoriented. I doubt that he was thinking clearly."

"I'm not so sure of that." Sam slipped the pistol beneath his jacket and went slowly back down the aisle. He stopped a short distance from the body and studied the spines of the dusty, leather-bound volumes on the shelves. "I assume he had a logical way of organizing his books?"

"Of course." Abby came to stand at the far end of the aisle. "Thaddeus devised a very elaborate system years ago. It was based on alchemical symbols and numbers. Each section is labeled. See that little placard on the end of each shelf?"

He glanced at the nearest bit of yellowed cardboard. There was a handwritten notation on it. The combination of old symbols and numbers looked like some ancient, incomprehensible alchemical formula.

"Can you tell what kind of books he kept in this section?" he asked.

Abby came down the aisle and examined the faded handwriting on the cardboard for a few seconds. "This is a history section. Reference books that were written about alchemy by late-nineteenth-century scholars. These would all be secondary sources, as far as serious collectors are concerned. Some are interesting, but none are unusually rare or inherently valuable."

"None of them are hot?"

"No. Most of them are available from other antiquarian book dealers or large academic libraries."

Sam studied a small gap on one of the shelves. "One of the books is gone."

"He probably sold it recently."

"No, look at the way the dust on the shelf is smeared. That was done by a hand groping for the book and pulling it away from the others. Whoever grabbed that volume was in a big hurry."

He went down beside the body again and took another look at the scene from the lower vantage point. A slim leather-bound volume lay just out of sight in the shadows beneath the last row of shelving. He retrieved the book, opened it and read the title aloud.

"*A Brief History of the Ancient Art of Alchemy,* by L. Paynter." He looked up at Abby.

"Paynter was a Victorian-era scholar," she said. "One of the first historians of science."

"I know."

"By that time, alchemy had long since fallen into disrepute. It was the province of crackpots and eccentrics. Anyone who considered himself a serious scientist or researcher was into chemistry and physics by then. But Paynter was of the opinion that if Isaac Newton had been intrigued by alchemy, there had to be something to it."

"Paynter was right." Sam handed the book to her. She paged through it quickly, pausing midway through the little tome.

"There's a page missing," she said. "It was ripped out, not cut out. The damage was done recently. You can tell because the crinkles and jagged edges haven't been pressed into place the way they would be if this book had been sitting unopened on the shelf for a few years."

"I knew I was missing something," Sam said.

The sense that an ominous darkness was closing in on them was getting stronger. *Spending time with a dead body will do that,* he reminded himself. *This is important. Take your time and think. You need to find whatever it is that you aren't seeing clearly.* He patted down Webber's pajamas and bathrobe. It was unpleasant work, but this was not the first time he had performed such a chore. When his palm passed over the pocket of the robe, he felt a small bulge. Probably a tissue or a handkerchief. There was a faint crackling sound. He reached into the pocket and drew out the crumpled page.

"That's it." Excitement quickened in Abby's voice. "That's the missing page. He tore it out of Paynter's history in the last moments of his life and stuffed it into his pocket."

"He knew we were on our way, that we would probably be the ones who found him. He did his best to leave us a message."

Carefully, he smoothed the old page and studied the illustration. The cold sleet of psi that had been stirring his senses all morning transmuted into an ice storm.

"What?" Abby asked.

"This message isn't for you. It's for me. He knew that I would be with you when you got here." He shoved the page into the inside pocket of his jacket. "Let's move."

"I don't understand. What does that drawing mean to you?"

"I'll tell you when we're in the car."

Mercifully, Abby did not question the decision. She followed him quickly out the front door. Newton dashed ahead, more than enthusiastic about the prospect of leaving the grim scene.

He got Abby and Newton into the SUV, climbed behind the wheel and drove swiftly back toward the main road. The icy-cold feeling on the nape of his neck was getting more intense.

"What's the rush?" Abby asked, fastening her seat belt.

"Damned if I know." He took one hand off the wheel long enough to rub the back of his neck. "Just a feeling."

"What is it about the page that Thaddeus tore out of the book that has you so worried?"

Sam reached inside his jacket. He pulled out the torn page and handed it to her. "Take a look."

She took the page and examined it closely. "It's an artist's rendering of an alchemist's laboratory. Competently done, but it certainly isn't Dürer's *Melencolia*. So?"

"Look at the setting."

"It's different from most pictures of an alchemist at work, because the setting is clearly Victorian," Abby mused. "Scenes of this type are usually set against medieval or Renaissance landscapes. This has got more of a *Frankenstein* vibe. The mad-scientist thing. But there is the usual mishmash of allegorical images from Egyptian and Greek mythology." She looked up from the picture. "What makes this illustration different?"

"That picture is not an artist's generic vision of an alchemist's lab. Take a closer look at the fire on the hearth."

Abby glanced down. She stiffened. "The flames are formed by the stylized wings of a phoenix. Oh, geez, Sam. The bird looks an awful lot like that tattoo on your shoulder."

"Where do you think I got the idea for the tat?"

"You've seen a copy of this book?"

"Not that particular text but some related writings. I told you that when Dad and his partners found the crystals, they did a lot of research into the scientific literature. They were trying to track down references to previous discoveries of similar crystals. They didn't find much that was useful, just some old alchemy texts. But they did come across a few notes made by the guy in the picture. Dad gave them to me."

Abby read the title under the drawing. *"Scene from Dr. Marcus Dalton's laboratory."*

"Dalton conducted some experiments on crystals that he called the Phoenix stones. Very little of his work survived, unfortunately. He sensed the latent power in the stones, but he never figured out how to access it. He theorized, however, that in the hands of someone who could tap the energy of the crystals, the stones could be used, among other things, as weapons."

"Like that crystal bug zapper you used on poor Nick?"

He let the *poor Nick* comment pass. "Yes, but on a much larger scale. The most I can do with my little zapper is temporarily paralyze certain currents in an individual's aura. It's probably similar to what you do when you channel the energy in an encrypted book into someone's aura. And I need physical contact to achieve the results. Dalton believed the crystals had the potential to create much greater destruction, and from a distance. But he also theorized that the crystals could be engineered to create a source of power."

"Which, presumably, is why your father doesn't want to destroy all the records of the experiments and why he doesn't want to obliterate all traces of the Phoenix Mine."

Sam smiled. "Good guess. The world is going to need new sources of power in the future. Engineered correctly, those crystals might be an answer."

"What happened to Dalton?"

"He was killed in an explosion that occurred when one of his experiments went out of control. All of the crystals he was working on at the time disappeared, and most of his notes were lost."

"Just like the explosion in the Phoenix," Abby said.

"Yes. I told you, those crystals are dangerous and highly volatile."

Abby thought for a moment. "So Thaddeus was trying to warn you that someone is after the lab book. But we already knew that."

"I don't think that's what Webber intended as the takeaway from his last message."

"What, then?"

"I think he was trying to tell me that someone has one of the Phoenix stones and has figured out how to turn it into a weapon. That's what the killer used to murder him."

"Oh, my God," Abby whispered. "Lander Knox."

"Maybe. I knew that Thaddeus Webber was murdered by paranormal means. Now I know the nature of the weapon. We need to find that lab book, Abby."

She took out her phone. "I'll see if any of the deep-end dealers have responded to my offer of a preemptive bid."

He drove very fast along the graveled lane and pulled out onto the main road, accelerating hard. He saw a car parked sideways, blocking both lanes, when he came out of the first turn. A man was slumped over the steering wheel.

The psi-chill that had been riding him hard for the last hour flashed into full-blown awareness of impending disaster.

"Hang on," he said.

Abby looked up from her phone and saw the car. "There's been an accident."

"I don't think so."

He hit the brakes, slamming to a stop. He heard dog claws scrabbling wildly on the rear seat.

He snapped the SUV into reverse and shot back around the turn.

The maneuver got them out of sight of the blocking car, but he knew that they had only a couple of minutes, at most. There was bound to be a second vehicle coming up from behind. A classic pincer move.

He braked again. "Out. Into the woods. Go."

Abby did not ask questions. She freed herself from the seat belt, opened the door and leaped to the ground, still clutching her phone. Sam followed. By the time he got out, Abby had freed Newton from the backseat.

"Head for the rocks," Sam ordered.

They ran up the hillside into the cover of the trees, aiming for the jumble of boulders that formed a natural fortress.

"What is going on?" Abby asked, panting alongside him.

"Not sure, but I think that whoever murdered Webber left some thugs to watch the house."

"But why?"

"Someone wants you, Abby. Someone wants you very, very badly."

18

HE PULLED ABBY DOWN BEHIND THE COVER OF THE MASSIVE rocks.

"Keep Newton quiet," he said. "I don't want him giving away our position. Whatever you do, stay down."

She nodded and tugged Newton down beside her. She put her hand on his muzzle. The dog seemed to comprehend that this was not a game.

"What's happening?" Abby whispered.

He did a fast assessment of the available evidence.

"I think this was supposed to be a simple carjacking followed by a kidnapping. In a minute or so, they'll realize that it's gone bad. Won't take them long to figure out which way we went. From this location, I will be able to spot them before they find us."

"And then what?"

He took the pistol out from under his jacket and settled onto his belly to peer through the narrow crack between two rocks. "Then I use this. With luck, they won't expect me to be armed. As far as most people are concerned, I'm just a guy who spends way too much time in a lab, studying rocks."

"Sounds like an excellent career path to me." Abby tightened her hold on Newton. The dog wriggled a little in her arms, trying to get free.

There was a fierce, all-too-familiar tension about Newton that Sam recognized. They were both experiencing the icy energy that accompanied danger, he thought, a unique kind of rush. He switched his attention back to the view of the road.

Down on the pavement, a man loped around the corner and into plain sight. It was the guy who had been slumped over the steering wheel of the blocking car. A second man got out of the chase car and joined his companion. Together they both looked at the open doors of the SUV, and then they turned to gaze up into the trees. One of them pointed at the pile of granite boulders.

"They just figured out that we're up here," Sam said.

"Not like we had much of a choice when it came to hiding places," Abby whispered.

Down below, both men took out guns and started up the hillside They separated, working their way toward the boulders, trying to use the trees for cover. But it was clear that they were not accustomed to moving through heavily wooded terrain. One of them skidded on a pile of needles and stones and nearly went down. Dead branches crackled under their feet.

City thugs, Sam decided. Guys like this were used to dealing drugs in back alleys, conducting smash-and-grab robberies and carjackings, crimes more suited to an urban environment.

They were out of their element today, and working under a major strategic disadvantage, whether they knew it or not. They were advancing uphill on an opponent who had the high ground, a fortified high ground at that. And they didn't know yet that the opposition was armed.

Sam settled into the zone. *I can work with this.*

The second man stumbled again and fell to one knee. "Shit."

In the deep silence of the woods, the curse was clearly audible.

Sam squeezed off a warning shot. A branch exploded above the second man's head.

"Shit," the second man yelped again. He lunged for the cover of the tree trunk. "He's got a gun."

The first man scrambled for cover. "Yeah, I can see that." He raised his voice. "You up there, the guy with the gun, listen, man. We're armed, too. But this doesn't have to get messy. We don't care about you. We want the woman. Send her out and everyone walks away from this now."

Sam let the silence echo. City thugs were no good when it came to the waiting game. They tended to be a jittery, impatient lot. They lacked the discipline for this kind of hunting.

"Hey, we're not going to hurt the woman if that's what you're worrying about," the second man shouted. "It's okay, man. We're just going to take her with us for a little while. We were hired to pick her up, that's all. There's this guy who wants her to do a job for him. When it's over, she goes home, safe and sound. Nobody gets hurt."

There was another long silence. The first man couldn't take it. He leaned around the tree and fired blindly. Most of the bullets plowed harmlessly into the ground. A couple zinged off one of the larger boulders.

When the silence became intolerable again, the second man called to his friend.

"Maybe he's out of ammunition," he said, sounding hopeful.

"Like hell," the first man responded. "He's going to wait up there and pick us off if we try to get to those rocks. Shit, this isn't going to work."

"I've had it," the second man said. "We didn't get paid enough for this. Let's get out of here."

"You up there in the rocks," the first man shouted. "You win. We're leaving. Don't shoot."

Sam let the silence lengthen once more.

Cautiously, both men edged away from the sheltering trees and half crawled, half stumbled back down the hillside toward the road. Sam fired two more shots by way of encouragement.

Newton exploded out of Abby's clutches. He charged around the tumbled boulders and raced down the hillside.

"Newton," Abby yelped, stricken. "No. Come back here."

"I knew that condo dog was going to be a problem," Sam said.

"Shit," the second man yelled. "There a dog."

The first man had reached the chase car. He jumped in behind the wheel and fired up the engine. The second man tried to open the passenger-side door, but Newton's jaws closed around his trouser leg. The guy yelled. He managed to kick free and get the door closed.

The chase car did a three-point turn and roared off, disappearing around a bend.

Sam got to his feet and went cautiously down the hill.

Abby followed quickly. "Newton, *Newton,* come here. Are you all right?"

Newton trotted back toward her, giving her a doggy grin. She went down on her knees and hugged him close.

"Good dog," she said. "Brave dog. You're the best dog in the entire world."

Newton licked her furiously.

"Always figured he'd go for the ankle, not the throat," Sam said.

"Let's get moving." He urged her toward the SUV. "I want to make a stop before we head back to the island."

"Where?"

"The Black Box lab."

"Don't forget, we have to make that nine-one-one call to report Thaddeus's body," Abby said.

"We'll stop at a gas station on the way back to Seattle," Sam promised.

19

SHE FELT THE HOT CURRENTS OF ENERGY SWIRLING INSIDE the lab as soon as she walked through the automatic doors with Sam. The interior of the Black Box facility, officially known as the Coppersmith Research and Development Laboratory, gleamed and sparkled with a lot of stainless steel and thick green-tinted glass. Instruments and high-tech equipment, including lasers that were clearly state-of-the-art and beyond, were arrayed on the workbenches. Computer screens glowed on every desk. Technicians in white coats hovered over chunks of raw ore and specimens of crystals and rocks.

There was a lot of heat in the room, Abby thought, and it wasn't all coming from the specimens. She was fairly certain that most, if not all, of the researchers and technicians were talents of one kind or another.

One of the techs looked up when Sam escorted Abby into the windowless room. He yanked his safety goggles away from his eyes and got to his feet.

"Mr. Coppersmith," he said. "Sorry, sir, didn't see you come in. It's been a while since you dropped by."

Several other members of the staff noticed Sam and greeted him with a mixture of surprise and friendly respect. They looked at Abby with veiled speculation.

"I know I haven't been around as often as usual in the past few months," Sam said to the technician. "But I've been keeping tabs on things from my private lab. Abby, this is David Estrada. David, Abby Radwell."

David nodded at Abby. "Nice to meet you, Miss Radwell."

"Abby, please," she said. "A pleasure to meet you, too." She looked around. "I've never seen anything like this place."

"Not a lot of labs like this one around," David said. He did not bother to conceal his pride. "Rumor has it that our competition, Helicon Stone, operates a decent version of their own Black Box, but I doubt if they've got anything we don't have."

"If you ever find out that the Helicon lab does have something we don't have, let me know," Sam said. "We'll get it for you."

David laughed. "That's what I like about working here. I get every toy I want."

"How are things going?" Sam asked.

"Humming along," David said. "I'm working on a very interesting piece of amber today. Definitely charged. Would you like to see it?"

"I would, but I don't have the time. We're on the way to the library. I just stopped by to say hello. Where's Dr. Frye?"

"I think you'll find him in the library," David said. He smiled, as if at some secret joke. "With Miss O'Connell."

There were a few scattered snickers around the room.

Sam took Abby's arm. "I'll catch up with him there. See you all at the tech summit next week."

"Wouldn't miss it for the world," David said. "My kids can't wait to go kayaking again. They're still talking about the experience last summer."

Sam guided Abby back through the automatic steel doors and down a hall. She studied the stone- and steel- and glass-clad walls, floor and ceiling.

Sam guessed her thoughts. "Stone, steel and glass are the three materials that do the best job of stopping psi-radiation and ultralight."

"Stone and steel I understand. But glass?"

"Glass is still something of a mystery, and it has a history of being unpredictable when it comes to paranormal energy, because it possesses the properties of both a solid and a crystal. But here in the Box we use a special type of glass that we designed ourselves. It doesn't always block psi or ultralight, but it does disrupt the oscillating pattern of the currents in many of the specimens. That works just as well as a solid barrier, in most cases."

He stopped in front of another set of steel doors and entered a code into the security system. The doors made almost no sound when they slid open, which, Abby decided, was why the two people at the far end of the room did not realize that they were no longer alone. The pair stood very close, their body language signaling an intimate relationship.

Abby looked around with a sense of spiraling excitement, her senses dancing to the beat of the hot energy in the room. Unlike the crystal-based heat in the lab, this was her kind of psi.

The Coppersmith Inc. technical library resembled the rare books and manuscripts room of a large academic library. The atmosphere was hushed and Old World. Leather-bound volumes graced the shelves. Some were quite ancient. Many of the hottest books were housed in glass cases. There were no windows, and the artificial lighting was kept to a minimum. Green glass shades covered the lamps on the reading tables. The difference was that many of the books in this library were hot.

Sam coughed discreetly. "Dr. Frye, Jenny. Sorry to interrupt."

The two people at the other end of the room jumped apart and turned quickly. The woman was clearly mortified. She appeared to be in her early forties and endowed with the scholarly, academic look that went with the library. Her silvering hair was cut in a sleek bob. She wore a navy blue skirted business suit and gold-framed glasses.

"Mr. Coppersmith," she said, flustered. "I'm so sorry. I didn't realize you were here."

"It's okay, Jenny," Sam said, moving forward with Abby. "Just stopped in to check on a few things and do a little research."

The man next to Jenny smiled. "Mr. Coppersmith. Good to see you again here at the lab. It's been a while."

"Been busy," Sam said. He sped through the introductions. "Dr. Gerald Frye, Jenny O'Connell, I'd like you to meet Abby Radwell."

Gerald Frye was obviously close to Jenny's age, but perhaps a couple of years younger, Abby thought. Thirty-nine or forty, although it was hard to be sure. It looked as if he had not bothered to run a brush through his shaggy mane of dark, graying hair that morning. His mustache and beard needed a trim. He wore heavily framed glasses and an unbuttoned lab coat that was liberally spotted with what appeared to be old coffee stains.

There was a polite round of *Happy to meet you.*

"Abby is an expert in hot books," Sam said.

"Is that so?" Jenny smiled warmly. "Always a pleasure to meet a colleague. There aren't that many of us who specialize in rare hot books. Do you work in one of the other Coppersmith labs?"

Here it comes, Abby thought. She braced herself for the inevitable reaction.

"No, I don't work in one of the other labs," she said. She gave Jenny her brightest professional smile. "I'm a freelancer."

Jenny blinked. Comprehension dawned in her expression along with ill-concealed disapproval.

"I see," Jenny said. "You work in the private market?"

"Right," Abby said.

Private market was polite code in the hot-books world for the paranormal underground market, and they both knew it. Professional librarians and academics who valued their scholarly reputations did not dabble in the underground market, or at least did not admit to dabbling in it. They had their own reputations to consider, and, besides, it was dangerous.

"Right now, Abby is working for me," Sam said.

Jenny's smile was stiff, but she kept her demeanor coolly polite. "I see," she said again.

Gerald Frye looked at Sam with a troubled expression. "I don't understand. Is Miss Radwell trying to find a specific book for you?"

"Yes, she is," Sam said. "It's one I want for the family collection, not the company library. It disappeared several years ago, but it's rumored to be coming up for auction. Abby has that covered. The reason we're here today is because I want to do some research."

"Yes, of course," Frye said. "In that case, I'll leave you to it. I need to get back to the lab." He bobbed his head at Abby. "A pleasure, Miss Radwell."

"Dr. Frye," Abby murmured.

Frye disappeared through the steel doors. Jenny gave Sam her own version of a professional smile.

"How can I help you, Mr. Coppersmith?"

"I'm looking for anything and everything you've got written by or about Marcus Dalton."

Jenny frowned slightly. "The nineteenth-century researcher who became obsessed with alchemy?"

"That's the one," Sam said.

"I'm afraid we don't have much. He was never considered a serious scientist. There is very little written about him in the literature, and as I recall, most of his own writings were destroyed in a fire or an explosion. Can't remember the details."

"Let me see what you've got, Jenny," Sam said.

"Certainly, sir."

It did not take long to exhaust the library's holdings on the subject of Marcus Dalton. An hour after Jenny produced a short stack of books, all secondary sources, Abby and Sam left the lab and walked across the parking lot to the SUV.

"Well, that was a waste of time," Sam said. "I had a feeling it would be, but I had to be sure."

"Jenny O'Connell was right," Abby said. "Marcus Dalton was not taken seriously in his own lifetime or by any of the historians of nineteenth-century science. Too bad so much of his own work was lost in that explosion."

Newton was waiting right where they had left him, his nose pressed to the partially open window in the rear seat of the SUV. Abby knew that he had probably been sitting there, his whole attention riveted on the entrance of the Coppersmith Inc. lab, ever since she and Sam had disappeared inside. He greeted them with his usual enthusiasm.

Sam got behind the wheel and drove out of the parking lot. "Not that it's any of our business, but did you get the impression that there was something personal going on between Frye and Jenny?"

Abby smiled. "Yep. We interrupted an office romance."

Sam looked thoughtful. "I hope it works for both of them. Jenny has been alone since her husband died a few years ago."

"What about Dr. Frye?"

"As far as I know, he's never been married." Sam took the interstate on-ramp, heading north toward Anacortes. "I saw Jenny's expression when you explained that you were a freelancer in the private market. Do you get that a lot?"

"Only if I deal with people like her, who work the academic and scholarly end of the market."

"How often does that happen?"

She smiled. "Not often. It's almost impossible for any of them to get a proper referral. Thaddeus held a major grudge against the academic world in general, because it disdained his insistence that the paranormal should be taken seriously. As a result, he almost never referred anyone from that world to me. On the rare occasion when I do agree to take on a client from any of the established institutions in academia, we rarely reach an agreement on my fees."

Sam grinned. "They can't afford you?"

"I always jack up my fees when someone from academia comes calling. Petty, I know, but we all have to have our standards."

"Guess I should be feeling lucky that you agreed to take me on as a client."

"Got news for you, Sam Coppersmith. Like it or not, you're from my world."

"I'm okay with that."

20

THE URGE TO CONFIDE THE FULL SCOPE OF THE DISASTER TO her special friend was almost overwhelming, but Orinda Strickland had resisted, at least until today. Some things simply could not be spoken of outside the family. Not that she didn't trust Lander Knox. He was a very discreet young man. He was the only one who really understood her. She looked forward to these luncheons so much. Nevertheless, one had one's pride. The loss of the family fortune and the possibility that Dawson might be facing bankruptcy, perhaps even prison, was simply too devastating to reveal. That sort of thing had to be kept secret.

"You look lovely today," Lander said. He held her chair for her.

She managed a light, gracious chuckle and sat down at the table. "You always say that. But thank you, anyway."

"I say it because it's true." Lander sat down across from her. "You radiate qualities that are increasingly rare in the modern world. Grace, style, dignity. And wonder of wonders, you can carry on an intelligent conversation. Do you realize how few women of any age can do that these days? That's why I savor our luncheons together so much."

It was shortly after noon, unfashionably early for lunch, but the advantage was that the downtown restaurant was only lightly crowded. That meant there was less of a chance that she would run into an acquaintance, Orinda thought. She would have preferred to lunch at her club on Lake Washington. The Stricklands had been members for several generations. But she knew that there would be raised eyebrows and a good deal of curiosity if she were to show up with a handsome, distinguished man who was young enough to be her grandson.

There was absolutely no reason for her to feel awkward about her relationship with Lander, of course. He was a friend, nothing more. They were intellectual companions with a wide range of mutual interests who, sadly, happened to be decades apart in age.

They had met quite by accident at the opera during intermission. Both of them had attended alone that evening. It had been obvious from the start that Lander was well-bred and well educated. He did not say much about his background, but it soon became clear that he was descended from an old, established East Coast family. The faint hint of a Boston accent was so charming.

The conversation that had followed had been the most stimulating one she had enjoyed in years. Her husband, George, had never enjoyed the opera or the symphony or high art. His greatest pleasure had been a string of yachts, each one larger than the last. She had never liked being out on the water. Their marriage had been conducted along parallel lines that had suited both of them. Losing him ten years ago had been a shock, but she had not truly mourned.

In spite of the sick dread that was eating her up inside, Orinda managed a smile. But the phone conversation with Dawson had left her thoroughly unnerved. The realization that Abby was the key to the family's financial salvation had come as a terrible blow. She had been forced to take an antianxiety tablet to calm herself.

Dawson and Diana were right, Abby viewed the situation as a golden opportunity to take her revenge against the family. Dawson had reported that she wanted more than a simple cash payment for her services. She would no doubt demand to be named as a full-fledged beneficiary of the family trust. It was unthinkable. The woman was not a Strickland. There was no blood connection whatsoever. And she was mentally unbalanced.

As incomprehensible as it seemed, Orinda was starting to believe that Abby actually wanted to see the family lose everything. *The ungrateful bitch. After all I've done for her. Brandon Radwell could never have afforded the tuition and fees at that special school on his own.*

"I see your son-in-law is having a signing event for his new book on Friday night," Lander said.

"Yes." Orinda shook out her napkin. "It's the start of his book tour. He'll be gone for almost a month. I understand the publisher has scheduled a number of appearances."

"Have you read *Families by Choice*?"

"I glanced through it." Orinda sniffed. "I'm afraid it's the usual psychobabble that passes for deep insight and wise advice these days. But my daughter tells me that there's a very good chance it will sell quite well, and may even lead to a TV show."

Lander's smile held both sympathy and condescending amusement. "It's all about marketing and packaging, isn't it?"

"I'm afraid so. My son-in-law is very good at both."

Orinda opened her menu and reminded herself to be careful what she said about Brandon. Not that Lander wasn't aware of her feelings on the subject. He never pried into personal matters, but over the past few months it had become very easy to talk to him about so many things.

Their luncheons were supposed to be reserved for conversations about opera, literary works and other cultural matters. But all too often she found herself confiding certain matters that really should be kept in the family.

She gave thanks yet again that Lander could be trusted to be discreet. In spite of the difference in their ages, they were similar in so many ways. He had a charming, poetical way of describing their relationship. *We are old souls who have found each other.*

21

SAM GAZED INTO THE GLOWING COMPUTER WITH THE BROOD-
ing air of an alchemist pondering his fires.

"There was no indication that anything was stolen from Webber's
home," he said. "The county officials have concluded that he died of
natural causes."

"Well, we knew that would be the official cause of death," Abby said.

She sank down into the corner of the massive leather couch and
curled her legs mermaid-style. Newton bounded up and settled down
beside her. She rubbed behind his ears, taking comfort from the physical contact with him.

The toxic mix of adrenaline and nerves following the discovery of
Thaddeus's body and the kidnapping attempt was starting to dissipate,
leaving exhaustion in its wake. But she had a feeling that a restful sleep
was going to be harder to come by than usual tonight.

"The local media mention that Webber appears to have been a

hoarder who collected old books related to the occult, magic and the paranormal," Sam said.

"That is absolutely wrong," Abby said. "Webber had no interest in the occult or magic. But I don't suppose it will matter. So many people don't understand the distinction between the paranormal and the supernatural. Regardless, those reports will be enough to fire up the rumor mill in collectors' circles. My competition will be looking very hard for Thaddeus's house."

Sam got up from the computer. "The police will have locked up the place."

"I'm sure they did," she said. "For all the good that will do. I think it's safe to say the authorities have no idea of the value of some of those books. They'll assume that Thaddeus was just another eccentric hoarder."

"Did he have any family?"

"Not that I know of," Abby said.

Sam crossed the room to where a bottle of white wine was chilling in a bucket of ice. A bottle of whiskey and two glasses sat nearby. "Did he make any contingency arrangements for his collection in the event that something happened to him? Is there a will?"

"I have no idea. He always dreamed of founding a library of paranormal literature for serious researchers, but he never had the money to start such an ambitious project, and no academic institution would accept his collection."

"If he made a will, it will be on file somewhere. I'll have someone in Coppersmith's legal department check into it." Sam took out his phone and keyed a number. "If we can locate a will and the lawyer who drew it up, we might be able to take action to protect Webber's books, or at least those in the vault, before it's too late."

He spoke briefly to whoever answered the phone, giving instructions with a relaxed authority.

160

"Thanks, Bill," he concluded. "Let me know when you've got something."

Sam ended the call and reached for the wine bottle. When he realized that Abby was watching him, he raised his brows. "What?"

"Must be nice to be able to pick up a phone and have a lawyer snap to attention like that for you," she said.

"There are benefits to having access to the resources of a privately held company." Sam poured wine into one of the glasses. "But guys like Bill don't come cheap, and they don't exactly snap to attention, sadly."

He splashed some whiskey into the second glass and carried both across the room to where Abby sat.

"Thank you for trying to protect Thaddeus's collection," she said. She swallowed some of the wine and lowered the glass. "It meant everything to him."

"We might be able to protect his books, at least for now, but if there is an heir and if he or she doesn't appreciate the value of the collection, the books will probably go straight into the used-book market," Sam said.

"Or a yard sale."

Sam drank some whiskey and sank down onto the couch next to Newton. Absently, he scratched Newton's ears.

Abby smiled proudly. "Newton was a real hero today, wasn't he?"

"You're not supposed to anthropomorphize," Sam said. "Dogs don't think in terms of bravery and cowardice. He recognized a threat, and he followed his instincts."

"He was trying to protect me."

"You're his pack buddy. Like I said, he was just going on instinct."

Abby took another sip of wine. "You were protecting me, too. You're human. Am I allowed to call you brave and daring and heroic?"

"Nope." He drank some more whiskey. "I was just doing my job."

"Heroes always say stuff like that, you know."

"In this case, it's the simple truth. You hired me to find a black-mailer. Now it looks like I'm dealing with a blackmailer who is getting desperate enough to commit murder and attempted kidnapping."

"And you hired me to find that lab book. Which reminds me." She reached into her tote, took out her phone and checked her email. "There are a few new messages. Let me see if any of them are from those dealers I contacted earlier."

She ran through the new mail. There was a note from her father, reminding her of the signing event, and a message from her stepmother, demanding that she get in touch immediately. Ignoring the first two emails, she opened the third. In spite of her exhaustion, she experienced another flash of adrenaline.

"Here we go," she said, trying to keep her professional cool. "The auction is scheduled for next week. No preemptive bids are allowed, but it has been noted that my client will try to top any bid. We are guaranteed the opportunity to do so."

Sam sat forward, eyes heating. Energy whispered in the atmosphere. Newton stirred and raised his head, ears sharpened.

Sam looked at the phone. "Which dealer is running the auction?"

"He calls himself Milton," Abby said. "But that's just his online alias. I don't know anything more about him, aside from the fact that he is one of the dealers who works with the most dangerous collectors and the most dangerous books. I've never done business with him, but he says he knows my reputation and trusts that my client is solid."

"I'll call one of the people in the IT department." Sam reached for his own phone. "See if he can trace Milton."

"I doubt that you'll be able to find him. Dealers like Milton don't survive this long unless they are very careful."

"Thaddeus Webber was careful," Sam pointed out. "Someone found him."

22

Imprisoned in the shadows, he watched her walk down the hall to the door of the lab. He called out her name, but in dreams there is no sound. He tried to move, desperate to stop her before she opened the door and disappeared inside the room where death awaited.

He managed to take one step and then another, but the darkness bound him as securely as a prison cell. He knew he would not get to her in time.

At the end of the hall, she stopped and looked back at him, her hand on the doorknob.

He said her name one more time, but she did not respond.

Cassidy.

She opened the door and entered the lab. The killer was waiting for her. . . .

SAM CAME AWAKE AS HE ALWAYS DID AFTER THE DREAM, BREATH-ing hard and drenched in sweat. He wrenched the covers aside and sat up on the edge of the bed. He forced himself to take a few deep breaths.

After a while he got up, yanked off his damp T-shirt, pulled on a pair of pants and opened the bedroom door. For a moment, he stood in the shadowed hall and studied the door across the way. Abby was inside that room. She had not invited him to join her. He had not pushed. His intuition warned him that she not only needed sleep, she needed time to come to terms with whatever had happened between them last night.

One night of hot, psi-infused sex did not a relationship make, he thought. Well, it had for him, but he could tell that Abby was having trouble with the concept. It was probably hard to focus on your personal life when you were worried about people with guns trying to kidnap you. A woman had to set priorities. So did a man, and keeping Abby safe was his one and only priority now.

He started down the dimly lit hall toward the stairs but paused when he heard the click of dog nails on the other side of Abby's bedroom door. Newton was awake and alert inside the room.

"It's okay," Sam said, keeping his voice to a whisper. "Go back to sleep."

He went downstairs to the kitchen, turned on a light and took the whiskey out of the cupboard. He poured a medicinal shot and drank it, leaning against the granite counter. The heat of the liquor burned away the last fragments of the dream.

When the glass was empty, he thought about going back to bed, but that would be futile. He would not sleep again tonight. He never did after the dream. He would be awake until morning, so he might as well do something productive.

He turned off the light, left the kitchen and went down to the basement. He walked along the hall, the same hall that appeared in the damn dream. The ghostly images of Cassidy walking this path to her doom were not from his memories. He had not been in the house that night. But he had imagined how it must have happened so many times that his reconstructed version of events had become as detailed and as graphic as a photograph.

He opened the door and went into the chamber. The energy in the room stirred all of his senses. The lab was drenched in darkness, but the specimens in the glass cases were all hot. They burned most strongly at night.

He jacked up his talent and walked through the dazzling rainbow of paranormal light. The hues ranged across the spectrum, from icy ultrablack to hot ultrareds and on into the silvery ultrawhite energy that the old alchemists had called the Hermetic Stream, *the water that did not wet the hands.*

The raw-amber pieces were especially powerful to his heightened senses. He stopped in front of a glass case and studied the copper-and-gold radiation given off by the specimen inside. The same color as Abby's hair, he realized. He smiled a little and reached out to open the case.

Soft footsteps and the click of dog nails sounded in the hall. He turned away from the case and saw Abby and Newton silhouetted in the doorway. Abby had a flashlight in her hand. The beam speared into the lab, illuminating one of the glass cases.

Newton trotted into the room and immediately began to investigate the space, his nose to the floor.

Sam looked at Abby. She had put on her robe and slippers. Her hair was a wild storm of curls around her face. His slightly jacked senses got hotter.

"Didn't mean to wake you up," he said.

She moved slowly into the room. "Are you all right?"

"I'm fine." He went to the desk and flipped the switch on the lamp.

"Not much in the way of lighting," she said. She switched off the flashlight. "I think of labs as being sterile, brightly lit places, like the Coppersmith Black Box."

"They often turn off the lights in the Box. Paranormal energy is more vivid to the senses in darkness."

"Yes."

She walked slowly toward him, gazing into the cases that she passed. He felt energy shimmer in the atmosphere and knew that she had heightened her talent. He would know her aura anywhere and in any light, he thought.

"What do you see when you look at these stones?" she asked.

He looked at her, not the gems and crystals that surrounded them. She dazzled his senses more than any of the rare stones in the room.

"Fireworks, rainbows and a thousand shades of lightning," he said.

"I can sense that they're hot. Anyone with a scrap of talent could figure that out." She stopped a short distance away. "But I don't see fireworks, rainbows and lightning."

"That's because you're not looking at what I'm looking at."

"What are you looking at?"

"You."

She took a step closer, and then another, until she was only a foot away. She raised her hand and brushed her fingertips across the phoenix tattoo that covered his shoulder.

"Why couldn't you sleep?" she asked.

"A dream woke me."

"A bad one," she said. It was not a question.

"A recurring one."

"Was it about the woman you were dating? The one who was killed here in this room?"

"Cassidy Lawrence. Good guess."

"Not a guess," Abby said. "Intuition. What really happened that night?"

"Damned if I know." He exhaled slowly. "I was on an assignment with that private contractor I told you about. I finished the job early and got the feeling that I needed to get back here to the Copper Beach house as soon as possible. I arrived sometime after midnight. Knew something was wrong immediately."

"Bad energy?"

"There was definitely some of that, but the really big clue was that the alarm system had been turned off."

"By Cassidy?"

"I don't know. I never gave her the code. Maybe she had some good hacking skills. But my theory is that it was the killer who deactivated the system. I entered the house. Nothing appeared to be disturbed, but I could feel the psychic residue that murder always leaves. Same thing I sensed today at Webber's house. Death leaves a calling card. I found Cassidy's body in here. There was no obvious sign of violence. The authorities and everyone else concluded that she had taken an overdose of some exotic club drugs."

"Suicide?"

"No. I'm sure of it. Trust me, Cassidy was not the type."

"But you never found the killer."

"No."

"What do you think happened that night?" Abby asked.

"I've gone over and over all possible scenarios, and I keep coming back to the only one that works. It was a setup right from the beginning."

"What do you mean?"

"Cassidy must have helped engineer the whole thing. I don't want to believe it, because it makes me look so damned stupid, but there's no other explanation that fits. Serves me right for breaking the rules."

"What rules?"

"Never date the employees."

"Where did you meet her?"

"At a gem-and-mineral show in Arizona. I hit most of the big events each year, because you never know what might show up. Once in a while, there's a hot stone. At that show, one of the dealers had a very interesting chunk of psi-infused quartz. It was obvious that he didn't realize what he had. In fact, the only other person in the vicinity who clearly recognized the nature of the quartz was the spectacular-looking woman standing next to me."

"Cassidy."

"Right. One thing led to another. She was smart, gorgeous and talented. And she was as obsessed with hot rocks as I am. She wanted a job with Coppersmith. I introduced her to the director of the Black Box. Frye hired her immediately. Talent like hers is hard to come by."

"But the two of you continued to date," Abby said.

"I started bringing her here on weekends. But she wasn't supposed to be on the island the night she died."

"Why was she here? Did you ever figure it out?"

"The only logical explanation is that she came here with her partner to steal the Phoenix stones."

"I don't understand," Abby said. "Why would she think they were here in your lab? You said that those stones disappeared in the explosion at the mine."

"That's only half true. The stones that Ray Willis had removed for analysis and experimentation vanished. But my father escaped from that mine with a small number of geodes containing hot crystals. The stone in my ring is from one of them."

Abby studied his ring, fascinated. "That's one of the Phoenix crystals?"

"Yes. Dad split one of the geodes and removed three of the smallest crystals. He had them made into rings and gave one to my sister, Emma; one to my brother, Judson; and one to me. But so far they've served mostly as reminders of our obligation to protect the stones. We can run a little psi through them, but none of us has been able to figure out how to tap the full power of the latent energy in the crystals. And we're not sure it would be smart to do so."

"But you can sense that energy?"

He glanced at the ring. "Yes. The three crystals are all different. Even though they came out of the same geode, they are not the same in color, and they appear to have different properties. Emma, Judson and I each responded differently to them. Each of us chose the one that compelled us the most. This was the stone that somehow resonated with me."

"Where are the rest of the Phoenix crystals?"

"They're in a vault here in the basement. But that's one of the problems with the scenario that I've been working on. I never told Cassidy about the stones. Never showed her the vault. As far as I knew, she had no knowledge of the Phoenix Mine or the rocks that Dad hauled out of it."

"Yet somehow she came to know your family secrets." Abby concentrated for a moment. "You said she was a talent with an affinity for stones that was similar to your own."

"Right."

Abby looked around the chamber. "She spent time in this lab with you. Maybe she could sense them."

"I doubt it. They don't actually give off a lot of energy unless you know how to tap into the heat. No one ever notices the one in my ring. It's the same with the crystals Emma and Judson wear. Besides, the stones in the vault are shielded behind an inch of steel. But maybe her accomplice knew something she didn't know."

"You're sure she had an accomplice?" Abby asked.

"It's the only answer. He's the one who killed her."

"Why would he do that?"

"That's one of the many things I don't know," he said. "The only thing I am sure of is that whoever was here that night, he or she did not get the vault open. The stones are still inside."

"Could be her accomplice wasn't all that good with locks," Abby said.

"Even a first-rate locksmith with some serious talent wouldn't be able to open the vault. It's got a one-of-a-kind crystal mechanism. Designed it myself." He held up his hand to show her the stone in his ring. "It can only be opened with one of the rings, and whoever did it would have to be able to push a little energy through the stone."

"What about explosives?" Abby asked.

"Sure, you could blow the safe, but it would be an extremely dangerous operation, due to the unpredictable nature of the stones inside. Whoever was here that night knew better than to try that approach."

"So Cassidy's partner got this far that night, realized he couldn't get into the safe and decided to cut his losses," Abby said. "He started with his accomplice, Cassidy, the one person who could implicate him."

"I think that's how it went down. I also think it's time you had a look at what this situation is all about." He walked toward the far end of the room.

Abby trailed after him. "You're going to show me the lock?"

"I'm going to open the vault and show you the stones. You're in this as deep as I am. You have a right to see what my family has been protecting for the past forty years."

He went to the far end of the room and pushed the concealed lever in the wall. A panel of fake stone slid open to reveal the steel door of the vault.

"That safe looks much newer than the rest of the house," Abby said.

"It is. For years Dad used a top-of-the-line security system designed by the head of our Black Box lab, Paul Lofgren. He was an old friend of my father's. Lofgren died a few years ago. After I moved into this house, I wanted something more secure. I designed a new one. It was made to order by a firm in Seattle. I played around with various crystal devices until I came up with the obsidian lock and the Phoenix keys."

Abby gave that some more thought. "Did anyone outside the family know that you changed the lock?"

"No. It was another Coppersmith family secret. You're thinking that whoever arranged the burglary that night expected to find the old lock in place, aren't you?"

"It might explain why things ended the way they did."

"That's my conclusion as well."

He held his ring to the chunk of obsidian that was set into the wall and pushed a little energy through the crystal. The black stone glowed with dark light. The thick steel door swung open slowly. Faint currents of ghostly energy wafted out into the lab. Newton growled.

"I see what you mean," Abby said. She moved closer to get a better look. "Whatever is inside doesn't feel particularly hot. The vibes are definitely strange, however."

Sam hit the switch that turned on the interior light. He watched her face when she saw the small pile of dull, gray rocks inside the vault. She looked disappointed. He smiled.

"Not very exciting, are they?" he asked.

"Nope. If I couldn't sense a little of the energy, I wouldn't give them another glance."

"Each one is a geode. The hot crystals are inside. Dad split one of them, removed the three crystals for the rings and then decided he didn't want to risk cutting into any of the other geodes. Too many unknowns."

"Which one did he open?"

"This one." He picked up half of the split geode and removed it from the vault. "Good old-fashioned rock on the outside, but take a look at what's inside."

He turned the cut geode to reveal the senses-dazzling interior.

Abby gazed in astonished wonder at the breathtaking array of multicolored crystals that filled the heart of the stone.

"Oh, my," she breathed. "This is nature's version of a Fabergé egg, except that the decoration is on the inside."

"We think it may be more like nature's version of a powerful furnace," he said. "The problem is that we don't know how to safely access the full force of the energy in even one of these geodes. We haven't got the technology needed to control this kind of paranormal power."

"You're able to control the crystal in your ring in order to open the lock on the vault?"

"Sure, I can run a little psi through it, do a few parlor tricks." He put the geode, cut side down, back inside the vault. "But I have no idea what would happen if I could channel the full power locked in it."

Abby watched him close the vault door.

"What do you see in your dream?" she asked.

He reset the vault lock. "I see Cassidy walking along the hall to this room. I know she is going to open the door and come face-to-face with her killer. I try to call out to her, to warn her, but I can't move, and she can't hear me."

"Tough dream," Abby said.

"I've had better."

"I know it won't help, but I can tell you that I've got something similar going on," she said.

He looked at her. "Bad dreams?"

"Worse than that. I've started sleepwalking. Gwen says I shouldn't worry about it. She says it's probably just temporary stress caused by the incident in the Vaughn library. But she also said that it might be my intuition trying to tell me that I'm overlooking something important."

"What do you see in your dream?"

"Nothing that looks like any kind of clue, that's for sure. I see Grady Hastings, the crazy guy who broke in with the gun that day. He reaches out to me. Begs me to help him. I want to, but I don't know how."

Sam pulled her into his arms and wrapped her close and tight.

"Maybe there's a lesson here," he said.

"What would that lesson be?"

He dropped a kiss into her hair, and then he moved his mouth to her ear.

"Maybe neither of us should be sleeping alone," he said.

She slipped her arms around his neck. "Do you think that sleeping together would stop the dreams?"

"Worked for me last night." He kissed her throat. "What about you?"

"Well, I had the dream before we went to bed together. That's what woke me up. But afterward, I went out like a light. I don't remember any dreams."

He nuzzled her throat. "What do you say we rerun the experiment again tonight and see if we get the same positive results?"

She smiled. "Is that the way you science guys talk when you want to get a lady into bed?"

"Depends. Is it working? If not, I'll try another approach."

"Don't bother." She brushed her mouth against his. "It's working."

The lovemaking was compelling and intense, just as it had been the first time, but there was something different about it tonight, Abby thought. Last night she had experienced what felt like a metaphysical as well as a physical intimacy at the height of her release. The short-lived sense of connection had been unlike anything she had ever experienced, but she had told herself it was a result of the paranormal energy involved. They had both been running a little hot last night.

The same alarming, enthralling sensation of psychical and physical intimacy swept through her again tonight. But this time when she shivered in Sam's arms and wrapped herself around him while he powered through a shuddering climax, she knew that the connection was not temporary. Something much more permanent was going on with their resonating auras.

Her last coherent thought before she tumbled down into sleep was that even if she did not see Sam again for the rest of her life, the link between them would endure to the end.

She did not know whether to be thrilled or terrified.

23

Grady Hastings was enveloped in dream fog. He reached out to her. "Help me. You're the only one who can save me."

"Please, you must tell me what you want," she said.

"Help me."

She tried to grasp his hand, but she could not get close enough. She tried to walk toward him through the swirling fog of energy, but some unseen force stopped her. . . .

"ABBY, WAKE UP," SAM SAID. HIS VOICE WAS QUIET BUT freighted with the weight of a command. "Can you hear me? You're dreaming."

Somewhere, a dog whined anxiously.

She came awake on the usual rush of energy, dismayed to find herself on her feet, almost halfway to the door. Sam was standing directly in front of her. He had both hands clamped around her shoulders. Newton pressed against her leg.

"Crap," she said. "I did it again. My own fault this time. I forgot to set my alarm."

"What alarm?"

"Gwen said I should set a psychic alarm so that I would go into the lucid dream state if I had the Grady Hastings dream again. She said that strong talents are especially good at manipulating lucid dreams, they just have to focus. She told me that if I took control of the dream I might be able to find out what my intuition is trying to tell me."

"So much for my theory that sex before sleep would ensure that you didn't dream," Sam said.

"Guess it's back to the drawing board."

"Let's not be too hasty here. We don't want to abandon the experiment just because we had one failure."

She looked at him. "I thought that doing the same thing over and over again and expecting a different outcome was the definition of insanity."

"Ah, but sex is never exactly the same." He pulled her into his arms. "Each time is different. I suggest that we keep rerunning the experiment until we get the right results."

She leaned into him. "The dream was stronger tonight, Sam."

He held her close against him. "Was there anything different about it?"

"No. But I have come to a conclusion."

"What?"

"I don't think there's any deep, hidden meaning in my dream. I think the message my intuition is trying to send me is very simple and straightforward."

"What is it?"

"We need to talk to Grady Hastings."

24

ABBY AWOKE WITH A START, AWARE THAT SHE WAS ALONE IN the bed. Funny how fast you could become accustomed to sleeping with someone, she thought. She had slept alone all her life and had concluded that she liked it that way. Two nights with Sam had changed a lot of things.

A cold, wet nose pushed against her hand. She opened her eyes and found herself face-to-face with Newton. He was standing beside the bed, gazing at her with a fixed expression.

"Okay, okay, I'm awake. I thought I told you to forget that psychic-command thing."

She pushed back the covers, sat up and rubbed Newton briskly. He chuffed a little, licked her hand and then, evidently satisfied that he had performed his duty, turned and trotted out the open door. She could tell that he was headed downstairs to the kitchen. The sounds and smells of breakfast wafted up from the floor below.

Sleeping with Sam definitely had a few perks, she thought. He was fixing breakfast for the second morning in a row. She could not recall the last time anyone had prepared breakfast for her. Tomorrow morning she would have to return the favor.

The summer dawn had arrived with rain, all in all, looking more like a midwinter dawn. Through the window she could see the steel-colored waters of the sea, but the neighboring islets and islands were lost in the mist.

She took a teal-colored cowl-neck pullover and a pair of gray trousers out of her suitcase and headed for the adjoining bathroom. She had not packed for an extended stay. On the next trip into Seattle, she would have to stop by her condo to check her mail and pick up some more clothes and necessities.

She grabbed her phone and checked her email. There was a new note from Nordstrom, announcing the advent of a summer sale, and a nice message from her very good friends at Zappos, telling her that new styles were available from one of her favorite brands of shoes. There were no new emails about the missing lab book or the upcoming auction.

Phone in hand, she went out into the hall. The aroma of freshly brewed coffee and a hint of cinnamon warmed the atmosphere. When she arrived in the kitchen, she found Sam at the stove, spatula in hand. His hair was still damp from the shower. The very interesting dark shadow of a beard that she had noticed in the wee small hours of the night was gone. He was dressed in dark pants and a black pullover.

Newton was sitting on the floor, ears perked, watching Sam's every move. He spared a moment to greet Abby again, and then returned to supervising the breakfast preparations.

Sam looked at Abby, eyes heating a little. "Good morning."

"Good morning," she said. "Did Newton get breakfast?"

She felt awkward, not exactly shy but not really comfortable with the intimacy of their relationship. This was unfamiliar territory, she reflected, more easily navigated at night than in the daylight. But if Sam had any problems with the rapidly evolving status of their relationship, he gave no indication of it. He was acting as if everything from the psi-infused sex to eating breakfast together was all quite normal.

"I fed Newton some of that fancy kibble you brought along," Sam said. "I think that he would rather have a slice of the French toast that we're going to eat."

"I told you, he's a very smart dog. And it's okay if he has a slice of French toast. Is the coffee ready yet?"

"Help yourself. Mugs are in there." Sam angled his head to indicate the cupboard.

"Thanks."

She opened the door of the cupboard and took down a mug. "Can I pour you another cup?"

"Yes, thanks." He scrutinized her closely. "Any more dreams?"

"None that involved Grady Hastings, thank goodness." She picked up the pot. "You?"

"None that involved Cassidy. I told you, we just need to perfect the experiment."

"*Mmm.*" She poured the coffee, trying to think of what to say next.

"You're not real good with the morning-after conversation, are you?" Sam said. "Yesterday I made allowances because your brother arrived."

"Stepbrother," she corrected automatically.

"But this morning we've got time to talk."

She sipped some coffee. "I thought men didn't like the morning-after conversation."

He flashed her a wickedly sexy grin. "Depends on what actually happened the night before."

She flushed. "In our case, there always seems to be a lot going on the night before. There was me almost setting fire to a red-hot book in my bedroom. A midnight intruder. Bad dreams. A vault full of weird paranormal rocks with unknown powers. To say nothing of the stress of some of our precoital activities, such as finding a body and escaping a carjacking and kidnapping."

"Our relationship sure as hell hasn't proceeded along a normal path. I'll give you that."

"Exactly," she said. "Maybe that's why I'm not sure how to have a morning-after conversation with you. Or maybe I simply haven't had a lot of experience in that department. I've had a few relationships, including one or two that I thought might have the potential to go the distance. But they've never lasted long, and I somehow know that going in, so I try not to get overly committed. For some reason, not spending the entire night with someone has always been my way of drawing the line."

"As long as you don't have to face him at breakfast, you can tell yourself it was just a date, not a relationship, is that it?" Sam asked.

"Something like that, yes. According to the counselors at the Summerlight Academy, I have serious trust issues. My father the shrink says I have commitment issues. The combination makes for a one-two punch when it comes to relationships."

Sam shoveled large stacks of French toast onto two plates. "Well, the counselors and your father sure got the diagnosis wrong, didn't they?"

She sputtered on a sip of coffee. *"What?"*

He put the frying pan down on the stone counter. "You don't have trust issues. You're just real careful about whom you trust. And you don't have commitment issues. You've made plenty of commitments, and you've stuck to them."

"What on earth are you talking about?"

"Years ago, you formed solid friendships with Gwen Frazier and Nick Sawyer. You've maintained those friendships for years. You trust both Gwen and Nick. You made friends with Thaddeus Webber, a reclusive, highly eccentric old man who trusted almost no one. But he entrusted you with his secrets, and you kept those secrets. You dutifully appear in book cover photographs to help your father uphold the image of the modern family by choice, even though it wasn't *your* family of choice. And last but by no means least, you are one hundred percent committed to your dog."

She looked at Newton. "One hundred and ten percent."

"See?" Sam set one slice of toast aside to cool. "You can and do make commitments. Ergo, the shrinks at the Summerlight Academy and your father have never fully comprehended you or your issues. But you already know that."

She blinked. "Ergo?"

"It's a technical term." Sam carried the plates to the table. "Thus ends the lecture for this morning. Let's eat."

She went to the table, sat down and studied the French toast. Each slice was thick and puffy and golden brown.

"This is the most beautiful French toast I have ever seen," she said.

"You are obviously hungry."

"Yes, I am. Starving, actually."

One thing about her association with Sam, she thought. She was getting plenty of exercise and burning a lot of calories.

She spread a large pat of butter on the French toast and poured some of the syrup over the top. Working carefully, she forked up a slice of the toast. She munched and swallowed. And immediately went back for another bite. And another.

They ate in a surprisingly companionable silence for a while, no conversation required.

Eventually, Abby put down her fork and picked up her coffee mug. "What about you?" she asked.

Sam paused the fork halfway to his mouth and gave her a look of polite inquiry. "Me?"

"You obviously know how to make commitments. You're certainly committed to keeping the secret of the Phoenix stones."

"So?" He ate the bite of French toast.

"What happened with Cassidy? You said yourself that the two of you were very involved, to the point where many people assumed that you were either engaged or about to be engaged."

Sam lounged back in his chair and stretched his legs out under the table. "The answer is that I did consider marriage for a time. Everything about the relationship with Cassidy seemed perfect, maybe a little too perfect. But something was missing. I kept waiting for the click, you know?"

"The click?"

"The sense that this is the one. I never got it with Cassidy. All I can tell you is that while I was away on that last job with the private contractor, I came to the conclusion that it was time to end things with her."

"Instead, you came home to find her body in the lab." Sudden comprehension flashed through Abby. "That's when you made your real commitment to her. You committed yourself to finding her killer."

"She wouldn't have died if she hadn't been dating me," Sam said. "It was our relationship that put her in harm's way. I've known that since the night she was murdered."

"But if she seduced you and set you up for the theft of the stones . . ."

"Doesn't matter. I'm the one who asked her out on that first date at the gem-and-mineral show. I'm the one who introduced her to Frye. And I'm the one who continued to date her, even after she was hired."

"I understand."

Sam watched her for a long moment.

"Yes," he said. "I can see that you do. You're the only one who does. I'll get some more coffee."

He went to the counter and picked up the pot. He used his free hand to toss a slice of cooled French toast in Newton's general direction. Newton made an agile leap and snatched the toast out of midair.

Abby's phone chimed. She picked it up and glanced at the unfamiliar number.

"I can't imagine who this could be," she said.

She stabbed the connect key.

"Yes?" she said.

"Abigail? Is that you?"

Orinda Strickland spoke in the same clipped, cold, supercilious manner that had frightened the thirteen-year-old Abby. Orinda was no less daunting now that she was in her eighties, but there was a faint rasp that betrayed her age and something else. It took Abby a few seconds to find the right word. *Panic*. It was Orinda who was terrified today, and trying desperately to conceal it.

Abby took a deep breath and silently repeated her mantra. *Show no weakness.*

"Mrs. Strickland. What a surprise. I didn't know you had this number."

"I got it from Dawson."

"I see. Did someone die?"

"That is not amusing."

"It wasn't meant to be. I just can't imagine any other reason why you would want to get in touch with me."

"Nonsense," Orinda snapped. "You're family. Why wouldn't I want to keep in touch?"

"I knew it." Abigail slumped against the back of her chair and contemplated the woods outside the window. Newton came to sit beside her. She put a hand on his head. "This is about Dawson and that investor he's trying to land."

"Dawson told me that he talked to you about finding some old book that he needs to close the deal. He said you refused to help him."

"It's not that simple, Mrs. Strickland."

"Dawson said you won't get the book for him because you still have issues about the past."

"Well, sure, who doesn't? But I repeat, it's not that simple."

"Abigail, you were a very troubled girl. We did what we felt was best for you and the family. You're an adult now. I would have hoped that by this time you would have realized that we had no choice but to send you to that special school. You needed treatment."

"Uh-huh."

"Do you have any idea of how much it cost to send you to the Summer Hill Academy?"

"Summerlight."

"What?" Orinda asked.

"The name of the school was the Summerlight Academy."

"Well, you can't expect me to remember the name of the school after all these years."

"Gee, that's funny," Abby said. "I've never been able to forget it. And no, in answer to your question, I don't know how much it cost you to dump me there."

"We spent thousands on tuition, room and board and counseling. You should be grateful for all that we did for you."

"Oh, I am," Abby said politely. "Very grateful."

She was aware of Sam watching her. He lounged against the counter, sipping coffee and listening to every word. Newton rested his head on her leg, offering silent comfort.

"The least you can do for the family is find that book for Dawson," Orinda said. "He tells me it is absolutely critical to closing the deal with the investor."

"Yes, he mentioned that. But you're going to have to trust me when I tell you that the book is dangerous."

"Nonsense. It's just a book, not even a very old one at that. We're not talking a medieval manuscript here. Evidently, the investor is obsessed with finding this particular book, however, and has made it clear that it is the price of doing business."

"A lot of people are searching for that same book, and at least one person has already been murdered because of it," Abby said.

"I don't believe that for a second. No one commits murder because of a forty-year-old book. You're making up stories, just like you did when you were a girl. This is about the money, isn't it?"

"No."

"Of course it is," Orinda said. "You have always resented Dawson's inheritance and the trust funds I established for the twins, even though I have explained that you have no right to that money because you have no biological connection to the Strickland line."

"I remember that talk. I told you then, and I'm telling you now, I'm not interested in the Strickland money."

"It's always about the money," Orinda shot back. Anger and conviction rang in her voice. "I would think that after all we've done for you, you would be willing to do this one small favor in return. If your sense of family obligation is so lacking, however, you have my word that you will be compensated for your efforts."

Maybe it was the rare show of emotion or simply the rising panic in Orinda's voice. Whatever the source, it triggered Abby's intuition. She straightened in the chair and braced her elbows on the table.

"This is as close to groveling as I have ever known you to come, Mrs. Strickland."

"I'm not groveling, you ungrateful woman. I'm trying to make you understand that you have a responsibility to help your brother in this crisis."

"Stepbrother," Abby said automatically. "No bloodline connection, remember?"

"That is beside the point. We are a family. Dawson says he could be looking at prison."

"Look, I understand that he's facing bankruptcy, but unless he was the one who was running the Ponzi scheme, I doubt that the Feds will charge him with a crime."

"Don't you understand?" Orinda said. "Whoever lured Dawson into that scheme made sure that when it fell apart, Dawson would take the fall."

"Okay, okay, calm down. Sounds like this all comes down to money. If Dawson is forced to pay off some clients, he can borrow the money from the Strickland trust. Surely he can get a loan from you."

There was a short, jarring silence.

"That is not an option," Orinda said in a flat voice. "The trust is almost entirely depleted."

"What?"

"I had Dawson invest almost the full amount into that damned Ponzi scheme."

"Oh, for pity's sake. I'm no expert on financial management, but didn't anyone ever give you the talk on diversification of assets? And what about the if-it-looks-too-good-to-be-true-it-probably-is-too-good-to-be-true speech?"

"Don't you dare lecture me, Abigail." Orinda's voice was electrified with anger and tension. "What's done is done. It's not Dawson's fault that the money is gone. Dawson was the victim of a scam. But as a result, the entire family is facing financial ruin. You have got to find that book, Abigail. It's the least you can do after all the trouble you caused us."

The phone went dead in Abby's hand. She looked at Sam.

"In case you didn't figure it out, that was Dawson's grandmother, Orinda Strickland."

"The one who made sure you knew that you were not going to inherit a dime of her money?" Sam asked.

"Yep. Evidently, there is no longer a dime left to be inherited. It

185

seems that she put virtually all of the Strickland money into the Ponzi scheme."

Sam whistled softly and shook his head. He did not say anything.

"I expect the next call will be from Dawson's mother."

"Your stepmother."

"Yes." Abby drummed her fingers on the table. "Although I suppose it's possible they'll get Dad to contact me. It's not like he was going to inherit anything, because he did sign that prenup, but as long as the marriage lasts, he gets to enjoy the many benefits of the Strickland money. If he knows the faucet has been turned off and that the twins' inheritance is at stake, he'll pay attention."

"You think he'll be worried about your half sisters' trust fund?"

"Jessica and Laura are Dad's do-over kids," Abby explained. "Part of the image of the modern family of choice. They're attending a very expensive private college. He won't want to see their tuition cut off."

"This situation," Sam said, "is getting complicated for you."

"Yes, it certainly is." She rose. "I'm going to take a walk. I need some fresh air to clear my head."

Newton sprang to his feet at the word *walk*.

"I'll come with you," Sam said.

Abby turned in the doorway. "I thought you said I'd be safe here on the island."

"You're safe." Sam put his empty mug on the counter. "I just want to go with you. Do you mind?"

"Suit yourself."

"So gracious," he said, not quite under his breath. "And after all I've done for you."

For the first time in her life, she knew what it meant to see red. She was so outraged, she could scarcely speak.

"Don't you dare try to guilt-trip me," she fumed. "I've just spent the past few minutes talking to a world-class expert."

Sam grinned. "Couldn't resist."

She tried to stay mad, but she just did not have the energy for it. She burst into laughter instead.

"Your sense of humor leaves a lot to be desired," she said.

The misty rain had cleared. The day was starting to warm slowly, but the air was still cool and damp. Abby bundled up in a jacket. Sam put on a windbreaker. Once outside, Newton dashed about madly, bobbing in and out of the trees, glorying in his newfound off-leash freedom.

"I think he hears the call of the wild," Abby said.

"For a condo dog, he certainly has adapted to the country life in a hurry."

Abby looked at the three other houses just barely visible through the woods. "So this is the Coppersmith family compound."

"One of them. There's another one down in Sedona."

Abby gestured toward the houses. "Who lives in those places?"

"My folks built that one for themselves." He pointed to a modern-looking house that overlooked the water. "My mother never did like the old house. Judson and Emma use the other two when they're on the island. We're a close family, but we like our privacy. Also, my parents have long-range visions of a large, extended family with plenty of grandkids."

"But none of you have married."

"Not yet. Mom is starting to push. I think that's why she and Dad got so excited about my relationship with Cassidy. They were so sure she was the one. They're convinced that I'm pining away here on the island, nursing a broken heart."

"I know you aren't brokenhearted, but do you think it's possible that when you were unable to solve the murder you may have become somewhat obsessed with your sense of failure?" Abby asked gently.

"Sure." Sam smiled, a slow, cold smile. "But everything has changed now. I'm on the trail, thanks to you."

They walked across the clearing and came to a halt at the top of the rocky bluff above the cove.

"Why did your mother name this cove Copper Beach?" Abby asked.

Sam's mouth kicked up at the corner. "One of these days you'll see for yourself."

Not far offshore, a pod of orcas sliced through the waters. The massive black-and-white creatures rose out of the waves in graceful, acrobatic leaps, only to disappear back into the depths.

"That's one of the resident pods," Sam said. "The researchers have them all identified, named and logged. No two orcas have exactly the same markings. Each pod even has its own dialect of the whale language."

"They're stunning when you see them up close like this," Abby said. "They look like they're dancing."

"They're hunting. Takes a lot of food to keep an eight-ton animal going. Looks like they've found a school of salmon. They'll work it as a team, driving the fish up against one of the underwater cliffs here on Legacy. Once the salmon are trapped, the orcas will pull out the knives and forks, otherwise known as very large teeth."

"Nature in the raw. Literally. I prefer my salmon cooked."

"Got news for you, the local fishermen often use the same technique to catch the salmon you eat. Hunting tactics don't vary all that much from one species to another." Sam's phone rang. He pulled it out of his jacket and checked the screen. Then he took the call. "Sorry, Dad. Nothing much to report. I told you I'd call as soon as I had something for you."

There was a short pause.

"That's not necessary, Dad," Sam said evenly. "You and Mom already have plans to come up here next week for the tech summit. No need to arrive early."

Another pause.

"I see," Sam said. He sounded resigned. He ended the call and looked at Abby. "That was my father."

"Bad news?" she asked, concerned.

"Depends on your point of view. He and Mom are on their way here to the island. They're due to arrive this afternoon."

25

THE COPPER BEACH DINER WAS NEARLY EMPTY WHEN ABBY arrived. By the time the young waitress brought the coffee to the booth, the place was half full, and more of the locals were ambling in every minute.

"You're good for business," the waitress said in low tones. "Between you and me, the boss is thrilled. Problem is, the only things people are ordering are coffee and doughnuts."

The server looked to be about nineteen. She was cheerful, friendly and unabashedly curious. Her blond hair was secured in a tight pony-tail. Her uniform consisted of a pair of jeans and a T-shirt. She was not wearing a name tag. In a town the size of Copper Beach, there was probably no need for one, Abby reflected. She had heard some of the other customers greet the waitress as Brenda.

"Don't knock the coffee and doughnuts," Abby said, in an equally soft voice. "High-profit items."

"Sure, for the boss. But people who only order coffee and doughnuts don't leave much in the way of a tip."

"Yes, I know. I've done this kind of work. Sorry about that. Maybe I should put up a sign that says minimum order of a hamburger required if you're here to see the stranger in town. And there will be an extra charge for viewing the dog out front."

Brenda snickered. Abby glanced around the crowded restaurant. Several pairs of eyes quickly slid away. The buzz of artificial conversation got louder. Most of it revolved around fishing and the state of the weather.

"I realize you don't get a lot of tourists here on the island," she said to Brenda, "but are they such a rare species that everyone in town turns out to view a specimen?"

Brenda giggled and leaned closer, on the pretext of collecting the menu. "It's true, we aren't exactly a destination stop in the San Juans. We're not Friday Harbor, that's for sure. Most folks don't even know that Legacy exists, and that's the way people around here like it. The biggest event here all year is coming up next week, that's the annual Coppersmith technical summit. The employees of the R-and-D lab and their families fill up the lodge and the bed-and-breakfast places. There is always a big barbecue on the last night. The whole town is invited."

"What makes me so interesting?"

Brenda winked. "The fact that you're staying out at Sam Coppersmith's place, of course."

"He doesn't have a lot of guests, I take it."

"Are you kidding?" Brenda straightened and did an eye roll. "He hasn't brought a lady friend here since his fiancée was murdered."

"The way I heard it, they were not engaged."

"Well, they weren't. She got killed before they could make it official.

191

But everyone on the island knew that Sam was going to marry her. Losing her like that just about broke his heart."

"I see."

"There was a lot of nasty talk after he found the body. Online, they were calling him Blackbeard. They said any smart woman should be scared to death of him."

"Bluebeard," Abby said.

"Huh?"

"Bluebeard was the name of the seventeenth-century nobleman who was in the habit of murdering his wives, not Blackbeard."

"Oh, yeah. Whatever. Anyhow, the fact that he brought you here is a very big deal. Means his broken heart is mending."

Abby watched Sam walk down the street toward the diner. He had just come out of the post office, but he wasn't carrying any mail. He nodded at the people he passed. They greeted him in a comfortable, relaxed manner.

Newton, secured to a post by his leash, spotted Sam approaching and got to his feet to greet him.

"No one from around here believed for a single minute that Sam had anything to do with that poor woman's murder, you know," Brenda whispered earnestly.

Abby watched Sam pause to scratch Newton behind the ears. "I understand. They believed he was innocent because they knew him and knew the family. They couldn't imagine him committing murder."

"Well, sure, everyone knows the Coppersmiths. They own most of the island. But that's not the reason we all figured Sam didn't kill his fiancée."

"What was the reason?" Abby asked politely. She braced for the answer she knew was coming.

"Simple," Brenda said, with an air of triumph. "Like my dad says, if one of the Coppersmith men decided to murder someone, you can bet there wouldn't be anything left behind to tie him to the scene. Either it would look like an accident or else the body would just disappear. Not that hard to make that happen around here." Brenda nodded in the direction of the small bay. "Lotta deep water out there."

"I've heard that theory," Abby said.

"Yeah, well, obviously you don't think he killed that poor woman. You wouldn't be here if you did, right? Oops, gotta go." Brenda grimaced. "The boss is giving me one of his get-back-to-work looks."

She whisked herself off in the direction of the coffee machine.

Sam opened the door and walked into the diner. Every head in the room swiveled in his direction. There were several rounds of cheerful greetings. Sam responded to the friendly gauntlet with the easy familiarity of someone who knows everyone in the room.

He made his way to the booth where Abby sat alone with her coffee, and lowered himself down onto the vinyl seat on the other side of the table.

Brenda materialized instantly, a thick mug and a pot of coffee in her hands.

"Morning, Sam," she said, her cheeks pink with excitement. "Coffee?"

"Yes, thanks, Brenda. How's your grandmother? Heard she was having some problems."

"She went to see that specialist in Seattle, like your mom suggested. They ran some tests, and he put her on some new meds. They seem to be working. Her blood pressure is under control again."

"Good. Glad to hear it."

Brenda poured the coffee and gave him a dazzling smile. "Can I get you anything else?"

"No, coffee is fine for now. We're waiting for my folks. Dixon is bringing them over from Anacortes. Should be here in a few minutes."

"It'll be nice to see them again," Brenda said.

She went back behind the counter and started to pour coffee.

The background noise of conversation that had faded for a bit returned in full force. Sam raised his mug to swallow some coffee. He stopped when he saw that Abby was looking at him.

"Something wrong?" he asked.

"No," Abby said.

"Okay." Sam shrugged and took a sip.

Abby glared. "Don't be dense. Do you realize that everyone in this diner, probably everyone in town, assumes that we're involved in a relationship?"

Sam struggled with that question for a few seconds and then gave up. "We *are* involved in a relationship."

"Maybe, but it's complicated." She tipped her head slightly, to indicate the crowded restaurant. "Your neighbors here don't understand the nuances. They think we're in a more personal relationship."

"Yeah." Sam drank some more and lowered the mug. He smiled. "That, too."

She leaned forward. "I'm concerned that there will be some widespread misunderstanding here, Coppersmith. This is your home, not mine. What about the gossip?"

"What about it? This is a small town and a small island. Gossip is the lifeblood of the community."

"You're not taking this seriously, are you?"

"What do you want me to do? Stand up and announce that we're sleeping together but that we're not involved in a personal relationship?"

She sat back and drummed her fingers on the table. "Don't say I didn't warn you."

"Relax. You don't care what anyone around here thinks. Once this situation is finished, you'll never see any of these people again, right?"

She did another staccato drumroll and narrowed her eyes. "Right."

"Good. Glad we got that sorted out."

She gave him a steely smile. "Like my dad says in his book on modern marriage, communication is the key to a good relationship."

"Absolutely. Here comes Dixon's water taxi." Sam put down his mug, got to his feet and pulled some money out of his wallet. He dropped the bills on the table. "Time for you to meet the parents."

Abby slipped out from the booth and collected her tote. She walked side by side with Sam, past the curious stares and polite farewells.

Brenda waved a casual good-bye. Abby wiggled her fingers in response. Outside, on the sidewalk, Newton greeted her in his customary over-the-top style. She freed him from the post and wrapped the end of his leash around her wrist.

They walked along Bay Street and watched the water taxi ease into the dock. There were only two passengers on board. The resemblance between Sam and the broad-shouldered, silver-haired man was unmistakable. Same fiercely etched features, same fiercely determined eyes, Abby thought. It was not all that hard to imagine Elias Coppersmith surviving a murder attempt and escaping an underground explosion with a cache of dangerous paranormal crystals. Not so hard to envision a man like this going on to found an empire like Coppersmith Inc., either.

A trim, attractive woman with discreetly tinted blond hair stood beside Elias Coppersmith. Her hands were thrust deep into the pockets of her jacket.

Abby looked at Sam. "Are both of your parents strong talents?"

"Dad definitely has some serious sensitivity for the latent energy in crystals. But he isn't nearly as strong as Judson and Emma and me. He can't run a little psi through any of the stones the way we can, for example."

"What about your mother?"

"I'd say Mom has above-average intuition, but what mother doesn't?

And she runs the Coppersmith Foundation like a forensic accountant. But I don't think her ability could be described as psychic. She's just very, very good when it comes to following the money."

"So where did you and your brother and sister get your talent for crystals?"

"Dad says it must have come from farther back on the family tree. Coppersmiths have been involved in mining of one kind or another for generations."

"Sounds like you don't buy that explanation."

"Let's just say that Judson and Emma and I have our own theory. We worked it out a few years ago, but we never told Mom or Dad, because we didn't want to upset them."

"Good grief. Surely you don't think you aren't your father's offspring. You've got your father's eyes, his bone structure . . ."

Sam grinned. "Not that kind of theory. But forty years ago, when that explosion occurred in the Phoenix, there was a hell of a lot of paranormal radiation released. We know that Dad and Knox must have caught a lot of it."

"Oh, my gosh." Abby felt her mouth fall open. She got it closed with an effort. "Are you telling me that you believe that the fallout from the explosion caused some kind of genetic mutation that manifested in you and your brother and sister?"

"Genetics are extremely complicated, even when you're dealing with the normal kind. We don't know much at all about the paranormal aspects."

"True."

"Promise me you won't say anything to Mom or Dad about the theory. Emma says they wouldn't handle it well."

"Okay," Abby said.

Sam went along the dock and grabbed the line that Dixon tossed to him. Then he caught the second one. He secured the water taxi with a few efficient, expert moves, straightened and took his mother's hand. Willow Coppersmith stepped lightly onto the dock. She gave Sam a quick maternal kiss, and then she turned to Abby with a warm smile.

"You must be Abby," she said.

Abby smiled. "Yes."

She started to put out her hand, but Elias bounded out of the bobbing water taxi, interrupting the polite greeting. He gave her a head-to-toe survey. Then he grinned, cold satisfaction glittering in his eyes.

"You got her." He clapped Sam on the shoulder. "Nice work, son. If she's half as good as Webber thought she was, we're going to get that damn book at last."

Abby gave him her best professional smile, the one she reserved for the most eccentric clients. "Nice to meet you, too, Mr. Coppersmith."

26

"YOU'LL HAVE TO FORGIVE MY HUSBAND," WILLOW COPPER-
smith said. "Well, actually, you don't have to forgive him for acting
as if you're just a useful employee that he can manipulate for his
own purposes. But there is an explanation for his rudeness."

"I understand," Abby said.

They were sitting in the living room of the house that Sam's parents
had built for themselves. It was not only much newer, it was a lot cozier
and warmer than the old house. The modern, two-story windows provided a spectacular view of the water and far more natural light than
those in the old stone house.

"To be honest, I thought Elias had abandoned the search for that old
notebook," Willow said. "Maybe it would be more accurate to say that I
hoped he had given up on it. But after he got the call from his old partner, Quinn Knox, he became obsessed with finding it all over again."

"I did get that impression, yes."

"If he does locate it, I know that he won't rest until he finds the crystals that went missing at the same time. He'll never believe that they were buried in the explosion, not now, after this business of the notebook surfacing."

"It's okay, Mrs. Coppersmith," Abby said, sticking with her polished, professional tone.

"Willow, please."

"Willow. The thing is, I'm accustomed to working for obsessed, difficult and eccentric clients. All part of the job, as far as I'm concerned."

"Ouch." Willow grimaced. "We're not just talking about Elias here, are we? You think Sam is a lot like his father in some ways."

"Well . . ."

Willow sighed. "I prefer to use words like *stubborn* and *determined* rather than *obsessed* and *difficult* to describe them, but you're right. They are good men, but I swear, once they set themselves an objective, it is almost impossible to make them rethink the whole idea."

"Not to worry, Mrs. Coppersmith," Abby said. "I've worked with even stranger clients, believe me. Collectors of the paranormal are always somewhat outside the mainstream."

Willow narrowed her eyes. "So are those who deal in the paranormal."

Abby kept her smile in place. "Takes one to know one."

Willow gave her an assessing look. "You're trying to convince me that your relationship with my son is strictly business, aren't you?"

"A business arrangement is the basis of our association. Sam and I made a deal, you see. He's trying to keep me from being kidnapped by some other collector who is after the notebook. In exchange, I'm trying to find the notebook for him. So far, he has upheld his end of the bargain. I'm still working on my half."

"If your relationship with my son is strictly business, I'm surprised you're staying in the old house. That's his personal residence."

"He had to stash me somewhere," Abby pointed out. "There weren't a lot of options. Someone did try to kidnap me, you know."

"Yes, I heard about what happened after you found Webber's body. That must have been a terrifying experience."

Abby pursed her lips. "I wouldn't say it ranked quite that high on my personal fear-and-panic meter. I reserve that category of terrifying for my step-grandmother. But the carjack incident definitely met the criteria for extremely alarming. Sam handled it brilliantly, though. Like I said, he is holding up his end of the deal."

Willow considered her with a thoughtful expression. "You are a very unusual woman, Abby."

"Just trying to do my job."

"Did Sam tell you that he's had some experience investigating paranormal crimes?"

"I think he said something about having done some work for the post office."

Willow's eyes widened. "The post office?"

"Never mind." Abby smiled. "Inside joke. Yes, he mentioned his consulting work."

"He told you about those jobs?"

"Not a lot," Abby admitted. "Between you and me, I think he was trying to reassure me that he does know what he's doing. Giving me his résumé, as it were."

Willow regarded her with a long, considering look. "Neither Sam nor Judson are in the habit of telling people about the nature of their consulting work. In fact, I would be willing to bet that Sam has never mentioned it to any of the other women he has been involved with in the past."

"To be clear, Sam and I are not exactly involved, at least not seriously involved. Not in the way you mean."

Willow brushed that aside. "I suppose you've heard about what happened to the last woman he dated."

"Hard not to know about it, under the circumstances. I got the first lecture on the subject from Dixon. Got another from a friend of mine who Googled Sam. Got the story from Sam. And last but not least, today I received yet another lecture on the subject from the waitress at the diner in town."

Willow's lips thinned. "I hate to hear that everyone is still talking about it."

"I understand."

"You don't seem concerned about the old rumors."

"Nope. Thaddeus Webber would never have sent me to Sam if he thought there was any danger involved. And my friend Gwen vouched for Sam."

"Who's Gwen?"

"She's a psychic counselor. Reads auras."

"Good grief. You decided to trust my son because your friend claimed to be able to see his aura?"

"Gwen is a genuine talent, and she is very, very good," Abby said coolly. "But I can see that even though you're married to a man who has a considerable amount of talent himself, and you've got two sons and a daughter with exceptional abilities, you don't really want to buy into the whole paranormal thing any more than is absolutely necessary."

Willow grimaced. "I've always realized that my husband and Sam and Emma and Judson all have unusual sensitivities. But I prefer to think of their gifts as being more in the nature of very powerful intuition."

Abby smiled. "You're okay with the concept of intuition?"

"Yes, of course." Willow moved a hand slightly. "I'm sure that most people have experienced a flash of intuition at one time or another in their lives. Unfortunately, they don't always listen to their inner voice."

Abby smiled. "That's true."

Willow's brows came together in a severe expression. "But that doesn't mean there is any need to resort to the concept of paranormal forces in order to explain my husband's and my sons' and daughter's abilities."

"Okay," Abby said.

"I don't want to debate the existence of the paranormal with you," Willow said quietly. "I want to make sure you understand my son. Cassidy's murder affected him very deeply. He did not realize that she was a complete fraud and had set him up until it was too late. He was heartbroken after he found the body."

"Well . . ."

"Now I'm afraid he no longer trusts his own judgment or his heart. In the past few months, I have become increasingly concerned about him. He has retreated into himself and that old house of his more and more. He only leaves the island these days when he absolutely has to go into the Black Box lab or when he takes one of those dreadful jobs for that private contractor. I think he uses the work to distract himself. He is not engaged with life, if you know what I mean."

"Hmm."

"What?" Willow asked, her tone sharpening.

"I agree with you that Sam has more or less imprisoned himself in the Copper Beach house. But it's not because his heart is broken or because he's afraid to love."

"No?" Willow watched her closely. "What, then?"

"You have to see the situation from his point of view. As far as Sam is concerned, Cassidy was a victim."

"She was a thief." Willow gripped the arm of her chair very tightly. "She seduced Sam so that she could steal the Phoenix crystals."

"He doesn't see it that way. He's the one who started the relationship and then continued it, breaking some unwritten rule about dating employees in the process. He blames himself for not getting a handle on the situation sooner. His heart isn't broken. But he's a man of honor, and he's got an over-the-top, steel-clad sense of responsibility. Plus he's just plain mad."

"He is not mad," Willow snapped. "Don't you dare say that."

"Sorry, I meant angry mad, not crazy mad. Poor choice of words. The thing is, it's intolerable to him that such a crime was committed in his home. He's been brooding over Cassidy's murder because he hasn't been able to bring the killer to justice."

"Good lord." Willow took a long moment to absorb that information. "You may be right. None of us looked at it from that angle. We were all so certain that Cassidy broke his heart with her betrayal."

"Don't worry, I'm sure it would take a lot more than that to break Sam's heart. Frankly, I'm not certain it's even possible."

"And here I was just starting to think that you knew Sam better than his own family does," Willow said. "You have a few things to learn about him as well, Abby."

27

ELIAS MATERIALIZED IN THE DOORWAY. "WELL? ANY MORE leads on that Milton character?"

Newton, napping beside Abby's chair, stirred, raised his head, and focused on Elias.

"Maybe." Abby pushed herself away from the glowing computer screen and got to her feet. "But if you keep interrupting me every five minutes, it will take me forever to follow up on them."

Elias beetled his brows. "I thought I made it clear, we don't have a lot of time. You need to find Milton before he holds that auction. I don't want to take the risk of losing that damn lab book."

"I'm doing my best, Mr. Coppersmith. But in the meantime, I've assured Milton that we will top any bid, and he has agreed to give us that option."

"If Lander Knox gets to him first, there won't *be* an auction. He'll murder the dealer the way he did Webber and take the notebook."

"I realize that we're in a time crunch here. Which is why I would prefer to work without someone looking over my shoulder. But since you have interrupted me, I'm going to the kitchen to get some coffee."

She walked toward Elias. Newton sprang to his feet and padded after her. Faced with the oncoming woman and dog, Elias reluctantly fell back into the hall. Abby slipped past him, Newton at her heels, and headed for the kitchen. Elias stalked after them.

"What did you mean by 'maybe'?" he demanded.

"I meant maybe, as in maybe I have a couple of leads." Abby walked into the kitchen. "You need to understand that I don't usually work with dealers like Milton. I know how to contact him, thanks to Thaddeus and my friend Nick, but I don't know anything else about him."

"Thaddeus is gone, but what about this Nick you mentioned? Does he deal with Milton?"

"Yes, but I can't ask him for more information."

"Why not?"

"Because currently he's my competition. He's after the lab book, too. Knowing Nick, by now he'll have lined up a client."

"Knox."

"It's possible, but I think it's unlikely," Abby said.

"Why?"

"The clients in the deep end are more dangerous than the ones I usually work with, but Nick is not stupid. He takes precautions. Lander Knox is an unknown in the underground market. He's not a regular collector. Nick wouldn't want to take him on as a client, especially if he's got options."

"Hah. Options like Hank Barrett or his son."

"The owners of Helicon Stone?" Abby picked up the coffeepot. "That's a much more likely possibility. Can I pour you a cup?"

"Yeah, sure."

"You're so very welcome," she murmured, going for excruciatingly gracious.

Elias was oblivious to the sarcasm. He started to pace the kitchen. "Maybe I've been too focused on Lander Knox. No question that he's after the lab book. But if Hank Barrett has heard the rumors, he or his son will be trying to find it as well. They might be a bigger problem than Knox, if for no other reason than that they have the money to pay top dollar."

Abby handed him a full mug as he stomped past her. "There are other problems with auctions like this. I think that Milton is reliable, but we have to allow for the possibility that the book he is going to auction off is a forgery."

Elias's face worked in outrage. "Are you telling me that someone might try to pass off a fake?"

"A shocking notion, isn't it?" Abby smiled wryly. "I regret to tell you that forgeries are actually quite common in the rare-book business."

"If someone thinks he can scam me, he'd better start running now."

"Mmm."

"What?" Elias stopped to glare at her. "You don't think I know how to deal with con men and scammers?"

"I'm sure you would be a very dangerous man to cross, Mr. Coppersmith," she said politely.

Elias finally appeared to notice that he was missing something in the conversation.

"Are you laughing at me?" he said with a growl.

"Wouldn't dream of it. As I told your wife, I accept the fact that tolerating difficult, eccentric, obsessive clients is a necessary aspect of my work, but I should warn you that I have some limits."

For a couple seconds, Elias looked bewildered. Then comprehension lit his fierce eyes. "Are you calling me difficult, eccentric and obsessive?"

Sam appeared in the doorway. "Take it easy, Dad. You get used to her after a while." He looked at Abby. "Bill, the lawyer, tracked down the name and address of the psychiatric hospital where Grady Hastings is undergoing observation. We have to go into Seattle tonight for your father's book-launch event. We'll stay the night at your place and interview Hastings first thing in the morning."

"Sounds like a plan," Abby said.

"Any coffee left?"

"Yep," Abby said. She picked up the pot.

Elias rounded on Sam. "She thinks we're both wackos."

"I never said anything of the kind." Abby frowned. "If I thought you were both out-and-out crazies, I would not have taken you on as clients. And I definitely would not have hired Sam to protect me."

"What's the difference between Sam and me and a couple of crazies?" Elias roared.

Abby nearly choked on her laughter. She looked at Sam and knew that he was having a hard time biting back a grin. She cleared her throat.

"An interesting question," she said. She turned around to pour the coffee. "Let's just say I know it when I see it."

"Are you sure you got the right Abigail Radwell?" Elias asked Sam.

"Oh, yeah," Sam said, with deep feeling. "No way there could be two of them, trust me."

The wicked, intimate certainty in his words thrilled Abby's senses. The pot in her hand trembled ever so slightly when she poured the coffee.

"I don't get it," Elias grumbled. "If you think Sam and I are such difficult clients, why did you agree to work for us?"

"You and your son certainly top my personal list of demanding clients," Abby said. She put the pot back on the burner and turned around to face the men. "Furthermore, I am convinced that either one of you would cheerfully commit murder if you felt the circumstances warranted it."

"What circumstances?" Elias thundered.

"If you thought it was necessary to protect someone in your family, for example," Abby said.

"Hell, yes," Elias said.

"Sure," Sam said. "So what?"

"I like that in a man," Abby said.

28

". . . TO SUMMARIZE, THE MODERN SO-CALLED BLENDED FAM-
ily, the family by choice, is nothing new." Dr. Brandon C. Radwell
surveyed his audience from the lectern. "There have always been
families consisting of children and adults who are related not necessarily by blood but by a complex web of social connections. The
major difference today is that while old-fashioned blended families
came into existence out of necessity, today's blended families are
formed by deliberate choices of the individuals involved."

"The *adult* individuals involved," Abby whispered to Sam. "The kids
rarely have any say in the matter. It's Mom and Dad who decide to get
divorced and start over with another spouse."

"Take it easy," Sam said. He patted her knee.

A couple of heads turned to glare at Abby. Someone shushed her.

Abby glanced at her watch. *Not much longer,* she thought, relieved.

The small auditorium was full. She and Sam were seated in the last
row. From her position, she could see her stepmother, Diana; the twins,

Jessica and Laura; and Dawson in the front row. The room was packed with her father's adoring fans. Each one clutched a copy of *Families by Choice*. A video crew was busy filming the scene.

Her father might be a serial monogamist, Abby thought, but he did have a way with a crowd. No wonder his publisher was delighted to send him out on tour. The man could sell books. With his good looks, charisma and a knack for the thirty-second sound bite, he was the ideal talk-show guest.

A burst of applause went up from the audience. Abby clapped dutifully and leaned closer to Sam.

"Told you he was good," she said.

"You were right," Sam said. "The man's a natural for television."

At the front of the room, Brandon bestowed a beatific smile on his audience. "Before I sign those books you all bought at the door, I want to introduce you to my own family by choice. My lovely wife, Diana; my son Dawson; my oldest daughter, Abby; and my two younger daughters, Jessica and Laura. I'd like them to come up here now, so that I can tell them in front of this audience how proud I am of each of them and how grateful I am to have the support of such a warm and loving family."

"This is the worst part," Abby confided to Sam. She got to her feet. "But it doesn't last long. See you in a few minutes."

"I'll be waiting," Sam said.

It was just a casual remark, but for some reason Abby suddenly felt a little more cheerful. She pasted on her best professional smile. Under cover of another round of applause, she went down the aisle. By the time she reached the front of the room, the others had already joined her father on the stage. She climbed the three steps and took up a position next to Jessica and Laura. Dawson studiously ignored her.

Jessica leaned closer to Abby. "Mom said you probably wouldn't show. But I knew you would."

"Not like I had anything better to do tonight," Abby whispered back.

Laura and Jessica giggled. Abby smiled. She hadn't spent much time with the twins. She had been packed off to the Summerlight Academy shortly after they were born. The difference in their ages and the long separation had put a lot of distance into the relationship. Nevertheless, Abby was fond of the pair. For their part, Laura and Jessica treated her like an aunt rather than a sister, but the arrangement worked for all three of them. Abby suspected that the twins secretly admired her because she held the role of the proverbial black sheep of the family.

At the lectern, Brandon clasped Diana's hand and raised it upward so that their wedding rings glinted in the light. He smiled again, an icon of Perfect Father and Ideal Husband. Abby and the others smiled dutifully and did their best to look like a happy family.

"This is what the modern family by choice looks like, my friends," Brandon said. "It functions the way family is supposed to function. Sure, there are the occasional conflicts and arguments. Building a family by choice can be hard work. But anything in life that is worthwhile requires hard work. The Radwells have done it, and so can you."

Another round of applause swept through the room. Abby and the others kept their smiles fixed in place.

Under cover of the applause, Laura edged closer to Abby.

"Mom and Grandma and Dawson are really pissed at you," Laura warned.

"I know," Abby said out of the side of her mouth. "But Dad made it clear that this was one of those command-performance gigs."

Jessica wrinkled her nose. "Not sure what's going on, but we think Dawson screwed up big-time. I heard Grandma telling Mom that he's trying to close a really important deal. She said that you could help him, but you won't on account of you're jealous because you didn't inherit any of her money. Is that true?"

"No," Abby said. "Not true."

"Hah." Jessica looked satisfied. "I knew there was more to it." She immediately switched subjects. "Who's the hot new boyfriend?"

"Boyfriend?" Abby repeated blankly.

"The guy you came here with tonight," Jessica hissed in a low voice. "The one at the back of the room in the leather jacket. Looks a lot more interesting than Kane Thurston."

Abby followed her gaze and saw Sam. He stood with his arms folded, one shoulder propped against the wall, watching her.

"Oh, him." Abby pulled herself together. "His name is Sam Copper-smith, and he is definitely a lot more interesting than Kane."

"Uh-oh," Jessica said.

Abby looked at her. "Uh-oh what?"

"We heard Dawson talking to Mom about someone named Copper-smith. He said the Coppersmiths have tons of money. They even have a private island in the San Juans."

Abby was saved from having to respond, because the moderator had moved to the lectern and was announcing that the author would now sign his book and that refreshments were available.

Abby stepped off the stage, followed by Laura, Jessica, Dawson, Diana and Brandon. They ended up in a small cluster.

Brandon looked pleased. He glanced at Diana. "I think that went very well, don't you?"

Diana smiled, but there was a strained expression in her eyes. "They loved you, dear."

The event coordinator, a small, spare, middle-aged woman with glasses and neon-red hair, materialized at Brandon's elbow. She was as focused as an air traffic controller. "I'll escort you to the table, Dr. Radwell."

"In a moment, Lucy," Brandon said. "Family comes first. I want to have a chat with my eldest daughter before I sign books." He winked. "It's a father thing."

Out of the corner of her eye, Abby saw Dawson grimace. Jessica and Laura rolled their eyes.

Lucy did not look happy about that, but she rallied. "In that case, I'll direct people to the refreshment table until you're ready."

"Good idea." Brandon gave Abby his patented paternal smile. "How about introducing me to the new man in your life, honey?"

A wave of anxiety swept through Abby. On the rare occasions when Brandon chose to play the concerned father, things rarely turned out well.

"Sam is a client," she said quickly. "There's nothing personal between us."

Brandon chuckled just loud enough so that people standing nearby could hear him. "You can't fool your dad. A father always knows when another man is interested in his little girl. I could tell from the way he walked into the room with you that there is definitely a very personal aspect to your relationship." He looked around, frowning a little. "Where did he go?"

Sam materialized out of the crowd directly behind Brandon.

"I'm right here, sir," Sam said. "Sam Coppersmith."

Brandon turned easily, radiating his charismatic smile, and extended his hand. "Brandon Radwell. A pleasure to meet you. I have a few minutes before I start signing. Why don't we find a quiet place for a quick chat?"

"Sure," Sam said. He looked at Abby. "Don't wander off."

"We don't have a lot of time," Abby said through her teeth. "Dad needs to sign books."

"This won't take long," Brandon said.

The two men walked through the crowd to a quiet corner of the room. Abby watched, deeply uneasy. When she turned back, she realized that Dawson had vanished.

"Done," Laura said, relief evident in her voice. "Jessica and I get to leave now, right, Mom? You said we only had to stay for the perfect family scene."

"Yes, you can go," Diana said. She looked at Abby. "I want to talk to you."

"I'm afraid I'm a little busy this evening," Abby said. "I've got plans."

"After all I've done for you," Diana said, her voice low and hard, "and after all I put up with over the years, the least you can do is give me a few minutes of your precious time."

Abby sighed. "I knew I shouldn't have come here tonight."

29

BRANDON SWITCHED OFF THE ENGAGING SMILE AND SLIPPED into concerned-father mode with effortless ease. The serious expression was just right, Sam thought. It consisted of a slightly furrowed brow, faintly narrowed eyes and a dash of paternal concern.

"My daughter tells me that you're one of her clients," Brandon said.

"Our relationship is complicated," Sam said.

One of Brandon's brows edged upward. "Aren't they all?"

"Good point."

Sam watched Abby and Diana disappear into a hallway. From where he stood, he could see that the corridor was lined with twin rows of offices. One of the doors was ajar. Abby and Diana went into the room. The lights came on. The door closed. *Not good,* Sam thought. But Abby had been dealing with her stepmother for a long time now. She could handle whatever was going down inside the office.

"How did the two of you meet?" Brandon asked.

"Through one of Abby's business connections," Sam said.

"She is in a rather unusual line of work."

"Antiquarian books that are associated with the paranormal. Yes, I know."

Brandon cleared his throat. "You collect those kinds of books?"

"I've got a few."

"I see. Has she told you that she doesn't just deal in books about magic, she actually believes in the occult?"

Annoyed, Sam jerked his gaze away from the closed office door. "Abby doesn't believe in the occult. Where the hell did you get that idea?"

"I don't know what my daughter has told you, but you need to know that she holds some weird theories."

"She believes in the existence of paranormal energy, not the occult."

"There's a difference?" Brandon asked drily.

"The occult is all about witchcraft, demons and magic," Sam said, impatient now. "Paranormal energy, on the other hand, is just that, energy. There's no magic, black or white, involved. Although there are a lot of fake psychics, mediums and dream analysts out there making a good living off the gullible."

Brandon's frown turned into a scowl. "Don't tell me you're into this paranormal crap, too?"

"I'm surprised to hear you say that, Dr. Radwell. You're in the psychobabble business. Surely you are aware that shared interests form the best basis for an enduring relationship."

Brandon's expression sharpened. "You read my book on marriage?"

"No. Just took a flying leap in the dark."

"Stop with the bullshit, Coppersmith. We both know why you're dating my daughter."

"We do?"

"You found out she's connected to the Strickland family, didn't you? You're not the first man to try to marry her for her inheritance. But there isn't one. The old bitch, better known as Orinda Strickland, controls the family money. Take it from me, she has gone to great legal lengths to make sure that Abby won't receive a dime. It all goes to my wife, and Dawson and the twins."

"I heard she cut you out, too."

Brandon snorted in disgust. "Prenup. And I was dumb enough to sign the papers. Thought that after the old bitch died, Diana would change her mind and tear up the agreement."

"But?"

"But at the rate she's going, Orinda may outlive me, and I've had it with the waiting game. Time to move on." Brandon glanced across the room. "Lucy is signaling. Got to go sign some books. Just remember what I told you. Abby has no blood connection to the old bitch. In fact, Orinda is downright embarrassed that Abby is considered a member of the family. That translates into no inheritance."

"You think I'm after the Strickland money?"

"That sure as hell was the agenda of that bastard Kane Thurston."

"Who is Kane Thurston?"

"The last man Abby dated seriously," Brandon said.

"I'll be damned. You're a complete con and a hypocrite, Radwell, not to mention a lousy father, but in your own stumbling, fumbling way, you're trying to protect Abby from me, aren't you? Guess I've got to give you some credit for paternal instincts."

Brandon's jaw sagged. Shock blanked his eyes for a few seconds, but he managed to pull himself together.

"Abby is an adult," he said, between gritted teeth. "I can't tell her what to do, but I'm going to warn her about you. Don't think I won't."

He walked swiftly away through the crowd. By the time he sat down to sign books, he had his warm, father-knows-best smile firmly back in place.

30

"THIS IS ABOUT DAWSON AND THE DEAL HE'S TRYING TO CLOSE, isn't it?" Abby said. "I've already explained to him that I can't help him."

"Keep your voice down." Diana glanced at the closed door of the office. "This is your father's breakout launch. I won't allow you to ruin it."

Abby measured the distance to the door. "I don't think this is a good idea."

The office was cramped and utilitarian. Metal file cabinets lined one wall. The window looked out over the street.

Diana folded her arms. "I'll come straight to the point. My mother says that she will redo the Strickland trust to include you if you agree to get that book for Dawson."

"Wow. She really is panic-stricken."

"That's putting it mildly. What's more, she's not the only one."

"The financial situation is that bad?"

"Yes," Diana said. "It's that bad."

"What about Dad's new book? If it sells well, that should help the family finances. And if the reality TV show comes through, that will be even better."

"The book and the TV project would both have to do phenomenally well to make up for what Dawson lost. Even if, by some fluke, the book does become a bestseller and the reality series takes off, the income will be Brandon's, not mine. That prenup my mother forced me to sign protects him, the same way it does me. He won't have to give me a dime."

"Oh, man. No wonder you and Orinda are having fits. Does Dad know what's going on?"

"No," Diana said, her jaw very tight. "I don't want him to find out. Do you understand? He married me for my money and my connections. I've known that for years. If he discovers that I'm on the verge of losing both, he'll be gone in a heartbeat."

"That is his pattern," Abby agreed. "His first wife dropped out of college to finance his Ph.D. He dumped her the day after he graduated. His second wife was one of his research assistants. That was my mother. He borrowed a lot of her work, which he published as his own. He divorced her to marry one of his wealthy patients. That would be you."

Diana reddened with fury. "Shut up. I know his history better than anyone, including you. That's why I know he's planning to leave me as soon as the TV show is a sure thing. In fact, I'm almost positive he's having an affair with the woman who is producing the pilot."

Abby said nothing. She looked down at her hands.

Diana made a soft, disgusted sound. "You were aware of that?"

"No, but I'm not surprised." Abby raised her eyes. "If you knew about his problem with monogamy, why did you stay married to him all these years?"

Diana's eyes glittered with barely subdued fury and frustration. "You haven't got a clue, do you? I divorced my first husband because he was an abusive man. My mother warned me not to marry him, but I didn't listen. But after Dawson was born, I realized I had to get out in order to protect him and myself. I married your father because I thought he truly cared for me and because I believed that he would be a good male role model for my son. Then the twins came along. Things were okay for a few years, but eventually I realized Brandon was having affairs on the side. I made myself tolerate his infidelity."

"For the sake of Dawson and the twins?" Abby said, surprised. "You didn't want to put them through a divorce? That was very self-sacrificing of you, Diana. I admit, I would never have guessed . . ."

"Don't be ridiculous. I didn't stay with your father because of Dawson and the twins. They could have handled a divorce. Half their classmates all through school were children of divorced parents."

"Right." Abby checked her watch again. "Okay, I get the picture. You're finally ready to divorce Dad, but suddenly you're trapped. You can't leave him, because you don't have the Strickland money to fall back on. And you think he's getting ready to leave you before his own ship comes in."

"Now do you see how important it is for Dawson to recover from the financial losses? I swear that if you help him get that book for his investor, I'll make sure that you receive a fair share of my mother's money."

"Always assuming Dawson can recover it for her."

"He will," Diana vowed.

"The thing is, I don't want your mother's money," Abby said quietly.

"Because you think you've landed on your feet with Sam Coppersmith? Don't fool yourself, Abby. It won't last." Diana went to the door and wrenched it open. She paused in the opening and looked back over her shoulder. "Money doesn't just follow blood. When it comes to marriage, it usually follows other money. There are occasional exceptions, but they rarely end well. Witness my marriage to your father."

Abby looked at her. "There's just one thing here I don't understand. If you wanted to leave Dad and you didn't feel compelled to stick with the marriage because of Dawson and the twins, why in heaven's name didn't you file for divorce a long time ago?"

Bitterness edged Diana's mouth. "In a word? Mother."

"Why was she a factor? She never approved of Dad, anyway. I would have thought she would have been delighted to see you split."

"Oh, yes," Diana said. "She would have been thrilled. You want the truth? I didn't leave Brandon years ago when I should have because I didn't want to give her the satisfaction of proving that she was right. Again."

Diana went out into the hall. Abby listened to the fading echo of high heels on the tile floor.

Sam materialized in the doorway. "Everything okay in here?"

"Sure," Abby said. "Just a little family chat. But I learned something tonight."

"What's that?"

"Even for a Strickland, it's not always about the money."

"Funny you should mention that. I just had a talk with your father and came to the conclusion that it's not always about the money for him, either."

"What do you mean?"

"He wanted to make sure that I knew you weren't going to inherit a dime from the Strickland trust. He was trying to protect you from being married for your nonexistent money."

"Oh." Startled, Abby took a moment to process that. "Huh."

"Can we leave now?"

"Yes," Abby said. "We can leave. In fact, I can't wait to get out of here."

31

SAM GOT BEHIND THE WHEEL, BUT HE DID NOT IMMEDIATELY fire up the engine. He contemplated the warmly lit windows of the auditorium across the street. There was still a large crowd inside.

"Tell me about Kane Thurston," he said.

Startled, Abby gave him a quick, searching look. "There's not much to tell." She buckled her seat belt. "He wasn't the first man I've dated who thought I was in line for a share of the Strickland money. People make that mistake all the time."

"Because everyone makes a show of pretending that you're all just one big happy family?"

"The power of branding."

"Who told Kane that you weren't fated to inherit the Strickland family fortune?"

"I did," Abby said. "As soon as I realized what he was after. Felt like an idiot for a while, because I can usually spot the con artists right away. But to give Kane his due, he is a very, very good con artist. He didn't fool Gwen and Nick, though. They saw right through him the first time they met him and warned me."

"You didn't doubt their verdict?"

"No, although I went into denial for a while before I admitted to myself that they were right. In the end, I knew I had to trust Nick and Gwen. And once I started looking at Kane with clear eyes, I realized they were right. Sorry you got the lecture from Dad. I've tried to make it clear to everyone in the family that you are just a client, but they all seem to be assuming the worst-case scenario."

"The worst-case scenario being that I might actually want to marry you?"

She winced. "I didn't mean it quite like that. Sorry. It's been a difficult evening."

"I assume your stepmother wanted to talk to you about Dawson's financial problems?"

"What else? She's desperate to recover the family fortune, in part because she wants to end the marriage to Dad. She figures my father already has one foot out the door, which is a logical assumption. If the book and the TV series do take off, he'll probably move on."

"He did say something about that. I think he's given up on plan A."

"Which was?"

"Hoping that Orinda Strickland would kick the bucket first. He seems to think that if she wasn't in the picture, he would be able to convince Diana to tear up the prenup."

"Maybe once upon a time he could have done that. Dad has occasionally been known to use his knowledge of psychology to manipulate others. Got a hell of a track record in that department. But it's too late now. Diana definitely wants out. The only reason she's hesitating is because she does not want to end up broke."

"Why did she stay with him this long?" Sam asked.

"Didn't want to give her mother the satisfaction of being able to say

I-told-you-so." Abby shook her head. "Can you believe it? Spend nearly two decades with a man because you don't want to admit your mother was right about him?"

Sam cranked the engine. "Families."

"A constant source of entertainment."

"They keep life interesting. You really think your dad hung around this long because of the Strickland money?"

"Sure. Even though he's not an heir, it has certainly made life very comfortable for him and provided him with a lot of social connections." Abby paused. "And to think that he doesn't yet know that it's gone. I wonder when they'll give him the bad news?"

"Good question."

Sam reversed the SUV out of the slot and drove onto the street, heading downtown. The lights of the city's office buildings, hotels and apartment towers glittered like watery jewels through the rain-splashed windshield.

"Just one more question about Kane Thurston," he said.

"What?"

"Was he ever there for breakfast?"

"Nope. Although I did meet him for brunch at a restaurant a few times. Does that count?"

"No," he said. "Brunch in a restaurant doesn't count."

Abby's phone chimed. She reached into her purse, grabbed the device and glanced at the caller ID.

"It's Nick," she said. Her tone was suddenly a few degrees brighter. She took the call. "Hey, Nick."

Sam heard the easy familiarity and affection in her voice and felt a tug of simple, primal jealousy. Knowing Nick was gay did nothing to assuage the response. Abby was closely bonded with her friends. She'd had years to forge the connections among herself and Nick and Gwen. He, on the other hand, was a newcomer in her life, and as far as she was concerned, their relationship was not easy to define. The passion was high-energy, but he knew she did not fully trust the intimacy that it generated. It was all happening too fast for her.

She needed time to recognize and accept the bond between them, he thought. But meanwhile, he did not have to like the fact that he was playing second fiddle to a cat burglar and a psychic who read auras for a living, to say nothing of the dog.

"Are you sure?" Abby's tone altered abruptly. Alarm edged her voice. She leaned forward in the seat, phone clamped to her ear. "Nick, wait, don't hang up. What do you mean? Tell me what's going on. . . . Okay, okay, I've got it. Code red. . . . Yes, he's with me. . . . Yes. Ten minutes. I promise."

She ended the connection and sat very still, phone clenched in one hand. She had been tense all evening, but what she was radiating now was off the charts.

"What's wrong?" Sam asked.

"There's a bar on a side street half a block off Broadway," she said urgently. "It's not far from here. We need to go there right now. Nick is waiting."

"What's with 'code red'?" Sam asked.

"It was the old signal that the three of us used when we were in the Summerlight Academy. It means what code red always means. Something very bad has happened."

32

LANDER KNOX STUDIED THE BACK-COVER PHOTO ON HIS COPY of *Families by Choice* while he waited in line. The smiling faces of the Radwell family stirred the deep wellspring of hot acid inside him. It was all he could do not to hurl the book at the author's head. *Just one big happy family.*

He took out the small bottle of acid-reducer pills and popped one into his mouth. The picture was deceptive, he reminded himself. Things were no longer quite so perfect for the Radwell clan, thanks to his financial games. The knowledge that he had caused some serious collateral damage soothed him.

Acquiring the lab book and a psychic who could break the code that protected his inheritance was still his primary objective. But the loss of the Strickland money was starting to send shock waves through the family. It was obvious that not everyone in the clan knew what had happened yet. But during their last lunch together, he had sensed the panic and helpless anger that seethed inside Orinda Strickland. The old woman was terrified. And tonight he had glimpsed the strain in Diana Radwell's eyes. *Not much longer now,* he thought. Soon they would all be forced to confront the enormity of their impending financial doom.

It would be interesting to see what happened when the bankruptcy ax fell. The old lady would probably have a heart attack, for starters. And it was a known fact that major financial problems often caused divorce. The Radwells' marriage would no doubt be the next casualty. Dawson was already awash in guilt and viewed himself as a failure. There was no telling where that might lead. It was not unheard of for a man who had lost everything to commit suicide. The pretty blond twins would no longer be able to afford the sky-high tuition at the private college they attended. In the end, the picture-perfect Radwell family would be devastated.

The hot acid sank back into the bottom of the well. Lander suddenly felt much better. The person ahead of him in line thanked Radwell for the signed book and moved out of the way. Dr. Brandon C. Radwell smiled.

"How would you like the book inscribed?" Brandon asked.

"Would you mind making it out to 'Lander, who will one day choose a family of his own'?"

"Certainly." Brandon wrote quickly and signed the book. "Good luck to you, Lander. Remember, family is everything. Choose wisely."

"I'll do that, Dr. Radwell."

33

FROM THE OUTSIDE, THE NIGHTCLUB LOOKED LIKE A LOW-rent dive. It resembled a lot of the other clubs in the Capitol Hill neighborhood. The door and the street-front windows were painted black. But when Sam ushered Abby inside, they were greeted with a comfortable, upscale space warmed by a large stone fireplace. The back bar gleamed with polished wood and glass.

A grand piano occupied one corner of the room. A middle-aged woman dressed in a beaded gown, her blond hair piled high, played a classic show tune. Her makeup was elaborate. Rhinestones dripped from her ears and draped her throat and wrists.

The clientele was a surprising mix of male and female, but the body language made it clear that the men and women at the tables were friends, not dates. The dress code was eclectic, tending toward high-end designer jeans, shirts and slouchy jackets for the men. The drinks were mostly variations on martinis and cosmopolitans.

A few heads turned when Sam and Abby walked into the room, but after a brief, discreet scrutiny, everyone went back to their drinks and conversation.

Nick sat alone in a booth at the back of the room. There was a blue martini on the table in front of him, but it appeared to be untouched. Abby slid onto the seat across from him. Sam sat down beside her. Nick gave him a bored look.

"I see you're still hanging around," Nick said.

"Sure," Sam said. "I live in hope that one day you and I will be friends."

"Don't count on it."

"I'm crushed, of course," Sam said. "But I'm sure I'll get over it."

Abby leaned forward. "What's going on, Nick?"

"As of five-thirty this afternoon, I am no longer your competition," Nick said. "I fired my client, and I stopped looking for that hot encrypted book. If you've got any sense, you'll quit looking for it, too."

"What happened?" Abby asked.

"Benny Sparrow had a heart attack and died in his shop last night."

"Not Benny, too," Abby whispered.

"Yeah." Nick took a small taste of his drink and set the glass down. "I was willing to overlook Webber's heart attack. He was an old man and in bad health. Stuff happens. But now that Benny has checked out the exact same way, we're looking at one too many coincidences."

"Who was Benny Sparrow?" Sam asked.

"One of the three or four deep-end dealers most likely to be using the alias of Milton," Nick said.

"The killer must have gotten Benny's name from Thaddeus," Abby said.

"Looks like it," Nick said.

"Do you think Benny had the notebook?" Sam asked.

"If he did, the killer has it now," Nick said. "We won't know one way or another until we find out if the auction is still on. So far, there hasn't been any update." He turned to Abby. "This thing is way beyond a deep-end deal. We're talking the Mariana Trench. Time to bail, my friend."

"I can't, Nick," Abby said.

"Listen to me, Abby. You need to dump Coppersmith here, and get the hell out of Dodge. Like right now. I'm leaving town tonight. You can come with me."

"If the book is locked in a psi-code, then leaving town won't do me much good," Abby pointed out. "If the killer does have the book and decides he needs me, he'll come looking. I can't run forever."

"I can set you up with a clean ID," Nick said. "I made new, updated sets for you and Gwen a while back, just in case."

"Thanks, but it would be hard for me to disappear permanently," Abby said. "My family may not be close, but trust me, a lot of my relatives would notice if I just up and vanished tonight."

"Not to mention me," Sam said. "I'd notice, too."

Nick glared at him. "You still think you can take care of her?"

"I'm in a better position to protect her than you are," Sam said.

Abby gave Nick a worried look. "Where are you going?"

"To Hawaii to join Gwen. Got a reservation on a red-eye. I'm taking an extended vacation until this auction is over."

"Who was your client?" Abby asked.

"Mr. Anonymous," Nick said. "I've done other jobs for him. Look, are you sure you don't want to come with me tonight, Abby?"

"I can't," Abby said.

"You may be in real danger here."

Abby sat back against the cushions. "I'll be okay."

Nick gave Sam a dismissive look and turned back to her. "You're sure?"

"Yes." Abby smiled. "I'm sure."

"You'll call me if you change your mind?" Nick asked.

"I'll call," Abby said.

"In that case, I'm gone."

Nick downed the rest of the blue martini and pushed himself out of the booth. He looked at Sam.

"Remember what I said, Coppersmith. If anything happens to Abby, you'll answer to me."

"I'll take good care of her," Sam said.

Nick turned on his heel and disappeared through the doorway marked *Restrooms*.

Sam looked at Abby. "I'm assuming he didn't just go to the men's room?"

"That hall leads to the alley exit," Abby said. "Nick must really be running scared if he was afraid to go out the front door."

34

THE ICY-FINGERS-ON-THE-BACK-OF-THE-NECK SENSATION hit Sam when they stepped out of the elevator on Abby's floor a short time later.

"Give me your key," he said quietly.

"Something's wrong, isn't it?" Abby whispered.

"Yeah."

She looked at the closed door of her apartment as if she expected to find a cobra on the other side. "I'm not sure this is a good idea."

He took the key from her. "Stay here," he said.

"Sam?"

"I don't think there's anyone inside now," he said. "Whoever was here is long gone."

He slipped the pistol out from under his jacket, just in case, and opened the door.

Shadows and a disturbing energy spilled out, but he did not pick up the subtle vibes that indicated the presence of someone hiding inside the apartment.

"Whoever was here is gone," he said.

"Ralph, the doorman, maybe."

"I don't think so."

He moved into the short hall and turned the corner. The city lights illuminated the chaotic scene in the living room. There was nothing professional about the search. The small condo had been ransacked by someone who must have been in a fit of rage at the time.

Books had been pulled off the shelves and dumped on the floor. The intruder had taken a knife to the cushions of the sofa and the reading chair. The contents of the desk drawers were scattered across the floor.

Sam did a quick tour of the bedroom and bath. Both rooms looked as if they had been hit by a tornado.

He headed back toward the living room, trying to think of a way to break the bad news to Abby. The hushed cry from the front hall told him that she had seen the disaster for herself.

He walked around the corner and saw her. She stood in the hallway, staring at her vandalized living room in shock and disbelief. Sam righted a lamp and switched it on.

"Why would anyone do such a thing?" She clenched her hands into small fists. "This was my home."

He did not miss her use of the past tense, but he decided not to comment on it.

"The question is, what was he looking for?" he said gently.

"Obviously, he was searching for that damn lab book or something that would tell him who has it." She walked slowly through the wreckage and looked into the bedroom. "Dear heaven, he even went through my lingerie drawer. How *dare* he do such a thing?"

"We can call the cops," Sam said. "But I doubt if it will do any good.

To them, it will be just another low-priority burglary. Not even that, because I doubt if anything is actually missing."

"Because what he wanted wasn't here for him to find. You're right. The cops will put this down as vandalism. They'll ask me if I know anyone who has a reason to be mad at me. How am I going to explain that some crazy guy with a paranormal ability to commit murder is after a forty-year-old lab notebook that's encrypted in a psychic code? They'll think I'm crazy. Then they'll find out about my time at the Summerlight Academy, and they'll know for sure that I'm a nut."

Sam walked to the sliding glass door and examined it. "Still locked from the inside. That means he got in through the front door. That settles it, this building definitely needs a major security upgrade."

"I can't stand it," Abby said. There was a strange tremor in her voice.

Sam turned quickly and went back to her. "Can't stand what?"

"I can't stand the fact that he was here, inside my home," Abby said. "I'll never be able to sleep here again. I'm going to list the condo with a real-estate agent tomorrow." She looked around. "No, wait, I'll have to get a professional cleaning firm in here first. I'll tell them to gather up everything and haul it to a charity."

"Hey, hey, hey, take it easy." He drew her into his arms and tried to think of something soothing to say. "It'll be okay. The bastard ripped up a few cushions and made a mess, but there's not a lot of serious damage."

"He touched my stuff." Abby was stiff with tension. She seemed unaware of his arms around her. "He was in my bedroom. My bathroom. My kitchen."

"I know. He'll pay for it, I promise you."

"This isn't about money, damn it."

He winced. "Bad choice of words. I didn't mean that he would pay financially. I meant I'll get him for you."

Abby took a deep breath and straightened her shoulders. "Okay, then. Thank you." She stepped out of his arms and went toward the door. "Let's get out of here."

"Don't you want to take some fresh clothes with you?"

"No." She did not look back. "I won't be able to wear anything that was here when he broke in. I won't be able to use any of the dishes or the silverware or the sheets or my new towels ever again. He contaminated everything."

She was already outside, punching the button for the elevator. Sam switched off the lamp. He stood for a moment, contemplating the violated space.

"Whoever you are, you just bought yourself a one-way ticket to nowhere," he said to the shadows. "You should never have touched her stuff."

35

ABBY WALKED OUT OF THE ELEVATOR INTO THE DIMLY LIT dungeon that was the underground parking garage. Her emotions were in turmoil. All she could think about was getting into the car and putting as much distance as possible between herself and her violated home. *No, not my home, not anymore.* Anger burned so hot within her that she did not register the ghostly prickle of awareness on the back of her neck until it was too late.

By the time she realized there was something wrong with the atmosphere in the garage, Sam's powerful hand was clamping tightly around her upper arm. She turned her head to look at him.

"What—?" she began.

"Quiet," Sam said, directly into her ear.

He drew her swiftly behind a massive SUV that was parked in the corner. The gray walls of the garage formed a barricade on two sides. The big vehicle provided additional cover.

Ominous energy whispered in the shadows. Abby was suddenly

chilled to the bone. Parking garages were always unnerving at night, and in spite of the condo's security measures, this one was no exception. Footsteps echoed eerily. There were too many dark spaces between the parked cars. She always walked through the gray concrete underworld as quickly as possible, keys in hand, all senses on high alert. But tonight she had been distracted.

The garage was far too quiet. There were no footsteps or voices, but her intuition warned her that she and Sam were not alone. Someone else waited in the shadows. Sam released her. She watched him take his pistol and a small chunk of silvery quartz that looked like a crystal mirror out from under his jacket. She wondered what the quartz was for but decided this was not the time to ask questions. There was the stillness of the hunter about Sam now. He was very focused, very intent. Very dangerous.

She did not know what to expect, a threat or a command from an armed gunman, perhaps. But there was only a strange, unnatural silence that seemed to deepen by the second. It was wrong. The pale glow of the fluorescent fixtures overhead was growing fainter. The garage was taking on a weird, dreamlike quality.

"Go hot," Sam ordered softly. "All the way."

She was already on edge, all of her senses, normal and paranormal, flaring in alarm, but she had made no effort to focus them. The problem with concentrating psychic energy for a prolonged period of time was that the exercise had a downside. The unpleasant jitters and, ultimately, exhaustion that followed a heavy burn were the least of her concerns. She could deal with those. What scared the daylights out of her in that moment was that the garage was starting to resemble the dreamscape of the Grady Hastings nightmare. It was bad enough to wake up and find herself standing beside her bed. What if pushing her talent too hard plunged her permanently into the dream?

Sensing her hesitation, Sam gave her an impatient glance.

"Do it," he ordered.

The garage was undergoing a bizarre transformation. The space around them was assuming an increasingly unreal aspect, as if it was sliding into another dimension. The rows of cars grew longer, stretching away into infinity. The concrete columns morphed into Möbius strips.

"Is it just me or is this starting to look like a bad dream?" she whispered.

"Looks that way to me, too."

She took comfort from that news. She wasn't in this alone. She wanted to explain the reason for her reluctance to follow orders, but this did not seem to be the time or place for an extended conversation. She had hired him as a consultant for situations like this. There was no point employing high-grade talent if you didn't follow up on the recommendations. Cautiously, she elevated her senses into the red zone.

Sure enough, the otherworldly distortion faded significantly as her para-senses took over. But the garage did not return to what passed for normal. When she was in the zone like this, she was able to perceive light from beyond the visible range of the spectrum. The scene was now illuminated in the radiance of ultralight.

In this eerily lit environment, human auras could be more easily perceived. The hot energy flaring in the shadows between two parked cars confirmed what she had already sensed. Someone waited in the darkness.

The senses-dazzling energy exploded out of nowhere. It was as if someone had lobbed a paranormal grenade directly in front of the SUV that protected them. Abby instinctively shut her eyes, but that did little to reduce the terrible glare. The explosion of searing ultralight affected her para-senses far more than it did her normal vision.

"*Don't waste your time and energy trying to fight it, Coppersmith.*" The dark voice came out of the shadows. It was masculine but strangely distorted. *"My little flash-bang is crystal-powered. It generates more energy than any human can. It will soon overwhelm your senses. My advice is to shut down your talent before you burn out."*

"Too late with the flash-bang gadget," Sam said. "I've already got the fix on it."

"It won't do you any good. But go ahead and try to overcome it if you like. When you're satisfied that the device is stronger than you are, we can get down to business. Assuming you're still awake, that is. I'm sure you are aware of the downside of a serious psi-burn."

"I'll try to stay up late tonight," Sam said.

Abby sensed another rush of hot energy in his aura and knew that he had done something with the mirrored quartz. She realized that he was pushing an enormous amount of energy through the stone.

There was a reverberating clang as an object struck the concrete floor. The ultrawhite-hot glare that had filled the space abruptly winked out of existence. When her dazzled senses cleared, Abby realized that the garage had returned to normal.

"Shit." The epithet was accompanied by a harsh gasp of pain.

The stranger's voice was no longer distorted. It was, however, clearly annoyed. "You're a real son of a bitch, Coppersmith. How the hell did you do that?"

"A tuned crystal can generate more steady-state energy than a person, but it takes a human mind to activate it. I didn't take the fix on your flash-bang device. I took it on you." There was a short pause before Sam added politely, "I got it while you were chatting about the cutting-edge wonderfulness of your gadget."

"Fortunately, I brought backup."

"A real gun?" Sam said. "Good thinking."

"I assume you have one, too?"

"What do you think?"

"That you've got one." There was resignation and irritation in the stranger's voice. "You destroyed my flash-bang. It was a prototype, the first and so far the only version that actually worked."

"PEC technology?"

"Sure. Do you have any idea how long it will take me to produce another? It requires months to grow a single crystal large enough to power the damn thing, and that's assuming nothing goes wrong in the process. You know how delicate para-crystals are."

"What kind of seed crystal did you use?" Sam asked.

"I might give you that information if you tell me what you're using to power that weapon you brought to the party."

It dawned on Abby that the conversation had veered off in the wrong direction.

"For Pete's sake," she hissed. "This is no time to get into a technical discussion."

"She's got a point," Sam said.

"Yes, she does. I hate to admit it, but I may have underestimated you, Coppersmith. My own fault. I was warned that you might be a problem."

"I try hard," Sam said. "Sometimes I succeed."

"So I see. The thing is, I need Miss Radwell. I give you my word she will not be hurt."

"Then why are you trying to take her by force?" Sam asked.

"Because, unfortunately, you are in possession of her at the moment, and I doubt that you'll give her up without a fight."

"Good guess."

"All right, then, let's try this in a businesslike fashion. Name your price for her. I'll top it."

"She's not for sale," Sam said.

Abby wanted to throttle both of them. "Stop talking about me as if I was a rare book up for auction, do you hear me?"

"In my own defense, I would like to point out that I did try to go about the business in a civilized way, Miss Radwell," the stranger said.

"I heard rumors of your unusual talent, but it was made clear that you only work by personal referral. I was unable to approach you in the usual manner, because I'm not closely acquainted with any of your other clients and Thaddeus Webber declined to recommend me. So I tried an indirect approach."

"The herbal," Abby said. "You sent it to me."

"It was a gift intended to assure you that I was qualified to become a client. But you never responded."

"I've been a little busy lately."

"I understand. I tried hiring my own freelancer to find the book. He's good at his job, but he can't break codes. I decided I would try to hire you to handle the encryption after the book was in my possession. But this afternoon I got a message from the freelancer saying that he was resigning. I can only assume he was put off by the recent murders. I concluded I had no choice but to take drastic measures."

"Yes, well, as you can see, your drastic measures aren't going to work," Abby said.

"Out of curiosity, did Coppersmith come to you with a proper referral?"

"Yes, he did," Abby said coldly. "And by the way, he is not only a client. I hired him to protect me while I look for a certain book."

"The forty-year-old lab notebook that is coming up for auction. Yes, I know. Your choice of a bodyguard is an odd one, to say the least. Rather like hiring the wolf to watch the sheep, isn't it?"

"Sam and I have an agreement."

"I will double whatever he is paying you."

"Sorry, I have to consider my reputation in the business," Abby said.

"I give you my word that you will be in no danger from me."

"Right," Sam said. "That's why we're standing around this garage in the middle of the night, holding a conversation that includes a couple of para-weapons."

"It would appear we have a standoff this evening," the other man said.

"Who are you?" Abby demanded.

"I think we'll wait on the formal introductions. Maybe we can do business together some other time."

Anger flashed through Abby. "You're the one who invaded my condo and contaminated it, aren't you? Just so you know, I will never, ever forgive you for that. And I definitely won't work for a bastard who would do that to a person's personal space. I'm going to have you arrested."

"Calm down, Miss Radwell. I admit that I took a quick look around your condo earlier this evening, but it was obvious that someone else had been there first. Either that or you are a very poor housekeeper."

"Why should I believe you?"

"If I had searched your condo, Miss Radwell, I would have been far more discreet about the process. I would not have left any obvious indications of my presence."

Sam shifted slightly in the shadows. "Any idea who did go through the condo tonight?"

"No, but it looked like whoever did it was in a tearing rage, probably mentally unbalanced. For Miss Radwell's sake, I suggest you assume that the intruder is the same person who murdered Webber and Sparrow. You do know that both men are dead, don't you?"

"Yes," Abby said. "Are you going to tell us that you're not responsible for those two killings?"

"Yes, that's exactly what I'm telling you."

"Both deaths were by paranormal means," Abby said. "It looks like you have the talent for designing the kind of gadgets that could be lethal."

"So does your bodyguard. While we're on the subject, Coppersmith, I don't suppose you would care to tell me what you used to destroy my flash-bang?"

"Sure. Right after you tell me what you used to turn this garage into a dreamscape."

"Sorry, proprietary secrets. You know how it is in the business world. Cutthroat. You can't trust anyone. To return to the subject of Sparrow and Webber, any idea who killed them?"

"There's a guy named Lander Knox running around in this thing," Sam said. "We've been trying to find him before he gets to the lab book."

"Webber and Sparrow were both very good at what they did. I will miss their professional services. But my chief concern at the moment is for Miss Radwell. I do not want to lose her, as well. Her talents are quite unique. But, then, you already know that, don't you? Take good care of her, Coppersmith."

"I'll do that," Sam said.

"Nice to know so many people are so concerned about my well-being," Abby grumbled.

"There are very few who can do what you do, Miss Radwell," the stranger said. "If for any reason you find yourself in need of a new bodyguard or a new client, please do not hesitate to contact me."

"Don't hold your breath waiting for me to get in touch," Abby said.

"You never know. Things have a way of changing. But since it appears that change is not going to happen tonight, I will say good-bye for now. I'll look forward to a future meeting."

"I suppose you want the herbal back?" Abby asked tentatively.

"Keep it as a souvenir. I'm not really into perfumes. But I would be interested to know if the Cleopatra recipe works."

Footsteps echoed in the shadows. Abby sensed Sam revving up his nearly exhausted talent. She knew that he was trying to catch another glimpse of the stranger's aura.

The alley door closed with a heavy metal clang that reverberated through the shadows. The garage went silent.

Sam got to his feet. "You asked him if he wanted the herbal back? What the hell was that about? Abby, that damn book was a bribe. You don't have to return bribes."

She rose quickly. "I told you, I have to think about my reputation."

"And you got upset with me because I talked a little shop with him."

"Are you okay?" she asked. "You took the brunt of that flash-bang blast."

"I'll survive."

"It must have been a very heavy burn. I can't even imagine how much energy you had to use to do whatever it was you did with that quartz. Are you sure you're okay?"

"Stop fussing," Sam said. "We don't have time. I'm going to crash soon."

"Right. Yes. Sorry. I suppose that was Nick's Mr. Anonymous."

"Probably, but he's not Mr. Anonymous as far as Coppersmith Inc. is concerned. We have another name for him."

"What?"

"The competition."

"That was someone from Helicon Stone?"

"Got a feeling we just took a meeting with Gideon Barrett, Hank Barrett's son. I told you that Dad and Hank have been feuding for years."

"Whew. Well, at least our side won tonight."

"Our side?" Sam sounded amused.

"Figure of speech," she said brusquely. "What now?"

"Now we find a place where I can crash for a few hours. Forget driving back to Anacortes. When I go down, I'm going to go down hard."

"I can drive."

"I know, but you'll be too vulnerable if I'm passed out on the backseat. I don't want to risk another carjacking."

Abby swallowed hard and braced herself. *Show no weakness.* Sam had used a lot of energy tonight. He would need to sleep, and soon. She had to be adult about this.

"We can go back to my condo," she said. "That's the nearest bed."

"No," he said, surprisingly gentle. "Not the condo."

36

HE CHOSE ONE OF THE BIG, ANONYMOUS HOTELS A FEW blocks away in the downtown core, and requested and got a room with no connecting doors. In the close confines of the elevator, he was intensely aware that he was not the only one experiencing the effects of a strong afterburn. There was a lot of edgy energy in Abby's aura. She had not taken the full force of the flash-bang blast because it had been focused on him, but she had caught some of the blowback. She was experiencing some of the downside, too.

"Are you okay?" he asked.

"I'll be fine," Abby said. "Just a little jittery. You know how it is. Probably just as well you didn't take me up on my offer to drive back to Anacortes tonight." She glanced at his duffel. "But if this keeps up, I may have to start traveling with an overnight bag the way you do. At least the hotel provided a few basics."

He looked at the small packet she clutched. The front desk clerk had given it to her. It contained a tiny toothbrush, toothpaste and a few other overnight essentials. She had refused to even take some of her underwear and a change of clothes from the devastated condo. All she had with her tonight was whatever she normally carried in her large tote.

The elevator doors opened. He followed Abby out into the hallway. He had to stay focused on getting her securely buttoned up for the night so that he could crash without having to worry about her safety.

"What was that flash-bang thing he used on you?" Abby asked.

"Damned if I know. The Barretts have their secrets, just like the Coppersmiths. I'd give a lot to know what kind of crystal he used to power that gadget, though."

Abby smiled.

"What?" he asked.

"In hindsight, there was a certain humorous aspect to that show-down in the garage."

"Yeah? I didn't notice anyone laughing, especially not me."

"Something about the way the two of you started to wander off into a discussion of crystal physics while you're both holding weapons on each other," Abby said.

"You think that was funny?"

"I guess you had to be there."

"I *was* there."

He concentrated on securing the room, but there was no getting around the fact that a part of him was consumed by the prowling tension that was the usual first phase of the post-burn syndrome. *You've been here before,* he thought. *You can handle it.*

The biochemistry of a heavy burn was complicated and not well understood. For males, there was a lot of adrenaline and testosterone involved, so the sexual arousal was predictable. But the hungry, urgent restlessness had never been this bad in the past. It didn't take a psychic to know why the sensation was so overwhelming tonight. It had a focus, and that focus was Abby.

He forced himself to go through the drill. He noted the location of the emergency exits and came up with two possible escape routes. His hand shook a little when he inserted the key card into the lock. If Abby noticed, she was too polite to say anything.

Inside the room, he secured the door and did a quick survey. No connecting doors, as promised. The sealed windows looked out over Sixth Avenue twelve floors below.

Satisfied, he unzipped the leather duffel and took out two small crystals.

"What are those?" Abby asked.

"Think of them as psychic trip wires. If anyone tries to come in through the door or the window, I'll know about it."

"More PEC technology?"

"Yes."

"Do you always carry those gadgets and your gun in your overnight bag?"

"Yes."

When he was satisfied that he had taken all possible precautions, he turned around and looked at Abby. She stood, contemplating the bed, arms folded. Something about her obvious uncertainty irritated him.

"What?" he asked.

She cleared her throat. "Nothing. I, uh, thought there would be two beds, that's all."

For some reason, the knowledge that she did not want to share the bed with him hit him harder than the damn flash-bang had. And then he got mad; not at Abby, at himself. That was another problem with the burn-and-crash routine. It pushed everything, including normal, logical thought processes, to the edge. It made for a real roller-coaster ride.

"Sorry." He knew he sounded brusque, but that was a hell of a lot better than begging her to sleep with him. "This was all that was available in a room that had no connecting door. No problem. I'll take the chair or the floor."

"No, you certainly will not." Her brows scrunched together in a severe look. "You need to sleep soundly. You can't do that in a chair or on the floor."

"Trust me, the way I'm going to go down tonight, I won't notice where I sleep."

"Forget it. Sorry I raised the issue. I'm a little tense. You've had a very deep burn. I thought that you would sleep better alone."

"I'm not going into a coma." He took his overnight kit, a fresh T-shirt and a clean pair of briefs out of the duffel bag. "I just need some sleep." He headed toward the bathroom.

"By the way, what is PEC technology?" Abby asked.

"What?" It was hard to focus on her question. The urge to pull her into his arms and lose himself in her warm, soft body while the after-math flames burned through him was growing stronger. What the hell was the matter with him? He had never been this close to the edge of control. Maybe Barrett's psychic flash-bang gadget had a few side effects.

"PEC technology," she repeated. "You and Gideon Barrett both used the term."

He stood in the doorway, staring into the white tile bathroom. "Stands for psi-emitting crystals. The paranormal equivalent of light-emitting diodes and liquid crystal displays."

"They're similar to LEDs and LCDs?"

"Yes, but the energy generated comes from beyond the normal range on the spectrum and has different properties. It's the kind of technology Coppersmith is working on in the Black Box lab." He moved into the bathroom and plopped the overnight kit down on the counter. "Do you mind if we save the science lesson for tomorrow? I'm beat. Not really in a good place to explain the physics of para-rocks right now. I need a shower."

"I was just curious."

That did it. Now he felt like a total brute. He closed the bathroom door.

He emerged a short time later wearing the clean underwear and the trousers he'd had on earlier. Abby was waiting, still fully dressed. She had the hotel vanity kit in hand.

It dawned on him that she did not have a nightgown.

"I've got a spare T-shirt," he said.

"Thank you." She looked relieved. "I'll take it."

He took a clean black T-shirt out of the duffel without a word and handed it to her. She slipped past him and disappeared into the small room. The door closed firmly. He heard water running in the sink. It ran for a very long time. He realized she was probably doing a little hand laundry. In the morning, he would probably find a pair of panties hanging on the towel rack. The vision heated his blood a little more.

He considered his options and went for the padded reading chair in the corner near the window. The sight of the ottoman cheered him in some macabre way.

"Damn perfect," he muttered. "Just doesn't get any better than this, does it, Coppersmith? You're in the middle of a burn. Abby is a few feet away, getting ready for bed, and you get to crash in a chair with an actual ottoman. You'll be able to prop up your feet. Wow."

The bathroom door opened a crack. "Sam, did you say something?"

"Just talking to myself."

"I understand. I do that sometimes, too. Well, actually, I talk to Newton. Maybe you should get a dog."

He realized that he was gritting his teeth. "I'll definitely have to think about doing just that."

The door closed.

He opened the minibar, chose two small bottles, the whiskey and the brandy. He yanked a pillow off the bed, turned off all the lights except the one by the bed and dropped into the chair. He propped his feet on the ottoman, twisted the top off one of the liquor bottles and swallowed some of the whiskey. He contemplated the closed door of the bathroom while he downed the medicinal alcohol. With luck, he would be unconscious by the time Abby came out.

The door opened quietly a few minutes later. Abby emerged wearing his T-shirt. It was much too big for her. The hem fell to her thighs. She looked sexy as hell in the shadows. An elemental thrill of possessiveness swept through him. He drank some more of the whiskey.

"Are you asleep?" she asked softly.

"Getting there."

"I told you to take the bed."

"I don't follow orders well."

"You don't have to be grouchy about it," she said. "I was just trying to make sure you'll get the rest you need."

"I'll sleep fine right here." *Eventually.*

"Are you drinking something?"

"Yeah." He opened the second bottle. "Helps take the edge off the afterburn buzz."

"You got into the minibar?"

"Uh-huh." He swallowed some of the brandy.

"I could use a glass of wine myself."

"Help yourself. There are a couple of small bottles of wine in the bar."

She crossed the room, opened the minibar and studied the assortment. Then she glanced at the printed card that detailed the prices of the items in the bar.

"Geez, look at the prices," she said.

"Go for it." He saluted her with the miniature whiskey bottle. "Live large. I'm paying for the room, remember?"

"Okay, thanks."

She chose the little bottle of white wine, untwisted the cap and sat down on the edge of the bed.

They drank in silence for a while. He saw no reason to try to engage in conversation. It would only make things more complicated.

"How are you feeling?" Abby asked.

"Coming down. Finally." It was the truth, he realized. The alcohol and time were working. He would sleep soon.

"Before you crash, I just want to say thank you again. This is the second time you've saved me from someone who wanted to kidnap me."

He closed his eyes. "I've told you before, I'm just doing my job. But in fairness, I don't think Gideon Barrett would have grabbed you against your will. He just wanted to get me out of the way for a while so that he could talk you into accepting his offer. And he would have made you one hell of an offer, trust me."

"Looked a lot like an attempted kidnapping to me. It's sort of scary knowing that people want to kidnap you."

"I know," he said, gentler this time. She had good reason to be afraid, he thought. "You're handling it well. Lot of folks in your position would be basket cases by now."

"If I'm dealing with it well, it's because I've got you watching my back. So thanks, anyway."

He opened his eyes. "Even if I do have my own agenda?"

She smiled. "Everyone has an agenda. I can deal with that, so long as a person is honest about it. You've been up front about yours from the beginning. Well, almost from the beginning."

The last thing he wanted was her gratitude.

"Finish your wine, turn out the light and go to sleep, Abby," he said.

"Okay."

She set the empty bottle on the nightstand, switched off the lamp and got into bed.

Sam contemplated the little brandy bottle and decided not to finish it. Too much alcohol might prolong the recovery phase of the crash. He set the bottle on the table beside the chair, leaned back and watched the shadows on the ceiling for a while. He thought about the array of people who were trying to grab Abby and the lab book.

"I'm missing something," he said after a while.

"What?" Abby asked from the shadows.

"Don't know. Can't think clearly tonight. But in the morning, I need to go back to the beginning of this case and look at everything from a different angle."

"You mean back to that first blackmail note?"

"No, back to what happened in Vaughn's library."

"You think that's where it all started?"

"The answer is there, somewhere."

"Maybe our chat with Grady Hastings tomorrow will give us a lead."

"I've never interviewed a crazy psychic," Sam said. "Should be interesting."

The deep sleep crept over him.

37

The woman walked down the endless basement hallway. He knew she was going to open the lab door, knew the killer was waiting for her on the other side.

He tried to go after her, but he was trapped in the shadows. He tried to call to her, desperate to warn her, but he could not get her name out.

At the door she paused, her hand on the knob. She looked back at him. For the first time, he saw her face. Not Cassidy.

"Abby."

"SAM, YOU'RE DREAMING. WAKE UP. IT'S ALL RIGHT. I'M HERE."

Energy shivered in the atmosphere, summoning him from the nightmare. He came awake on a surge of adrenaline and psi, aware of the warmth of Abby's hand on his bare arm, aware of her comforting energy.

He opened his eyes and saw her bending over him. Her anxious concern was a palpable force in the atmosphere. He had probably scared the hell out of her. Bodyguards weren't supposed to sleep on the job in the first place, and they definitely were not supposed to suffer from nightmares. There were rules about that kind of stuff somewhere.

He took his feet down off the ottoman and sat forward, scrubbing his face with his hands. He willed himself to full wakefulness.

"Abby," he said again.

"I'm here."

She was safe. She was not caught in the endless loop of the damned lab dream.

Automatically, he raised his para-senses and was relieved to discover that they responded instantly. He did not know how much time had passed, but it was clear that he had recovered from the heavy exhaustion that followed a hard burn. He glanced at his watch. The black crystal numbers glowed. He had slept for nearly three hours.

"Sorry," he said. His voice sounded rough, as if he had dragged it out of the fog of the nightmare. "Must have been dreaming."

"Yes. You called my name."

He tried to think. "It was the recurring dream I told you about tonight. But it was different this time. Sorry. Didn't mean to wake you."

"I was already awake."

He got to his feet. "Couldn't sleep?"

"No." She stepped back, out of his way. "Well, actually, I didn't try. I was a little worried after you fell asleep. You seemed feverish, so I decided to stay up until it looked like you were through the burn and sleeping normally."

First he had to deal with her gratitude. Now she was treating him as if he was an invalid. This relationship was going downhill fast.

"Just the afterburn fever," he said, trying to sound cool and in control, like a man who could handle his job. "I'm not ill. You've been through a burn. You know how it is."

"I know how it *feels,* but I've never been close to anyone else who is going through it, so I didn't know what it looked like. I didn't realize that it had some of the symptoms of a high fever."

"Aura heat."

"Yes, but you were giving off *a lot* of energy," she said. "I have to tell you it was a little unnerving. I was afraid that flash-bang gizmo might have caused some sort of delayed psychic stress."

"I told you, I'm all right." *Great.* Now he was snapping at her again. "You don't have to play nurse."

"I was just looking out for you while you slept off the burn." She was starting to sound annoyed. "I didn't mean to offend your macho self-image. Do you always wake up in a bad mood like this?"

"No. But everything seems to be different with you."

"Keep in mind that I had a bad day, too, and unlike you, I haven't had any sleep yet. I am in no mood for sarcasm."

He took a few beats to ponder that. "Does it strike you that we seem to be arguing over nothing again?"

"Yes, it does." She folded her arms. "Any idea why that is happening?"

"Sure. I want to have sex with you, but every time I turn around tonight, you're either thanking me or trying to take care of me. So I provoke an argument because it makes you mad. See, I'd rather have you mad at me than pointing out the fact that I'm a decrepit bodyguard."

There was stunned silence for a few seconds. Abby finally got her mouth closed.

"Good grief," she said. "That is . . . very insightful."

"For a man, you mean?"

"For anyone. I'm impressed."

She started to giggle. She covered her mouth with her hands and turned toward the window. The giggles turned into muffled laughter.

"Now you're laughing at me," he said, resigned. "You know, you can be hard on a man's ego."

She sobered, dropped her hands and turned back to face him. Her eyes sparkled with the tears generated by her laughter.

"Good thing yours isn't too fragile," she said.

"Every man has his limits."

"So does every woman. You were only half right, you know."

"Yeah?"

She smiled ruefully. "The arguments aren't all your fault. I may be pushing things a bit, too."

"Why?"

"For the same reason," she said.

He went still. "Yeah?"

"I want to sleep with you, but part of me thinks that is a very bad idea."

"Why?"

"Because something weird seems to happen when you and I make . . ." She broke off and coughed discreetly. "When you and I have sex."

"Define weird."

She spread her hands. "I don't know how to explain it, but it feels like something to do with our auras. It's as if my wavelengths are somehow resonating with yours. It's a very *intimate* sensation. Probably just my imagination at work. But I've been wondering . . ."

"Wondering what?"

She sighed. "If you must know, I'm wondering if it's some aspect of the psychic stress I experienced when I broke the code on that book in Mrs. Vaughn's library. Maybe some energy from the dreamstate is affecting my normal senses or something."

"Ah," he said. He smiled.

She frowned. "What is that supposed to mean?"

"You're wondering if having sex with me is making you crazy," he said. He was grinning now. "It's an intriguing question. One that will require a lot more research and experimentation."

"You're laughing at me, aren't you?"

"Yeah. That resonance thing going on with our auras? I feel it, too."

She brightened. "You do?"

"If you're going crazy, so am I. But unlike you, I'm not worried about it."

"You've experienced that kind of thing before during sex?" she asked, hopeful now.

"No." He smiled and moved closer to her. "Maybe that's why it feels so good. Personally, I've gotta tell you that I'm not going to lose any sleep over this."

"But what do you think is going on?" she asked. "The para-physics involved, I mean. It certainly isn't normal."

"You want the truth? I don't give a damn about the para-physics."

"You don't?"

"No."

He put his hands around her shoulders. Beneath the fabric of the black T-shirt, she felt sleek and warm and soft and like all that was feminine. Her scent clouded his senses, intoxicating and compelling. He tightened his grip on her and drew her to him. She did not resist.

Her lips were slightly parted. He jacked up his talent a little and saw that her eyes burned with a little psi-light. He could sense the heat in her aura, too. Sexual energy was so hot that it burned across the spectrum from the normal range into the paranormal. It was the raw energy of life. And he had never felt more alive than he did right now.

"Abby," he said.

"You're the scientist here," she said. "I guess if you're not worried, I should stop worrying, too."

"I like your logic."

He plunged his fingers into the storm of her hair and captured her mouth.

She wrapped her arms around his neck and kissed him back with a feminine heat that ignited a wildfire within him. It was all he could do to hold on to his control.

He wrenched his mouth free from Abby's and kissed her throat. Her hands moved down from his neck and slipped up under his T-shirt. Her palms felt good on his chest, soft and very warm.

"You feel feverish again," she said.

"No kidding. You're running a fever, too."

"Feels good."

"Yes," he said. "It does."

She pushed the T-shirt upward. He yanked the garment off over his head and tossed it aside. She kissed his shoulder, her mouth warm and damp on the phoenix tattoo. He took a step back and got rid of his pants and briefs. When he turned to her, she was smiling at him. He could already sense the intimate resonance pattern of their auras.

"*Yes,*" he said. "Damn right, it feels good."

He tugged off the T-shirt she wore, scooped her up into his arms and fell with her onto the bed. He rolled onto his back, dragging her down across his chest. She made love to him there in the darkness, raining spicy wet kisses from his throat to his belly, and then she ventured lower. He groaned when her fingers closed around him. When she took him into her mouth, he sucked in a sharp breath and sank his hands into the thick, tangled curls of her hair.

She used her tongue on him, and he thought he would go mad. When she pressed gently against the ultra-sensitive place directly behind his testicles, he knew he had reached his limit.

"My turn," he breathed.

He eased her onto her back and came down on top of her. She was as damp as he was, slick with perspiration. He kissed her firm, dainty breasts until she was arching against him and clutching at him. Satisfied, he worked his way slowly down her body, savoring the taste and scent of her.

When he reached the tight little furnace between her legs, she cried out and dug her nails into his shoulders. He sensed the gathering tension in her and stoked the fires until she was fierce and breathless. He gripped her sweet ass in both hands and anchored her so that she could not escape his mouth.

She came undone in a storm of energy that dazzled all of his senses. "Sam. *Sam.*"

"Right here," he breathed.

He shifted position, holding his weight on his elbows. He captured her face between his hands and plunged his tongue into her mouth at the same time that he thrust deep into her still-clenching passage. The convulsions of her release pulled him over the edge within seconds.

He gave himself up to the rushing freedom of the climax with a hoarse, muffled groan of satisfaction that seemed to echo forever.

A long time later, Abby became aware of the weight of Sam's thigh on top of hers. His arm was flung across her breasts. She turned her head on the pillow and saw that his eyes were closed. He looked to be sound asleep. Cautiously, she tried to edge out from under his sprawling weight. He tightened his arm around her, trapping her, but he did not open his eyes.

"You're awake," she accused.

"I am now." Reluctantly, he rolled onto his back. "You know, we should do this more often."

"What? Meet weird guys in parking garages who try to whack you with psychic flash-bang gadgets so that they can kidnap me?"

"Must you always focus on the negative? I was referring to the hot sex."

She smiled. "Oh, that."

He folded his arms behind his head. "Yeah, that."

She turned onto her stomach and levered herself up on her elbows. "How was it different tonight?"

"The sex?" He gazed up at the ceiling. "Let me count the ways . . ."

"Not the sex. The dream."

"The one you interrupted?"

"That's the one, yes." She paused. "You called my name."

"Probably because you weren't supposed to be in it."

"What was I doing in it?"

"Scaring the hell out of me," he said.

"Explain."

"It's the same dream that I told you about."

"The one in which poor Cassidy walks down the hall to open the lab door?"

"Yes. Usually, it's like some damned video loop. It keeps repeating, over and over again. Always the same. Until tonight."

"What was different about tonight's version?"

He looked at her, his eyes burning a little in the shadows. "Tonight you were the woman walking down the hall, about to open the lab door. I called out to you. Tried to stop you. But you couldn't hear me."

"You're worried about protecting me, and that concern came through in the new version of the dream." She leaned over and brushed her mouth against his. Then she pulled back. "But it's okay. I'm not Cassidy. If you called out to me or tried to warn me, even in a dream, I would hear you."

"Would you?"

"Yes," she said. "I heard you tonight, didn't I?"

He stroked her cheek with the back of his finger. She turned her head and kissed his palm. He wrapped one arm around her and drew her back down to him.

38

"WHAT DID YOU MEAN LAST NIGHT WHEN YOU TOLD ME THAT we needed to go back to the start of this thing?" Abby asked. "You said you were missing something about the incident in the Vaughn library."

They were eating omelets and drinking coffee in the hotel restaurant. Abby was feeling surprisingly well rested. Which only went to show that if you had clean underwear, a toothbrush and a sexy bodyguard, a woman could handle anything, she decided.

For his part, Sam showed no signs of exhaustion. He looked sated and satisfied. He also appeared energized.

"You told me that the day of the home invasion, Grady Hastings specified that he was after a particular encrypted book," Sam said.

"Yes. Morgan's *The Key to the Latent Power of Stones.*"

"According to what little there is about him online, there's no indication that Hastings was in the hot-books market. He doesn't have the money for it, for one thing."

"He told me that he needed *The Key* to help him with his research. Evidently, he's really into crystals."

"Like me," Sam said.

Abby smiled. "Like you without the Coppersmith money to fund his work."

"And without the Coppersmith connections in the rare-books market. And yet he somehow discovered that an obscure, psi-coded book on crystals was in the library of a private collector. How would that be possible if he wasn't tapped into the underground book world?"

Abby put down her fork and thought about it. "He said a voice in a crystal had told him how to find the book and that it was encrypted."

"Did the voice tell him about you?"

"Yes."

"Think we can safely assume he is delusional? He may have fantasized about hearing a voice in the crystal, but the information about you and the book was accurate. He got it from some source. Any ideas?"

"I don't know. I certainly don't advertise, and Mrs. Vaughn didn't put the contents of her library online. She is not dangerous, but she is as secretive as every other collector I've ever worked with."

"But serious collectors, dealers and freelancers like you would be aware of at least some of the more valuable books in her collection, right?"

"Oh, yes. That kind of gossip is always floating around. All of us who work that market keep close track of auctions, sales and rumors about recent acquisitions. What are you thinking?"

"Your dream intuition has been right all along. I'm thinking it is past time to talk to Grady Hastings."

39

"IT WAS THE VOICE IN THE CRYSTAL THAT TOLD ME THAT *The Key* was in Mrs. Vaughn's library," Grady Hastings said. "I couldn't believe it at first, but I heard it over and over again, so I knew it had to be true. I didn't mean to hurt anyone. At least, I don't think I meant to hurt anyone. Can't remember, exactly, to be honest. The doctor tells me I have to remember that part, but I can't."

"Why did you want *The Key* so badly?" Abby asked. "Do you remember that?"

They were sitting in the spare, utilitarian room the psychiatric hospital reserved for meetings between visitors and patients. An orderly stood some distance away, surreptitiously checking email on his cell phone. *Or maybe playing a game,* Abby thought. Whatever the case, it was obvious that he was not interested in the conversation. The woman who had led Abby and Sam to the visitors' room a short time earlier had explained that they were the only people who had come to visit Grady since he had been admitted.

Abby and Sam were on one side of a wide table. Grady sat across from them. He was no longer radiating the wild, chaotic energy that had swirled around him on the day he had invaded the Vaughn home. He still gave off the vibes of an individual who marched to his own drummer, but he was not scary today. Abby found herself feeling sorry for him. He seemed very worried, very young and very lonely. He was dressed in hospital-issue garb, a loose-fitting shirt, trousers and slippers.

"I needed *The Key* to complete my experiment," Grady said. His expression became animated for the first time. He straightened in his chair. "I was so close to the final step, you see, and the voice told me that the answer was in *The Key*." His enthusiasm faded as quickly as it had materialized. He sagged back in defeat. "I can't believe I thought I was hearing a voice in one of my crystals. I must have been crazy, just like everyone says. I screwed up, and now I'll never know if I was on the right track or not."

Sam looked at him. "What was the nature of the experiment?"

"I was trying to grow crystals that could be used as hearing aids. My mother was deaf. I used sign language from the cradle. When I was still a kid, I told her that one day I would find a way to help her hear. She believed in me. She died when I was fourteen, but she made me promise that I would never give up my goal of inventing a new kind of hearing technology. But they won't let me have a lab in here. When I asked them for some of the crystals that I was working on at home, the doc said that the fact that I believed crystals had some kind of special powers was another indication that I needed more treatment."

"Your doctor doesn't think there is power in crystals?" Sam asked.

"Nah." Grady grimaced. "He thinks it's all woo-woo stuff."

"Did you remind him that it's crystal technology that makes it possible for him to have a personal computer and carry a phone that can access the Internet?" Sam asked. "Did you mention lasers? LCD screens?"

"Sure," Grady said. "But I was working with crystals that have some paranormal properties, and the doctor can't grasp the concept."

"He's not alone," Abby said.

Sam folded his elbows on the table and fixed Grady with a deeply interested expression. "You were working with crystals to invent hearing devices?"

"Yeah." Grady came alive again. "According to my theory, almost anyone could use them. You wouldn't have to have a lot of talent. If I'm right, it will take very little psi to make my hearing devices work. Everyone produces *some* energy. But I was missing a critical element. I knew there was a problem, but I couldn't get at it. Do you know that feeling?"

"Yes," Sam said. "I know it well."

"One day I started hearing this voice telling me that I needed *The Key*." Grady rubbed his forehead. "It sounds freaky, I know. But I just got this feeling that if I could find that book and the woman who could crack the encryption, I could make the breakthrough that I needed."

"You said the voice came from a crystal?" Sam asked. "One in your collection?"

"Yes." Grady frowned, bewildered. "I think so. But I can't remember which one. I don't understand why I can't remember that, either."

"What color was the crystal?" Sam asked.

"I don't . . ." Grady stopped. "Wait. It was green. I'm almost positive that it was one of my green stones."

"The voice in the green crystal told you that *The Key* was in the Vaughn library?" Abby asked.

Grady gave her a plaintive look. "I guess so. I told you, I can't remember exactly. But how else could I have known that?"

"You had never met Mrs. Vaughn before you went to her home to get *The Key*?" Sam asked.

"No." Grady snorted. "Get real. How would a guy like me meet someone like that? I don't know anyone who has that kind of money."

"Where did you get the gun?" Sam asked.

"Huh?" Another troubled frown came over Grady's face. "I'm not sure."

"Did you buy it?" Abby asked.

"No." Grady rubbed his forehead. "I think I found it somewhere. Maybe on the front seat of my car. Can't remember."

"Did the voice tell you where to find the gun, and that you had to use it when you went to get *The Key*?" Sam asked.

"Maybe." Grady Hastings winced. "I'm sounding crazier by the minute, aren't I?"

"No," Sam said. "You're sounding more and more like a man who was set up."

Abby looked at him. "You think Grady was somehow hypnotized to go to the Vaughn house that day?"

"That's what it feels like," Sam said.

"But why? *The Key* is an interesting book, but the only thing that makes it really valuable is the psi-encryption."

"The contents of the book weren't important," Sam said. "The idea was to test you to see if you really could break a psi-code."

"Good grief," Abby said. "This is starting to make some sense."

"You and Grady were both unwitting participants in someone's experiment," Sam said. "The experiment was a success. Whoever conducted it is now after you."

"The blackmail notes," Abby said.

"Wait," Grady blurted out. "I don't understand."

"Neither do I," Sam said. "Not all of it. But I think I'm finally getting close."

Abby looked at Grady. "Sam is an expert on paranormal crystals."

Grady nodded. "I was starting to figure that out." He looked at Sam. "You're one of those Coppersmiths, aren't you? You're connected to the family that owns Coppersmith Inc."

"That's right," Sam said.

"Your labs must be awesome," Grady said wistfully. "State-of-the-art and then some."

"And then some," Sam agreed. "We do a little R-and-D work with hot rocks, too."

"You mean paranormal crystals, right?"

"Yes."

"*Awesome.* I'd give anything to have access to a lab like that." Grady looked around the bare visitors' room, his gloom deepening. "But I'll be lucky to get out of here someday, and even if I do, there won't be anything left of my lab. I'll have to start over."

"Why do you say that?" Abby asked.

"My equipment and my crystals are in the shed in back of the house I'm renting," Grady said. "Lease is up next month. I don't care about my furniture and clothes, but as soon as the rent comes due, the landlord will clean the place out. He'll probably put my crystals and lab instruments into a yard sale. All my stuff will be gone."

"I know exactly how it feels to have someone else mess with your stuff," Abby said. She sat forward. "If you like, Sam and I can pack up your rocks and your lab equipment and store it for you."

Grady looked startled. "You'd do that for me after I pointed a gun at you?"

"Yes, because I don't think you ever really meant to point that gun at me. By the way, Sam is not just a crystal expert, he is also a security expert."

"Yeah?" Grady was curious now.

"He's investigating what happened to you and me at the Vaughn house," Abby explained. "He's been working for me for a few days, and as of now he's working for you, too. Isn't that right, Sam?"

Sam looked at her, brows elevated. "Well."

Abby turned back to Grady. "Consider yourself one of Sam's clients."

Grady processed the new data. For a few seconds, he looked hopeful. Then his eyes went flat. "I can't afford to hire a private investigator."

"Lucky for you I work cheap," Sam said. "Like Abby said, consider yourself a client."

"Yeah?" Grady started to look hopeful again. "Just like that?"

"Just like that," Sam said.

"And you'll pack up my lab stuff before the landlord sells it?" Grady asked urgently.

"Don't worry," Abby said. "We'll take care of your stuff."

"All part of the service," Sam said. He got to his feet. "I don't suppose you still have the key to your house?"

"No key," Grady said. "They took that away, too. But the lock on the porch door is nothing special. You shouldn't have any trouble getting inside the house. The hard part will be getting into the shed out back. I installed my own door and security system, mostly to keep my landlord out."

"Give me the code," Sam said.

"See, that's the tricky part," Grady said. "It's not an off-the-shelf system. It's PEC-based."

"Yeah?" Sam looked intrigued.

Grady glanced around the room and then lowered his voice. "You'll need a crystal to work it."

"What kind of crystal?"

"Doesn't matter. You just have to be able to generate a little energy through it. Find a resonating frequency, and the lock will open."

Sam moved his hand, calling subtle attention to the fire crystal in his ring. "Will this do?"

Grady studied the copper stone. Abby felt energy hum briefly in the atmosphere.

"Sure, that will work," Grady said. "Nice stone. I don't recognize it."

"Synthetic," Sam said easily. "It was grown in one of the Coppersmith labs."

"Awesome."

Abby rose before Grady could ask any more questions. "We'll report back as soon as we have some information."

"That would be cool," Grady said, brightening. "I don't get many visitors. In fact, you're the only ones I've had."

Abby frowned. "You don't have any family?"

"Not that you'd notice. I think there are some people on my mom's side somewhere, but I never heard from them after she died."

"What about your father?" Abby asked.

"He skipped out before I was born."

A chill of intuition twisted through Abby. "Did you go into the foster-care system after your mother died?"

"For a while," Grady said. "But everyone decided that I was on the crazy side, so I ended up in a special school for wackos."

Abby stopped breathing for a couple of heartbeats. Her talent flared. She was aware that Sam was motionless. His eyes were a little hot.

"Was the name of the school by any chance the Summerlight Academy?" Abby asked.

"Yeah." Grady widened his eyes. "How'd you know?"

"I'm a graduate, too."

"No kidding?" Grady sighed. "Well, I guess we both survived."

"Yes," Abby said, "we did. And when this is all over, I will introduce you to some other graduates. You can join our alumni club if you like."

Grady started to smile. The smile stretched into a grin. "A club for graduates of the Summerlight Academy? That would be sort of cool."

Outside, in the parking lot, Abby got into the SUV and fastened her seat belt. She waited until Sam climbed in beside her.

"Given what we know of the laws of para-physics, what are the odds that Grady Hastings and I both have the Summerlight Academy in common?" she asked.

"Realistically, the odds probably aren't all that bad, given your psych profiles and the diagnosis that you both got when you were in your teens," Sam said. "I doubt that there are a great number of boarding schools in the Seattle area that accept students with your unusual issues."

"Okay. What are the odds that both of us wound up together in Vaughn's library that day by sheer luck or coincidence?"

Sam started the SUV and snapped it into gear. "Zero."

"I was thinking the same thing. Where does that leave us?"

"Looking for a psychic who knows how to locate other genuine psychics in the Seattle area. Someone who has access to the Summerlight Academy records."

"If he has access to the records," Abby said, "he would have a lot of information about the students' psych profiles and their personal situations. I'll bet that bastard picked poor Grady because he knew he was not only a talent but also alone in the world. There is no family to worry about him or to protect him."

"The son of a bitch would also know that you have a complicated relationship with your family. I'm guessing he would have preferred to use someone like Hastings, a loner, to break the psi-code, but he doesn't have much choice. There aren't a lot of sensitives with your kind of ability running around the Pacific Northwest. There are others who can find the lab book for him, but it would be almost impossible to find another code breaker."

"In other words, he was stuck with me."

"Something like that, yes."

"It's always nice to be appreciated for one's talent."

40

THE HOUSE GRADY HASTINGS HAD LEASED WAS A RUN-DOWN bungalow in West Seattle. The rental looked as sad and depressed as Hastings had looked sitting in the locked ward at the psychiatric hospital, Sam thought. The place was in desperate need of a fresh coat of paint. The small lawn was patchy and studded with weeds. Yellowed shades were pulled down to cover the grimy windows.

Sam went up the concrete steps and set down the stack of packing boxes he had picked up at a container store. He checked the lock. Grady was right. It was standard-issue and probably original to the house. It took less than thirty seconds to open it.

"Doesn't look like Grady's landlord has put much money into upkeep," he said. He twisted the old-fashioned knob and opened the door.

"No." Abby followed him up the steps. She had a large roll of Bubble Wrap tucked under one arm. "Why bother? I doubt if Grady was a demanding tenant. All he cares about is his work with crystals."

"True. As long as he had his lab, he was probably content."

Abby smiled a secret smile.

He eyed her with suspicion. "What?"

"Nothing. It just occurred to me that Grady isn't the only person around who is content so long as he has his lab."

"Yeah, well, I'm not the one sitting in a psychiatric hospital."

"There is something to be said for that." Abby followed him into the house, put down the roll of Bubble Wrap and closed the door. When she turned around and saw the nearly empty space, she froze. Outrage heated the atmosphere around her.

"There's hardly any furniture left," she yelped. "Someone stole Grady's stuff."

"It's possible," Sam said. "Empty houses are magnets for thieves. But I think it's more likely the landlord jumped the gun and started clearing out Grady's things."

"Bastard. I hope he wasn't able to get into the shed in back. Grady will be crushed if his lab stuff is gone."

Sam walked through the kitchen and opened the back door. The shed sitting in the yard looked like a ramshackle wooden fortress. The one window was boarded up. The gleaming new metal door was closed.

He walked across the weed-infested yard and examined the lock on the door. Abby followed him.

"Doesn't look like anyone has gotten inside yet," he said. "But it's probably a good thing we're here. Got a hunch the landlord will be taking a blowtorch to this door when he figures out that a regular locksmith can't open it."

He raised his ring to the dull, gray crystal embedded in the metal on the wall next to the door. Cautiously, he focused a little energy through the Phoenix stone. He sensed the familiar tingling current of power. The lock crystal began to heat with violet-hued ultralight.

There was a sharp click as the lock disengaged. Sam opened the door.

"The kid's good," he said. "Very, very good."

"And certainly not as crazy as everyone, including me, believed," Abby said.

"Maybe not."

He found a switch on the wall. The lights came on, revealing a battered metal workbench and a number of old metal cabinets. The concrete floor was bare.

He examined the lab with professional interest. The small space did not gleam with steel and polished equipment like the Coppersmith labs. There were no state-of-the-art computers. The chemistry equipment on the workbench looked as if it had been assembled from various do-it-yourself science kits and then seriously modified. An old burner designed for heating the contents of test tubes sat on one corner. A cumbersome, obviously hand-built laser occupied the far end of the bench.

"You know," Abby said, gazing around the crowded room. "If anyone else, members of the media, say, or the shrinks at the psychiatric hospital, saw this place, the first words that would spring to mind would be *mad scientist.*"

"I was just thinking that this lab looks a lot like mine," Sam said.

Abby cleared her throat. *"Mmm-hmm."*

He went to the bench to examine the laser. "Not as high-end, but most of the basics are here."

"Mmm-hmm."

He glanced back and saw that her eyes were sparkling with amusement. He sighed. "Go get the boxes and the Bubble Wrap. I want to take a look around before we pack this equipment."

"Okay." Abby turned and hurried back up the steps.

When she was gone, he went slowly, methodically, through the shed, opening cabinets and drawers. He discovered a number of stones and crystals, most of which would have been overlooked by the average rock hound. But with his senses mildly jacked, he could tell that several of the stones were hot.

He was holding one half of a split geode, studying the glittering crystals inside, when Abby reappeared.

"Find something interesting?" she asked.

"Nothing yet that would explain the voices that Grady heard." He put the geode down and took another look around. "He said the voice came from a crystal."

"A green crystal."

"I found several varieties of green quartz, a small piece of green tourmaline and some green andradite, but none of it was giving off enough energy to explain the voices he was hearing."

"Shall I start wrapping up the equipment while you look around?"

"All right. But I'd better dismantle the laser for you."

She smiled. "It looks like he found it in a scrap yard."

"He probably bought the various parts online and assembled them himself."

Sam started back to the workbench. A faint hiss of energy made him pause in mid-stride. To his slightly heightened senses, it sounded as if a small insect was buzzing somewhere nearby. He turned on his heel, searching for the source, and caught a flash of green out of the corner of his eye. When he tried to take a closer look, he discovered he could not focus clearly on the object that was giving off the energy.

"What is it?" Abby asked.

"I'm not sure yet." He stopped trying to see the object with his normal vision and raised his talent to the max. The dull gray of the concrete floor and the faded paint on the walls were abruptly transformed. The basement was now lit with ultralight. The rocks and crystals in Grady's collection glowed, bathing the space in a paranormal rainbow.

The buzzing-insect sound grew louder but not more distinct.

"Got it," Sam said.

"What?" Abby asked. "Where? I don't see anything except the rocks and equipment that you've already checked."

"Go hot. You'll hear it, too."

Energy warmed the atmosphere as she went into the zone.

"Good grief," she said. "You're right. It sounds like a scratchy old audio recording of some kind."

"That's exactly what it is." Sam went to the filing cabinet and examined the array of precision-cut objects on top. "A recording. It's emanating from one of these."

"Those aren't crystals or rocks. They look like modernistic glass sculptures."

"They're prisms," he said. "Very special prisms. Grady probably used them to focus energy as well as light."

"There's a recording inside one of those prisms?"

"That's the only explanation that fits," he said. "It must have been laid down with psychic energy, and probably tuned to Grady's wavelengths. That's why we can only detect a faint buzz but not distinct words."

He picked up a heavy green glass prism. The shiver of energy got a bit louder but not much. "It's very weak to our senses, but it was probably a lot louder, stronger and clearer to Grady."

Abby moved closer. "I've never seen a prism like that one."

"It's called a retroreflector, a trihedral prism. It's designed to reflect energy or a beam of light back to its source, regardless of direction. Standard equipment in labs. But this particular prism focuses paranormal energy, not the normal kind. If it was tuned to Grady's aura, it would focus on him whenever he was in the vicinity."

"Once it acquired the fix, it activated the recording?"

"I think so, yes. The prism detected our presence and triggered the psychic message when we entered the room, but since it isn't tuned to either of us, we can barely sense the recording. Grady was never able to tell where the voice was coming from, because every time he tried to look at the prism, it reflected his own psychic wavelengths right back at him, blinding him while simultaneously playing the message."

"Sheesh. Over time, that would have driven anyone nuts."

"I think it would be more accurate to say that it had a hypnotic effect on Grady. Let me have some of that Bubble Wrap."

Abby picked up the scissors she had brought and cut off a length of the wrap. "I've never heard of a psi-recording. I didn't know such a thing was possible."

"The technology is in the experimental stage. This prism came out of a very sophisticated, cutting-edge R-and-D lab."

She handed him the Bubble Wrap and glanced around the room. "What about the gun? Where do you think Grady got that?"

"Whoever recorded the hypnotic message in this thing probably made sure the gun was conveniently at hand when Grady went to Vaughn's house that day."

"Poor Grady. That thing looks valuable."

"It's worth a fortune to certain people."

Abby frowned. "Think it came from your competitor's labs?"

"No." Sam peeled off a strip of packing tape and secured the Bubble Wrap around the prism. "This didn't come from the Helicon Stone labs."

"You're sure?"

"Trust me."

"So who else is running a hotshot R-and-D lab that could turn out something like that prism?"

Sam looked at her. "Take a wild guess."

"Oh, yeah, right. Coppersmith Inc."

"Yes."

"Oh, geez. This is not good."

"No," Sam said. "It's not good."

"You said the prism was valuable. Wonder why the guy who gave it to Grady didn't come back for it?"

Sam picked up the bundled prism. "Maybe because he couldn't get through the crystal lock on the door of this shed."

Sam stowed the last taped and sealed box in the cargo bay of the SUV.

"Where are we going to store all of this stuff?" Abby asked.

"We'll take it back to the Copper Beach house for safekeeping until we figure out how to spring Grady from the hospital."

Abby looked at him. "We are going to get him out, aren't we?"

"Yes. But right now he's safer where he is."

"What do you mean?"

Sam closed the cargo door. "As long as everyone assumes he's crazy, he's not a threat to whoever set him up."

"Oh," Abby said. "I see what you mean."

Sam started toward the shed. "I'll be right back."

"Where are you going?"

"I want to see if I can remove the crystal from the lock that Grady used to secure his lab door. It's a nice piece of engineering. I'd rather not leave it behind."

"Good thought."

She followed him back around the house and checked her email while he studied the lock. He would have to dismantle the whole mechanism, he concluded, which meant using a screwdriver and some other tools.

He was in the process of removing the lock when he heard Abby's sharp exclamation.

"Sam, we got it."

He eased the lock out of the door. "Got what?"

"The lab book."

"But the auction was set for two days from now."

"Not any longer," she said. "Our preemptive bid has been accepted."

He gripped the lock in one hand and looked around the edge of the door. "Are you sure?"

"Not until I actually see it." Abby was aglow with triumph and excitement. "But I just got a message from Milton, who claims that he wants to unload the lab book as quickly as possible and he's giving my client first crack. Actually, we're getting first and last crack. He wants to know if we're still interested."

"Why did we get lucky?"

"In a word, me. I told you, my reputation is good. The bottom line here is that Milton is running scared and wants to unload the lab book as quickly and safely as possible."

"He figures I'm the safe bet, because you wouldn't be working for me if you thought I might be untrustworthy."

"That's pretty much what it comes down to," she said. "He's decided to trust you because he trusts me. But he wants to move fast. I get the impression that he is very nervous. Believe me when I tell you that it takes a lot to make someone like Milton nervous."

Sam pulled the lock mechanism out of the wall. "Get the details. Tell him the money will be wired into whatever account he wants as soon as we have verified the authenticity of the journal."

She sent the message. A moment later, she looked up from the screen.

"Done. Milton just sent the code for the pickup location and his bank-account information."

Sam headed for the door. "Where is the pickup point?"

"A place where no one ever thinks twice about someone collecting a package."

41

"I LEFT A SHOPPING BAG HERE A COUPLE OF HOURS AGO," Abby said. She held up the claim ticket that she had found in a sidewalk planter in front of the museum.

The woman behind the coat- and package-check desk smiled. "I'll be right back." She took the ticket and disappeared into a back room.

Sam glanced around. "Isn't this a risky way to conduct business?"

"Beats the old locker routine at the bus station," Abby said.

Sam surveyed the monumental glass-walled forum in which they stood. There was art everywhere, some of it hanging from the high ceiling. "Definitely more upmarket."

The woman reappeared. She held out the shopping bag with the familiar department-store logo on its side. "Here you are."

"Thanks," Abby said.

She took the bag and opened her senses a little. Currents of energy swirled in the atmosphere. The object inside was hot. She looked at

Sam and knew that he had picked up on the heat. Without a word, he took the shopping bag from her. They walked through the front doors onto First Avenue and turned right toward the Pike Place Market.

"This better be the right lab book," Sam said.

"I'm sure it is."

"Wonder where Milton is? Think he's watching us?"

"No," Abby said. "I think he's on a plane out of town as we speak. I told you, he was scared."

"Like everyone else involved in this thing."

"Except us, of course," she said proudly.

"Speak for yourself."

"Hah. Nothing scares you, Sam Coppersmith."

"You're wrong. I've been running on the edge of panic since that first day you came to see me on the island."

"I don't believe that for a minute."

"Believe it," he said.

"Why?"

"Because I've known from the start that you were in danger."

She glanced at him. "And that scares you?"

"Like nothing else I've ever encountered in my life."

"Oh," Abby said. She was not sure what to do with that information. "I've known some people who were scared *of* me but not *for* me. Except for my mom, of course. But she's been gone a long time."

"Trust me, I'm scared for you. That's why we're headed back to the island."

"Okay," Abby said. "For now, I mean. I appreciate it. But I can't stay there forever. After I break the code on this book for you, my job is done. I've got things to do. I have to find a new place to live, someplace that will take dogs. Got to put my old condo on the market. Then I have to get back to work."

"We'll take it as it comes."

A brisk wind whipped Abby's hair. She could see a bank of ominous dark clouds moving in over Elliott Bay.

"It's going to rain soon," she said.

"I understand it does that a lot around here."

It was clear that Sam's mind was not focused on the weather.

"How will we know?" Abby asked after a while.

"What?"

"How will we know when this thing is over? It will be easy to get the word out that the lab book has been acquired by a new owner and that the code has been broken. Heck, I'm sure it's already out in the underground. But we can't be sure that will be the end of the matter. What if whoever tried to kidnap me decides to try to steal the book from you?"

"I don't think the killer will risk trying to steal the lab book from my vault. He knows that he can't get through my lock."

"You're still convinced that whoever is after the book is the person who murdered Cassidy, aren't you?"

"I'm sure of it."

"Now what?"

"Now we go home. Can't miss the annual tech summit and the big barbecue."

"I didn't realize you were looking forward to it."

"The weekend is going to be a lot more interesting than usual this year."

"Why?"

"The killer will be there."

42

THE COPPERSMITH FAMILY COMPOUND WAS ABLAZE WITH fiery grills. The annual Black Box technical summit was concluded, and the big barbecue was in full swing. The weather had cooperated, with plenty of sunshine and temperatures in the mid-seventies. The long summer day was drawing to a close, but there was still some light in the evening sky.

Abby stood at the edge of the crowd, a glass of sparkling water in her hand, and tried to shake off the chill that was lifting the hairs on her neck. Everything looked normal. There was a line in front of the open bar set up under a large tent. Elias and Willow Coppersmith were mingling with their guests. The sound of laughter and conversation rose up into the trees. All appeared as it should, except for one thing. A few minutes ago, Sam had disappeared.

Earlier that afternoon, he had given a series of tours of his lab, answering an endless string of questions. Abby had been amazed at his patience with the children and teenagers. Afterward, he had done his duty, socializing with the employees and their families. But now he was gone.

She took a sip of the sparkling water. She hadn't had anything stronger to drink all afternoon, even though she could have used something to calm her nerves. A strange darkness was gathering at the edges of her senses. Every time she tried to focus on it, the eerie shadows flickered out of sight. But the sense of wrongness was intensifying. The only thing she knew for certain was that it was linked to Sam. He had set his trap, and now he was waiting for the killer to walk into it.

She had assumed the snare involved catching the killer on camera in the lab. But now she was having doubts.

Jenny O'Connell materialized out of the crowd. She had a glass of wine in one hand.

"I've been looking for you, Abby," she said. "I wanted to apologize for my behavior the other day, when you and Sam came to the Black Box library. To be honest, I was a little taken aback, or maybe just plain insulted, that Sam Coppersmith was using a freelancer to go after a hot book for his family's personal collection."

"I understand," Abby said. "It's okay. I know what librarians and academics think about those of us who work the underground market."

"It's hard enough having serious academic degrees and just enough talent to know that the paranormal is real. Most of us in that category have to pretend that we don't really believe in the existence of extrasensory perception, psychic energy or any of the rest of it. We tell people that we study the sadly deluded folks who do believe in it and examine the effects of such bizarre beliefs on culture and society."

"I understand," Abby said again. She couldn't think of anything else to say.

"Unlike many of my colleagues, I was lucky enough to get a job in a scholarly collection like the Coppersmith company library, where the paranormal is taken seriously. And what did I do? I treated you the way my old academic colleagues would have treated me if they had realized that I actually do believe in the paranormal."

"I get that," Abby said. She smiled. "My father has spent a lot of time in the academic world. I have a sense of how things work there. Please don't worry. I accept your apology."

"Thank you." Jenny sounded grateful and relieved. "I really would like to know more about your end of the field. I have to admit that I've always had a great curiosity about the private collectors' market. It's such a mystery, and so intriguing. Perhaps we can talk shop one of these days?"

"Sure," Abby said.

"Wonderful. I'll look forward to it."

Jenny wandered off in the direction of the bar. Abby watched her go and then turned to search the crowd once more. There was still no sign of Sam.

There was something else that was bothering her now, as well. Jenny O'Connell had been in the company of Gerald Frye for most of the evening. Now she was alone.

43

SAM SAT IN THE CHAIR, ANKLES STACKED ON THE CORNER OF his desk, and listened for the sound of footsteps in the hall. His gun was on top of the desk. So was the green prism.

It was just a matter of time. He had seen the killer make his way to the edge of the crowd a few minutes ago. Sooner or later, he would show up in the lab.

The desk lamp was switched off, but Sam was jacked. The crystals and stones in the display cases glowed in the darkness, casting the strange shadows that could be created only by ultralight.

The footsteps he had been waiting for echoed in the hallway at last, faint at first and then louder as they neared the door. There was a short pause.

The door opened slowly. A figure appeared, silhouetted in the opening. A toxic mix of fear, panic and desperation burned in the atmosphere.

The intruder hesitated, then moved quickly into the room and closed the door. There was a sharp click. A penlight beam arced through the darkness and came to rest on the packing boxes in the corner.

"You don't have to go through the boxes, Dr. Frye," Sam said. "I've got what you're looking for here on my desk."

Gerald Frye froze. "Sam."

"I had a feeling you would be the one who came here tonight, but I had to be sure."

"I was looking for you, Sam. Your mother noticed that you had disappeared from the party. She's worried because you've been so depressed lately. She asked me to see if you'd retreated here to your lab. I told her that you probably just wanted to get away from the crowd for a while, but that I'd make sure you were okay."

"Skip the bullshit," Sam said. "You're here to get the prism that you used to manipulate Grady Hastings. Must have come as a shock today when I mentioned during the tour that I had packed up the contents of the lab of a small-time researcher named Hastings."

"I don't know what you're talking about."

"The prism is the one thing that connects you to Grady Hastings. You realized that if I ever examined it closely, I would know that it had probably come from the Black Box lab. You were right."

"You're not making any sense," Frye said.

"I recognized the para-engineering immediately. Knew it could only have come from our facility. But there's a large staff in the Black Box. It took me a while to go through the list of suspects. I had a hunch you were the one who had created the hypnotic recording and tuned it to Grady Hastings's aura, though. You're one of the very few people in that lab with the technical expertise and the talent to do it. But that didn't mean that you were the killer. There was always the possibility that someone else had used your device. Trust me, I know how it feels to be set up. I didn't want to make a mistake, so I ran this little experiment tonight."

"I don't know what you're talking about." Frye edged toward the door.

"There's no point trying to run. It's over. Just a couple of things I want to get clear. Whose idea was it to try to steal the crystals? Yours or Cassidy's?"

"I'm not going to answer any of your questions. If you lay a hand on me, I'll scream bloody murder. There are a couple hundred people outside."

"We're in a concrete basement. No one will hear you scream." Sam took his feet down off the desk, sat forward and rested one hand on the glowing green prism. "But I'm not going to touch you. We're just going to talk."

"Why would I do that?"

"Because you want me to know how brilliant and how talented you are."

There was stunned silence. A great calm descended on Frye. He moved to the nearest display case and examined the cut geode inside. The blue ultralight from the glittering crystals embedded in the rock etched his face in eerie shadows.

Frye grunted. "Everyone said you were heartbroken, but I knew you were just pissed off because you had let Cassidy get so close to your family's secrets."

"That was part of it." Sam got up and walked around to the front of the desk. He leaned back against the edge and folded his arms. "So whose idea was it to try to steal the crystals?"

"Mine. I recognized Cassidy Lawrence for the opportunist she was the first time I met her. We were two of a kind. I dropped a few hints about the Phoenix stones. Imagine my surprise when I found out that she was already aware of them. That's why she set out to seduce you at that gem-and-mineral show."

"Guess that explains a few things."

"Cassidy, of course, thought she was using me. She was accustomed to being able to manipulate every man she encountered. She certainly dazzled you."

"How did she learn about the crystals?"

"The rumors of the Phoenix Mine have had forty years to turn into a legend. Cassidy came from a long line of crystal talents. She paid attention to that kind of chatter. She picked up the whispers of the Phoenix a year ago and started doing some serious research. She arranged to meet you at that gem-and-mineral show. The next thing you know, you're giving her a tour of the lab and she's filling out a job application."

"You started working for us before Cassidy did. How did you learn about the Phoenix Mine and the crystals?"

"Ray Willis filled up more than one lab notebook with the records of his experiments," Frye said. Cold triumph rang in his words.

"I'll be damned. Willis kept more than one notebook?"

"There were two, the one he showed to your father and Knox, and a second one in which he kept his own private records. Shortly before the explosion in the mine, he sent the second one to my mother for safekeeping."

"Why would he send it to your mother?"

"The two of them were lovers at the time that your father and the others discovered that vein of crystals," Frye said. "He realized the true value of the stones immediately, and wanted to conceal some of the results of his experiments from his partners."

"Did your mother have any idea of how dangerous the stones are?"

"No, of course not. The first lab book wasn't encrypted, but it might as well have been, as far as she was concerned. The notes are all written in the form of para-physics equations and technical jargon. I found it when I went through her things after she died a few years ago. But there was nothing in the notebook concerning the exact location of the Phoenix Mine."

"But after you found the lab book you knew who did have that information, though, didn't you? Your father's partners, Elias Copper-smith and Quinn Knox."

"I managed to track down Knox," Frye said. "He was deep into the booze and the pills by then. I tried to question him, but I couldn't get much out of him. His brain was mush. He told some very tall tales about the Phoenix Mine, but he had long since forgotten the coordi-nates, or pretended that he had forgotten. All I got from him was that it was somewhere in Nevada."

"Lot of desert in Nevada."

"Knox did let slip one other interesting bit of information. He told me the story of how he and your father had escaped from the mine after Willis tried to murder them. He said that they both nearly died because your father insisted on carrying out a sack of rocks."

"You realized that my family probably still had the crystals."

"I decided my best bet was to get a job with Coppersmith Inc.," Frye said. "With my talent, it wasn't hard to work my way into the Black Box facility."

"You became a trusted employee, but you couldn't find what you wanted most, the location of the Phoenix. And there was no record of the geodes that my father had carried out of the mine the day of the explosion."

"Since the stones were not housed in the lab vault, I knew they were most likely either here on the island or down in Sedona," Frye said. "Couldn't see the Coppersmith family letting the crystals get too far out of sight. After a couple of visits here, I realized that your private lab was the most likely place."

"But my security is good, and you didn't even know where the vault was located. You needed to get someone inside. And then Cassidy came on the scene, and you saw your opportunity. How did she find the vault in the wall?"

"There aren't that many firms that specialize in high-end vaults and safes here in the Northwest. I eventually tracked down one that had a record of an installation here on Legacy a few years ago. There weren't many details, but a contractor had left some handwritten notes that made it clear the safe had been installed in a basement wall."

"Cassidy had the freedom of the whole house when she stayed here with me. But I still don't know how she found the vault. I never showed it to her."

"Finding it wasn't that hard," Frye said. "I knew there had to be a phony wall somewhere, and that the vault would be behind it. I gave Cassidy one of the high-end metal detectors we use in the lab. It didn't take her long to find the lever that opens the wall."

"After that, the two of you figured you were home free. You weren't concerned about your ability to crack the vault. Given your lab equipment and your talent, you assumed that would be a piece of cake. You chose a night when you knew that I was going to be away from the island on a consulting trip."

"When you go off on one of those trips, you're generally gone for several days," Frye said. "We knew we'd have plenty of time."

"You and Cassidy came to the island in a private boat. You anchored in one of the small pocket beaches to make sure no one in town witnessed your arrival. You made your way here and managed to disarm my house security system."

"I've always had a talent for locks, and yours had come straight out of a Coppersmith lab," Frye said. "That part was easy. Cassidy and I came down here to the basement. She showed me the mechanism that opens the fake wall."

"You got the wall open, but then you discovered that there was a new lock on the safe, one you couldn't hack."

"That damn crystal lock is your own design, isn't it?" Rage flashed in Frye's voice and in his aura. "I realized immediately I wouldn't be able to open it. The only option was to blow it. That's what Cassidy wanted me to do. But I hadn't come prepared for that. I knew enough about the crystals to know they were volatile. The last thing I wanted to do was use an explosive device. She was screaming at me."

"So you cut your losses and murdered her."

"I had to kill her," Frye said. "I had no choice. She was raving mad, furious with me for failing to get into the safe. She said I was a screwup. I'm pretty sure she intended to kill me. I acted first."

"Plan B, stealing the crystals, had fallen apart. You went back to plan A, trying to find the Phoenix Mine. This time, you decided to go at it using a research approach. You spent a lot of time in the Coppersmith company library. You even started a relationship with the librarian, Jenny O'Connell."

"Jenny knows a great deal about the hot-books market," Frye said. "Between you and me, she's fascinated with it. She even hangs out in some of the underground chat rooms. I asked her to help me search for a forty-year-old lab notebook rumored to contain some experiments performed on some rare earths from an old mine in Nevada. She got a real kick out of the challenge."

"Does she know why you wanted to find that notebook?"

"No. Of course I didn't tell her anything about the Phoenix or my connection to it. I had to be very careful. Jenny's a true-blue company employee. She would have gone straight to someone in the Coppersmith family if she had suspected that she was prying into your family secrets."

"Good to know," Sam said.

"Jenny suddenly caught nibbles of a forty-year-old book that was rumored to be coming up for sale in the private market. The underground chatter was that the book was a notebook containing records of some crystal experiments and that it was encrypted. I knew I had to get hold of it. But Jenny didn't have the kind of connections required to do a deal deep in the underground market."

"Her lack of connections didn't matter, anyway, because you didn't have the kind of money you needed to go after an encrypted book. They're expensive. You had to find another angle."

"Yes," Frye said. "I needed someone in the underground market who could not only find the book for me but also break the code."

"So you set out to find your own freelancer. You got lucky and came up with Abby."

Frye rocked a little on his heels. "How did you put it together?"

"You made one critical mistake. You used the Summerlight Academy student records to find the local talent you needed."

"You know about that? I admit, that does surprise me."

"You were obviously aware that the Summerlight Academy had more than its share of talents among the alumni, because troubled teens with certain para-psych profiles often ended up there. How did you discover that? Were you a student at the academy?"

"No," Frye said. "My mother was one of the counselors at Summerlight for years. She had some talent herself, enough to realize that several of the so-called troubled teens in the school were actually psychically gifted. She wanted to follow them and study them over time. She even went so far as to shape the admissions criteria to ensure that families dealing with teens who displayed certain kinds of psychological issues were encouraged to enroll their kids in the academy."

"In time, she created a very handy database of talents throughout the Pacific Northwest."

"For all the good it did her," Frye said. "Most of the real talents at the school either dropped out of sight after they graduated or refused to cooperate in her research study."

"But you were able to use the records to trace Abby."

"The files were very complete," Frye said. "I found family names and addresses, and the name of the college she had attended. With all that to go on, the investigator I hired had no trouble locating her. After all, she had never left Seattle."

"Before you contacted her, however, you wanted to be certain that she could actually deal with serious psi-encryption."

"I certainly didn't want to risk another disaster like the Cassidy Lawrence fiasco," Frye said.

"So you set up an experiment to test Abby's abilities."

"When she took the job cataloging Vaughn's library, I saw the opportunity to conduct my test. Thanks to Jenny, I knew that Hannah Vaughn was rumored to have a small collection of encrypted books in her collection, including *The Key*."

"To run your experiment, you needed another talent, someone you could manipulate with the prism. You chose Grady Hastings out of the Summerlight files, too. How did you get the prism into his lab?"

Frye snorted. "That was simple. I mailed it to him, explained it was a free sample from an online company that made scientific and research equipment. Miss Radwell passed the test with flying colors."

"But you knew that you couldn't afford her, even if you could get someone to refer you, so you started sending blackmail notes. Abby, however, immediately contacted Webber. By then he had heard the rumors about the lab notebook. He realized that Abby might be in danger. He sent her to me."

"I couldn't believe it," Frye hissed. He slammed a fist on the nearest workbench. "It was as if there was a conspiracy against me."

"It was a classic example of the oldest law of engineering. Anything that can go wrong will go wrong, and at the worst possible moment."

"No, it was your fault, you son of a bitch," Frye snarled. "When luck breaks, it always breaks in your favor. You should have been arrested for murder after you found Cassidy's body. But you walked away. When the rumors of the lab book started circulating, who does Abby run to for protection? *You.* I set up a careful, controlled experiment, and you figure it out because you believed the wild story of a kid who has been declared certifiable."

"For the record, Grady hasn't been declared crazy yet. He's still undergoing observation. But yeah, I figured it out. What are the odds?"

"Don't you dare laugh at me, you bastard," Frye said. "I have as much claim on those crystals as you or anyone else in the Coppersmith family."

"In that case, maybe you should have been up front about those claims instead of hiding your true identity, infiltrating Coppersmith Inc. and murdering an innocent young woman."

"Cassidy Lawrence was no innocent, but that aside, I had no choice. I knew that you would never give me my share of those crystals or tell me the location of the mine."

"Because the stones are dangerous."

"I'll be damned." Frye was amused. "You're afraid of them, aren't you? You and the rest of the Coppersmiths are prepared to let them sit in that vault forever, rather than discover their properties and find out what they can do."

"We're not afraid of them. We're being cautious with them. We need more advanced technology and instrumentation before we risk running experiments on them."

"Your family doesn't deserve those crystals." Frye reached into his pocket and took out an object. "So I'm going to take them. Now."

"A gun, Frye? That's a little over-the-top."

"Not a gun. Something a lot more interesting. A weapon that only I can use, because I'm the one who constructed it. One that won't leave any evidence. You Coppersmiths aren't the only guys who can work crystal."

Dazzling energy flashed from the object in Frye's hand. An icy shock wave lanced through Sam's senses. He tried to move and discovered that he could not even unfold his arms. The glowing stones and crystals in the cases did not dim, but the atmosphere took on an eerie, foglike quality.

"What made you think that I created only one prism?" Frye asked. "The one you found in Grady Hastings's house was a simple version I designed to deliver hypnotic commands. But this one is far more sophisticated. It throws the subject into a trance that is more like a true dreamstate. You will know what you are doing, but you won't be able to resist my orders. You will open the vault for me, and then you will take your own life using your own gun. For the record, this is what I used on Cassidy. While she was trapped in the dreamstate, I gave her an injection of a fast-acting drug that stops the heart but leaves no trace in the body."

The crystals and stones in the display cases were drifting in and out of the paranormal mist now. Sam fought to focus his para-senses and discovered that he no longer had any control over them. He could hear every word Frye said, but he could not respond.

"The difference between a true dreamstate and your present condition is that under the influence of the prism, you are aware that you are locked in a dream." Frye walked slowly through the maze of glowing specimens. "Aware that you are powerless."

Sam watched one of the glowing rocks in the gallery burst into flames. The fire wasn't real. He knew that. But in his dreamstate, it seemed very real.

"I did bring a gun," Frye said. "But this time, we'll use yours."

He went behind the desk and picked up the pistol. Sam watched, helpless to stop him.

Frye's words echoed in his head. *You are aware that you are locked in a dream. . . .*

That was the definition of a lucid dream. According to Abby's friend Gwen, strong talents were especially good at manipulating lucid dreams: they just had to focus.

With an effort of will, he succeeded in pulling his attention away from the burning stone. The paranormal flames were abruptly extinguished. But now the darkly glittering interior of one of the geodes summoned him into an endless black hole in the universe. In the distance, he heard a labored *thud-thud-thud*. His heart. He was using a harrowing amount of energy to overcome the effects of the prism.

A spark of fire caught his eye. He managed to look down and saw that the stone in his ring was burning. *Real energy. Not part of the dream.*

"You will open the vault for me now," Frye said.

Slowly, painfully, Sam began to unwind his arms. Each tiny movement required enormous effort. It was like moving through quicksand.

And then he heard the light footsteps in the outer hall. A woman.

Abby.

"That will very likely be Miss Radwell, come to see what's keeping you," Frye said. "I didn't plan this, but it's going to work out well. When your new girlfriend walks through that door, she will be silhouetted against the light, a very easy target. You will kill her, and then you will open the vault. Afterward, you will turn the gun on yourself. Given your recent history of depression, no one will be terribly surprised."

The footsteps drew closer. Now he could hear a familiar clicking sound. Dog nails. Abby had Newton with her.

Sam tried to call Abby's name, but he could not get the words out.

It was the damned recurring nightmare made real.

The footsteps and the clicking stopped. Frye moved out from behind the desk and aimed the gun at the door.

Sam pulled hard on his senses. This dream was going to have a different ending.

And suddenly he knew intuitively how to shatter the trance. He focused everything he had left through the Phoenix stone. It was all he had to work with, his only chance to save Abby.

He found the resonating frequency buried deep in the heart of the stone, the latent power that he had always known was there. In that moment, it was his to command.

The Phoenix crystal blazed with dark fire, swamping the energy that Frye was using to maintain the dreamstate. Sam came out of the paralysis on a wave of raw power.

Paranormal lightning arced from the ring, igniting Frye's aura. Psi-fire blazed around him, enveloping him in flames. He opened his mouth in a silent scream. His body stiffened, as if electrified. The gun and the prism fell from his hands. Violent convulsions racked his body.

He crumpled and collapsed without making a sound. The paranormal fire winked out. So did Frye's aura.

The door of the room slammed open. But it was not Abby who stood silhouetted in the doorway. Newton charged into the shadows, low to the ground, silent and dangerous. He locked his jaws around Frye's right ankle.

"Abby," Sam said. "Call off your dog."

Abby appeared. "Newton. That's enough."

Newton released the ankle and trotted back to her.

"See?" Sam said. "He goes for the ankles every time."

Abby ignored that. "Everything okay in here?"

Sam glanced down at his ring. The crystal was no longer burning. He looked at her. "It is now."

44

"WELL, OF COURSE YOU SHOULD HAVE KNOWN THAT I WOULDN'T do something dumb like open the door and make a perfect target out of myself," Abby said. She patted Newton's head. "I watch TV like everyone else. You don't charge into an unknown situation. But Newton is a lot shorter than me. I knew that no one would be expecting a dog to be the first one through the door."

Newton licked her hand. She fed him another treat, his fourth or fifth, Sam thought. He had lost count.

Sam raised his glass. "Here's to Newton."

"To Newton," Willow said.

"To Newton," Elias repeated.

The four of them were sitting in the living room of the big house. A fire burned brightly on the wide stone hearth. The Coppersmith employees and their families had returned to their island lodgings, preparing to leave in the morning. The county sheriff and a deputy had come and gone, taking Gerald Frye's body with them.

Everyone seemed to think that Frye had died of a heart attack. There was, Sam thought, nothing to indicate otherwise. He looked at his ring and thought about the raw power he had pulled from the small Phoenix crystal. So much energy from just a tiny stone.

"Not to take away anything from Newton's act of derring-do," Abby said, "but it's obvious that Sam had the situation under control before Newton and I arrived."

"Don't be so sure of that." Sam swallowed some of his whiskey and set the glass down on the arm of his chair. He gazed into the flames. "In a weird way, I think it was knowing that you were coming down the hall and that you would open the door that gave me the juice I needed to break through the trance."

"You would have escaped from the dreamstate with or without me," Abby said, with conviction.

Willow smiled. "You have a lot of confidence in my son."

Abby raised her glass. "Another professional."

Elias studied her with keen interest. "How did you know?"

"Know what?" Abby asked.

"That Sam was in danger?"

Abby rubbed Newton's ears. "I just knew. And there was a huge sense of urgency about the knowing. I knew he had set a trap in the lab, so that was the logical place to go first." She glared at Sam. "I thought you had set up cameras to photograph the killer when he went after the prism."

Willow frowned. "Yes, that was the plan."

"I changed the plan," Sam said. He took his attention off the flames and looked at Abby. "Did you know that Frye was in the lab with me?"

"I wasn't certain, but I had a feeling he might be there, because Jenny O'Connell was alone. Frye had been with her most of the day, but suddenly she was on her own. When I realized the door was unlocked, I flattened myself against the wall, just like they do on the cop shows, and sent Newton in." She smiled, not bothering to conceal her pride. "And it worked great. Except that you had already taken out Frye, so in the end, it was something of a nonevent."

"Trust me, it was not a nonevent from my perspective," Sam said. He drank some more whiskey. He was still riding a post-burn buzz, but he was going to crash soon.

Elias scowled at him. "Why didn't you tell us that you suspected Frye was the one who would walk into your trap?"

"He didn't tell you because he didn't want to get it wrong," Abby said quietly. "Sam knows what it's like to be falsely accused."

Willow sighed. "I understand. So does Elias. It's just that you took such a risk, Sam."

"A calculated risk," Sam said. He drank some more whiskey. "What I did not factor into the equation was the possibility that Frye might have another prism weapon. Also, I didn't factor in Abby."

"Or Newton," Abby said.

"No," Sam said. He smiled and rested his head against the back of the chair. The exhaustion was starting to seep through him. "I didn't make allowances for Newton, either."

Elias shook his head in disgust. "There were a few things that I failed to factor in, too. All these years I've been watching for a single lab book to surface. Knox and I were aware of only the one notebook containing the record of the experiments. It never dawned on us that Ray Willis had filled up a second notebook with the results of experiments that he ran in secret."

"The question now," Sam said, "is where did Gerald Frye stash the other notebook?"

"With luck, it will be among his personal possessions," Elias said. "We need to get someone inside his house as fast as possible to search the place."

"I can do it after I've had some sleep," Sam said.

"Forget it," Elias said. "I'll handle the search first thing in the morning. According to Frye's personnel records, he had no close family. No one will think it strange if his employer takes charge of his personal possessions until someone arrives who is authorized to claim them."

"Which may be never," Sam said.

Elias shook his head. "I still can't believe that we spent the past few days thinking that the threat was coming from Lander Knox. When all along, Gerald Frye was right there in the Black Box lab, plotting against us."

"I think we've still got a problem with Lander Knox," Sam said.

"You're right," Abby said. "There are a lot of unanswered questions here. Did Gerald Frye kill Thaddeus Webber and that other book dealer?"

"No," Sam said. He steepled his hands and contemplated the fire. "He didn't have the connections in the underground market to identify those dealers, let alone locate them. Someone else murdered those two people."

"What about the thugs who tried to kidnap me? Do you think Frye hired them?"

"No. Whoever murdered Webber sent that pair to keep watch for you."

"Lander Knox," Elias said grimly. "He's still out there."

"I agree with you," Sam said. "We'll find him. But the process of connecting all the dots will have to wait until morning. I can't think clearly enough to do that tonight."

"You need sleep," Willow said.

Abby nodded. "Yes, you do."

"I'm not arguing." Sam pushed himself up out of the chair. "If you will all excuse me, I'm going to crash."

He started toward the bedroom stairs.

"One more thing before you leave," Elias said.

Sam paused and turned back. "What?"

"You said Frye told you that his mother had an affair with Ray Willis and that Willis entrusted her with that other notebook."

"Yes," Sam said. "Willis didn't want you and Knox to know about those experiments."

"What about the missing crystals?" Elias asked. "The ones he used in the field tests? Knox and I searched for them after the explosion, but we never found them."

"I don't have the answer to that question," Sam said. "All I can tell you is that Frye made it clear he did not have them. That was one of the reasons he was so desperate to get his hands on the Coppersmith crystals. He felt that he had been deprived of his inheritance."

"His *inheritance*?" Willow's eyes widened. "You mean . . ."

"Of course," Abby said quietly. "It all makes sense now, including the psychic genetics. Ray Willis was Gerald Frye's father, the father he never knew."

45

ABBY AWOKE TO THE KNOWLEDGE THAT SAM WAS NO LONGER in the bed. She opened her eyes and saw him standing at the window. His strong, bare shoulders were silhouetted against the moonlight. His hard face was in shadow. He was not alone. Newton was beside him, front paws braced on the windowsill. Together, both males contemplated the darkness.

Abby sat up against the pillows and wrapped her arms around her knees.

"Did you have another one of your nightmares?" she asked.

"No." Sam looked at her. "I woke up a while ago and couldn't get back to sleep."

"You had a rough evening. We all did, but you endured that dream-state experience and nearly got killed. That kind of stress takes some time to get over."

"That's not why I couldn't sleep. I started thinking about some of the missing answers."

"You said they could wait until morning. The main thing to focus on tonight is that you solved Cassidy Lawrence's murder. That should give you some closure."

"Closure. Good word," Sam said. He turned away from the window and moved back toward the bed. "It does feel a lot like a door has been closed somewhere, this time for good. But there is another door still ajar. I think your stepbrother is standing on the other side."

"Dawson?"

"We need to find that investor, the one who is pressuring him to acquire the lab book."

"You think the investor is Lander Knox, don't you?"

"I think there's a strong possibility of that, yes."

"Even if you're right, Knox has to know the chase is over and that he lost. The lab book is no longer on the market."

"If he's killed two people to get it, he's unlikely to stop now. We need to find him."

Abby shivered. "I can call Dawson in the morning, tell him what's going on. Maybe he'll believe me and cooperate with us to help find the investor."

"Yes."

Newton dropped his front paws to the floor and trotted to the door.

"He wants to go out," Abby said.

"And then he'll want to come back in."

"It's the way of all dogs."

Sam went to the door and opened it. "Remind me to install a dog door this week."

Abby watched Sam and Newton disappear into the darkened hallway.

Remind me to install a dog door. She smiled. A gentle warmth spread through her. Installing a dog door sounded like a long-term plan, as if Sam was envisioning a future that included her and Newton.

She listened to the kitchen door open and close. Sam came back to the bedroom alone, got out of his pants and got into bed. He reached for Abby and drew her across his chest.

"Tonight, in the lab," he said, "when I heard you coming down the hall and realized that I could not stop you, I think I went a little crazy."

She framed his face between her palms and kissed him firmly on the mouth, silencing him. "No, that's not what happened. You need to remember events correctly. What *happened* is that, in an emergency, you pulled on psychic energy that you did not know you possessed because you've never had to use that much of it before. You broke free of the trance in time. If I had been dumb enough to open that door, I would have been okay, because you clocked Gerald first."

He put two fingers over her mouth. "You didn't let me finish."

She sensed his amusement and winced.

"Sorry," she said. "So what were you going to say?"

"That when I went a little crazy trying to break free of the trance, I suddenly realized that I could use the ring to do it."

"Really?" She pushed herself up on her elbows and peered at his ring. She could not see it in the shadows, so she jacked up her talent a little and studied the tiny aurora of energy that leaked out of the stone. "You figured out what it can do?"

"I think it acts as a kind of psychic laser." Sam raised his hand and examined the ring. "At least that's what happened tonight. I was able to channel my own energy through it and focus it in a way I've never been able to do before. I could feel the currents overwhelming Frye, setting his aura on fire."

"You didn't say anything to your parents tonight about using the ring."

"Because I'm still not sure what happened. I'll talk to Dad in the morning, though. We need to run some experiments." Sam paused.

"Very careful experiments. And I need to contact my brother and sister, warn them that the rings appear to have laserlike properties and that they can be deadly."

"Maybe you'll know more when I break the code on the lab book."

"Yes." Sam thrust his fingers into her hair and wrapped them around the back of her head. "There's something we need to talk about."

"The lab book?"

"Not the damn lab book. The real reason I was able to pull the extra energy I needed to break the trance tonight was you."

"Me? But I was out in the hall."

"I knew you were there. And you were running hot. There's a connection between us, Abby."

"I know. It's weird, isn't it?"

"No, it's love."

She froze. Her mouth went dry. *"Sam."*

"I needed some additional power, and I drew it from the link between us."

"I realize there's some kind of psychic vibe going on here. But there might be a very straightforward explanation involving the resonating frequencies of our auras. Or something."

He touched the corner of her mouth. "I'm the expert here. If I wanted a para-physics explanation for what's going on between us, I'd have come up with it. But I don't need one. I love you. I have from the moment you stepped out of Dixon's water taxi. It was as if I'd been waiting for you all of my life and you had finally decided to show up."

Warmth and wonder sparkled through her. "Oh, Sam."

"You were like some fabulous new crystal, glowing with unknown fire and mystery. And you were in danger, and I had so much damn baggage."

"Well, to be fair, I had a lot of baggage, too."

"I know. Someone was trying to grab you."

"That wasn't the kind of baggage I meant," she said. "I'm talking about more serious baggage."

"What the hell is more serious than someone trying to kidnap you?"

She cleared her throat. "I have never been one to take risks when it comes to romantic relationships."

"Oh, yeah, right. The commitment-and-trust-issues thing."

"Yes. But I've always suspected that the shrinks and the counselors were wrong. I was pretty sure that I was just waiting for the right man to walk into my life. I knew I'd recognize him, you see."

Sam traced her bottom lip with one finger. "Did you?"

"The instant I turned and saw you coming toward me along the dock that first day. I recognized you, but I told myself I had gotten it all wrong. There was so much drama going on all around us. Everything was happening way too fast. For Pete's sake, we had sex the first night that we were together. I never do things like that."

"We made love that first night. Big difference."

"Sure, but at the time all I could focus on was the weird feeling that there was some kind of psychic connection forming between us. It was very confusing. I was afraid to trust what my senses were telling me. But now I know that what was really going on was that I was falling head over heels in love with you."

He drew her mouth down to his. Abby felt him open his senses. She responded, heightening her own talent. The kiss was dark and profound, the kind of kiss that sealed a vow.

The heat built quickly. Energy burned in the room. Sam rolled Abby onto her back and came down on top of her. She pulled him close, savoring the weight of him crushing her into the bedding. The power that charged his aura challenged and aroused and thrilled her in ways that she could not begin to explain or understand. She knew on some level that he was as compelled and captivated by her energy as she was by his.

Sam raised his head so that his mouth was only an inch or so above hers. In the shadows, his eyes heated.

"You and me," he said. "Forever."

She wrapped her arms around him. "Forever."

He took her mouth again. The night burned. So did the Phoenix ring.

She awoke to the muffled whine of an impatient dog.

"Newton," she said.

"Your turn," Sam said into the pillow. "I let him out."

"Okay, okay. But definitely a dog door."

"For sure. This week."

She got out of the warm bed, wrapped her robe around herself and slid her cold toes into her slippers. She left the bedroom, went downstairs into the kitchen and opened the door.

Newton trotted over the threshold and paused, radiating a hopeful air.

"All right," Abby said. "You're a hero. I guess you deserve a snack."

She opened the bag of doggy treats, took out a goodie and tossed it to Newton. He seized it out of midair and crunched with enthusiasm.

When he was finished, they both went back upstairs. Abby heard the chimes of her phone just as she arrived in the bedroom doorway.

"What in the world?" she said.

Sam levered himself up on one elbow. "Your phone."

"Yes, I figured that much out all by myself."

She grabbed the phone off the bedside table and looked at the glowing screen.

"I don't believe it," she said. "It's Diana."

"At this hour?" Sam grumbled. "It's four o'clock in the morning."

Abby took the call.

"If this is about Dawson and that book he wanted me to find for his client . . ." she began.

"Abby, shut up and listen to me." Diana's voice rose to a near-hysterical pitch. "Dawson has been kidnapped."

"What?" Abby's stomach clenched. "Please tell me this is some kind of really sick joke."

"I just got a call demanding a ransom."

"Let me guess. The lab book?"

"He's going to murder Dawson if you don't give him that damned book. Dawson's life is in your hands."

"You said we needed a plan," Abby said. "I just gave you one."

"It's a lousy plan," Sam said.

"Got a better one?"

"No. And yours just might work if we tweak it a bit."

46

DAWSON WAS SLUMPED IN A CHAIR IN THE YACHT'S MAIN cabin. His wrists were fastened behind him. His legs were bound to the legs of the chair. He looked up when Abby walked on board. Disbelief flashed across his face.

"What the hell are you doing here, Abby?" he said. "I told him that you wouldn't come."

The good-looking, sandy-haired man with the gun chuckled. "But I was sure she would. She's your sister, after all."

"Stepsister," Dawson said dully. "I explained that she's not a blood relative. She doesn't even like me."

"But you're all part of Dr. Radwell's modern blended family, his family by choice. I admit I don't get the family-loyalty thing, but it can certainly prove useful."

Abby stopped just inside the cabin, the package containing the lab book in her hands. She looked at the man with the gun. He was polished and well groomed, the kind of a man who was at ease with money and the sort of people who possessed a lot of it. His open, classically handsome features invited trust. He was dressed from head to toe in iconic yachting attire, a dark blue polo shirt, well-cut white trousers and deck shoes. The ring on his hand was set with a large diamond. The watch was gold, the kind of timepiece that, according to the ads, was meant to be handed down to the next generation. The ads did not usually mention that in a pinch the watch could be pawned to buy a ticket to a no-name island if the Feds came to the door.

"You must be Lander Knox," Abby said.

"So you figured that out, did you?" Lander looked amused.

"Sam Coppersmith is the one who worked out your real identity."

"I see. Well, no harm done. When this is over, I will disappear again, just like I did a few years ago, when I wanted everyone to think that I was dead."

Dawson shook his head. "You shouldn't have come, Abby. He's a total psycho. Now he'll kill both of us."

"No," Lander said. "I'm not going to kill either of you, not unless you force me to take extreme measures."

"Bullshit," Dawson muttered.

"Why should I kill you or your sister?" Lander asked, in a voice of perfect reason. "She followed all the rules today. She came alone, as instructed. Paid a private charter service to drop her off at the cabin. She knows what will happen if I hear or see another boat or if there's any sign of a floatplane, don't you, Abby?"

"Yes," she said. "You'll kill Dawson."

"Exactly right." Lander gave her an approving smile. "But if everyone sticks to the plan, you both will walk away from this meeting, and I will sail away. You won't ever see me again."

"Why the gun?" Abby asked. "You've already murdered at least two book dealers by paranormal means, and I'm betting that you've killed others the same way."

"I have discovered that people tend to take guns more seriously than they do the paranormal. A gun concentrates the attention."

"Sam said something similar."

"And those people you say I murdered were all victims of cardiac arrest. There is nothing to tie me to their deaths." He glanced at the gun. "Certainly not this device."

"Device?" Abby took a second look at the weapon in his hand.

"It looks like a gun, but it isn't a traditional pistol. It's crystal-powered. Kills without leaving a trace."

"He's lying about letting us go," Dawson said wearily. "He's a damned psychopath. He lies as easily as he breathes. He's been stalking you for months, using Grandmother and me. He's the one who set up the Ponzi scheme and suckered Grandmother and me into investing in it."

Lander gave Abby a warm, charming smile. "I don't want to have to kill anyone. All I want is the lab book. Once you've broken the encryption and I've verified that it's the right book, we'll take a short cruise. I'll put you and Dawson ashore on one of the uninhabited islands here in the San Juans. It may take you a while, but sooner or later you'll manage to flag down a passing boat. Plenty of time for me to disappear."

"What if we go to the police?" Abby said.

Lander shrugged. "They wouldn't believe you. There was no ransom paid. No money changed hands. At best, the kidnapping story will be viewed as a publicity stunt designed to help your father sell more books. Speaking of books, let me see Willis's notebook. I want to be sure you brought the right one."

"Afraid of being scammed the way you scammed Dawson?" Abby asked.

"You wouldn't take the risk," Lander said. "You know that it would cost your brother his life, and your own as well. But after going to all this trouble, I want to be certain that the book you found is the right one. You know how it is in the collectors' market, so many frauds and forgeries out there."

"True." Abby put the package down on the desk and started to peel off the tape she had used to secure the wrapping paper. "How will you know if this is the right lab book?"

"I'll know," Lander said. He moved closer to the desk to get a better look at the package. "In fact, I can already sense some energy around it."

"Encryption energy." Abby finished unwrapping the book. The atmosphere inside the cabin heated a little, but she knew that it wasn't all coming from the lab book. Lander had heightened his talent. He was powerful. The strange gun in his hand was suddenly a luminous green. A new chill went through her.

"You used a crystal from the Phoenix Mine to power that weapon," she said.

He followed her gaze to the gun and gave her another approving smile. "Very good observation. My father thoughtfully kept one crystal as a souvenir. I ran a lot of experiments on it before I finally realized what it could do."

"That's what you used to kill Thaddeus Webber and the other dealer."

"Yes. I know the East Coast hot-books market quite well. I've been dealing in it anonymously for some time now. But sadly, I lacked connections here in the Pacific Northwest."

"But your contacts back east knew how to find Thaddeus."

"It took some doing, but once I located him, I was able to get the names of the most likely auction dealers from him before he suffered his heart attack."

"Before you murdered him, you mean. You sent those two men to kidnap me."

"I had hoped to avoid violence, but when it became clear that you had another client and that your dear brother was not going to be able to convince you to work for him, I realized I had to take more drastic measures. I wasn't absolutely certain that you would show up at Webber's house, but it seemed likely. I didn't have time to watch the place myself, so I hired that pair to pick up any female seen leaving his place. Obviously, they did a very poor job of grabbing you. I assume you had Coppersmith with you that day?"

"Yes."

"That explains why you got away," Lander said. "Never mind, what's done is done, and it's all ending the way it's supposed to end. Let's have a look at the lab book."

He opened the leather cover and examined the first page.

"There's Willis's name," he said. "The dates are correct." He turned one page and then another. His eyes tightened. "This is a record of experiments conducted on rare earths and crystals taken from a mine, but there's no mention of paranormal properties or the location of the mine."

"The book is still encrypted," Abby reminded him. "It won't make any sense to you until I break the code."

He closed the book with a snap. "Do it now."

"You promise you'll let us go?"

"I promise," Lander said. Anger flashed in his cold eyes. "I told you, I have no reason to kill either of you."

"He's lying, Abby," Dawson said.

Lander aimed the gun at him. "It occurs to me that now that I have your sister, I don't have any more use for you."

Dangerous currents swirled in the atmosphere. Dawson started to sweat. He gasped for breath.

"No." Abby grabbed the lab book. "You said you wouldn't hurt him. I'll break the code for you."

"Do it," Lander snarled.

She jacked up her energy, found the frequencies and held out the lab book.

"Okay," she said. "It's done. Here, take the book and let us go."

Lander reached for the book, ignoring her plea. His fingers closed around the spine. Abby seized the energy of the encryption and sent it into his aura.

Lander stiffened. His eyes widened in dawning horror.

"No," he screamed. He tried and failed to let go of the book. "You can't do this to me. I'll kill you first, I swear it."

His left hand was still frozen to the book. Abby sensed that the energy of the unlocking code was channeling straight into his aura. But he was so much stronger than she had realized. He managed to let go of the lab book. Gaining strength, he turned the pistol toward her.

"Bitch," he screamed.

The barrel of the pistol glowed hotter. Icy currents flowed around her heart.

Sam came through the doorway, the Phoenix ring on fire. Paranormal lightning crackled across the small space, igniting Lander's aura. Ultralight flames blazed. Lander jerked and twitched and writhed.

He stared at Sam from the heart of the inferno. "*No.* It can't end like this. The crystals are *mine.*"

In the next instant, he crumpled to the floor. His aura and the psi-fire winked out with a terrible finality.

Sam scooped up the crystal gun and looked at Abby.

"I told you this was a bad plan," he said.

"I thought it all went quite well," she said. Her voice sounded far too high and thin.

She hurled herself against Sam's chest. His arms closed fiercely around her.

47

"I DON'T GET IT," DAWSON SAID TO SAM. "HOW DID YOU MANAGE to sneak up on Knox? He watched Abby's arrival with his binoculars and made sure that she was the only one who came ashore from the floatplane. That island wasn't much larger than a big rock. We would have heard even a very small outboard engine."

They were back at the Copper Beach house. Sam had used his phone to summon the floatplane that had been standing by to pick them up. The pilot was a resident of Copper Beach. He had asked no questions about the unusual charter.

Abby sat in a chair near the hearth. Newton was on the floor at her feet. Willow had made coffee for everyone. She and Elias were following the conversation with sharp-eyed attention.

"I came partway out on one of the whale-watching charters," Sam said. "Figured Knox wouldn't be overly concerned if he happened to catch sight of a boat full of sightseers in the distance."

"I understand," Dawson said. "But how did you get the rest of the way to the island?"

"Kayak," Sam said. "They make almost no noise. I came ashore on the far side of the island and walked the rest of the way. I stayed out of sight and kept an eye on things from the trees. The plan was for me to move in as soon as Abby started to unlock the psi-code. We knew that even if she couldn't take him down with encryption energy, she would probably be able to distract him long enough for me to get on board."

Dawson shook his head. "I still don't understand this whole code thing. Knox kept talking about how he'd need Abby not just to get the book for him but to unlock it. At first I assumed he meant a real code, one with secret meanings for certain letters and numbers. When I realized he thought the book was encoded with some kind of psychic energy, I figured he was just flat-out crazy."

"I think he was, in a way," Abby said.

"But you aren't." Dawson looked at her. "You never were. The family is wrong about you. There is something to this whole paranormal thing, isn't there?"

Abby smiled. "What makes you believe that?"

"I felt something weird happen when Knox turned that strange gun on me, and again when you gave him the book. It was as if there was some kind of invisible storm inside the cabin. The air seemed somehow charged." Dawson looked at Sam. "When you came in, the sensation got a thousand times worse. I've never experienced anything like it. Except maybe once."

"When was that?" Abby asked.

"The day you burned the book in the bathtub and Mom decided that you had tried to set fire to the house."

"In hindsight, I have to admit that she had some reason to be concerned," Abby said. "I was just coming into my talent. I had no idea what I was doing."

"What really frightened Mom was the fact that you seemed to believe you had set fire to the book with some kind of mental energy. But that's exactly what happened, wasn't it?"

Abby sighed. "Pretty much."

Elias looked at Sam. "We need to find the missing crystals. We've got one lab book, a good shot at getting the second one if it's with Frye's things, and we've got Knox's crystal gun. That will give us a lot to work with."

"Still got a long way to go," Sam said. "We're going to need Judson's and Emma's help. They are the only ones we can trust, the only ones who have a sensitivity to the Phoenix crystals."

Willow picked up her coffee cup. "What did you do with Lander Knox's body and his yacht?"

"I made sure there was nothing on board that tied any of us to the boat, and then I sank it," Sam said. "The water is very deep off that island. I doubt that the wreckage or the body will ever be discovered, but if they are, it won't cause much of a stir. Just one more tragic summer boating accident in the San Juans."

Abby looked at him over the top of her cup.

"What?" he asked.

"I was just thinking of what Dixon told me about you the first time he brought me here to the island."

Sam raised his brows. "That would be?"

"I was given to understand that if you ever had to get rid of a body, it would disappear for good," she said. "Something to do with all the deep water around these parts and the cleverness of Coppersmiths in general."

"Damn straight," Elias growled.

Sam let that go. He turned back to Dawson. "Are you going to tell your grandmother that she was giving out details about the family finances to a killer?"

"I don't think that I'll mention that he was a killer." Dawson tapped one finger on the arm of the chair. "That gets complicated."

"Yes," Sam said. "It does."

"I doubt that she'd believe me if I did tell her the whole truth, anyway," Dawson continued. "But I do plan to let her know that the guy she was doing lunch with on a regular basis for the past few months was the architect of the Ponzi scheme that she insisted I invest her money in. I'm also going to make it clear that it isn't Abby's fault that Knox was a fraud and a scam artist."

Willow exchanged a look with Elias. Abby was sure she saw some unspoken message pass between them. Willow looked at Dawson.

"It might be possible to recover whatever is left of the money that you invested with Knox, assuming he didn't spend all of it," she said.

"He didn't have time to go through that much money," Sam said. "He was focused on acquiring the lab book and getting the encryption broken. Depriving the Stricklands of the family fortune was merely a means to an end, collateral damage."

"In that case, I'll see what I can do," Willow said.

Elias grinned proudly. "My wife has a real talent for following the money," he said to Dawson. "If your grandmother's fortune is out there, she'll find it."

Dawson looked at Willow. "That's very kind of you. I might be able to help. I've got a little talent in that arena myself."

"Excellent," Willow said. "We'll work the project as a team."

They finished the coffee in silence. The flames crackled cheerfully on the hearth. Outside, the long summer day came to a close. Darkness settled on the island.

"I told Knox that he had miscalculated," Dawson said to Abby. "I explained that he had misjudged the family dynamics. I said you had no reason to risk your neck for me. But he was convinced that you would come. For a smart psychopath, he sure had a blind side. He actually bought into the image in that photo on the back cover of *Families by Choice*. Thought the happy Radwell family was the real deal."

Abby smiled. "Like Dad always says, family is everything."

48

ABBY STOOD WITH SAM ON THE BLUFF ABOVE THE SMALL COVE. Sam was on his phone. Newton was exploring some nearby rocks.

Sam concluded the call and slipped the phone into the pocket of his leather jacket. "That was the lawyer I had looking into the status of Thaddeus Webber's estate. Turns out there is a will."

"So Thaddeus did take steps to make sure his most valuable books went to a library?" Abby smiled. "That's great."

"He didn't leave his collection to a library. He left everything, including the contents of his book vault, to a single individual."

"He had some family after all?"

"According to his will, he left his collection to the person he looked upon as a daughter, although, given the age difference, maybe he should have said granddaughter. He left it all to you, Abby."

"*What?*"

Sam smiled.

It took her a few seconds to find her tongue. "But some of the volumes in that collection are worth a fortune."

"They're all yours now. The lawyer is making certain that the collection is guarded until it can be packed up and transported here to Copper Beach. You'll have to open Webber's vault, though. You're the only one who knows the code."

"This is amazing. I can't believe it. First your mother and Dawson track down the bulk of the Strickland fortune in that offshore bank and arrange to get it back. Then one of your fancy lawyers manages to spring Grady Hastings, who is scheduled to start work in the Black Box facility on Monday."

"Good talent is hard to come by," Sam said. "Don't like to see it wasted."

"And now I find out I'm inheriting all of Thaddeus's books. On top of everything else, I actually got a phone call from Orinda Strickland today, informing me that she intended to make provision for me in the Strickland family trust."

"You told her you didn't want to be named in the trust, didn't you?"

"How did you guess?"

"I know you, Abby. The money isn't important to you. All you've ever wanted was to be part of the family. Don't worry, when you marry me, you're going to have all the family you can handle."

The late summer sun was setting, streaking the clouds with fiery light and turning the water to a sheet of hammered copper. Abby watched the spectacular sunset, aware of a glorious sense of happiness and certainty.

"Now I know why they call this place Copper Beach," she said.

Sam drew her into his arms. His eyes heated. "I told you that you would understand one of these days. Think you can call this island home?"

"Home is wherever you and I are together," she said. "Well, and Newton, too, of course."

"Newton, too," Sam agreed.

He kissed her there in the warm copper light of the summer evening. Abby opened her senses to the powerful energy of the love that she knew would bind them for a lifetime.

The Phoenix crystal burned.

*Turn the page for an extract of the new novel by Jayne Ann Krentz
writing as Amanda Quick*

CRYSTAL GARDENS

Coming soon from Piatkus

CRYSTAL GARDENS

A LADIES OF LANTERN STREET NOVEL

THE MUFFLED THUD OF THE SHATTERED LOCK ECHOED LIKE a thunderclap in the deep silence that drenched the cottage. Evangeline Ames recognized the sound at once. She was no longer alone in the house.

Her first primal instinct was to go absolutely still beneath the covers. Perhaps she was mistaken. The cottage was old. The floorboards and the ceiling often creaked and moaned at night. But even as the commonsense possibilities flitted through her head, she knew the truth. It was two o'clock in the morning, an intruder had broken in and it was highly unlikely that he was after the silver. There was not enough in the place to tempt a thief.

Her nerves had been on edge all afternoon, her intuition flickering and flaring for no obvious reason. Earlier, when she had walked into town, she had found herself looking over her shoulder again and again. She had flinched at the smallest rustling noises in the dense woods that bordered the narrow lane. While she was shopping in Little Dixby's crowded high street, the hair had lifted on the back of her neck. She had felt as if she was being watched.

She had reminded herself that she was still recovering from the terrifying attack two weeks ago. She had very nearly been murdered. Little wonder her nerves were so fragile. On top of that, the writing was not going well and a deadline was looming. She dared not miss it. She'd had every reason to be tense.

But now she knew the truth. Her psychical intuition had been trying to send a warning for hours. That was the reason she had been unable to sleep tonight.

Cool currents of night air wafted down the hall from the kitchen. Heavy footsteps sounded. The intruder was not even bothering to conceal his approach. He was very certain of his prey. She had to get out of the bed.

She pushed back the covers, sat up quietly and eased herself to her feet. The floorboards were chilly. She stepped into her sturdy leather-soled slippers and took her wrapper down off the hook.

The assault on her person two weeks earlier had made her cautious. She had considered all possible escape routes when she had rented the cottage. Here in the bedroom, the waist-high window was her best hope. It opened onto the small front garden, with its lattice gate. Just outside the gate was the narrow rutted lane that wound through the dense woods to the ancient country house known as Crystal Gardens.

Out in the hall, a floorboard creaked under the weight of a booted foot. The intruder was moving directly to the bedroom. That settled the matter. He had not come for the silver. He had come for her.

There was no point trying to silence her movements. She pushed one of the narrow casement windows wide, ignoring the squeak of the hinges, and clambered through the opening. With luck, the intruder would not be able to fit.

"Where do you think you're going, you bloody stupid woman?" The harsh male voice roared from the doorway. It was freighted with the accents of London's tough streets. "No one slips away from Sharpy Hobson's blade."

There was no time to wonder how a London street criminal had found his way to Little Dixby or why he was after her. She would worry about those questions later, she thought, if she survived the night.

She jumped to the ground and stumbled through the miniature jungle of giant ferns that choked the little garden. Many of the fronds were taller than she was.

To think she had come to the countryside to rest and recuperate from recent events.

"Bloody hell, come back here," Hobson howled from the bedroom window. "Make things difficult, will ye? I'll take my time with ye when I do catch you, just see if I don't. You'll die nice and slow, and that's a promise. Bloody little bitch."

A string of savage curses told her that Hobson was finding it impossible to squeeze through the casement window. A tiny whisper of hope swept through her when she did not hear the pounding of footsteps behind her. Hobson would be forced to use one of the two doors in the cottage. That meant she had a little breathing room, time enough, perhaps, to make it to the only possible sanctuary.

There was no escape through the woods that bordered the lane. The moon was nearly full, but the heavy canopy of summer leaves blocked the silver light that should have dappled the forest floor. Even if she'd had a lantern she would not have been able to make her way through the dense undergrowth. She knew just how impenetrable the vegetation in the vicinity of the old abbey was because she had attempted to explore it during the day. The trees and undergrowth around the ancient ruins flourished in what the locals whispered was an unnatural manner.

She found the graveled garden walk and flew down it, the hem of the

JAYNE ANN KRENTZ

wrapper flapping wildly. She paused long enough to unlatch the gate, and then she was out in the moonlit lane, running for her life. She knew that Hobson would see her as soon as he emerged from the cottage.

Heavy footfalls thudded behind her.

"I have ye now, ye silly bitch. Ye'll soon get a taste of Sharpy's blade."

She risked a quick glance over her shoulder and saw the dark figure bearing down on her. She would have screamed, but there was no point wasting her breath. She ran harder, heart pounding.

The ancient stone walls that protected the vast grounds of Crystal Gardens appeared impregnable in the moonlight. She knew from previous explorations that the massive iron gate was locked.

There was no point trying to run the length of the long wall to the front door of the sprawling country house. There was no time. Hobson was gaining on her. His footsteps were closer now. She could hear his harsh breathing, or perhaps it was her own labored gasps that she heard.

She reached the back wall of the ancient abbey and raced toward the mound of overgrown foliage that concealed the jagged hole in the stone barrier. She had discovered the opening a few days ago and had decided to indulge in some discreet exploration before the new owner had arrived to take up residence. She could not help herself. Her sense of curiosity was linked in some ways to her psychical talent and the mystery of Crystal Gardens that had fascinated her from the start. It was the reason she had chosen to rent Fern Gate Cottage instead of one of the other properties available in the countryside around Little Dixby.

The fact that the rent on the cottage was considerably cheaper than it was for the other suitable lodgings in the area had also been a factor. But she had discovered soon enough why the little house was a bargain. The locals feared the abbey and the woods around it.

She slammed to a stop in front of the concealing foliage and pulled aside a curtain of cascading greenery. The jagged opening in the stone was about two feet above ground level. It was large enough for a person, even a man the size of Hobson, to squeeze through. But if he did pursue her onto the grounds, she might have a chance.

She looked back one last time. Hobson had not yet rounded the corner of the wall, but he would at any second. She could hear him—his thudding footsteps and his harsh breathing—but she could not yet see him. She had a few seconds.

She put one leg over the broken stone and then the other, and then she was inside the grounds of Crystal Gardens.

She caught her breath, transfixed by the eerie scene that surrounded her. She had seen enough of the strange gardens by day to know that there was something bizarre about the energy inside the walls and that the vegetation was not normal. But at night the paranormal elements were unmistakable.

The foliage on the vast grounds glowed with an eerie luminescence. In the very center of the gardens, where the ruins of an ancient Roman bath were said to be located, the psychical light was as dark and ominous as a violent storm at sea.

She knew from the guidebooks that she had purchased from Miss Witton, the proprietor of the bookshop in Little Dixby, that Crystal Gardens was divided into two sections. The outer region in which she stood was called the Day Garden on the maps. It surrounded the walls of an elaborate maze, which, in turn, encircled the interior portion of the grounds known as the Night Garden.

In the nearly two weeks during which she had resided in Fern Gate Cottage, she had not ventured much farther into the gardens than where she was tonight. But she had seen enough to know that the peculiar nature of the atmosphere inside the walls would provide her with her best chance of escaping Sharpy Hobson's knife.

There was a steady stream of curses, as Hobson yanked and clawed at the foliage.

"No little whore gets away with making Sharpy Hobson look the fool. I'll teach you to show some respect, see if I don't."

She looked around, summoning up a mental image of the layout of the gardens. The maze was the obvious place to hide. Her talent would very likely ensure that she did not get lost inside. But on a prior expedition, she had discovered that a locked gate blocked the entrance to the labyrinth.

She started toward the gazebo. The graceful domed roof and the pillars glowed with a faint blue light that seemed to emanate from the very stone of which it was constructed. She hurried but she did not run. She wanted Hobson to see her.

He finally scrambled through the hole in the wall, grunting and swearing. She stopped and looked back, wondering how much of the paranormal light he could perceive. There was a shocked silence as Hobson took in his surroundings.

"What the flamin' hell?" he growled. He rubbed his eyes.

Then he saw her and promptly forgot about the strangely luminous landscape around him. He yanked a knife out of the leather sheath at his hip and lunged toward her.

"Thought you'd get away from me, did ye?" he growled.

She whirled back toward the gazebo. Her goal was the darkly gleaming pond in front of the structure. With luck, Hobson would not be able to see it until it was too late. Her senses told her that if he tumbled into the gleaming black pool, he would quickly lose interest in her. There was something nightmarish about those waters.

She was so focused on her plan to lure Hobson to the pond that she was unaware of the presence of the man in the long black coat until he walked out of the shadows and into the moonlight. He stopped directly in front of her, blocking her path.

"Is it the custom around here for visitors to call at such an unusual hour?" he asked.

His voice was as dark as the obsidian surface of the pond and charged with a similar chilling power. It stirred all of her senses. In the strange moon-and-energy-lit shadows, it was difficult to make out the man's face clearly, but there was no need to see him. She recognized him immediately. Indeed, she thought, she would know him anywhere. Lucas Sebastian, the mysterious new owner of Crystal Gardens.

She stumbled to a halt, trapped between Lucas and Sharpy Hobson.

"Mr. Sebastian," she said. She was breathless and her heart was pounding. She struggled to identify herself; afraid he would not recognize her in the darkness, dressed, as she was, in her wrapper and nightgown, her hair falling around her shoulders. They had met only the one time, after all. "Sorry to intrude like this. Evangeline Ames, your tenant at Fern Gate Cottage."

"I know who you are, Miss Ames."

"You did say to call upon you if I had a problem. As it happens, I do have one."

"I can see that," Lucas said.

Hobson pulled up short. He made a slashing motion with the knife. "Get out of my way and ye won't get hurt. I just want the little whore."

Lucas regarded him with what could only be described as detached curiosity. "You are trespassing. That is a very dangerous thing to do here at Crystal Gardens."

"What's going on in this place?" Hobson looked around uneasily.

"Haven't you heard the stories?" Lucas asked. "Everyone around here knows that these grounds are haunted."

"Sharpy Hobson ain't afraid of no ghosts," Hobson vowed. "Won't be hanging around long enough to meet one. All I want is this bitch."

"What do you want with Miss Ames?" Lucas asked.

Evangeline was floored by Lucas's matter-of-fact tone. It was as if he was only casually interested in Hobson's reasoning.

"None of yer bloody business," Hobson snarled. "But I can tell ye she's worth a nice bit of blunt dead and I'm not going to let anyone get in my way."

"You don't seem to comprehend the situation," Lucas said. "The lady is my tenant and therefore under my protection."

Hobson snorted. "I'm doing you a favor taking her off your hands. The way I heard it, she's a lying little bitch."

"Someone hired you to kill her?" Lucas asked.

Hobson was starting to appear uncertain. Matters were evidently not proceeding the way they usually did when he went about his business.

"I'm not wasting any more time talking to you." Hobson leaped toward Lucas, knife ready to slash. "Yer a dead man."

"Not quite," Lucas said.

Energy, dark and terrifying, flashed in the atmosphere. Evangeline had just time enough time to realize that Lucas was somehow generating it, and then Hobson was shrieking with raw, mindless panic.

"No, get away from me," he shouted. He dropped the knife and clawed at something only he could see. *"Get away."*

He whirled and fled blindly into the gardens.

"Damn it to hell," Lucas said quietly. "Stone?"

A second figure glided out of the shadows. "Here, sir."

The voice sounded as though it emanated from the depths of a vast underground cavern, and, like Sharpy Hobson's voice, it carried the accents of the London streets.

In the strange light provided by the subtly glowing foliage, Evangeline could see that Stone suited his name. He was constructed like some ancient granite monolith and looked as if he would be just as impervious to the elements. The moonlight gleamed on his shaved head. The shadows and the eerie luminescence around them made it difficult to estimate his age, but he appeared to be in his early twenties.

"See if you can grab Hobson before he blunders into the maze," Lucas said. "Whatever you do, don't try to follow him if he gets that far."

"Yes, sir."

Stone broke into a run, moving with a surprising lack of noise for such a large man.

Lucas turned back to Evangeline. "Are you all right, Miss Ames?"

"Yes, I think so." She was still trying to calm her rattled senses and rapid pulse. "I don't know how to thank you—"

A high-pitched, keening scream echoed from somewhere deep in the gardens. The unearthly cry iced Evangeline's nerves. She stilled, unable to breathe.

It ended with horrifying suddenness. Evangeline was shivering so violently it was all she could do to remain on her feet.

"Sharpy Hobson," she whispered.

"Evidently Stone did not get to him in time to prevent him from entering the maze," Lucas said.

"Is he—" She swallowed and tried again. "Is he dead?"

"Hobson? Probably, or he soon will be. It's unfortunate."

"Unfortunate?" she managed. "That's all you can say about the man's death?"

"I would like to have questioned him. But as that does not seem likely to happen, you and I will talk instead."

She tried to compose herself. "Mr. Sebastian, I'm not at all sure what to say."

"There will be nothing complicated about our conversation, Miss Ames. You will come inside with me now. I will pour you a glass of medicinal brandy for your nerves and you will tell me what you are doing here in my gardens at this hour of the night and why a man with a knife was trying to murder you."

"But that's what I'm trying to tell you. I have no idea why Hobson attacked me."

"Then we must reason it out together."

He shrugged off his coat and draped it around her shoulders before she could summon up further protest. When his fingers brushed the nape of her neck, a thrill of awareness stirred her senses. The heavy wool garment was still warm from the heat of his body. She caught a trace of his masculine scent. It caused her senses to flare in a way that she had never before experienced.

Stone appeared. "Sorry, sir. He saw the open gate and ran straight inside. Probably assumed it was a way out of the gardens."

"I'll deal with the body later," Lucas said. "I wish to speak to Miss Ames first and then I will escort her back to the cottage."

"Yes, sir. Will you be needing anything else?"

"Not at the moment."

"Yes, sir."

Stone moved into the shadows. Evangeline watched him disappear. She was starting to wonder if she was caught up in some bizarre dream. Perhaps she was hallucinating. It was not beyond the realm of possibility, she thought. Her employers and her friends were convinced that her nerves had been badly strained by the attack two weeks earlier. Perhaps they were right.

Lucas's powerful hand closed around her arm. The shock of the physical contact made her flinch. Her talent was still flaring wildly and it was linked to her sense of touch. She could perceive Lucas's aura now quite clearly. The fierce bands of ice-and-fire energy took her breath.

"Relax, Miss Ames," he said. "I will not hurt you."

There was nothing in his aura to indicate that he was lying. She was safe enough, she decided, at least for the moment. She pulled herself together and lowered her talent.

"This way, Miss Ames." He steered her around a large bush. "Watch your step. There are a number of hazards on the grounds, including those roses."

The power she had glimpsed in Lucas's aura warned her that he was probably a good deal more dangerous than anything in his strange gardens.

Sharpy Hobson had stopped screaming, but she knew that she would hear the echoes of his last horrified cries in her nightmares for a long time to come.